NIGHT
WARRIORS

ALSO BY GRAHAM MASTERTON

HORROR STANDALONES

Black Angel
Death Mask
Death Trance
Edgewise
Heirloom
Prey
Ritual
Spirit
Tengu
The Chosen Child
The Sphinx
Unspeakable
Walkers
Manitou Blood
Revenge of the Manitou
Famine
Ikon
Sacrifice
The House of a Hundred
Whispers
Plague
The Soul Stealer
Blind Panic
The House at Phantom Park

THE SCARLET WIDOW SERIES

Scarlet Widow
The Coven

THE KATIE MAGUIRE SERIES

White Bones
Broken Angels
Red Light
Taken for Dead
Blood Sisters
Buried
Living Death
Dead Girls Dancing
Dead Men Whistling
Begging to Die
The Last Drop of Blood

THE PATEL & PARDOE SERIES

Ghost Virus
The Children God Forgot
The Shadow People
What Hides in the Cellar

THE NIGHT WARRIORS

Night Warriors
Death Dream
Night Plague
Night Wars
The Ninth Nightmare

SHORT STORY COLLECTIONS

Days of Utter Dread

NIGHT
WARRIORS

GRAHAM
MASTERTON
THE NIGHT WARRIORS 1

HEAD
ZEUS

An Aries Book

First published in the UK in 1986 by Sphere Books

This edition first published in the UK in 2023 by Head of Zeus,
part of Bloomsbury Publishing Plc.

9 7 5 3 1 2 4 6 8

A catalogue record for this book is available from
the British Library.

ISBN (PB): 9781035903986
ISBN (E): 9781035903979

Cover design: Matt Bray / Head of Zeus

Typeset by Siliconchips Services Ltd UK

Printed and bound in Great Britain by
CPI Group (UK) Ltd, Croydon CR0 4YY

Head of Zeus
First Floor East
5–8 Hardwick Street
London EC1R 4RG

WWW.HEADOFZEUS.COM

Out of Innocence Came Forth Unspeakable Evil ...

Henry *was* the first to reach the body, while Gil and Susan walked cautiously closer, and then stood watching. It was the body of a beautiful young girl, naked, like a peacefully sleeping mermaid. Never in their most traumatic nightmares could they have imagined the convulsive violence which followed ...

Then each is visited by a mysteriously androgynous figure who reveals that the girl had been used as innocent host to the most hideous malevolence known to man, a horrific presence that, through grotesque acts of impregnation, is madly insinuating itself into the bodies and minds of thousands of unsuspecting people. The only hope is to destroy the original evil seed and together, Henry, Gil and Susan become NIGHT WARRIORS, an ancient Order of men and women charged with the power to enter and search for the abomination in a fantastic dream world of soaring exhilaration and searing terror, driven by the inescapable reality that if they fail to find the beast, then the beast will certainly find them ...

'For one thousand years, Devils shall live in the dreams of men, and hold dominion over the dark realms of the night. But then shall come a company whose name shall be the Night Warriors; and it shall be charged unto them to banish the Devils and to rid the darkness of all evil influences forever. And those who are Night Warriors shall be secret, and their names shall not be known. Nevertheless they shall be counted as the greatest heroes of any age, and they will be remembered in the chronicles of Ashapola for all eternity.'

The Great Book of Darkness, Chapter IX, published by the Camden Society, 1844.

Chapter One

The three of them approached the body on the beach as if their meeting had been preordained. Henry was the first to reach it, and he hunkered down beside it, but wouldn't touch it, while Gil and Susan walked cautiously closer, and then stood silently watching, with their bare toes half buried in the sand.

'No doubt that she's dead,' said Henry, in his clear lecture-room voice. He brushed back his white windblown hair with his hand.

'I thought it was a dog, at first,' said Gil. 'You know, an Afghan or something.'

Henry stood up. 'I guess we'd better call the police. There's nothing that *we* can do.'

Susan kept her arms folded close across her tee-shirt, and shivered.

Henry said, Would you and this young man like to go call the police? I'll stay here and make sure that nobody disturbs it.' He hesitated, and looked down at the body, and then corrected himself by saying, 'Her.'

Susan nodded, and the two of them jogged away across the beach. Henry remained where he was, his hands clasped behind his back, tall and stooped in the silvery mist of the early morning. Almost unseen, the grey Pacific disobediently roared as the moon tugged it inch by inch away from the shore, and seagulls shrieked like anxious women as they swooped for fish. It was April, but it was chilly, and the sea-mist would probably envelop the coastline for most of the day.

Henry hadn't yet been to bed. He had been sitting in the study of his beach-house all night, under the light from his brass-shaded lamp, working on his new article for *Philosophy Today*: 'The concept of life after death', by Professor Henry Watkins. He had been writing in thumb-cramping longhand, and rewarding himself after the completion of every page with a large vodka and tomato juice; and so at six o'clock he had taken a walk along the beach not only to clear his mind often centuries of philosophical morbidness, but the cumulative effects of twelve large Bloody Marys.

And here she was, lying dead on the sand, a naked young woman. Stark and direct proof that everything he had been writing all night was pretentious nonsense; hot-air balloons and horsefeathers. He felt almost as if he had been fated to find her; as if stern gods had directed his footsteps this way, to show him in the most jarring way possible just how ridiculous his theories were. Nobody can ridicule the living quite as effectively as the dead.

She was lying face down, her bare skin covered in fine grey grit. Her long blonde hair was ribboned with seaweed, and fanned out on the beach like a mermaid's. One dead hand seemed to be clutching at the sand as if she had been trying to stop herself from being dragged out to sea again, as if to be drowned twice was more than she could endure. Her body was so white that in the pearly-grey mist it was almost luminous.

Henry walked around her. Alone, he felt suddenly so sad for her that he found that his throat was tightening up, and that the sea-wind was bringing tears to his eyes. Perhaps he was drunk, but she could have been any one of his philosophy students, she was so young. Although her face was hidden, she couldn't have been more than nineteen or twenty years old. She had a long, well-shaped back, and wide-flared hips. One of her legs was drawn up, so that he could glimpse blonde bedraggled pubic hair. There was a fine silver chain around her left ankle, but that was all the jewellery she wore. The white blue-veined curve of one half-exposed breast showed that she had the kind of figure that most men would turn around to look at twice.

The sea foamed briefly around her outstretched foot, and then retreated, as if it had sourly decided that it had done enough.

Henry thrust his fists into the pockets of his fawn-coloured windbreaker and deliberately turned away, towards the cliffs. He had never had children of his own. His four-year marriage to a lady oceanographer from the Scripps Institute had been barren in every conceivable sense. He had learned to drink during that marriage; he had also learned to be alone. Now he taught philosophy to successive waves of cheerful young men and women, and occasionally played chess with his next-door neighbour; and that was sufficient to make him feel fulfilled.

At least, it was sufficient to stop him from taking two bottles of sleeping-pills and going to bed with a copy of *Thus Spake Zarathustra*.

His students at UC San Diego called him Bing, because of his faint resemblance to Bing Crosby. He had grown his hair to try and make himself look more like Timothy Leary than Bing Crosby, but the nickname had stuck.

After five minutes or so, Gil and Susan came back down the concrete ramp which led up to the oceanside parking-lot, and half jogged, half walked across the sloping beach.

'The police are on their way,' Gil said, breathlessly.

'Thank you,' Henry acknowledged.

Susan said, 'I never saw anybody dead before.'

'She was young, too,' Henry remarked. 'Nineteen, twenty.'

They waited, uncomfortable and fidgety. There was no sound of a police siren yet. The sea kept on snarling, and the seagulls fluttered silently against the wind.

Gil said flatly, 'I was just jogging, you know? I really thought it was a dog at first.'

Susan couldn't take her eyes away from the body, from the fanned-out hair and the clutching hand, and the shoulders sparkling with grit.

Gil was one of those young Southern Californian men who defy immediate classification. He could have been a student or an automobile mechanic or a barman or anything at all. He was very thin, very tanned, with a narrow serious face and a prominent freckly nose. His hair was thick and dark, and mussed up into a fright-wig by the wind. He wore a navy-blue sweatshirt with *Crucial* stencilled on it in white, and sawn-off denim shorts.

Susan had all the hallmarks of the spoiled but rebellious daughter of a middle-class family. Her fair hair was cut short and spiky, and she wore a white Italian-style tee-shirt with red and green lightning flashes on it, and white satin running-shorts that were tighter than tight. She was plump faced but pretty. Henry could see that in two or three years some very striking features would emerge from that teenage roundness. Her eyes were already large and blue and dreamy lidded, like the eyes of one of those girls in a romance comic.

'I guess the police will want us to make statements,' said Henry.

Now they could hear the whip-whip-whip-whooo of a distant police siren, followed by the scribbling of an ambulance.

'What can we say?' asked Susan. 'We just found her here, that's all.'

'That's all we have to say,' Henry reassured her.

The police car drove right down the ramp on to the beach, and drew up only fifteen feet away. It was hotly pursued by an ambulance from the county coroner's office. Henry and Gil and Susan waited in silence as three detectives climbed out of the police car, and two medics noisily dragged a folding stretcher out of the back of the ambulance. A second police car arrived, slewing across the sand, and two uniformed officers got out.

The detectives came over and looked down at the body, standing with their hands on their hips. Two of them were big bellied and white, Tweedledum and Tweedledee; the third was lean as an adolescent wolf, a dark-eyed Hispanic with a drooping black moustache and a cinnamon-coloured three-piece suit that looked as if it had been chosen by his wife at Sears.

'Lieutenant Ortega,' he announced himself. 'These are Detectives Morris and Warburg.'

'Henry Watkins,' said Henry.

'And these young people?'

'We haven't had time to introduce ourselves.'

'You don't know them?'

'This is the first time we ever met. I guess we all caught sight of the body at the same moment.'

'Your name, please?' Lieutenant Ortega asked Gil.

'Gilbert Miller.'

'And yours, young lady?'

'Susan Sczaniecka.'

Lieutenant Ortega said over his shoulder, 'You get those names?'

Detective Warburg said, 'No, sir.'

Lieutenant Ortega let out a short, testy breath, and then went across to inspect the body. He stared at it for a very long time; then walked around it; then peered at it close with his hands on his bended knees, still without touching it.

'Any of you people know this girl's identity?' he asked, without looking towards them.

'No.' they replied. Henry felt strangely guilty that he didn't; but he supposed that everybody felt the same when they were interviewed by the police.

'Looks like a straightforward drowning t'me,' said Detective Morris, clearing his throat as if he were about to give a recitation. 'Kind of early in the year, but the pattern's familiar. Nude bathing off Cardiff Beach, too much to drink, and there's a pretty sharp undertow there, once you get out a ways. You get pulled out to sea. It's cold in April, you die of hypothermia in less than ten minutes – that's if you can swim. Then the tide brings you down here.' He checked his watch. 'Right on time, I'd say.'

Lieutenant Ortega stood up straight. 'You people were

down on the shoreline exceptionally early,' he said, waving his finger loosely from Susan to Gil to Henry.

'I was jogging,' said Gil. 'I hurt my leg in a motorcycle accident last December. I have to jog for a couple of hours each day to exercise it. Early morning is the only free time I get.'

Lieutenant Ortega raised his eyebrows at Henry.

'I, um – I was working on a magazine article all night,' Henry explained. 'I live right up there ... the cottage with the white-painted balcony. I finished up around five-thirty, then I decided to take a walk.' He hoped Lieutenant Ortega couldn't smell his breath.

Lieutenant Ortega turned to Susan. 'How about you?' he asked her. 'Exceptionally early to be down on the shoreline, wouldn't you say?'

Susan said, 'Guess it is.'

'So what were you doing here, so exceptionally early?'

'Walking, that's all. Thinking.'

'You had a row with your parents?'

'My parents are dead. I live with my grandparents.'

'You had a row with them?'

'I just went for a walk, that's all.'

Lieutenant Ortega worried something out from between his front teeth with his thumbnail. Then he sucked at his teeth, and said, 'Okay. I want you all to make statements to my officers here; full statements: how you found this dead person here, everything.'

'Straightforward drowning,' Detective Morris repeated.

At that moment, two more cars arrived on the beach, a dilapidated Buick Regal and an olive-drab station-wagon from the coroner's department.

'Ah, the photographer,' said Lieutenant Ortega, rubbing his hands together. 'And the medical examiner, too, remarkably prompt for a change.'

The photographer was a dour young man with a monk-like tonsure and a repetitive sniff. He began work straight away, laying out measurement markers and then photographing the young woman's body from all sides. The medical examiner, a short bull-necked man in a loud black-and-white hound's-tooth sports jacket, whistled tunelessly between his teeth while he waited for the photographer to finish.

'Straightforward drowning, what do you think?' Detective Morris asked him.

The medical examiner stared at him. 'Do *you* want to do the post mortem, or are you going to leave it to me?'

Detective Morris gave him a hesitant grin. 'No, sir, you go right ahead.'

'Can we turn her over now?' asked Lieutenant Ortega. 'I'd like to see what she looks like.'

The medical examiner didn't answer him, but carefully brushed the sand away from the dead girl's shoulders, and ran his hands down the length of her bare back. He stood up straight, and frowned, and then he looked out along the beach.

'Do any of you know this beach at all well?' he asked, thoughtfully.

'Yes, sir,' said Detective Morris. 'I've lived here just about all of my life.'

'Have you attended drownings here before?'

'Five or six.'

'Can you recall how far up the beach those other five or six bodies were discovered?' the medical examiner asked him.

Detective Morris looked puzzled. 'On the waterline, I guess, just like this one.'

'You take a look at that washed-up weed and that other debris,' the medical examiner told him. 'See where it lies. Most of it's lighter than a body, and far less bulky; yet it's way down the beach by comparison.'

Lieutenant Ortega came forward and looked down at the body uneasily. 'So what do you infer from that?' he asked the medical examiner.

'I don't know, I'm just making an observation,' the medical examiner replied.

'You observe that the body is lying further up the beach than the seaweed and the logs and the other trash?'

'That's correct.'

Lieutenant Ortega sucked at his teeth again. His earlier efforts obviously hadn't succeeded in dislodging the fragment of food that was worrying him. 'You observe that the body is lying further up the beach than the seaweed and the other trash, and from this observation you conclude that the girl was not drowned at all, but that she died in some other way and was left on the beach, either by accident, or with the deliberate intention of making it appear as if she had drowned?'

'You said it, not me,' replied the medical examiner, palpating the dead girl's right leg, and watching to see what finger-marks he made. He snapped his fingers and one of the gum-chewing medics brought him his alloy medical-case, and opened it up for him. He rummaged around inside it until he found his thermometer, which he lubricated, and then unceremoniously inserted into the body's anus. 'If she's been floating around in the ocean all night, the probability is that her body temperature will be far lower than if she's been lying on the beach. That will depend when she died, of course; but this beach is pretty well crowded right up until sundown, isn't that true?'

'Yes, sir,' Detective Morris agreed. 'Sometimes well after sundown, too, when the kids have cookouts.'

The medical examiner waited patiently for the girl's body temperature to have its effect on the mercury in his thermometer. Meanwhile he looked up at Henry and Gil and Susan, and said, 'Who are these people? Gawkers, or what?'

'These people found the body,' said Lieutenant Ortega.

The medical examiner asked Henry, 'Ever see anybody dead on this beach before?'

Henry shook his head.

'Fine way to start the day, finding a body,' the medical examiner remarked, as casually as if he were discussing the weather. He withdrew his thermometer and frowned at it carefully. 'Sixty-one degrees.'

'And what does that mean?' asked Lieutenant Ortega.

'It means that the temperature inside the body is sixty-one degrees,' said the medical examiner.

'But what do you conclude?'

'Conclude? I don't conclude anything. It's up to you to make the conclusions. But you could take into consideration the fact that the air temperature here is something like fifty-five or fifty-six degrees, and that the ocean temperature is something like forty-two to forty-eight degrees.'

'So, if the body had been floating in the water all night, her body temperature would have been lower than sixty-one degrees?' said Lieutenant Ortega.

'Possibly,' the medical examiner replied.

Lieutenant Ortega let out another of his short, testy breaths. 'All right,' he said. 'Now can we turn her over?'

The medical examiner stood up, and fastidiously brushed the sand from the knees of his pants. As he did so, the two medics came forward, and positioned themselves on either side of the body. Henry, watching, was gripped by an irrational feeling of dread, and he had the strongest urge to turn and look the other way. Somehow, however, he found that he couldn't, that he had to watch. Otherwise the girl on the beach would remain faceless forever, and when he dreamed about her at night, which he inevitably would, he would see nothing but that mermaid hair, tangled with weed, and nothing but that long pale back.

'Be careful,' the medical examiner instructed the medics. 'I don't want any extra bruising.'

He came over and stood next to Henry and Gil and Susan. 'You didn't touch her at all, or try to move her?'

Henry shook his head. 'I don't think I would have had the nerve.'

Susan ventured, 'Do you suppose that somebody might have killed her? I mean, on purpose?'

The medical examiner pulled a face. 'Girls of this age are always susceptible to being killed, either on purpose or accidentally, or else through carelessness. Pretty girls especially. They have more power than they know. Their youth and their looks give them power. The trouble is, they never know how to use it. Not safely, anyway.'

With exaggerated care, the two medics eased the girl's body out of the sand, and then rolled her on to her back.

Her arm fell against the wet beach with a slapping sound

and then one of the medics said, in a peculiar voice, 'Jesus Christ.'

Henry stared, but at first he couldn't understand what he was staring at. The medical examiner moved forward at once, and stood over the body, his face disassembled into no recognisable expression at all. Fear? Horror? Fascination? The two medics took a step back, one of them holding his hand over his mouth, and looking watery eyed. Lieutenant Ortega had been standing with his back to the body, talking to Morris and Warburg; but then Warburg nudged him and he turned around and saw what the girl really looked like.

Her face was almost beautiful, in spite of the fact that it had been swollen by the sea. A classic blonde, with classic American bone-structure, the sort of girl who could easily have found herself an acting part in *Matt Houston* or *Magnum, P.I.* or even *Dynasty*. Wide shouldered, large breasted; but beneath her ribcage the horror began. Henry suddenly understood what he was looking at, and whispered, 'Oh, God,' and Susan buried her face in her hands.

The girl's abdomen had been completely ripped out, from her ribs to her pelvis, and inside her abdominal cavity scores of silvery-black eels were writhing; a tumultuous nest of slithering creatures, twining and untwining themselves, blindly feeding on what was left of the dead girl's softer organs.

Gil turned away, buckled at the knees, crouched on the sand, and retched. The uniformed policemen stared in alarm and helplessness; even the photographer crossed himself. For minutes on end, there was nothing that any of them could do but watch the knotted tangle of eels as they heaved and twisted and wriggled, and the pale emotionless face of the girl whose'body they were slowly devouring.

The medical examiner turned to Lieutenant Ortega with widened eyes. 'Ever see anything like that, *ever!*'

Lieutenant Ortega abruptly shook his head.

'Me neither,' said the medical examiner. Then he turned to the medics and said, 'Get rid of those things.'

The medics looked unhappily down at the body. 'You mean …?'

'Whatever they are, those eels. Those snakes. Get them out of there.'

One of the medics picked up a stick from the beach, and approached the body gingerly. He leaned forward, and prodded the eels with the tip of it, just once. Immediately, the eels wriggled and twisted even more furiously, and the medic jumped back with a high-pitched '*aah!*' of irrepressible disgust.

The medical examiner impatiently took the stick away from him and circled around the body himself. While everybody else watched him with flesh-crawling apprehension, he prodded the eels two or three times, and each time they boiled in the dead girl's stomach with the same slippery fury. Suddenly, however, the medical examiner managed to hook the end of the stick underneath one of them and flip it out on to the beach.

The eel was almost three feet long, with a flat chisel-shaped head and tiny blind eyes. It flapped and writhed on the surface for a while; then it burrowed its head into the sand, and within seconds it had disappeared, leaving nothing on the sand but a slight indentation. Almost immediately, the remaining eels poured out of the dead girl's pelvis, and scattered in all directions, burying themselves deep into the sand.

'Catch one!' the medical examiner shouted, urgently.

One of the uniformed policemen snatched at the tail of the last eel to disappear, and tugged at it furiously.

'Give me a hand for Chrissake!' he gasped to his uniformed partner. His partner came hurrying across and gripped the eel's body nearer to the sand, and between them, cursing and grunting, they gradually managed to drag the creature backwards out of the hole it had been burrowing for itself.

As soon as its head was clear, though, the eel lashed and looped and twisted wildly around in the air. Henry saw its teeth flicker; and then it wriggled like a whip, and caught one of the policemen directly in the face, clamping its jaws over his upper lip and part of his nose.

The policeman shrieked out loud, and snatched at the eel's head, trying to prize its jaws apart. Henry watched in horror as the man danced around the sand, the silvery-black eel wriggling from his face like a carnival nose. Bright-red blood began to sprinkle all around them.

Lieutenant Ortega dodged forward, and seized the officer from behind, tripping him up so that they both fell heavily on to the ground. The policeman was screaming wildly, and his legs were jerking like an epileptic marionette. Lieutenant Ortega reached around to the officer's face, and clutched the eel right behind its chisel-shaped head, squeezing the gills closed so that the creature would be unable to breathe. Then he held up his free hand and yelled, 'Knife, for God's sake!'

The medical examiner dug hurriedly into his pockets, and came up with a single-bladed clasp knife. Lieutenant Ortega snatched it from him, and then cut into the welter of blood in front of the policeman's face. The policeman screamed again and again while Lieutenant Ortega sawed through the eel's body. The eel's own blood spurted out dark, like bile, and splattered all over Ortega's hands and arms. Its tail lashed furiously from side to side, right up until the last moment when Ortega cut its spinal column, and flung its body across the sand. The headless body lay twitching and jerking, and the medics cautiously stepped away from it.

The medical examiner knelt down on the sand and examined the policeman closely. The policeman was shivering and trembling and Lieutenant Ortega was doing everything he could to soothe him. The eel's severed head was still gripping the policeman's face, and when the medical examiner quickly dabbed away the blood with cotton and distilled water, he could see that the creature's teeth had already detached half of the policeman's nostril and most of his upper lip. The eel's jaw muscles showed no signs of relaxing; it was plain that any attempt to pull its head away would make the injury far more severe than it was already.

Henry came up, and although he was trembling himself, he said, as steadily as he could, 'You know what they used to do in Vietnam, to get the leeches off?'

'That's right,' said the medical examiner. 'They used to burn them off with lighted cigarettes. Does anyone here have a cigarette?'

Everybody looked at each other. In the end, Detective Warburg said, 'Nobody smokes, sir.'

'Jesus,' said the medical examiner. 'Only in Southern California.'

'Perhaps a cigarette-lighter, from one of the cars,' Henry suggested.

Detective Morris jogged off to the nearest car, and came back a minute or so later with his belly bouncing, and a glowing cigarette-lighter held up in his hand. He handed it to the medical examiner, and the medical examiner immediately touched it against the eel's raw neck.

There was a sharp sizzle, a sickly odour of burning; then the eel's jaws clamped convulsively tight and bit away the whole of the policeman's upper lip and nostril, dropping on to the ground in a sudden spurt of blood. The policeman let out a tight, choked shriek, his upper teeth hideously exposed, and Lieutenant Ortega had to wrestle him down against the sand.

'Plasma!' the medical examiner shouted. 'And you!' he ordered the injured policeman's partner. 'Take that head and cut the damn thing in half, and get your buddy's face out of its mouth!'

It took the medics less than five busy minutes to bandage the policeman's face and set him up on to a plasma drip, to reduce the effects of shock. While they worked, the policeman's partner manhandled a pair of bolt-cutters out of the trunk of his patrol-car, and nudged the eel's head around on the sand so that he could position it between the blades. He tried twice to cut it in half, but both times the head slipped out. Then Gil came forward and rested the head against the toe of his shoe, so that it wouldn't roll away. There was a sharp, crisp crunch, and the eel's skull was chopped apart. The medical examiner stooped down and extracted the bloody rag of flesh that the creature had wrenched away from the policeman's face.

'I want that bastard in a plastic bag,' he told Detective Morris. 'Head, tail, and anything else you can find.'

Lieutenant Ortega looked at his watch. 'It's almost seven. Let's get this beach cordoned off. Warburg – call for some back-up. I want a digging detail. If those eels killed that girl, I want them dug out and destroyed. I want the coastguard alerted, too. They'll probably want to put up a temporary ban on swimming. Morris, you go along with the M. E. I want the fastest post mortem in the history of the world.'

'Is there anything that we can do?' asked Henry.

Lieutenant Ortega stared at Henry as if he had never seen him before. 'You? Oh, you can go home. Give your name and address to Detective Morris here, he'll come and talk to you later. And, please, don't leave the area, not until you've made your statement. And don't talk to the newspapers or the television. This is one of those situations that causes panic, you understand me? I'd rather we kept the whole thing quiet, just for now.'

Henry said to Gil and Susan, 'That's it. I guess we can leave.'

Susan was very pale. 'I think I'm going to faint,' she said.

'Sit down for a moment,' Henry told her. 'Put your head down between your knees.'

While they waited for Susan to recover, Henry looked across the beach at the body of the girl they had found. From where he was crouching, next to Susan, he was unable to see the gaping cavity of her stomach; the girl could have been lying serene and naked in the mist, waiting for the sun to break through. She was really quite beautiful, Henry thought to himself, and somehow that made her death seem even more horrifying.

'I'm all right now,' said Susan. She tried to get up, and Gil gave her his arm.

Henry was watching the medics lift the girl's body off the beach, and zipper it up in a body-bag. Against the mist, the figures looked like an Oriental shadow-play. 'I never saw anything like that before in my whole life,' he said. 'Those eels – did you ever see anything like that? And I used to be married to an oceanographer.'

They walked up the beach together. When they reached the boardwalk, Henry suggested, 'Come and have a drink. That's my cottage, right over there. I expect you could use something to settle your nerves.'

'I think I want to get home, thank you,' said Susan. She glanced back down at the beach and her eyes were staring with repressed hysteria.

Gil asked her, gently, 'Where do you live? I could take you.'

'Do you have a car?'

'Sure, that Mustang convertible right across the street.'

'Okay, then, thank you.'

They walked off together, Gil and Susan, leaving Henry standing alone. After a while, Henry shrugged, and walked the sixty yards back to his cottage, unlocking the door with the key which he always kept around his wrist. He went through to the living-room, opened up the glass-fronted cocktail cabinet, and poured himself a very large vodka, straight up, no ice, and drank it.

He coughed as the vodka burned its way down his throat. Then he filled up his glass again, and walked over to the wide sliding windows which led out on to the balcony.

He could see the police cars from here, with their flashing lights, and Lieutenant Ortega in his cinnamon-coloured suit. Further down the beach, towards Del Mar, two uniformed policemen were already dragging trestles across the beach, marked **Police Line – Do Not Cross**.

Henry watched the police activity for almost twenty minutes. Then he went back into the cottage and sat down on the white-painted bamboo sofa, and stared at himself in the shiny glass door of the stereo cabinet on the opposite side of the room.

Life after death? The only life in that poor dead girl had been those wriggling eels; and what kind of life did *they* represent?

He thought about the morning's events and all he could see was a series of frightening still pictures. The girl's hand, clutching at the beach. The silver chain on her ankle. The whiteness of her back. Then the eels, in their complicated Chinese-puzzle pattern. And the severed head of that single captured eel, gripping the policeman's face like an ancient symbol of evil persistence.

He finished his third glass of vodka, and then tilted across to the cocktail cabinet to drain the bottle into his glass. 'Stolichnaya,' he pronounced, with what he liked to think was a thick Russian accent. Then, '*Zdarovya.*'

With inebriated care, he went to the bookshelf at the end of the room, under the window, and ran his finger along the spines of all the marine books that his less-than-dear departed wife had left behind her. At last he came across a large illustrated volume entitled *Anguilliformes: Migration & Life-Cycles of Common Eels.* He tugged it out, took it over to the coffee-table, and opened it up.

It was the quotation on the opening page that caught his attention first of all. It said simply, 'The eel was eaten in olden times because it was thought to give exceptional potency. In certain parts of ancient Scandinavia, shoals of eels were described by a single mystical word which meant "sperm of the Devil".'

Henry was about to take another drink, but he paused, and read the quotation again. Then he looked towards the balcony, and out towards the beach, and frowned.

Chapter Two

Gil and Susan said very little as they drove back to Del Mar Heights Road, where Susan lived. Gil glanced across at Susan from time to time, but he could see that she was still shocked by what had happened at the beach. He was pretty queasy himself, thinking about those eels writhing silvery-black in that woman's white body, and how that policeman's face had been half bitten off.

Susan said, 'Here – here it is,' and Gil steered the shiny yellow Mustang up the steeply angled concrete driveway, and yanked up the handbrake. He hopped out of the car without opening the door, and went around to the passenger side to let Susan out.

'This your grandparents' place?' he asked her. It was a small Mexican-style house, with a balcony overlooking the garden, and rows of pink-painted arches. Three lizards watched them from the clay-tiled roof, blinking in prehistoric small-mindedness. Outside the back door there were six or seven recently watered azaleas, in terracotta pots, and matching rocking-chairs, in white-painted cane.

'Thank you for driving me home,' said Susan. 'I really felt nauseous.'

'You're welcome,' Gil told her. He nodded, and smiled, but made no immediate move to get back into his car.

Susan glanced behind her. 'I'd invite you in, but – well, my grandparents are kind of old fashioned. They'd want to know everything about what happened, you know; and right now I just don't feel like talking about it at all.'

Gil scuffed his trainers on the concrete path. 'You're going to want to talk about it sooner or later. You're going to have to.'

She stood with her hand on the wrought-iron balcony rail, looking at him with one of those distinctively teenage expressions, bored, curious, go-on-show-me; her eyes in shadow. From inside the house, they could hear a vacuum-cleaner ruminating from room to room, and a television turned up loud so that whoever was using the vacuum-cleaner could listen to *Josie and the Pussycats*.

'Could I call by later?' asked Gil.

'Well, I don't know,' said Susan. She turned toward the house. 'I mean, no offence or anything, but I really want to forget it.'

'Well, I'll tell you what,' Gil suggested, 'I'll leave you my number, and then if you want to talk about it you can call me. Or even if you *don't* want to talk about it, I don't mind.'

Susan thought for a moment, and then said, 'Okay. But I have to go in now.'

'Do you have a piece of paper?'

She picked up a piece of chalk from the flowerbed. 'I'll write it with this.'

'Okay, then. It's 755-9858.'

'Where's that?'

'Solana Beach, on the Boardwalk. My father owns the Mini-Market.'

'Oh, really? Okay, then.'

At that moment, Susan's grandmother came out of the house, a small porky woman with strawberry-ice hair done up in curlers, and a strawberry-coloured tracksuit.

'Susan?' she said, querulously. 'You came back quick.'

'Oh, Gil here gave me a lift.'

'Gil?' demanded her grandmother, and lifted up the gold-framed spectacles which she wore around her neck on a long gilded chain.

'Gil Miller, ma'am,' said Gil, giving her a wave. 'Nice to meet you.'

'Have I seen you before?' Susan's grandmother wanted to know.

'Could be, ma'am. My father owns the Mini-Market down at Solana Beach. Sometimes I serve behind the deli counter.'

Susan's grandmother lowered her spectacles and allowed her face to subside into a soft blancmange of disapproval. 'Susan's dating a medical student from Scripps,' she told Gil. 'A fine boy, with a fine career in front of him. Irish.'

Gil said, 'Well, ma'am, that's excellent,' even though he could see that Susan was desperately embarrassed. He waved his hand again, an odd Howdy-Doody wave that he hadn't really meant to do at all, and then he swung himself back into his car and started up the engine.

'Grandma,' Susan protested, under her breath. Then she called out, 'Thanks for the ride, Gil.'

'Yeah. You're welcome,' said Gil, and backed himself out of the driveway.

Susan watched him turn around in the roadway, all screaming torque and squealing tyres, and roar off back towards the beach. Then she followed her grandmother into the house, making sure that the screen door banged noisily behind her. In the kitchen, her grandfather looked up from his *San Diego Tribune* and said, 'Your friend Daffy's here.'

'Yes, and I was ashamed to let her into your room,' her grandmother admonished her. 'The mess! I never saw anything like it. You have drawers for your clothes, don't you, and shelves for your books?'

'Oh, Grandma, I can't keep everything immaculate, the way that you do.'

'It's a state of mind,' her grandmother told her. 'If your mind is tidy, then your house is tidy. Goodness knows what Daffy thinks of you.'

'Daffy thinks I'm very neat. You should see her room. World War Eight isn't in it.'

Her grandmother hovered by the doorway. Susan could tell that she was torn between going back to her vacuum-cleaning and broaching the subject of Gil Miller. She went over to the icebox and poured herself a large glass of Mountain Spring water, topping it up with ice cubes. She drank almost the whole glass without once taking a breath.

'That boy,' said her grandmother, 'you won't be seeing him again, will you?'

'Is there any reason why I shouldn't?'

'Well, what will Carl say?'

'Grandma, it's none of Carl's goddamned business.'

'Suzie,' put in her grandfather, taking off his half-glasses. 'In this house, we don't use words like that.'

'Well, it's none of Carl's blank-censored business, then. Grandma, we're not even dating.'

'You should. He's a very well-mannered person.'

'I know, but I happen not to like him. And anyway, he's not Irish, he's Armenian.'

'His mother is half Irish.'

Susan closed her eyes and leaned against the icebox and her grandmother knew that there wasn't any point in nagging any more. Her grandfather shrugged and smiled. 'She'll find somebody nice, don't worry about it. The whole planet is wall to wall with eligible men.'

'It's these boys from the beach, that's all,' Susan's grandmother complained. 'These surfers. One day, some surfer is going to make her pregnant, and then what? It's a responsibility, bringing up your own daughter's child. Sometimes I think it's too much.'

Susan opened her eyes. 'Grandma,' she said, 'I am not going to get pregnant by any surfer.'

Her grandmother shook her head, and went off to finish her vacuum-cleaning. Every morning, she vacuum-cleaned for at least two hours, and watched the television at the same time. Those were her two principal obsessions in life: cleaning the house and watching TV. She thought it was mandatory that her house should sparkle like the houses in the Lemon-Kleen commercials, and that she should live her life according to the gospel of Richard Simmons. She had once appeared on *The Price Is Right and* won three hundred dollars and a lawn-sprinkler. That was six years ago, and she still talked about it.

Susan's grandfather held out his hand, and hooked his arm around Susan's waist.

'You'll find somebody, you wait and see. You're young yet, you haven't even finished your education.'

'Grandpa, I'm not actually panicking to get married,' Susan told him. Unannounced, unwanted, a vision of the dead girl on the beach suddenly flashed in front of her eyes. White breasts, coated in grit. Squirming eels. She pulled herself away from her grandfather, went to the sink to rinse out her glass, and stood there for a moment to steady herself.

'You all right?' her grandfather asked her.

'Sure, I'm all right.'

'You look like you're upset. Your mother used to look like that, when she was upset. Kind of chalky, know what I mean? Wasn't anything to do with that boy, was it?'

'It's not morning-sickness, if that's what you're trying to suggest.'

'Well, I wasn't,' said her grandfather, offended.

He glanced towards the hallway door, where Susan's grandmother was vacuum-cleaning in surge after surge of roaring decibels, and then he stood up and came over to the sink, and laid his hand on Susan's shoulder. He was short and tubby, like Susan's grandmother; but unlike her grandmother he was quite content to look his age, which was sixty-six. His bald head was varnished like a candy-apple from hours of sitting out in his rocking-chair and watching the bouncy golden schoolgirls go by.

'Your grandma means well,' he told her, in a low voice.

Susan nodded. 'Yes, I know.'

'She's only trying to protect you from making a mistake.'

'Yes, I know.'

Her grandfather didn't know what else to say. He fiddled with the cuff of his droopy grey cardigan. Then he shrugged, and went and sat down, and picked up his paper again, although he kept his eyes on Susan. The newspaper headlines warned of more earth tremors mainly centred on Tijuana.

Susan went across the hall to her bedroom. Her grandmother looked up from her vacuum-cleaning with a hurt, impatient expression, but Susan tried to ignore her. It wasn't *her* fault that she had to live here, and just as soon as she possibly could, she was going to move out. She briefly glimpsed the dead girl's face again, and somehow it became tangled up with her mother's face, crushed and lopsided after the accident. She opened her bedroom door with the flat of her hand.

Daffy was sprawled across Susan's divan-bed, her legs kicked up, engrossed in *Cosmopolitan.*

'Oh hi, Suze, You're early. Did you read this thing about the sponge?'

Susan went straight across to the washbasin and brushed up her hair in the mirror. Her grandfather had been right: she did look chalky.

Daffy turned over and said, 'It says here that it's only seventy per cent safe.'

Susan frowned at herself in the mirror. 'What is?'

'The sponge O deaf ears. Can you imagine that? Seventy per cent! That means for every hundred times you make love, you get pregnant thirty times. My God, I'll have ninety children before I'm eighteen.'

Susan found that she was crying. Silently, but bitterly, so that the tears ran down her cheeks and dripped down the sides of her mouth. Daffy didn't notice at first, and went on reading, but then Susan let out a high-pitched sob.

Daffy jumped off the bed. 'Suze – what's the matter? What's happened?' Outside the door, the vacuum-cleaner was still roaring, and banging at the skirting-boards. 'It's not *her* again, is it?'

Susan shook her head. She dragged two tissues out of the box beside her basin, and noisily blew her nose. Then she dragged out another one and wiped her eyes. 'I don't know what it is. It's probably nothing, just my period.'

'I was going to ask if you wanted to come to my house. We're having a barbecue, and some of the kids from Escondido are coming over.'

'I don't know. I feel kind of weird.'

'Weird? Why?'

'It's – I don't know, it's something that happened down on the beach. I'm trying not to think about it but it won't go away.'

She sat down on the edge of the divan-bed and Daffy sat down beside her. 'Well?' asked Daffy, with incandescent curiosity.

Susan dabbed at her eyes again. 'I'm not sure that I can tell you.'

'Was it a boy? You weren't raped, were you? You definitely look like you could have been raped.'

'It wasn't anything like that'

'Then what, for Christ's sake?'

Outside the door, the vacuum-cleaner suddenly whined to a stop. There was silence, even the television had been turned off, and both girls listened in case Susan's grandmother had heard Daffy taking the name of the Lord in vain. Susan's grandmother prayed in front of the television every Sunday morning with Dr Howard C

Estep, and Dr Howard C Estep sternly disapproved of anyone taking the name of the Lord in vain.

Susan whispered, 'I saw a body, a dead body.'

'You're kidding!'

'No, I am not kidding. It was a girl, she was drowned or something. The police were there, and the ambulance, and everything.'

'Oh, my God,' said Daffy, shocked and sympathetic but still desperate to hear all the details. 'You must have been absolutely paralysed! I mean, what was she like? I never saw a dead body before.'

'Daffy,' said Susan, in an uncontrolled voice, 'she had eels in her stomach, where her stomach was supposed to be, and they were eating her.'

Daffy stared in shock. 'Eels! You're kidding? Oh my God, that's absolutely disgusting! What did you do? Were you sick?'

Susan couldn't even speak. She kept thinking about those eels twisting and wriggling and sliding underneath the dead girl's ribcage; and then the policeman dancing in agony with the eel whipping out of his face. She clasped her hands over her eyes and forced herself to cry, her chest heaving, her throat clenched tight, trying to wrench out of herself all of the fright and all of the horror, trying to exorcise all of the nightmares that she knew would come crowding in on her, come nightfall.

She had dreamed for months of her mother's distorted face. She knew that she would dream about the dead girl on the beach for ever and ever.

Daffy put her arms around her and held her close, shushing her, rocking her gently backwards and forwards as if she were a small child. In the hallway, the vacuum-cleaner started up again, and began to harvest the dust next to the living-room door. Daffy was younger than Susan by four months and two days exactly, but she was much more mature. She was a tall, skinny, brown-skinned girl, with masses and masses of curly brunette hair, and one of those pouting provocative mouths that every senior in high school had wanted to kiss. She had wanted to write to Hugh Hefner and offer herself as Playmate of the month, but her mother, although she was broad minded, had said no. Her mother had brought up Daffy on her own. Her father had gone to work on the oil pipeline in Alaska and never quite managed to come back, and so Daffy's mother was generally not in favour of male exploitation of women. She had brought up Daffy to be pretty and suspicious and worldly wise, not to take rides from strangers, and to take the pill.

Susan stopped crying as suddenly as she had begun, and sat in Daffy's arms looking around the room.

'Are you okay now?' Daffy asked her.

'I guess. I wasn't really crying. It was just thinking about it. That poor girl, you know, all gnawed away by eels. And one of the eels bit a cop, too, right in the face.'

'What were they, some kind of man-eating eel? What do they call them, moray eels? There was one in that movie. You know that movie with Nick Nolte? Anyway it bit some guy's head off. Don't you think that Jerry looks like Nick Nolte, if he had a moustache, I mean?'

Susan stood up, and mechanically took off her tee-shirt and her running-shorts, so that she was naked except for her socks. She dropped her shirt and shorts on to the floor, next to yesterday's skirt, a copy of *Rolling Stone* which she had been cutting up for pictures of Bruce Springsteen, her badminton racquet, her hairdryer and the sleeve of her new Eurythmics album.

'Are you sure you're okay?' Daffy asked her, worried.

Susan nodded. Her eyes were still reddened and watery. 'I just want to go take a shower; then we'll go over to your place.'

Daffy waited while Susan went to the bathroom. She paced up and down the bedroom for a while, nudging with her sneakers at discarded clothes and dismembered magazines. Then she went to the window and looked out into the yard, a small paved area with sunbeds and a stone fountain that didn't work, or only rarely. It was a hot clear day, and lizards were poised in the shadows of the undergrowth.

From here, it was possible to see a small part of the street outside, and Daffy's attention was caught by a young man in a black sports jacket and white tennis slacks sitting on the wall outside Susan's grandparents' house, smoking a cigarette. He looked as if he were waiting for somebody, because every now and then he lifted his wrist and Daffy could see a spark of reflected light from the face of his watch. His eyes were masked with impenetrably dark sunglasses.

She watched him for almost five minutes. Cars passed him by on both sides of the street, but nobody stopped for him, and it occurred to Daffy that he wasn't watching out for any particular car, either. He remained where he was, never turning his head, smoking and occasionally checking the time.

She turned away from the window and suddenly realised that Susan had stayed in the shower for an awfully long time.

She walked through to the hallway, where Susan's grandmother was now burnishing her collection of brass figurines of Mexican dancers, and down the end to the bathroom.

'Is Susan going to your barbecue?' her grandmother asked, busily flapping her duster.

'She said she would,' Daffy replied. She hesitated by the bathroom door, and then knocked. 'Susan? Are you okay?'

'She's taking a shower,' said her grandmother, testily. 'Of course, I've only just cleaned up the bathroom. Now what am I going to get, soap all over the tiles and hair in the wastepipe. Not to mention the wet towels all over the floor. She really has to be the messiest girl ever.'

'Susan?' Daffy repeated.

'Go on in,' said Susan's grandmother. 'She probably can't hear you because of the water.'

Daffy opened the door and peered into the bathroom. The shower was clattering loudly and the room was clouded with steam.

'Susan?' she called again, and stepped inside. For some reason, she began to feel frightened, and she suddenly thought about the story that Susan had told her. The dead girl, eaten by eels. The policeman, whose face had been half bitten off. The glass door of the shower-stall was obscured with steam, although Daffy thought that she could make out a pink shape on the other side of it, which must be Susan.

Her throat was constricted with alarm. She slowly approached the shower, and knocked tentatively at the glass. 'Susan? Suze? Are you okay?'

At that moment, there was a hair-raising moan, and

Daffy jumped away from the shower and whispered, 'Oh, Jesus.' But then the moan was followed by an anguished, suppressed sobbing, and Daffy tugged open the shower door to find Susan crouched on the tiled floor, her legs drawn up, her hands clutched over her head, shivering and weeping with delayed shock.

Daffy turned off the faucet, and then reached over to the rail and dragged a large bath-towel off it, which she wrapped around Susan's shoulders.

'Susan, come on; you're upset, that's all. Susan, it's Daffy. Come on, baby, let's get you out of here.'

Susan numbly and shakily allowed Daffy to lift her up, and half carry her out of the bathroom. They encountered her grandmother as they came down the hallway, and for one split-second the old lady was going to protest about Susan's wet feet on the carpet, until she saw how white and distressed Susan was, and how determined the challenge was on Daffy's face.

'What on earth's the matter?'

'She fainted, that's all. Her period.' For some reason Daffy was reluctant to tell Susan's grandmother about the body on the beach. Between them, they helped Susan into her bedroom, and quickly dried her off. Susan's grandmother searched through the untidy heaps of clothes in her closet drawers, until she found a striped nightshirt, which Daffy pulled over Susan's head.

'Maybe I ought to call Dr Emanuel,' said Susan's grandmother, anxiously.

Susan opened her eyes. Her fragmented thoughts were beginning to slide back into place again, like the film of a car-bomb explosion being played slowly in reverse. She found that she could focus again, and that sounds coagulated into words. She recognised Daffy, sitting on the end of the bed smiling at her. She recognised her grandmother, peering at her from a safe distance through her gold-framed spectacles, as if she were worried that whatever she was suffering from might be contagious.

'Did I faint?' she asked, with a dry mouth. 'I thought I was someplace else.'

Daffy squeezed her hand. 'You're okay now. You'll live. But you gave me a scare, I can tell you. Would you like some coffee?'

Susan nodded. 'That would be great.'

Her grandmother said, 'I'll fix it,' pleased to have something to do that didn't actually involve nursing. She fretted endlessly about her own ailments, but she was totally squeamish when other people were sick. She wobbled off to the kitchen in her bright pink tracksuit, leaving the door open.

Daffy told Susan, 'Get under the blanket. You need to keep warm.'

Susan said, 'I'm okay now. Really.'

'It must have been shock, you know, from seeing that body.'

Susan shook her head. Her hair was tangled and wet. 'It was kind of like shock, but there was something else too. I don't know how to describe it. I thought I could hear somebody's voice, very loud and echoing. Then I was travelling very fast; it was like I was in a helicopter or something, speeding over the surface of the sea. It went so fast that I couldn't keep my balance, and I fell down. The next thing I knew, I was back here with you.'

'Shock,' Daffy pronounced. 'Now, will you keep warm? The Pink Panther's going to be bringing you some coffee in a second.'

It took Susan a little over a half-hour to stop shivering. Then she dressed slowly, in a green tee-shirt and white pedal-pushers, and combed out her hair.

'You're sure you're going to be okay?' Daffy kept asking her. 'I mean, you don't have to come to the barbecue if you don't want to. I won't be offended.'

'Daffy, I *want to* come. I'm not an invalid.'

'You just take good care of yourself,' her grandmother instructed her.

'Yes, you take good care,' her grandfather echoed.

They left the house and walked down the sloping driveway in the hot mid-morning sunshine. Daffy lived ten minutes' walk away, in one of the new houses on Jimmy Durante Boulevard. Usually she borrowed her mother's Seville to drive around in, but this morning her mother had gone to her beautician in La Jolla to have her face jacked up another inch, as Daffy put it.

They had almost reached the intersection with the main road when a clear man's voice behind them said, 'Pardon me, are you Susan Sczaniecka?'

Susan and Daffy turned around. It was the man who had been sitting on the wall outside Susan's grandparents' house. He was tall – taller than Daffy had imagined – with dark wavy hair. He took off his sunglasses and both girls had to admit to themselves that he was undeniably good looking. Thin faced, brown eyed, with one of those slightly amused faces that can make you feel both excited and at ease – at least if you're a seventeen-year-old girl.

'Didn't I see you sitting on the wall?' said Daffy, in a tone that meant the man ought to establish his credentials before either she or Susan would start talking to him.

'Sure you did. I was waiting for you to come out.'

'Why didn't you call at the door?' asked Susan. She had to close one eye against the bright sunshine.

'I didn't want to disturb your grandparents, that's all. You know what they're like.'

Susan frowned. 'Sure I know what they're like. But how do you know what they're like?'

'It's my job. I'm a newspaper reporter. Here – here's my card. Paul Springer, *San Diego Tribune.*'

'You're really a reporter?' Daffy asked him, squinting at the card.

'Sure. Why else do you think I've been staking out your grandparents' house?' 'To rape us?' Daffy suggested.

'You don't have to sound so hopeful,' grinned Paul.

Susan handed his card back. 'Is this about what happened on the beach this morning?'

Paul gave a reserved, down-and-sideways glance. 'Kind of. That's part of it.'

'How did you know about that? The police said they were keeping it out of the media.'

Paul continued grinning and shook his head. 'If the police had their way, *everything* would be kept out of the media. Except successful drug-busts, of course, and police baseball-team scores.'

'I don't really have anything to say about it,' Susan told him. 'I didn't see any more than anybody else.'

'It was pretty horrifying, wasn't it?' said Paul.

Daffy butted in: 'My friend here doesn't actually want

to talk about it, you know? She was very sick this morning because of what happened. So, you know, do you mind? We're on our way home, and we'd just like to get on with it.'

But Susan said, 'Come on, Daffy, it's okay. He's not bothering me.'

'May I walk along?' asked Paul.

They continued northwards along Camino Del Mar, between the rustling yuccas, waving occasionally to kids they knew who were hanging out beside the bars and hotels and stores along the strip. One group was gathered around a VW Beetle which had just been resprayed in ruby metallic flake and decorated with airbrushed pictures of surfers and Western heroes. There was a strong smell of marijuana in the air, mingled with pina-colada suntan lotion.

Paul seemed incredibly straight, and yet Susan felt that there was something strange about him, something almost unreal. When he spoke, she felt that she could anticipate everything that he was going to say, and in a peculiar way she felt that she had met him before, although she wasn't sure when. It didn't seem to be necessary to get to know him. They talked from the very beginning as if they were long-time acquaintances.

'I've been assigned by the *Tribune* to write a series of feature articles on young people' said Paul. 'Each of the articles is supposed to cover a different aspect of the way that young people think and react. I guess you might call it a kind of psychoanalysis of youth. Well, it sounds pretty corny stuff, but I think that if it's written and researched properly, it doesn't have to be. In fact, I think it could be really enlightening.'

'You want to write about *me!*' asked Susan, more curious than flattered.

'Well – to come straight to the point – one of the articles has to do with death, and how young people cope with it.'

'How do you mean?' Susan asked him.

'I mean, how young people come to terms with losing somebody they love. Their parents, maybe, like you did –'

'How did you know that?'

'I'm sorry. I thought I recognised your name when the police passed me the list of witnesses to what happened down there on the beach. I looked you up in the morgue. Your parents were killed in a car-crash, weren't they, over at Lake Hodges?'

Susan nodded. 'I didn't realise I was quite so famous,' she said, not without a touch of bitterness, although she knew that Paul hadn't meant to upset her.

'The thing is,' Paul continued, 'you not only lost your parents, you saw a complete stranger lying dead on the beach. It would be interesting for me to compare your reaction to each of these events: the death of someone you loved, and the death of someone you didn't even know. I'd like to know how you really felt, and how you feel now.'

'Isn't that pretty ghoulish?' Daffy demanded.

'Well, maybe it is,' Paul admitted, 'and if Susan doesn't want to have anything to do with it – that's as far as it goes. But death is a part of life, and there isn't any point in trying to hide away from it. I think that other young people – if they read about Susan and how she's handled those tragedies – well, they may find it easier to cope with their own experiences of death.'

Daffy pulled a face. 'Sounds like bull time, if you'll pardon my French.'

But Susan said, 'I don't know. Maybe we could talk about it some more.'

'Maybe this evening?' Paul asked her. 'Supposing I buy you dinner, on the *Trib*.'

'Okay, then. Where?'

'You know Bully's North? I'll meet you there at seven.'

Susan thought about it, and then nodded yes. 'Okay. The only thing is, I have to be home at nine-thirty. That's the house rule.'

'I know,' said Paul.

Daffy was frowning ferociously – her 'for-Christ's-sake-be-careful' face. But Susan, without knowing why, felt safe with Paul, and reassured. She didn't even think to ask him how he could possibly have known that she had to be home by half-past nine.

'I left my car at the Oceanside Hotel,' said Paul. 'I'll catch you later, okay?'

He crossed the street, and made his way back along Camino Del Mar towards the Oceanside. Susan watched him go, while Daffy waited a little way away, an exaggeratedly sceptical expression already prepared on her face.

'What a bull artist,' said Daffy.

'I don't think so,' said Susan, without even noticing the special face that Daffy had put on for her.

'You don't mean to say that you fell for all that stuff

about death and things? My God, Suze, he wants your body, that's all.'

'Don't be so ridiculous. He doesn't even know me.'

'Oh, no? Well, he knows your name, and he knows that your parents died in a car-crash, and he knows that you were down on the beach this morning, and he knows that you live with your grandparents, and he knows what time you're supposed to be home, and he also seems to know that your personal favourite restaurant is Bully's North. Now, if he's telling the truth, he only got your name from the cops about an hour ago. How did he find all *that* out in just one hour?'

Susan looked towards the ocean, glittering between the buildings on the opposite side of the road like smashed diamonds. 'I don't know,' she said.

'Well, don't *you care!* I think it's scary.'

'No,' said Susan, and in her own mind she was quite sure of this. 'It's not scary. But something's going to happen. Something's going to change. I can feel it.'

'Brother!' said Daffy, shaking her head. 'The lightning bolt of true love has struck you straight in the brain.'

'No,' Susan emphatically. 'It's more important than love.'

Chapter Three

Gil swerved his Mustang into the parking-lot across the street from his father's Mini-Market, gunned the engine, and then switched it off. He sat where he was for a moment or two, thinking, and then he hopped out of the driver's seat, and crossed over Highway 101, jingling his car-keys in his hand.

The Mini-Market was a single-fronted store, wedged between the Mandarin Coast Chinese restaurant and Freddy's Instant Print Service. It was the kind of store that sold absolutely everything from ice-cream to cans of Chef Boy-ar-dee Spaghetti Bolognese to shoe-laces to golfing hats to Jewish get-well cards. It had a wonderful aroma to it; an aroma of feta cheese and Hungarian salami and penny candy and Superman comics. Gil's father was a qualified engineer, and could have brought in four times as much money designing braking systems for hospital trolleys and hydraulic controls for locomotives, but he had dreamed about owning a store like the Mini-Market ever since he was a kid, and he wouldn't have lived out his life any other way.

Gil's mother used to say that he must have had a deprived childhood, to want to run a general store, but she knew how happy he was, and that made her happy, too. She stocked the shelves and kept the store clean and even made quiches for the deli counter. Along the strip, Gil's father and mother were known as the 'M&Ms' – Mr and Mrs. Miller.

Gil's father was standing behind the checkout, packing a week's groceries for old Mrs. Van Buren who lived on the other side of the Santa Fe Railroad tracks. He was tall and big boned, like Gil, with wiry grey hair and one of those husky-looking outdoor faces like Lloyd Bridges. He wore a striped blue storekeeper's apron with his name sewn on to the pocket, *Phil*.

'Hi, Dad,' said Gil.

'How're you doing?' his father asked him. 'You're back early.'

'I didn't feel like swimming, that's all.'

'They closed off the beach, somebody told me,' said Phil Miller. 'Did you want the barbecue-flavoured beans, Mrs. Van Buren, or the vegetarian?'

'Yeah, I think somebody drowned or something,' Gil remarked.

'There were ambulances and police cars coming in from all directions,' said Phil, reaching down for another paper sack, and opening it out.

'I heard that it was a girl,' put in Mrs. Van Buren. 'Some girl, drowned on the beach. Nude, that's what I heard.'

'Taking dope, if you ask me,' said Phil. 'They take dope, they swim, and they think they can swim all the way to Japan.'

'I guess we were just as crazy in my day,' said Mrs. Van Buren. 'In those days, of course, it was bootleg liquor. We used to drive up and down the Pacific Highway in a De Soto CK Six, high as kites on McNamara's home-brewed whiskey, and see how far we could get without putting our hands on the steering-wheel. First person to grab for the wheel was a chicken.'

Phil laughed. 'Why now, Mrs. Van Buren, I didn't know you were a juvenile delinquent.'

'You show me a juvenile who isn't,' said Mrs. Van Buren, 'and I'll show you a juvenile who's never going to get anywhere in life, not anywhere at all.'

'I don't know about that,' said Gil. 'This girl only got as far as the beach.'

Phil glanced across at his son questioningly. Gil was conscious that he had sounded as if he had known the girt, or seen her. He deliberately changed the subject by rubbing his hands together briskly, and saying, 'Want me to slice up some ham, Dad?' 'Sure thing, and maybe some of that Italian salami, too, the dry salami.'

Gil walked between the shelves of groceries to the back of the store, to the glass-fronted deli counter. He went around it, ducking his head to avoid the plastic cloves of garlic which hung from the ceiling, and through to the stockroom, where there was a washbasin and a mirror. He washed his hands thoroughly, and dried them. In the mirror, his face looked detached and expressionless, and not at all like the face of somebody who had just witnessed a hideous death and a frightening accident.

Back at the counter, he hefted up a large Maryland ham, covered in golden breadcrumbs and positioned it on to the slicer. He switched on the motor, and began to slide the slicer backwards and forwards, heaping up thin pink stacks of aromatic ham. His father had finished with Mrs. Van Buren, and came down to the back of the shop, wiping his hands on his apron.

'By the way,' he said, 'some girl came by, asking where you were.'

'Some girl? It wasn't Gina Chappell, was it?'

'I don't know; I don't know what Gina Chappell looks like.'

'Blonde, gappy teeth, very small tits.'

His father grunted in amusement. 'No, this wasn't Gina Chappell. This one was tall, and dark, and I have to say that she had very big –' He left the word unspoken, but held out his hands as if he were comparing the weight of two large cantaloups.

Gil switched off the slicer, and lifted the ham with a spatula. 'Don't know who that could have been.'

'She seemed quite anxious to see you. She said she'd have a cup of coffee down at the bookstore, and then she'd come back.'

Gil smiled at his father, and switched the slicer back on again. 'Maybe it's my lucky day. For the first time in my life, a beautiful girl has come chasing *me*.'

'She's probably an officer of the court, trying to serve you with a summons for all those parking tickets of yours.'

'Don't shatter my illusions, Dad.'

Phil watched his son for a moment or two, and then said, 'Are you okay?'

Gil glanced up. 'Okay? Why shouldn't I be okay?'

'I don't know. You look kind of worried about something.'

'Worried?'

'Well, I don't know. You look like you've got something preying on your mind.'

Gil shook his head. 'Nothing that I can think of.'

But his father didn't seem to be satisfied. He stayed silent a little while longer, and then he said, 'It's not like you, to miss out on your swim.'

'I jogged. The jogging was enough.'

'Your leg isn't hurting?'

'My leg is fine. What is this, the third degree? You're going to beat a confession out of me with a Hungarian salami?'

Phil laughed again, but without much amusement. 'I know you. I know you better than you know yourself. That's because you're just like me. And when I'm worried about something, I behave just like you. I laugh, but all the time it's false. And that's how *you're* laughing. I knew something was wrong the moment you walked into the store.'

'God protect me from an understanding father,' said Gil. 'Do you think that's enough ham? There's about three and a half pounds there, in half-pound batches.'

'That's enough; you can always slice some more later.'

Gil's mother came in, carrying two cartons of Coco-Puffs from the storeroom at the back. 'Oh. Gil, I'm glad you're back. You can stack these on the shelf for me.'

Gil took the cartons, and carried them around to the cereal display. His mother followed him, and stood beside him. She was a small woman, still handsome at forty-four. Phil said she reminded him of a statue, a Greek statue, not the one without the arms but the other one, with the classic face and the classic figure. She was smiling as she watched Gil cut open the cartons and take out the boxes of cereal.

'Who's the girl?' she asked him.

'You mean the girl who came around looking for me?'

'There's another girl?'

'Well, Dad told me about her, but I don't know who she is.'

'She's very pretty,' said Fay Miller, looking at her son closely to see if he was telling the truth.

'That's what Dad said.'

'And you really expect us to believe that you don't know who she is?'

Gil slapped his hand over his heart. 'Mom, believe me, I wish I did.'

About ten minutes later, Gil's friend Bradley came in. Bradley's father ran a fishing-tackle store in Encinitas, a few miles up the coast. Bradley was lanky and funny and almost invariably wore Hawaiian-style beach shirts and Bermuda shorts. He and Gil had been classmates in grade school, and although Bradley was now studying to be a computer programmer, while Gil was taking business studies, they saw each other practically every weekend and all through the summer vacation, and went fishing, and swam, and told each other absurd jokes.

Bradley lifted the new issue of *Hustler* off the revolving rack and appreciatively leafed through it. Gil's father had made sure that his general store had an adult magazine rack. He derived benign amusement out of watching teenage boys pluck up enough panicky courage to buy themselves a copy of *Chic* or *Penthouse*, paying for it red faced and then rushing out of the store as quickly as they could. The adult magazine rack was part of a general store's mystery and excitement, along with the strange bottles of Japanese cooking ingredients, the lurid candies and the peculiar kitchen gadgets.

'How're you doing, Bradley?' asked Gil. He took a quarter from a small ginger-haired boy who had carefully been counting out eight liquorice whips, and gave him a penny change.

'Oh, bored, pretty much,' said Bradley. 'Did you hear about what happened at the beach?'

'Yeah, I heard. "They've still got it cordoned off. Jellyfish warning, that's what they're saying now.'

'Oh, yeah?'

Bradley opened up *Hustler's* centre-spread. He was silent for a very long time. Then he said, 'Do you know something, it isn't fair. It just damn well isn't fair. Some guy got paid for taking this picture. *Paid*, can you imagine that? And I couldn't get to see a girl like that with her legs wide open if I crawled all the way to Mount Palomar and back pushing a rat's turd with the end of my nose.'

'Well, that explains it,' Gil told him. 'Girls like that don't really go for guys who push rat's turds up and down mountains with the ends of their noses. Didn't anybody tell you that? Your social science teacher?'

Bradley swatted at Gil with the rolled-up magazine.

'Hey, you take care of that,' warned Gil. 'Some jerk-off is going to want to buy that.'

'I'd buy it myself, but I just couldn't stand the unfairness.'

Gil shook his head, and said, 'You're a real dork, sometimes, Bradley. I hate to think what the inside of your brain is like.'

'Listen, I have to tell you this joke,' said Bradley. 'What do you get if you let an elephant walk across your living-room?'

'For God's sake, Bradley, I don't want to know about that.'

'No, come on, what do you get if you let an elephant walk across your living-room?'

Gil sighed in exaggerated exasperation. 'I don't know, Bradley. What *do* you get if you let an elephant walk across your living-room?'

'You get a thick pile on your carpet.'

Gil said, 'I should throw you out of here, right on your head, you know that?' But then he turned around and there she was, standing in the doorway, with the sunlight shining brightly behind her so that Gil had to narrow his eyes to make out what she looked like. Bradley turned around too, and was suddenly silent. Gil's father had been quite right. She was tall, almost as tall as Gil, and dark haired. Her hair was brushed and clean and shining and it reached right down over her shoulders. Her eyes were wide and her lashes were extravagantly long; her mouth was slightly parted as if she were about to say something or as if she were about to kiss somebody. She wore a tight white tee-shirt which clung to her overfull breasts, and it was obvious from the way that the darker tint of her nipples showed through the cotton that she was wearing no bra. She wore white rolled-up shorts and white sandals, and that was all.

'Gil Miller?' she said.

Bradley whispered, 'My wish has been granted. Did she say Bradley Donahue?'

Gil looked the girl up and down, trying to be steady, trying to be cool, but with an extraordinary tightness around his heart.

'*That's –*' he began, in a choked falsetto. Then, much deeper, 'That's me.'

The girl stepped into the store, and smiled at him.

'My name's Paulette Springer. I hope you don't mind my surprising you like this.'

'Well, uh, no,' said Gil, wiping his hands on his denim shorts. 'No, no. My folks told me you called by earlier. I'm just sorry I wasn't here.'

'I know, you had to take Susan Sczaniecka home. But that's all right. I had a cup of coffee at the second-hand bookstore. That's quite a place, isn't it? I bought a book called *De Sortilegio*.'

Gil glanced at Bradley, but all Bradley could do was look baffled.

Paulette came closer. Gil couldn't help noticing the tantalising sway of her breasts underneath her tee-shirt. Close up, he could smell her perfume, which was like sweet-peas and roses and something else altogether, something subtle and arousing and barely perceptible, like the smell of a warm clean body.

'I was hoping you could help me,' she said. 'Well, sure,' Gil told her. 'Anything, you name it.'

'I'm writing an article for *San Diego* magazine about the different things that get washed up on the beaches.'

'Oh, yeah?' Gil's heart still felt tight; in fact it felt tighter than ever.

'I know it sounds silly,' said Paulette, 'but actually it's going to make a pretty interesting piece. You'd be amazed what gets washed up. I mean apart from whales and driftwood and things like that. There's an old man who lives about a mile north of here, and he's furnished his whole cottage with chairs and tables and beds that were washed right up on the beach.'

Gil drummed his fingers on the top of the cash-register.

'That's pretty interesting. The only thing is, what does it have to do with me?'

'Well,' Paulette smiled, her eyes sparkling at him, 'you go down to the beach every morning, don't you? You have to jog, because of your leg."

'That's right,' Gil agreed. 'It's part of the therapy. But I still don't see –'

She lifted a finger to silence him. He didn't know why, but he was silent. She said, quite sweetly, 'You're almost always the very first person down on the beach, aren't you? Sometimes you' re down there as soon as it's daylight. So if anything was washed up during the night, anything at all, you'd be the very first person to find it.'

Gil looked at her closely. Then he looked away, and jammed his hands into the back pockets of his sawn-off jeans, and made one of those faces that means hey, hold up a minute, what exactly in hell is going on here? Paulette watched him, her soft smile never wavering once, and Bradley watched Paulette. His face was saying, it isn't fair. The nearest living thing I've ever seen to a *Hustler* centre-spread walks right into my life, and wants to talk to Gil, not me.

Gil said, at last, 'Have you been talking to anybody?'

'I don't know what you mean.'

'Have you been talking to Susan Sczaniecka? Or that old guy who lives along the beach?'

'Who's Susan Sczaniecka when she's at home?' Bradley wanted to know.

Paulette didn't answer Gil's questions, but said in the simplest of voices, 'You've found one or two interesting things washed up on the beach, haven't you?'

'I found a case full of Johnny Walker once. My dad made me hand it over to the Coastguard. I expect they drank it. I'm pretty damn *sure* they drank it.'

'And then of course you found what you found today.' Paulette's mouth may have been smiling, but the expression in her eyes was completely serious.

'You talked to Lieutenant Ortega?' asked Gil.

'Gil,' Paulette coaxed him, 'all I want to do is to write my article. You don't have to be mentioned by name. All you have to do is describe what happened to you, how you felt about it.'

There was no doubt that Paulette was almost irresistibly attractive. If Gil had seen her in a crowd of girls, he would have picked her out straight away. She was exactly the type of girl that turned him on the most. Long brunette hair, sooty-lashed eyes, and the kind of figure that just had to be felt to be believed. She was standing even closer now, so that her breasts were almost touching his arm, and he could see the tiny green flecks in the irises of her eyes.

The tip of her tongue ran lightly across her lower lip. Gil melted inside, into white-hot liquid boy. He was confused by Paulette, and irritated by how much she knew about him. She even frightened him just a little. But he knew that whatever she suggested, he wouldn't be able to refuse, because a girl who looked like this would probably never walk into the Mini-Market ever again, not in a grillion years, and what a dork he would look if he chased her away.

Who cared what she knew? Who cared what she wanted? His throat was dry and his shorts were uncomfortably tight and she was so goddamned nice, as well as sexy, as well as beautiful, and, if she went to the second-hand bookstore and bought books with names like *Day Sortie Ledgey*, as well as intelligent, too.

'What exactly do I have to do?' Gil asked, cautiously.

'You have to answer some questions, that's all,' Paulette told him. 'There's nothing to it.'

'Questions about ... what I found on the beach?'

'Uh-huh.'

'You really want to know about that?'

There was a look in her eyes that warned him not to ask her any more, not in front of Bradley, at least.

'We can't do it here,' she said. 'Why don't you meet me this evening? We could talk over dinner.'

'Sure, if that's what you want. Sure.' He tried to sound off-hand.

'Okay, then,' said Paulette. 'Meet me at seven at Bully's North. You know Bully's North?'

'Well, yes, but I can't afford to buy you dinner there.'

'That's okay,' Paulette smiled. 'The magazine will pay for the meal. Expense account.'

Just then, Phil Miller came up to the front of the store. He nodded to Paulette, and then said to Gil, 'Aren't you going to introduce me?'

'I'm sorry Dad. This is Paulette Springer, from *San Diego* magazine. She wants to write an article about some of the things that people find on the beach. Paulette, this is my dad.'

They shook hands. 'Good to know you, Mr. Miller,' said Paulette. 'How's your insurance problem?'

'Oh, I guess we'll get the money eventually,' said Phil. 'The insurance company's been arguing that a brown-out doesn't constitute a black-out, and so none of our freezer-food was covered; but our lawyer seems pretty hopeful about it.'

He suddenly stopped himself, and frowned at her. 'How do you *know* about that?' he asked her.

She smiled at him, half knowingly, half provocatively. 'Word gets around,' she said, winking.

'Word gets around about three hundred dollars' worth of spoiled pizzas?'

Paulette wouldn't say any more, but gave Gil's hand a squeeze and told him, 'I'll see you later. Don't be late. Bully's North, at seven.'

'I'll be there,' Gil promised.

All three of them watched her walk out of the store, and the way that she moved in her tight white shorts. Bradley whispered, in a reverential voice, 'No panties, did you see that? Not a pantie-crease in sight.' He stared wide eyed at Gil, and clenched his fists, and said, 'God! I could hit myself in the face with a brick.'

'It might do you some good,' said Phil.

Gil just stood behind the cash-register staring at the open door of the Mini-Market as if he couldn't believe that Paulette had actually been real.

Phil said, 'You're seeing her tonight?'

Gil nodded. 'She's buying me dinner.'

Phil laid his arm around his son's shoulders. 'You know something?' he said. 'There do seem to be times when you can fall on your feet.' He glanced behind him, but Gil's mother was still in the stockroom. 'Just make sure, you know, that you take all the necessary precautions. She might be a lovely young lady, but I don't know her well enough yet to entrust her with my first grandchild.'

Bradley wrenched his golfing-hat down over his head. 'Precautions! What are you doing to me? I could hit myself in the face with two bricks.'

Phil laughed, and gave Bradley a playful punch in the stomach. Bradley coughed and spluttered and pretended to expire.

'Listen,' said Phil, 'I'll do you a favour. You can have that *Hustler* at fifty per cent discount.'

'While he goes out with Miss Super Bosom, 1986? Are you kidding?'

Gil served behind the deli counter until lunchtime. Then he made himself a salt beef and onion submarine, and took off for San Pasqual Valley, out by the San Diego Wild Animal Park, where his friend Santos Ramona lived. Santos had briefly attended the same business college as Gil, but after two semesters his father had been hospitalised with emphysema, and he had been obliged to give up his education and work in the San Pasqual vineyards to support his family. Bradley was fun; but Santos was the man to see if you felt serious or reflective. Santos had sampled peyote and yage, the mind-expanding drugs taken by the Jivaro Indians. Santos claimed that he could see the future.

Gil ate the salt beef submarine as he drove one-handed along the winding road that led up from Solana Beach to Rancho Santa Fe. Beyond the quiet retirement community of Rancho Santa Fe, with its whitewashed houses and its neat streets, the road ribboned out into more mountainous country, around the edge of Lake Hodges, and out into the San

Pasqual Valley. Hot and sheltered, with slopes of dry, tawny soil, the San Pasqual Valley was ideal for growing grapes. The vines stood hand-in-hand on the hillsides, their green leaves fluttering in the afternoon breeze like tattered shirts.

Santos Ramona's house was set close by the road, in a steep sloping hollow, so low down that its clay-tiled roof was almost on the same level as the pavement. Gil steered the Mustang down the dusty gradient into Santos's front yard, and five or six chickens scattered around his wheels. Santos himself was out back, with a spanner in one hand and a can of Mexican beer in the other, staring without much optimism at a battered John Deere tractor, and occasionally wiping the sweat from his forehead with the back of his arm.

Gil brought the Mustang to a halt, and a cloud of sandy-coloured dust drifted away through the eucalyptus trees which shaded the back of Santo's property. Gil jumped out, and walked over to stand next to Santos and join him in staring at the tractor.

'What's wrong?' he asked Santos.

'You've been eating onions,' Santos remarked.

'So what? What's wrong with the tractor?'

'Won't go.'

'Do you know what's the matter with it?'

Santos swallowed beer, and then spat into the dust. 'If I knew what the matter with it was, I'd fix it.'

'Maybe the fuel line.'

'Maybe the fuel line what?'

'Well, maybe it's clogged. That happens with tractors, working in dirty conditions.'

Santos stared at the tractor for a moment or two longer,

then let the spanner drop on to the ground with a clank. 'Come inside,' he said. 'Do you feel like a beer? Where have you been for so long? These past two months, I've hardly seen you.'

They walked into the house. It was shadier inside, but not much cooler. In the blue and yellow-tiled kitchen, Santos's mother was making empenadas, and occasionally flicking away flies with the fringe of her black embroidered shawl.

'How're you doing, Mrs. Ramona?' Gil asked her.

'Phoof, don't ask me,' Mrs. Ramona replied. Her face was thin and wrinkled and her eyes were as black and glittering as two beetles, nestling in the sockets of her skull. 'My husband is still sick, you know; the winery is cutting their workforce; who knows what will happen?'

Santos went to the icebox and took out two more beers. He lobbed one across the kitchen to Gil, and Gil caught it left-handed.

'Come through,' said Santos, and they walked through to Santos's bedroom. Santos kicked the door shut behind them, and suddenly Gil felt peaceful and quiet and very enclosed.

To look at Santos, it was almost impossible to guess that he had a room like this. He was short and podgy, and his shirt was always hanging out of his jeans. He had one of those Mexican faces that reminded Gil of Mayan masks, flat as a pancake, and featureless. His black hair was combed into a 1950's crest at the front and duck-tailed at the back. He spat a lot, by way of punctuation.

His room, however, was almost monastic. It was white painted and cool. The bed was neatly draped with a plain light-blue cover. There was a pale oak closet with brass hinges and a shelf with half a dozen books on it, all in Spanish and all concerned with mysticism. On the wall between the two shuttered windows there was a large gilt and enamel crucifix, set with red glass rubies and pieces of mirror. The Christ that hung on it was like a pink-painted doll, with an almost ludicrously agonised expression on His face.

'Well, what worry brings you here?' asked Santos, prizing off his sweaty loafers and sitting cross-legged on the bed. He tugged the ring-pull of his beer-can, and sucked at the opening before it could foam out too much.

'Does it have to be a worry? Maybe I just felt like shooting the breeze with my old friend Santos.'

'You sound more and more like a bad cowboy movie every time you come here. What's the matter? You're forgetting those times we had, those bottles of wine we drank, those things we talked about?'

Gil shook his head. He hadn't opened his beer yet. He kept the ice-cold can pressed against his chest. 'It was because of those things we talked about that I came this afternoon.'

'Which things in particular?'

'Magic. You know, people who can work magic. Shamans, medicine men, people like that. People who can make themselves invisible, and people who know everything about you even though they've never met you before.'

'Oh, yeah?' asked Santos. He seemed unimpressed, but Gil could tell that he was interested.

Gil said, simply, 'I went out jogging on the beach this morning. I found a dead body. Well, me and this girl and this old professor-type guy, we found it together. It was a girl, a naked girl, and she was way up on the sand, way beyond the weed-line.'

Carefully, with very little embellishment he told Santos all about the girl's body, and the eels, and what had happened to the policeman. Then he told him about Paulette Springer, especially the way that Paulette Springer seemed to know everything about him.

'Do you know something?' he said. 'I've been thinking about this on the way out here: she was *exactly* my type. Can you believe that? The more I think about her, the more it hits me. She was my dream girl, my fantasy girl, come true. I loved her face and I loved her body and I loved the way she dressed. I loved the way she talked and I loved the way she laughed. Jesus – if I met a girl like that and she really liked me, I'd marry her tomorrow. I'd marry her this evening.'

Santos listened to this carefully. Then he reached into his pocket and took out a key. He unlocked his closet, and from one of the shelves near the top, he brought down a tin box, with a plaid pattern printed on it. Originally, it had contained Genuine Scottish Petticoat Tails. Santos opened it up and inspected its contents. About a half-ounce of marijuana, a packet of cigarette-papers, and some shag tobacco.

'We should smoke,' he said. 'Then maybe we can find out what's going on here.'

'I'm not sure I want to.'

'I can't help you if you don't,' Santos told him, matter-of-factly.

Gil glanced up at the crucifix, and then said, 'Okay. But I'm not getting totally stoned. I want to get back and meet this girl this evening.'

'You'll get back,' Santos assured him.

Gil watched silently as Santos rolled a joint. Then he

closed the tin box and reached into his shirt pocket for matches. He lit up unhurriedly, and blew smoke across the room. 'This is good stuff. I got it from Benes. You remember Benes, who used to come down to the college sometimes?'

'Sure,' said Gil. He waited while Santos drew in a deep, sharp breath of marijuana. Then he said, 'You must miss college pretty bad.'

Santos shrugged, his mouth leaking smoke. 'What's to miss? Look what I got here. A tractor that won't go, a mother who never stops complaining, grapevines, heat, dust, and fucking chickens.'

He passed over the joint. Gil hesitated, and then inhaled, dragging the aromatic smoke deep down into his lungs. He closed his eyes and waited, then he slowly allowed the smoke to roll out of him. He took another drag, and then passed the joint back to Santos.

Gradually, as they smoked, the room seemed to Gil to openout, to expand. Before he knew it, the tiny adobe cell was like a vast cathedral, echoing and empty. He could see Santos, but Santos appeared to be very far away, and shrunken, as if he were nothing more than a half-developed embryo with a checkered shirt and a pompadour.

Santos said, slowly and loudly, 'You have to tell me what she said ... exactly what she said.'

Gil tried to think of Paulette. For a moment, he couldn't assemble any kind of picture of her in his mind, but then he forced himself to remember the very first moment he had seen her, standing against the sunlight that irradiated the street outside the Mini-Market door.

In a blurry voice, he told Santos, 'She said ... Gil Miller. She spoke my name.'

'Then what did she say?'

'She said ... I'm sorry to surprise you ... she said, I've had a cup of coffee and I've bought a book ... She told me the name of the book. She seemed to think that I would know what it meant, like it was a secret message or something.'

'What was the name of the book?' asked Santos. He sounded distant and metallic.

'It was foreign, I didn't understand it. I can't remember it now. *Day* something.'

'Remember,' Santos urged him. 'It could be important.'

Gil closed his eyes and tried to recall the name of the book. *Day* something. *Day* something. *Day After Day. Day For Night. Day of the Triffids.*

He heard a voice, different from Santos's voice, and he opened his eyes again. He was startled to see that the floor of the room was bright blue, and swirled with streaks of white that looked like horsetail clouds. One second he was sitting still, the next he was travelling over the floor at what seemed like sixty or seventy miles an hour, the clouds flashing past underneath him. The voice said, '*Remember nothing. Remember nothing.*' And then he was hurtling even faster, even though he was still sitting with his legs crossed.

There was a flash of ultimate speed. Then the opposite wall of Santos's room came rocketing towards him, and hit him straight in the face. He was conscious of falling, tilting sideways. Then he looked around him and he was lying on the tiles, and there was blood splashed everywhere. Santos was kneeling beside him, staring at him in fright.

'Hey, you're not dead?' Santos asked him, anxiously. His high seemed to have vaporised.

Gil touched his nose, and then his forehead. His fingers came away bloody, and his head pounded.

'What happened?' he croaked.

'What happened? I wish I knew. One minute we were sitting there talking, the next minute you jumped up like a fucking space shuttle and banged your face straight into the wall.'

'Did you hear anything?' Gil asked him, gripping hold of the edge of the bed, and sitting up.

'Hear anything? Like what?'

'Like a voice, another voice. Not yours, and not mine.'

'I didn't hear anything like that, but what I did hear was quite enough.'

Gil tugged out his handkerchief, and dabbed at his nose. He hoped his face wasn't going to be bruised for this evening's date.

'What did you hear? You mean you heard something from me?'

'Sure, you said the name of the book.'

'Well. Day something was all I could remember,' Gil told him.

'No, no, you said the name. And, believe me, that's all I needed to hear. *De Sortilegio*.'

'Hey, that was it!' Gil responded. '*De Sortilegio*. That was the book she bought.'

Santos shook his head. 'No way did she *buy De Sortilegio* at any second-hand bookstore in Solana Beach. You were right, she was giving you a message. Pity you were too dumb to understand it.'

'Well, what is it, then, this *De Sortilegio?* Sounds like some kind of Italian cookbook.'

Santos said, '*De Sortilegio* was written by some guy called Paul Grilland in fifteen – something. It's a famous book, if you're into mysticism and magic and all that kind of stuff. You don't find it in any second-hand bookstore, though. No way, Jose. It's rare, and what's more it's all in Latin, because it's so dirty.'

'What are you trying to say? This Paulette was trying to talk dirty to me in Latin?'

'Are you kidding? *De Sortilegio* is only dirty because it explains how the Devil, who happens to be a spirit, can have physical sex with mortal women. I mean it tells you how he uses living ectoplasm to provide himself with a viable dick.'

Battered and sore as he was, Gil was still a little bit high. He kept a straight face as long as he could, but then he burst out laughing, and rolled on to the bed, laughing so much that he could scarcely breathe.

'Oh, God, Santos, you had me fooled with that one! Oh, God, I can't stand it! A viable dick! Oh, God, that's the funniest thing I ever heard!'

But as Gil laughed, and pounded his fists on the bed, Santos remained unsmiling. He waited for Gil to finish, and kept his eyes fastened on the crucifix that hung on the wall of his room.

He closed his eyes for a moment, and prayed, and then he crossed himself twice.

Gil abruptly stopped laughing, and stared at him, his forehead marked with a glaring crimson bruise, his upper lip caked with dried blood from his nose.' What are you doing?' he asked, in a hollow-sounding voice.

'I am praying for my own protection,' he said.

Gil turned toward the crucifix, and then back toward Santos. 'Protection from what?' he demanded. 'Come on, tell me, protection from *what*?'

Chapter Four

Henry was asleep on the couch when Lieutenant Ortega called around. At first, he thought that the persistent buzzing of the doorbell was a large mosquito, and he flapped at the air several times to get rid of it. Then he opened his eyes and saw the sunlight and the ceiling and the half-empty bottle of vodka on the table, next to Andrea's book on eels, and he was jolted back to reality like a man arriving at the lobby of a cheap hotel in a badly serviced elevator.

He opened the door. Lieutenant Ortega was standing on the concrete doorstep, neat and smart in his cinnamon-coloured suit and his cinnamon-coloured necktie, his hands clasped behind his back, inspecting Henry's thermometer.

'Eighty-two already,' be smiled. 'Looks like we're in for a hot afternoon.'

Henry smeared his hand all over his face, trying to reassemble his features. The older he got, and the drunker he got, the larger his face seemed to spread, and the less disciplined its component parts seemed to become. His forehead felt like a ploughed field that it would take hours to walk across. His jowls seemed to hang like theatre curtains. The bags under his eyes were hammocks, in which fat and indolent matelots swung.

'You'd, uh,' he said, gesturing behind him, 'better come in.'

Lieutenant Ortega walked past him into the living-room. His suit may have looked cheap but his after-shave was Giorgio of Beverley Hills. He stood in the centre of the carpet, carefully tugging his cuffs and looking around him. Henry closed the door. He was pretty sure that Lieutenant Ortega had immediately taken note of the vodka bottle and the book on eels.

'What happened this morning on the beach, that was very distressing,' said Lieutenant Ortega. His Latin accent was soft but distinctive.

'It was not only distressing, it was *unnatural*,' said Henry. He walked across the room, tucking in his shirt-tails, and collected up the bottle of vodka. He tightened the screw-cap, and put the bottle back in the cupboard.

'I will be talking later to the two young people who were with you,' said the lieutenant. 'But I thought first of all that I would like to discuss the matter with you. You are, after all, a man of learning, are you not?'

Henry shrugged, and sniffed. 'Learning, yes. Wisdom, only possibly.'

Lieutenant Ortega leaned over the book of eels. Henry had been reading about their dietary habits. Henry watched him for a moment, and then volunteered, 'There doesn't seem to be any record of eels attacking a human being *en masse*, the way those eels did.'

'Well, it's something of a mystery,' Lieutenant Ortega admitted. 'We still have the beach cordoned off, and we have asked the people from Scripps to come along and dig out the remaining eels for us. Then perhaps we can find out how to deal with them.'

'It could be a serious problem, couldn't it, killer eels, just before the vacation season?'

Lieutenant Ortega smiled distantly. 'I don't think we have a *Jaws* situation on our hands, Professor Watkins. This is probably an isolated tragedy. Some deep-sea eels which were brought close to shore by the current. We've been having some unusual tides here lately; you know for yourself how uncharacteristic the weather has been.'

'What does your medical examiner think?' asked Henry. 'He seemed like a pretty opinionated kind of guy.'

'Oh, him. John Belli. Don't take too much notice of him. He would run the whole investigation single handed, if we allowed him. He watches too much *Quincy* on television.

He's good, yes, I have to confess, but he sometimes fails to see the whole picture. How and when somebody died is usually not half as important as *why*.'

Henry said, 'What do you think I can do for you? Would you like some coffee?'

Lieutenant Ortega nodded. 'Yes, some coffee would be appreciated. Black, please.'

Henry went through to the kitchen, which was an untidy jumble of washed-up dishes that hadn't yet been put away, cups, glasses, boxes of cereal, and sprawled-out newspaper sections. He rinsed out the coffee jug, filled it, and unfolded a fresh filter-paper.

'Mocha. You like mocha, lieutenant?'

'Perhaps you should call me Salvador. I'm not much of a stickler for formality.'

'Salvador, okay. My name's Henry. Well, you know that.'

They shook hands. Henry looked around the kitchen and said, 'Excuse the – well, I was working all night. The place doesn't usually stay too tidy when I'm working.'

'You were thinking about the eels this morning, then?' asked Salvador.

'Yes, I was thinking about the eels.'

'And what line of thinking were you pursuing? Is it possible for you to tell me that?'

'Well,' frowned Henry, 'it struck me that the eels were unusually aggressive. I mean, although that eel that attacked your officer was only trying to defend itself, it was particularly fierce, and it was unusual that when its head was cut off, instead of its jaw muscles *relaxing*, as they would have done under normal circumstances, they actually *tightened*. So here we have a creature that attacks, and goes on attacking, even after it has been mortally injured. You don't find that very often in nature – that kind of, well, ferocity.'

'Go on,' said Salvador, watching him with steady dark-brown eyes.

'If you try to work out what must have happened to the dead girl,' said Henry, 'you end up with pretty much the same pattern of blind aggression.'

'What do you mean?' Salvador asked him.

'Well – she couldn't have been in the water all that long, could she? She wasn't swollen up, or anything like that. I'm not an expert, by any means, but I can remember the body of a fisherman they dragged out of the harbour at San Diego two or three years ago, and he was bloated up like a blimp. Maybe your medical examiner will prove me wrong, but I wouldn't have thought she was floating around for more than a few hours.'

Salvador said, 'You're right. Mr Belli's first opinion was that she hadn't been immersed for longer than two or three hours, possibly less.'

'Fine – then that bears my theory out. It says in this book on eels that they have been known to devour the flesh of drowned bodies, when those bodies are trapped on the seabed, and well decayed. But apart from an occasional attack by moray eels, they hardly ever go for living people who are swimming around in the water, or even for bodies that are floating on the surface. What these eels did to that girl was completely outside the normal feeding pattern of marine teleosts. They attacked her either when she was alive, or when she was freshly dead and still floating around. It wasn't as if her body was down on the sea-bed for a while, where the eels could have gotten at her, and then bobbed up and floated into shore later.'

The last of the water dribbled through the filter into the coffee jug. Henry found two clean blue pottery mugs, and filled them up to the brim. Then he led the way back into the living-room, and sat down on the couch. Salvador sat facing him, clasping his mug in both hands.

'I have to say that I subscribe to the idea that she didn't float into shore, but was dragged,' Salvador said. 'You remember what Mr Belli pointed out – that her body was lying higher on the beach than the rest of the flotsam?'

Henry thought about that. 'There were no footprints, though, were there?' he said. 'If somebody had dragged her up beyond the tideline, there would have been footprints. But the sand was completely smooth.'

'Ah, yes,' said Salvador.' But the sea *did* reach up that far, at the very turn of the tide, and so any footsteps would have been washed away. I personally believe that she was dragged, footsteps or not, because the water that far up the slope of the beach would have been far too shallow for her body to float in.'

Henry sipped a little coffee, then stood up and went over to the drinks cabinet, and took out the bottle of vodka again. He poured a large dose into his mug, without offering any to Salvador. Salvador said nothing. He was used to drunks, both civilian and police. Who was he to criticise those people who couldn't manage to get through the day without being half blinded?

Henry said, 'What does that leave you with? A naked girl, her stomach eaten by eels, lying in a place where somebody must have dragged her?'

'That's right,' said Salvador. 'And a million questions, such as who dragged her, if anybody? Her murderer, if she was murdered, or a would-be rescuer, who then decided she was beyond saving, and left her where she was? Also, was she killed or knocked unconscious or drugged perhaps before she went into the water – Mr Belli will be able to tell us this. What's more, did the eels attack her before or after she was dead? Were the eels themselves responsible for her death, or were they simply predators on a body that had already expired? Then, we still don't know who she is, or where she came from, or why nobody has reported her missing.'

Henry was silent for a very long time. He finished his coffee in three large gulps although it was still scalding hot.' Best cure for a hangover I know,' he said, at length.

Salvador said, 'Perhaps I shouldn't trouble you with this matter. Perhaps it would be better if I went.'

'I don't have any answers, of any kind,' said Henry. 'My questions are the same as yours.' He paused for a moment, and then he said, 'What are you going to do if you can't find out any more?' 'All cases of homicide have some kind of handle on them, somewhere,' said Salvador. 'It is simply a question of groping for it, and recognising it when you have found it.'

Henry nodded. Then he looked away, and stared out of the window at the beach and the ceaselessly grumbling ocean.

'I must go,' said Salvador. 'But it has been interesting to talk to you. I was fairly sure that, as an educated man, you would apply your mind to what had happened. I would very much appreciate it if you would continue to think this tragedy through, and call me if you happen to think of anything. Every problem is more susceptible to solution by two minds, rather than one.'

'I'm afraid I'm a philosopher not a detective,' said Henry.

'This tragedy may have something to do with philosophy,' Salvador replied. 'To a greater or lesser extent, most man-made tragedies do. At least the ones which I have to deal with.'

'What kind of detective talks like that?' Henry asked him, with a sharp look in his eyes.

Salvador buttoned up his coat, and smiled. 'The kind of detective who is tired enough to search not just for causes but for reasons.'

'Well,' said Henry, 'I'm not sure that there *are* any reasons. You know what Kierkegaard said, that there are only two ways: one is to suffer, and the other is to become a professor of the fact that somebody else has suffered. Believe me, be a professor.'

Salvador Ortega left. Henry stood by the window, holding the slats of the Venetian blind apart, and watched him drive away in his bright green Datsun sports car. He wasn't sure why, but the Mexican detective had disturbed him deeply. Perhaps it was because he had been unable to do what Henry expected the police to do – and that was to come up with a rational explanation for a very irrational event. He expected his police to be factual to the point of pig-headedness. He wanted them to insist that everything was normal. Violent, yes. Frightening, yes. But *normal*.

Whatever Salvador had said about every homicide having a handle, it was obvious to Henry that he didn't have very much faith in being able to find one, not in this case. There was too much weirdness, too little evidence. And then there were the eels.

He went back to the book. He poured himself a large vodka, and leafed through the book again. Page after page of staring, shining eels. Then he came across a reference to hagfish, any of the marine fishes of the family Myxinidae, order Cyclostamata, class Agnatha. Hagfish *look* like eels, he read, with no lateral fins and a slight median fin at the end; but unlike eels they attack other fish, like haddock or cod, and cling on to them, rasping away their flesh with their tooth-studded tongues. All they leave of their prey is the skeleton. When they are not hunting for food they bury themselves in the mud on the ocean floor. He read the paragraph twice. Then he swallowed some more vodka, reached for his telephone, and punched out the number of the Scripps Institute of Oceanography at La Jolla.

'Doctor Andrea Steinway,' he requested.

'May I ask who's calling her?'

'Jacques Cousteau.'

'Could you hold on a moment, please, Mr Cousteau?'

After a long wait, Andrea's extension was picked up and her brusque, mannish voice said, 'Yes, Henry, what do you want now?'

'Andrea, how are you doing?'

'Don't ask, Henry. You don't really want to know, and I don't really want to tell you. What do you want?'

'Andrea, it's to do with fish,' Henry explained, trying to sound both apologetic and desperately in need of expert advice.

'What kind of fish?' Andrea demanded. 'The only kind of fish that you were ever interested in was baked flounder.'

'No, no, Andrea – this is different. This is eels.'

'Eels?' she repeated, suspiciously.

'Well, I came across an eel on the beach this morning. It must have been washed up by the tide. I tried to pick it up but it bit me. I mean, I washed the bite out with antiseptic and everything, but I was wondering what kind of an eel it was, that might do that. I mean, if it's dangerous, maybe I ought to warn the coastguard about it.'

Andrea said, 'You're lying, Henry.'

'What are you talking about? All I want to know is, what kind of an eel could this be?'

'You and the county police department and just about every newspaper and television reporter for two hundred miles around. Come on, Henry, I know all about it. Three of my colleagues are down at the beach now, trying to dig the eels out of the sand. The remains of one of the eels is being sent up here this morning, so that we can examine it.'

'And?' asked Henry, because it didn't sound to him as if Andrea had finished.

'And I'm expressly forbidden to discuss any of this with anybody, including my ex-husband, until the police give me permission.'

'Come on, Andrea, the police themselves have been round here this morning, talking about it. They want every scrap of assistance they can get.'

'They won't get much from you, will they? Maybe the regurgitated thoughts of Bertrand Russell, God help them.'

'Andrea,' said Henry, trying very hard now to be patient, 'I looked up eels in that Kaiser & Cohen book you left behind, and it mentioned hagfish. It occurred to me that since these eels were so vicious, they might not be eels at all, but hagfish.'

'Yes?' asked Andrea. 'And what else?'

'Well, that's it. It just occurred to me, that's all.'

'I see. All right then, thank you.'

'But what do you think?' Henry persisted.

'I think you'd better stick to what you're good at, which is drinking and thinking in that order. Hagfish, for your information, have four sets of tentacles around their head, which they use to grip on to their prey. Although I haven't yet had the opportunity to see it for myself, I know for a fact that the eel which the police are asking us to examine has no such tentacles.'

'All the same, it could be some kind of mutation.'

'Henry, for God's sake! You don't know anything about

it. Now, put the phone down, there's a good boy, and pour yourself another Vodka Collins, and philosophise.'

'Philosophy isn't a theory, it's an activity,' Henry retaliated.

'Ludwig Wittgenstein,' Andrea countered. 'You used to quote that every time you cut classes to go play golf.'

'I've given up golf.'

'Well, that's a pity,' said Andrea. 'You were always a great deal better at golf than you were at philosophy.'

'Andrea,' said Henry, 'will you do me a favour? Will you call me, if you and your colleagues find out what kind of a creature that eel happens to be, and let me know? You know you can trust me.'

Andrea drew in a long, impatient breath. Then she said, 'I'll consider it. I do owe you for letting me have the Volkswagen, I suppose.'

'Is that what our relationship has come down to?' Henry asked her. 'A trade-off?'

'All relationships are trade-offs,' said Andrea. 'If you'd understood that from the start, maybe our marriage would have worked better.'

Henry was about to reply, but managed to keep his sudden surge of hostility to himself. Just repeat after me: we weren't suited. That's all. There was no animosity between us. We never threw crockery, we never blasphemed. She was into oceans and I was into vodka, and that was all there was to it.

'Andrea' he said, 'Maybe we should have dinner together sometime.'

'Sure,' she replied. 'And maybe we shouldn't.'

He put down the phone, and sat back in his leather-upholstered captain's chair, and swung from side to side.

He pictured that girl on the beach, with her hair fanned out, and her hand clutching the sand. Somebody's daughter, somebody's friend, somebody's lover. But what events had led her to Del Mar and death? And *why!*

He was just reaching over to pick up his drink when he caught sight of a man standing smoking a pipe outside his cottage, just beside the wooden railings that separated the promenade from the beach below. There was something about the man that attracted Henry's attention. He was elderly: there were white curls protruding from under his yachting-cap, and he sported a busy white moustache. He seemed at peace with himself; his hands were thrust into the pockets of his mid-length coat, and he was puffing at his pipe and staring out to sea. But there was more than that. He had some indescribably reliable look about him, as if he were a man of considerable certainty and confidence.

Henry didn't know how he could tell that the man was so reliable, but somehow he just knew that he was.

The man seemed to be in no hurry to continue his walk along the promenade, but remained outside Henry's cottage, contentedly smoking. Henry watched him for a very long time, and then at last felt impelled to go outside and speak to him. He found his door-keys, shuffled into his sandals, and then walked around the side of the cottage into the steady breeze that blew from the sea.

The man remained where he was, smoking, hands in pockets, staring out at the foaming breakers. Henry walked up to him, and said, in not quite the right tone of voice, 'It's a fine day, wouldn't you say?'

The man took his pipe out of his mouth, licked his lips, and looked Henry up and down. It suddenly occurred to

Henry that the man might think he was a faggot making a proposition. The man himself might be a faggot, and then what was Henry going to do – say, 'Pardon me, on second thoughts, it's a terrible day,' and rush off?

But the man smiled, and said, 'Well, then, Henry Watkins. I've been waiting for you to come out and say hello.'

'Do I know you?' asked Henry, perplexed.

'Well, you do and you don't. I used to go to your evening classes in modern philosophy, those ones you used to hold up at Encinitas. You probably don't remember me now – my name's Springer. But I remember you. In fact, there's hardly a day goes by when I don't think about you.'

Henry said, 'I'm sorry. I have a terrible memory for faces. Springer, did you say?'

The man held out his hand. 'Paul Springer. You can call me Paul if you want to. I was one of your keenest students, I have to tell you.'

They shook hands. Then Paul Springer said, 'Maybe we could walk a little. I always find it refreshing, walking along here. Do you have the time? We could talk a little, too.'

'I'm, uh – free for most of the day,' said Henry.

'Well, that's good to hear,' smiled Paul. 'Everybody should take their leisure regularly and take their leisure seriously. Do you know who taught me that?'

Henry shook his head. 'I'm sorry, I don't.'

'You should do, Professor, because *you* did. You said it in class and you even wrote it down. Remember that essay you wrote for *Time* magazine, April 1978? The philosophy of leisure. That was a good essay, that. I tore it out, and stuck it on the back of my galley door.'

'You're a yachtsman?' asked Henry.

'A kind of a yachtsman, you could say that, yes.'

'You live around here?'

Paul sucked at his pipe for a little while, his eyes looking amused, and then said, 'Kind of. You could say that. Yes.'

'Was there anything in particular you wanted to talk about?' asked Henry. Although the day was sunny – and in the shelter of the cottages it was hot – the wind that blew off the shining back of the ocean was quite cool, and Henry was beginning to feel like another stiff vodka, to give him warmth and maybe courage, too.

The man reached a break in the railings, where steep wooden steps went down to the sand, and he stood there for a moment, watching the coastguards and the police as they systematically searched the distant beach with long pointed sticks, probing for the eels. 'Somebody told me that you were the first to find the body,' Paul remarked.

Henry said, 'Yes,' in a voice catchy with phlegm. He cleared his throat, and added, 'How did you know about that?'

'Oh, it's in all the papers.'

'How can it be? None of the papers have talked to me yet. The police said they wanted to keep it quiet, in case of a panic.'

'Panic?' Paul smiled. 'I don't think people are capable of panic these days. Panic is the response of untutored masses to the sudden threat of deadly danger. These days, everybody knows what to do about the sudden threat of deadly danger; they've seen it time and time again on television. *Earthquake, The Towering Inferno, The Poseidon Adventure*. The women should scream without stopping and the men should get hold of a gun and shoot indiscriminately in all directions. So, whenever danger threatens, that's exactly what people do. At least, that's what naturally hysterical people do. The rest of them do what they've always done, which is to sit and stare and wait for further instructions.'

They walked a little further along, and then Paul said, 'You don't think the girl died from natural causes? She didn't drown, is what I'm trying to suggest.'

Henry said, 'I don't know. I wish I did. The police are still waiting for the medical examiner.'

'Was she beautiful?'

Henry stopped, and stared at Paul, and frowned. 'Yes,' he said. 'As a matter of fact, she was.'

'Do you know something,' said Paul, abruptly changing the subject, 'there was something you said in class which I could never quite understand. I mean I *understood* it, but I could never quite grasp the wider implications of it.'

'What was that?' asked Henry. For some reason, in spite of the stranger's off-handedness, there was something about him which Henry found very friendly and comfortable. He seemed like the kind of fellow who could easily become a close companion, sharing an evening drink and talking about philosophy and listening to Rossini overtures. The kind of fellow who asked for nothing except your opinion and your liquor.

Paul puffed furiously at his pipe for a moment, to keep it alight, and then said, 'You talked about the world being the sum-total of our vital possibilities.'

'That's right. I was quoting Jose Y Gasset.'

'Well,' said Paul, 'I have all sorts of thoughts about that.' He looked around, as if he had heard somebody calling his name, and was trying to see where they were. 'But, you know, this isn't really the time or the place, is it?' He looked back at Henry. 'To discuss philosophy, I mean? One should have a good meal, and a bottle of wine, and a pleasant atmosphere. That's when philosophy really becomes fun, don't you think? Your mind can take flight. But not out here, in the middle of the day, with the ocean interrupting, and all these damn joggers.'

Henry said wryly, 'It's a few years since *my* mind took flight, I can tell you.'

'Perhaps it's time it did, then,' Paul suggested. 'Look – I know this sounds impudent. You may not like the look of me at all. You may think that I'm a bore, or some kind of tedious eccentric. But I would very much like to talk about Y Gasset a little more. You were so *clear* when you brought up his philosophies in class!'

Flattered, Henry said, 'Well then, what do you suggest?'

'Perhaps I could buy you dinner this evening. Do you know Bully's North? The prime ribs are excellent, and the bar's well up to standard.'

'Sure, I know Bully's North.'

'Could you meet me there this evening, at seven, say?'

Henry thought about it, and then nodded. 'Okay.' The idea of spending an evening eating and drinking and talking about philosophy seemed irresistibly warm and attractive; Paul Springer had just the kind of voice that he liked to listen to, and just the kind of face that appealed to him. Oddly, Paul Springer reminded him of his father. It was a look about the eyes, keen and kindly. 'Okay,' he repeated. 'I'll see you at seven.'

Paul Springer walked away. When he reached the first

footpath that led from the promenade up towards the Camino del Mar, he turned and waved. Henry waved back.

Henry turned and walked slowly northwards again. The wind blew sand across the pathway with a soft sizzling sound, and up above his head the gulls kept turning and turning. Someone had once said that gulls are the lost souls of people drowned at sea, and that they have to search and search forever for the loved ones they left behind. That's why their cries sound so sad.

He had almost reached the short flight of concrete steps that ran up alongside his cottage when he saw a girl walking towards him. She was wearing a colourless cotton shawl draped over her head so that it was impossible to see her face. She passed Henry by so closely that he could have touched her without reaching out. It struck him as peculiar that she was wet. Even her shawl was wet, and clung to her shoulders. He looked down and saw that she had left wet footprints on the sidewalk.

He slowly raised his head and focused his eyes on the beach. The sun was glaring off the sea now, and he had to shield his forehead with his hand. The beach was still closed; there were police trestles at every access point, and lifeguards driving backwards and forwards in jeeps to keep people away. He could see a knot of policemen, and a group of men in tee-shirts and jeans, who were probably the marine biologists from Scripps. He saw a cinnamon-coloured suit, and recognised Salvador Ortega.

But if the beach was closed, and there was no swimming, how had that girl got herself wet?

Henry turned, and a sensation like 220 volts of electricity prickled down him from his scalp to the soles of his feet.

The girl was gone, but her wet footprints led all the way down to the pathway where Paul Springer had left him.

There had been something familiar about that girl. Something about the whiteness of her skin, something about the fine gritty sand that had stuck to her calves and her ankles. And something more. A fine silver chain around her ankle.

Henry began to jog back along the promenade. The wind was gradually drying the girl's footsteps away, so that they looked like nothing more than question-marks, printed on the tarmac. Henry jogged faster, and reached the corner of the footpath out of breath.

He looked up towards Camino del Mar. In the distance, at the head of the footpath, he could see Paul Springer. He recognised him by his sailor's cap and his white hair. But there was no sign of the girl at all, even though her footprints turned around here, and made their way uphill. There were two dilapidated cars parked by the side of the footpath, a '76 Caprice and a bronze Firebird with oxidised paint. On the other side, there were fences made out of corrugated iron and concrete slabs painted white; spiky grass and trailing vines; and a stunted row of shabby-looking yuccas. A white bull-terrier that had been gnawing at an old beef bone pricked up its ears and stared at Henry balefully.

Paul Springer had disappeared from sight now. Henry stayed where he was for a moment, and then began walking slowly back to the cottage. There was no sign of the girl's footprints, and he was beginning to think that he must have hallucinated.

He reached the cottage, unlocked the front door, and went straight to the bottle of vodka. He poured himself half a glassful, draining the bottle, and dropping it noisily into the metal waste paper basket with the picture of galleons on it. He walked over to the window and stared up and down the promenade. When he drank, he found that he was shivering.

He left his drink on the table and went through to the kitchen. Perhaps he needed something to eat. All this drinking without eating, it was bound to give rise to hallucinations. He rummaged through the icebox, through half-finished packs of longhorn cheddar; left-over chicken-legs; pre-packed salads turning brown at the edges; strawberry yoghurts that had been 'best before' the last time he had gone to the theatre. He found a reasonably fresh pack of Oscar Mayer's bologna, and made himself a sandwich, with too much French mustard and a large pickle to eat on the side.

He came out of the kitchen arguing silently with himself whether hallucinations were fractionally less troubling than indigestion. Then he looked up and said, '*Aah!*'

The girl was standing by the window. This time, she had let her shawl fall down to her shoulders, and he could see her face quite clearly. He stayed where he was, with his sandwich and his pickle, staring at her. Her wet hair clung to her head. One side of her face was marked with sand.

'*Are you afraid?*' she asked him, in a light, transparent voice.

He cleared his throat. 'I think so,' he said. He was. His heart was running up and down inside his ribcage, and he could hear himself panting.

The girl took a step forward. Behind her, the sun came out, and diffused her outline, so that Henry found it more difficult to see her face. 'Are you real?' he asked her.

'*Real?*' she whispered. '*I am as real as you want me to be. Or as imaginary.*'

'Was it you, on the beach this morning?'

'*In a way,*' she said.

Henry put down his sandwich and his pickle on to a side-table. 'You know what I'm thinking?' he told her. 'I'm thinking that I'm drunk, and that I'm hallucinating.'

'*I know what you're thinking,*' the girl said, softly.

She came nearer. She seemed to be able to approach him without moving her legs. Her eyes were strangely blank, like the eyes of a fibreglass model in a fashion-store window; as if she were talking to him, but wasn't thinking about him at all. He remembered that look in Andrea's eyes, in the last few months of their marriage.

'What does this mean?' Henry asked her.

'*I don't understand.*'

'Well, does it mean that you're still alive? Does it mean that you're a ghost? Or does it mean that I'm going mad?'

She smiled. She had such a beautiful, sad smile. It looked to Henry like the kind of smile that might have touched the lips of Annabel Lee or Lenore or any one of Edgar Poe's limpid loves, in the kingdom by the sea.

'*I am your own creation,*' she said, and touched him, although he felt no touch. '*I am here to remind you of what you must do. Springer will see to it.*'

'You know Springer?' asked Henry, baffled and still very frightened.

The girl lifted her shawl over her head. It came up in a curious snaking way, like a film being run in reverse. She said, as softly as before, '*I know Springer now.*'

'You scare me,' he said.

She smiled that smile. '*Then you are only scaring yourself.*'

'But you said you were here to remind me what to do.'

'*I am, and you will know it when Springer mentions it.*'

Henry didn't know what else to say. The girl moved towards the door, still smiling at him. Then she opened the door – and even though he could have sworn afterwards that she opened it no more than an inch – she disappeared out of it, as quickly as smoke disappears, when it is blown by a sudden draft.

Henry looked over towards the window, towards his large glass of vodka.

'Something's happening,' he said to himself, out loud. Then, 'I'm frightened.' Then, after a long pause, 'God help me.'

Chapter Five

In spite of the heat of the day, the sea-fog closed in early that afternoon along the north beaches of San Diego County, and by six-thirty the world was prematurely gloomy and almost unbearably humid. Cars travelled slowly along Camino del Mar with their lights on, an endless funeral procession rolling through the fog. Speed restrictions were in force on Interstate-5, and coastguards advised small boats to stay tied up in harbour until the fog had lifted.

Susan was feeling better, almost light headed. She took a shower, and then she put on her white low-waisted dress with the red and yellow and green splotches on it, and blow-dried her hair while she watched her portable television.

Her grandmother knocked on her bedroom door and came in before Susan could invite her. She stood watching Susan for three or four minutes, waiting until Susan had switched off her hair-dryer, and then she said, 'You wouldn't be going out tonight, if it was up to me.'

'Grandma, I'm absolutely *fine* now,' said Susan, tweaking her hair with styling-gel to give it that fashionable raggedy look. 'I was just feeling faint this morning, that's all. I'm not sick or anything.'

'Well, you make sure you're not too late. I'm responsible for you – just remember that. If anything happens to you, it's me who has to answer for it.' She paused to pick up Susan's discarded tee-shirt, grunting with the effort of it. Then she said. 'This man, too, I'd like to know more about him. Picking you up in the street like that.'

'Grandma,' Susan sighed, with concentrated seventeen-year-old impatience. 'He works for the *San Diego Tribune*, he's the nicest person ever, and we're only going to Bully's North for something to eat. I promise, promise, cross my heart and hope my eyes will drop out, that I shall be back by nine-thirty, alive and well and unraped.'

'You don't have to talk like that,' her grandmother protested.

'I'm sorry,' said Susan, primping up her hair, and pouting at herself in the mirror. 'But I *can* look after myself. I'm not a child any more.'

'If only you knew,' her grandmother told her.

'Grandma, I can drive a car, I can almost vote, I can almost get married without consent.'

Her grandmother looked resigned. 'All right, go. Your mother was the same. You're a good girl, Susan, I know that. Untidy as all fall down, but good. Well, at least I hope so.'

The phone rang. She heard her grandfather answering it. He said, 'Yes, okay,' three or four times, and then he put the phone down again.

'Who was that?' asked Susan. Most of the phone calls were for her.

'Your friend Daffy. She said not to forget to call her when you get back from dinner tonight, and tell her all about it.'

'Hah! Did she think that I *wouldn't!*'

Her grandmother came closer, and watched her putting

the finishing touches to her lipstick. 'Are you going to have your picture in the *Tribune?*' she wanted to know.

Gil meanwhile had been up in his bedroom for almost an hour, shaving and combing his hair and trying to make up his mind whether he was going to dress up suave and elegant or whether he was going to go for the Rambo look. He dressed and undressed four times – each time becoming increasingly bad tempered – until at last he settled on a pair of dove-grey cotton slacks and a short-sleeved white shirt and a charcoal-grey Italian-cut jacket. He sprayed on Signoricci eau-de-toilette and accidentally squirted himself in the left eye, so when he came downstairs he was holding a wadded-up handkerchief against it.

'You're crying already,' his father teased him. 'You haven't even said *hello* to her yet, let alone goodbye.'

Fay shushed him, and asked Gil, 'What did you do?'

Gil said, 'Aftershave,' and blinked furiously. 'Is it bloodshot?' he asked his parents.

'Bloodshot? You look like the teenage son of Dracula,' said Phil Miller, cheerily.

'No, he doesn't!' said Fay. 'Your eye looks a little watery, that's all. Have you splashed some cold water into it?'

'It's okay,' Gil told her, waving her away. 'I'll get over it.'

'I'll unlock the door for you,' Phil offered.

They walked together through the darkened store. Phil laid his arm around his son's shoulder, and said, 'Have a good time, won't you? But, you know, don't forget about the precautions, if it comes to that.'

'Okay, Dad.'

Phil unlocked the store door, top and bottom, and let his son out into the street. He stood on the sidewalk for a while, his hands on his hips, inhaling the fog. 'Be careful how you drive, won't you? This stuff looks like it's getting thicker.'

'Yes, Dad.'

'And don't drive drunk, you understand me? If you have too many beers, get somebody else to drive you home – or call me. I'd rather be woken up by you telling me you can't drive than by some cop telling me you're dead.'

'I got you, Dad.'

Gil jogged across the street to the parking-lot, where his Mustang was waiting. He folded back the sheet of blue yachting plastic which he used to cover the seats and then vaulted into it. He started up the engine, switched on the lights, and pulled out of the cinder-surfaced parking-lot in a long slithering skid. He blasted his two-tone horn, waved to his father, and then disappeared into the fog in the direction of Del Mar.

Phil watched him go, and then shook his head. Kids. But he knew that Gil wasn't crazy, not like some of the boys who hung around the beach. Some of those kids would surf when they were high, and ride their motorbikes right off the road and on to the sand, even when families were sunbathing there. Some of them would speed all the way along Camino del Mar, which was intersected by over a dozen side-streets, and run every stop sign from Jimmy Durante Boulevard to Carmel Valley Road. Five boys had been killed last year, head-on collision.

Phil went back into his store, closed the door, and locked it.

Henry meanwhile was already walking along Camino del Mar towards the restaurant. He wore a grey turtle-neck sweater which made him look greyer than ever, and a black-and-white houndstooth jacket. His head was thumping, and his tongue felt as if it was lying curled up in his mouth, as hairy as a Persian cat. He was carrying a copy of *The Revolt of the Masses*, by Jose Y Gasset, with the spine missing, and also a copy of his own pamphlet, *The Necessary Evil*.

His hallucination this afternoon had badly shaken him, even though he was now quite convinced that it had been caused by nothing more than too many glasses of undiluted vodka. He had almost decided not to meet Paul Springer at all, but to call up the restaurant and make some Byzantine excuse. However, by five o'clock he had begun to feel a little more composed; and the more he thought about meeting Paul Springer again, the more the idea appealed to him. He was also vain enough to want to hear what somebody else thought about *The Necessary Evil*, which he had always considered to be one of his most original pieces of work.

He had walked along the beach promenade, partly to see if the beach was still cordoned off, and partly (he had to admit it) to see if the wet-footed girl was anywhere around. The police lines around the beach were marked by flashing amber beacons; they winked through the fog like hopeless messages. There was scarcely any wind, and the surf sounded flat and clattering as the tide came in. He was passed by two gasping joggers and a rotund woman walking her pet Weimaraner, but there was no sign at all of the girl.

I am your own creation, she had told him. *If you are scared, then you are only scaring yourself.*

He walked up one of the narrow sloping side-streets to Camino del Mar. In one of the houses close to the top of the street, a man and a woman were shouting at each other in

Spanish. In the room next to them, a television was blaring out *Galeria Nocturna*. When he reached the corner, Henry dropped a quarter into the newspaper-vending machine, and bought himself a copy of the *Tribune*. He shook it open with one hand and read the headlines.

'*North Beaches Closed by Jellyfish Threat*,' was the main banner. Henry skimmed through the front-page story, and recognised it for the blatant cover-up that it was. Lieutenant Salvador Ortega must have been working overtime, he concluded.

The story said: 'Police and coastguards today cordoned off several miles of north county beaches from La Jolla to San Elijo Lagoon after the body of a young woman was washed up at Del Mar, apparently having been stung to death by jellyfish.

'The young woman – who was probably attacked while she was enjoying a nude midnight swim – has not yet been identified. Police say she was "blonde, beautiful, and well-proportioned" and that she wore a silver chain around her left ankle.

'Lt. Salvador T Ortega, in charge of investigating the girl's death, warned that there could be 'scores more' jellyfish swarming off the beaches. He has called in marine biologists from the Scripps Institute to assist in identifying the deadly creatures. They could be "sea-wasps" – scientific name *chironex fleckeri* – which are usually found off the coast of Australia, but which may have migrated to Southern Californian waters. Sea-wasps can kill a human being in eight minutes. Bathers and surfers were warned this afternoon that –'

Henry folded up the paper, and tossed it into a trashcan

without breaking his stride. So, Salvador had successfully managed to persuade the media that the beaches had been closed off because of jellyfish. Well, he supposed that Salvador was not to blame. Jellyfish at least were explicable. There was nothing explicable about those eels.

Just as he reached the entrance to Bully's North, he was surprised to see Gil's yellow Mustang turn into the entrance; and then, as he reached the doorway, he saw Susan Sczaniecka arrive, in her splotchy white dress.

He waited by the doorway without opening it. A middle-aged couple pushed past, and the woman frowned at him for getting in the way. From inside the restaurant he heard laughter and the clinking of glasses. A man came out and, standing next to Henry, said loudly to his companion, 'We can lease for half that. Why do you want to buy, when we can lease?' Up above his head, green neon flashed the name *of Bully's North*.

Susan Sczaniecka came up the steps towards the doorway, and it was obvious that she didn't recognise Henry at all. She must have been very shocked this morning by what she had seen down on the beach. Probably, all that she could remember with any clarity were the body and the eels.

Just as she passed him by, Henry said, 'Susan?'

She stared at him. Her face was blank. Then she suddenly realised who he was. 'Oh, *hi!*' she said, breathlessly. 'I didn't recognise you! You look so much smarter now!

Listen, I have to thank you for being so kind to me this morning. I thought I was going to pass out. In fact, I *did* pass out, when I got home. Zonk!'

'You look fine now,' he told her.

'Well, thank you, I have a date.'

'So do I,' said Henry. 'That's why I waited for you. And look –' he pointed across the front lot, to where Gil was taking his parking check from the car-hop. 'Our friend has a date here, too.'

Susan turned to look at Gil, and then she turned back and stared at Henry. 'Can this be coincidence?' she asked him, in a soft, alarmed whisper. 'I mean, all three of us meeting on the beach this morning, and now coming here?' Gil came up to them, and stopped and stared just as they were staring at him. 'Well,' he said, 'I sure didn't expect to find you two here.'

'And we sure didn't expect to find *you* here, either,' Susan told him.

'Well ... as a matter of fact, I was invited here,' said Gil.

'Me too,' said Susan.

'And me,' added Henry.

'This is weird,' Gil protested. 'I never saw either of you before today, and yet here you both are, waiting for me. You're sure this isn't some kind of a practical joke?'

'If it is, *we're* not playing it,' said Henry. 'We're just as much victims of it as you are.'

'Who invited you?' asked Susan. 'I was asked to come here by a newspaper reporter, from the *Tribune*.'

'Well, it was a girl who asked me,' said Gil. 'She said she was writing an article for *San Diego* magazine.'

Henry lifted up his philosophy books. 'That settles it. It must be nothing more than an incredible coincidence. The fellow I'm supposed to be meeting used to be one of my evening-class students, when I was teaching up at Encinitas.'

Gil shook his head. 'Some coincidence, huh? I mean, the three of us meeting on the beach, and now meeting here.'

Henry turned and peered inside the restaurant doorway. 'I hope that nothing's *wrong*,' he remarked.

'Wrong?' asked Susan. 'What do you mean?'

'I hope that what we saw on the beach wasn't something that we weren't supposed to see.'

'In what way?' said Gil.

'Well, just supposing that girl wasn't drowned by accident. Just supposing those eels didn't drift in to shore on a freak current, or whatever it was that the police were trying to suggest. Just supposing those eels were actually bred as killers – deliberately bred to attack swimmers or divers or anybody going into the water. You have your Scripps Institute just down the road here, and you have your naval base at San Diego. Supposing the Scripps people have been working on a government project to supply the Navy with man-eating eels. And just supposing we saw the result, and now we've all been invited along here to be dealt with. You know, like Karen Silk wood.'

'Boy, do you have an imagination!' Gil whistled. Then he laughed, and said, 'Are you serious, or are you just trying to scare us?'

Henry said, a little too pompously, 'I'm a philosopher, Gil. I'm trained to use my mind. I'm trained to hypothesise, to think problems out from every conceivable angle. All I'm saying is that the idea of specially trained eels is a conceivable angle.'

'But Karen Silkwood was killed,' said Susan, worriedly.

'This is nothing like Karen Silkwood,' Gil protested. 'We don't have any evidence at all. It's just a theory, right? And if I know anything at all about theories, the real explanation will be uninteresting. That's one thing you learn about life, that the explanation for just about everything is really uninteresting.'

'So cynical, so young,' smiled Henry, but not patronisingly. He agreed with Gil almost one hundred per cent. In his experience, the wildest phenomena always seemed to have the most mundane solutions. Like Bridey Murphy, or the *Mary Celeste*. He nodded back towards the restaurant door, and said, 'All we have to decide for ourselves is whether we are in any kind of personal danger here.'

'I can't see how we could be,' said Gil. 'I mean, this girl from *San Diego* wasn't threatening in any way that you could possibly think of. Just the opposite.'

'Well, you may be right,' said Henry. 'My philosophy student wasn't exactly your stereotypical hit-man.'

Susan said, 'I vote we go in and see what happens. Nothing ventured, you know.'

Henry thought about it, and then shrugged. 'Come on, then.'

Inside Bully's North, it was noisy and dark and crowded. The television was tuned to the Padres, playing at home, and people were smoking and laughing and drinking beer.

The three of them walked the length of the cocktail bar, and up to the young blow-dried maitre d', who was answering the telephone and handing out menus at the same time.

After a moment, the maitre d' hung up the telephone and grinned, and said, 'Good evening. Can I help you folks? Table for three?'

'Well, we're not together, as a matter of fact,' said Henry. 'Each of us is meeting somebody.'

He turned to Susan, and said, 'What was the name of your *Tribune* reporter?'

'Springer,' Susan told the maitre d'. 'Mr Paul Springer.'

Henry looked at Gil and his expression was shocked. 'That was the name of my philosophy student,' he said, in bewilderment.

'And the girl from *San Diego*, her name's *Paulette* Springer,' said Gil.

The maitre d' stared at them as if they were playing some kind of lunatic party game. 'You're not together, each of you is meeting somebody, but each of those "somebodies" happens to have the same name?'

'It appears so,' said Henry, in a tight, constricted voice.

The maitre d' skimmed down the list of names on his clipboard. Halfway down, his pen came to a stop. 'Here it is, Springer. Table nine.' The pen went down further, right to the bottom of the page, and then the maitre d' shook his head. 'Only one Springer. I'm sorry.'

Susan glanced at Henry anxiously. 'What you said outside. You don't think that – ?'

'I don't know,' said Henry. 'I think we'd all better stay together, and see which Springer we've got here, mine, or yours – or Gil's.'

The maitre d' whipped out three menus. 'You all want to go to the same table?' he asked them.

'If there's only one table booked in the name of Springer, I don't think we have a lot of choice,' said Henry.

The maitre d' led them between the crowded tables, where diners were laughing and drinking wine and tucking into ribs and cracked crab. At the very back of the restaurant, beside a frondy coconut-palm in a wicker basket, was table nine; and at table nine sat a single figure in a black Homburg-style hat and a black three-piece suit. The brim of the hat was lowered so that as they crossed the restaurant they were unable to see the figure's face. But Henry immediately noticed the hands, which were spread flat on the salmon-coloured tablecloth. They were very white, the same hue as blanched almonds, and very long fingered.

'Here you go, then,' said the maitre d', and dragged out three of the four chairs. 'Mr Springer? One of these people is a guest of yours. Well, I don't know – maybe they all are.'

Henry and Susan and Gil stood around the table apprehensively as the figure very slowly raised its face towards them, in the way that a white-petalled flower raises its face to the sun. 'Yes,' said the figure, quietly but distinctly. 'They *all* are.'

Henry was transfixed. The figure's face was pale and smooth and androgynous, like the almond-shaped face of a portrait by Modigliani. Yet despite its smoothness and despite its sexlessness, it was quite clearly Paul Springer, the same Paul Springer that he had met outside his cottage on the shore. It was not so much the detail of the face that carried his character, but the personality that it projected. The difference between the man he had met on the beach and this man here was the difference between a highly finished portrait and a deft but accurate sketch.

Gil slowly sat down. To Gil, the figure was Paulette. A severely dressed Paulette, with her hair scraped back, away from her face, yet undisputably the same girl who had called round to the Mini-Market and asked him out for dinner. He understood that she was different, although he would have found it difficult to say exactly how. Her eyes were still the same, her cheekbones were still the same, her mouth was just as tempting as before. She attracted him just as much, yet she was something else now, apart from Paulette. She wasn't less than she had been before, but '*more.*'

Susan said, shyly, 'Hello.' Because for her, too, the figure was the same Paul Springer she had met outside her grandmother's house. A changed Paul Springer, certainly – more mysterious, more remote, and much less chatty – but the same presence, the same personality. The same calm and penetrating eyes.

'Please, all of you, sit down,' said Springer. 'You're confused, I understand that, and you're concerned for your own safety. But I hope that I can set your minds at rest, and that you will forgive me for playing some little tricks on you.'

Henry dragged out a chair, and sat down. Susan hesitated for a moment or two, and then perched herself on the edge of the chair next to him.

'You're one and the same person,' said Henry, his voice thick and off-balance.

'You're three people, all rolled up into one. Not all the same sex, either. Now, how do you do that? How come I think you're my old philosophy student, and Gil here thinks you're a lady journalist, and Susan believes you work for the *Tribune!*'

Springer removed his, or her, hat. Underneath, his hair had been razored very short, and combed straight back. The style was completely neutral, completely sexless, just like his clothes. He laid his hat on the table and rested his long pale hands on either side of the brim.

'Let me put it this way,' he said. 'It was necessary for me to appear to each of you in a guise which you would find irresistible. You all had a severe shock this morning, when you came across that girl's body. None of you were in the mood for going out to dinner with a complete stranger. Because of that, I considered it more effective to use my particular facility for appearing – how shall I put it? – all things to all men. And women, of course,' he added, nodding to Susan.

Gil said sharply, 'All right, then. Just exactly what kind of a trick is this? You've got us all here. Now what?'

Susan stood up. 'I'm going home. I don't like this at all.'

Springer raised one hand, palm outwards. He lifted it towards Susan's face almost as if he had a mirror hidden in it, because Susan found herself staring at it as if she were mesmerised. She hesitated, and then she sat down again. Henry laid a hand on her arm, and said,' What's the matter, Susan? Are you all right?' but all she did was nod, and whisper, 'I'm all right,' and touch her fingers to her forehead.

'What did you do to her?' Henry demanded. 'What was that? Hypnotic suggestion?'

'Nothing of the kind,' said Springer, gently. 'I simply assured her that there was no need for her to be afraid. There is equally no need *for you* to be afraid, either.'

A waiter came up and asked them what they wanted to drink. Henry ordered a large vodka; Gil asked for a beer; Susan wanted a fruit punch. Springer said, 'The driest white wine that you can find.'

Gil said, 'Are you a woman or a man or what?'

The waiter heard that, and turned around to stare at Springer curiously. Springer waited until he had gone to fix their order, and then he said quietly, 'I am neither. I am an agent of sorts. A messenger. I am neither man nor woman, flesh nor spirit. I am not even "I" in the sense that you would normally understand it.'

'So what are you?' Henry asked him. 'If you're not either of the Paul Springers, and not Paulette Springer, and not a man, and not a woman, and not flesh, and not a spirit, what in Heaven's name *are* you?'

'Are you hungry?' asked Springer.

'Not exactly,' said Henry. 'Gil, how about you?'

Gil shook his head. 'I couldn't eat if you held a gun to my head.'

Susan said, 'Me neither.'

'All right, then,' said Springer. 'Let us all take a walk somewhere quiet, where we can talk. I have one or two things to show you. Things which will startle you, perhaps, but which you will find most fascinating.'

Susan had been watching Springer very closely. Just as the waiter brought their drinks, she said, 'Could I touch you? I mean, could I touch your hand?' Springer turned his eyes towards her without moving his head. 'Why do you ask?'

'I don't know. There's something about you that makes me want to touch you, that's all.'

Springer edged his left hand across the table and laid it on the tablecloth right in front of her. 'Go ahead.'

Gingerly, Susan reached out, until her fingertips were only a quarter of an inch away from the back of Springer's hand.

'Don't be afraid,' Springer encouraged her.

Susan stroked his knuckle. There was no outward evidence of it, no visible sparks, but she felt as if she had brushed a bare terminal, fizzing with electricity. The sensation was shocking, but at the same time curiously pleasant, as pleasant as having your scalp massaged or somebody's fingers drawn lightly down your naked back. She stared at Springer, right into Springer's eyes, and Springer said, 'Touch me again. Lay your hand right on top of mine, and hold it there.'

Susan turned to Henry and Gil, but Henry and Gil said nothing. Slowly, tentatively, she laid her hand fully on top of Springer's hand, and stared into his eyes again, waiting and watching for something to happen.

For a moment, nothing did happen. Then suddenly Susan felt as if she had been plucked out of her chair and hurtled at enormous velocity right the way across the restaurant, right through the doors, which slammed open and then slammed shut again behind her, right through another set of doors, which also slammed open and then slammed shut, and then another and another and another, door after door after door. And at the end of the rows of doors – she took her hand away. She stopped. She was still at the table, with Henry and Gil and the extraordinary person called Springer.

'What happened?' she asked. 'I felt like I was flying, almost. Flying through all these double doors, and they opened and closed to let me through. I could actually hear them banging!' Henry lifted his glass, and swallowed a large mouthful of neat vodka, without taking his eyes off Springer and without offering any kind of toast. 'You're a hypnotist,' he told Springer. 'I don't know what you've been trying to do to us, and I don't think I'll be very enthralled when I find out, but I for one would like some kind of coherent explanation for this evening's tittle get-together, or else I'm finishing off this drink and going home.'

'Finish your drink and come with me,' said Springer.

'Where do you have in mind?' asked Henry. 'Mugger's Cove? Or Dope's Leap?'

Springer shook his head. 'I will not harm you. I think you are conscious of that already. There *is* harm around us; you *are* threatened, but not by me.'

'Then by whom?'

Springer finished his dry white wine, and raised his hand towards the waiter. The waiter turned towards them, but as soon as he caught sight of Springer he turned away again. 'Come along,' said Springer, and he stood up, and helped Susan out of her chair.

'Aren't you going to pay?' asked Gil.

Springer shook his head. 'I have no money. But there is no question of theft. They will find when they check their inventory that they are missing nothing, no wine, no beer, not even a measure of Smirnoff.'

Henry looked at Springer interrogatively, but kept his questions to himself. He preferred to hold back, and see how this confrontation with Springer turned out. But there was no doubt that it was deeply disturbing. At least forty-seven degrees of stress on the Holmes-Masudu scale. He kept his eye on the waiter and the maitre d' as the four of them walked towards the exit without making any attempt to pay for their drinks. Nobody noticed them. They might have been invisible. Henry passed only inches away from the maitre d', and the man didn't even turn to bid him goodnight, or ask why he was leaving only five minutes after he had arrived.

Gil said, 'This is weird with a capital "W".' Susan said, 'It's just like they can't even see us.' She paused for a moment, and went over to the bar, and peered straight into the face of a leather-jacketed man who was sitting alone drinking Pina Coladas. She stared directly into his eyes – first, from about a foot away then closer and closer, until her nose was almost touching his. He remained completely motionless, unblinking, as if he couldn't see her at all. But just as Susan was about to turn away from him, and rejoin the others, the man unexpectedly kissed her on the tip of the nose, and laughed. 'You want a kiss, sugar, you only have to ask.'

Susan, red faced and furious, stalked out of the restaurant in front of Henry and Gil and wouldn't even look at Springer. Henry and Gil both chuckled; and even Springer seemed to allow himself a neutral smile.

'We are not invisible, I regret,' said Springer. 'We have simply failed to make an impression on the memories of the staff.'

They left the restaurant. Susan was sulking, but didn't want to go home, not yet, especially if the others were staying. Springer beckoned, and they followed him along Camino del Mar as far as the block just before the Bennett Coast Hotel. The night was still foggy and humid, although a light wind was getting up. In the middle of the block, in between Cord Realty offices and Eleganza fashion boutique, there stood a three-storey stucco-fronted house, its shutters tilting from corroded hinges, its pink paint stained black with damp, its front yard densely overgrown with wild bougainvillaea, its railings broken and rusty. It was a house that spoke silently but eloquently of neglect, and decay, and lost lives.

'In here?' asked Gil, wrinkling up his nose in distaste. 'Come on, man, this has to be a put-on. Either that, or the most creative mugging I ever heard of.'

'Follow me,' said Springer, and walked up the weedy

concrete path. He unlocked the front door, and hesitantly the three of them followed him inside. The door closed behind them, quite silently. Springer crossed the hallway, found the light switch, and flicked it on. The interior of the house was completely bare. No furniture, no carpets, only naked light bulbs dangling from the ceiling. At one time, it must have been a house of considerable elegance. The mahogany staircase curved down to the hallway in a graceful sweep, and all the doors were solid panelled oak, with detailed beading. Despite the decrepitude of the outside, inside the rooms seemed dry and clean, as if they had been freshly swept. Their footsteps clattered and squeaked on the bare boards, and their voices echoed as if the house were already occupied by furtive spirits. There was a strong and curious smell of laurels.

'We have to go upstairs,' said Springer. Without hesitation, he led the way up the staircase, one long-fingered hand trailing on the banister rail. Henry, who came up close behind him, noticed that his shoes were more like moccasins than street shoes, black leather made all of a piece.

They crossed the upstairs landing, and Springer opened a door on the opposite side, which led into a large room with two french windows at one end. These windows were as black as ink now, but during the day they must have offered a wide view of the gardens behind the house, and beyond, possibly, as far as the sea-shore. Henry and Gil and Susan could see themselves reflected in the glass, the anxious occupants of a strange and empty room.

The walls of the room had been painted turquoise, many years ago. There were rectangular marks where pictures had once hung, and scars on the plaster where light-fittings had been removed from the side of the fireplace. Springer closed the door, and then turned to face Henry and Gil and Susan, his straw-coloured eyes as pale as the dry white wine he had been drinking.

Henry said, 'All right. Here we are. Now, are you going to tell us why you brought us here?'

'This house is built at one of the nine hundred key locations in America,' said Springer. When he saw that they didn't understand him at all, he explained, 'There are nine hundred places in the United States where the power may be tapped, and this is one of them. "Power"?' asked Henry, suspiciously.

'The power that created me, and ultimately, the power that created you,' said Springer. He pointed upwards, to the ceiling.

'Are we talking about the power of God?' asked Gil. 'Is that what we're talking about?'

Springer smiled. His hand made a brushing motion in the air, as if he were stroking a soft, invisible animal. 'You may call it the power of God, if you wish, but that is to suppose that it is wholly good. That is the popular human conception of God. A divine Being without fault and without weakness. The reality is rather different, as most realities are. The reality is that there is a power which is capable of being turned against those who rob and those who murder and those who corrupt the lives of the young, but this power is only *relatively* good. It would not be effective if it were wholly good – good without compromise – because no war can be fought on terms of totality. Extremism in the name of whatever cause is the most destructive of all human characteristics. It is equally the most destructive of all spiritual characteristics. No, my friends, this power is wise and this power is terrible and this power is hugely creative, but this power is not perfect.'

Henry asked, with undisguised scepticism, 'Does the power have a name?'

Springer nodded. 'The power is called Ashapola, after the ancient word which means avenger of great wrongs.'

Susan, in a thin, quiet voice said, 'Are you trying to tell us that Ashapola is God?'

'God is whatever you want Him to be,' Springer explained. 'But the true power of creation is not "God" or "Buddha" or "Gitche Manitou"; it is Ashapola, who embraces all of these deities, and more. It was Ashapola who made man in his own image, with all of his own strengths and weaknesses. Unlike the deity you worship as God, who is forever punishing his children for failing to be perfect, Ashapola recognises their imperfections as his own, and teaches them instead to overcome them, to use their weaknesses as strengths.'

Henry thoughtfully rubbed his chin. 'Well,' he said, 'I think I've heard just about everything I need to hear. In my opinion, Mr Springer, you're cracked. You're welcome to your own religion, your own point of view. This is a free country. But I regularly turn the Mormons away from my door, as well as the Seventh Day Adventists; and while you've found a much more novel way of claiming my attention, I'm afraid that Ashapola doesn't impress me any more than Moroni or Boroni. I'm going now, and I expect these two young people will want to come with me.'

He took a step towards the door, just one step, and it was then that Springer lifted his right arm, straight up in the air, and the room began to darken, until Henry could scarcely see anything but the glistening reflection of Springer's eyes, and the whiteness of his upraised hand. There was a soft crackling, spitting sound, like a fire burning, or cellophane being crumpled, and the atmosphere inside the room grew dense with the smell of laurel.

Gil said, 'Jesus Christ, Henry, what's that?' and Susan sharply drew in her breath.

In the centre of the room, a tall transparent figure had suddenly appeared, indeterminate at first, but quickly growing clearer and clearer. Henry stared in horror. The crackling sound grew louder, until it sounded more like ferocious radio interference; and then louder still, so that they could scarcely hear themselves speak.

The figure was white, and naked. It was the figure of a young girl, with her back towards them. Her blonde hair fanned out in the air as if she were floating in water, rather than standing in the centre of a room. Springer stepped away from her, but his hand was still upraised, and his face was set into an expression of intense concentration.

'*Springer! Do you hear me, Springer!*' Henry bellowed. '*We've had enough of these tricks, you understand me? We're going! Now, stop this nonsense and put on the lights!*'

Springer ignored them. Instead, he made a twisting gesture with his left hand, and the figure of the girl began slowly to turn around. '*Springer, what the hell is going on here?*' Henry roared at him. The crackling noise was louder than ever.

The girl gradually turned to face them. As before, she was beautiful. This time, her eyes were open, and she was staring at the three of them with an expression so sad and so hurt that Henry was completely silenced. Gil jerkily reached out and gripped Henry's left shoulder – out of fear, out of a need for companionship; out of the plain fact that he didn't know what to do, and all he could hope for was that Henry might somehow be able to guide them out of the room, away from Springer, away from the girl who was staring at him so pitifully, although she was dead, drowned dead, eel-eaten dead, and couldn't be standing here at all.

The girl's hair undulated in the air. Her features appeared to change and shift, as if they were watching her through water. She opened and closed her mouth several times, giving Susan the impression that she wanted to say something, that she was trying to appeal for help.

'*This is how it happened ...*' blurted Springer's voice, penetrating the crackling noise with all the distorted bass of a public-address announcement. '*This is what she was like in the beginning ... look at her closely ... see how beautiful she was ...*'

In spite of their fear, in spite of their anger against Springer, Henry and Gil and Susan looked at the girl intently. Her face was beautifully structured, the face of a fashion model. Her breasts were large; white globes patterned with tree-traceries of blue veins, and rippled with palest pink. Her waist was slim, uncreased: she had obviously never had a baby. Her thighs were slim and well shaped. She wore a thin silver chain around her left ankle.

'*We know nothing about her ... not even her name ... but she is the first,*' said Springer. '*Watch what happened to her.*'

Gradually, the girl's expression altered. She gave a smile, a little distant, but still a smile. She held out her arms, and although they could see nobody else there, she appeared to be holding somebody, and kissing them, some invisible lover. Her thighs rubbed rhythmically together in a slowly quickening erotic rhythm, and she kissed the air in front of her more and more fiercely, using her tongue and her teeth.

She opened her mouth wide now, and began licking at the empty air in the lewdest and most suggestive way. Her tongue ran down some invisible length; then her lips stretched wide to contain something delicate and pendulous, which she lightly thrummed with the tip of her tongue. After a while, her mouth went deeper, and her tongue protruded stiffly into some tight but unseen crevice. All the while she was doing this, she squeezed her breasts with her own hands until the nipples rose so hard that they jutted between her fingers, and her hips rotated around and around and around.

Now she arched her head back, and let her hands slide down her stomach and between her thighs. She opened herself up with her fingers, just a little way at first, pinkish glistening folds; but then she kissed and kissed and kissed again, and with each kiss she stretched herself wider and wider open.

Then – as Henry and Gil and Susan watched her in fascinated horror – something extraordinary happened. She appeared to be penetrated by something invisible, but huge, and she was stretched even further to accommodate it. She squeezed her eyes tight with pain, and opened her mouth in a silent scream, but the remarkable thing was that there was nothing there – at least nothing that Henry and Gil and Susan could see. The girl began to buck her hips backwards and forwards, holding her arms outwards with her hands clenched as if she were tightly gripping the back of some furious assailant. Her thighs were wide apart now, and she was opened up beyond anything that Henry had ever seen.

The girl's bucking movements reached a frenzied crescendo. She shuddered, and twisted and she was abruptly flooded with pints of viscous white fluid, so much of it that it coursed down her thighs. Then she closed her eyes, and crossed her hands over her breast and for a long time she was motionless, as if she were sleeping. '*Time passes ... days pass ...*' said Springer's voice. The light in the room flickered on and off, swivelling as it did so from one side of the room to the other. Henry suddenly realised that he was watching a living diary; a record of passing days, with the sun rising in the east and setting in the west, over and over and over again, like a speeded-up movie.

Almost imperceptibly, the girl's stomach began to swell. She woke and slept, woke and slept. Her stomach grew larger and larger, until it was the size of a woman three or four months pregnant. It was then that it began to show movement. Not the uneven bumping movement of a baby's arms and legs and shoulders, but an extraordinary twitching, writhing movement.

The girl's eyes opened. She registered pain. Her stomach began to knot and twist and ripple. Her eyes opened and closed. She clenched her teeth in agony. She opened her eyes again. She was screaming, then she stopped screaming. The days poured past, sun rising, sun setting. Her stomach began to heave and churn. Her eyes bulged. She opened her mouth in a long shriek that never seemed to finish.

Henry and Gil and Susan could hear nothing, but they could see her face, and they knew that the pain she was suffering was intolerable. The scream never seemed to come to an end.

There was a strong, convulsive jerk in her stomach, a localised movement quite near to the girl's navel. Suddenly, her skin rose in a narrow chisel-shaped protrusion, dark grey like a cancer. But this wasn't cancer. The dark grey was the head of an eel, showing through her last few layers of skin. And then the skin burst open, and a vivid streak of blood slid quickly down her stomach, and the waggling head of an eel appeared, staring out at the daylight with its yellow slitted eyes, its scales slicked with blood.

'*Do you want more* ...?' asked Springer, as three or four more eel-heads burst out of the girl's stomach like obscene asparagus. '*Do you want everything* ...?'

'*Stop it.*' roared Henry. And as quickly as she had first materialised the girl disappeared. The lights in the room abruptly brightened, and everything was back the way it was.

Susan screamed at Springer, 'You're *sick!* Do you know that? You're *sick!*' She was shaking all over, and her tears had streaked her eye make-up.

Gil stepped towards Springer and demanded, 'What are you, some kind of perverted person or something? Somebody who gets kicks out of – what was that? – some kind of 3D stuff movie or something?'

But Henry held Gil's arm, restraining him. 'Whatever we feel about Mr Springer, Gil, I don't think you ought to misjudge him. Nor you, Susan. What he just showed us was disgusting, but it was also true. It was a playback of what happened to that girl we found on the beach. I don't know how it was done, but I expect Mr Springer can explain it to us.'

'A small but comprehensive sample of DNA taken from the girl's brain was quite sufficient to help me recreate her memories,' said Springer, without emotion.

'It sounds as if the Lord Thy God is a scientific God,' Henry commented, not altogether kindly.

'Science is only the human discovery of everything Ashapola created,' retorted Springer. 'I call it DNA because that is the name by which you will recognise it. Ashapola calls it something else altogether.'

Henry said, 'I read something in my ex-wife's book on eels. It said that in ancient Scandinavia, eels were sometimes referred to as the "sperm of the Devil".'

Springer nodded, almost with relief. 'What you saw – those images – they were an exact recreation of what happened to that girl in the last few months of her life. In late February of this year, she had intercourse, as you so graphically saw. As the year progressed, she became increasingly gravid, but not with child. At least, not with *human* child. Whatever she had intercourse with, she was impregnated with creatures that appeared to be eels. Eventually, they killed her. How she got into the sea, I don't yet know. But I suspect she may have been dumped there, in order to make her death seem less suspicious.'

Susan whispered, 'You don't know what – what it was that had sex with her?'

Springer shook his head. 'Henry referred to the Devil. But the opponents of Ashapola take on many different forms, some of which you would identify as animals, others as men. This girl's memory has been blotted out – by shock, perhaps, or by the deliberate intervention of the creature that had sex with her, or by a version of the same spiritual technique that I used in the restaurant to avoid being remembered by the waiters. Whichever it was, she remembers the sexual act, but she cannot remember what it was that had sex with her, human or animal or something else altogether.'

Henry saw that Susan was still trembling with shock and disgust. He put his arm around her shoulders and held her close. He looked at Springer defiantly.

'Very well. You've shown us what happened to that girl we discovered. You've told us that she was – well, that she had sex with something. We've seen what the consequences were. I think I can speak for all of us and say that we believe you, although I must question the necessity of your showing it to us so graphically, especially to poor Susan here.'

'And?' asked Springer, bland-faced. 'What is your point?'

'I have no point, except that we believe you, and that we wish logo now.'

'I second that,' put in Gil. 'There might have been some kind of a reason for that little picture-show, but what it was sure beats me.'

Springer laid one hand flat across the other, and carefully examined his fingernails. 'The reason for it was simply this, my friend. It was necessary for me to make you believe me; and none of what I have been telling you is easy to accept. I am not only asking you to believe in Ashapola. I am asking you to understand that it is desperately urgent that the beast which impregnated this girl is found.' 'Not by us, Charlie,' Gil told him, sardonically.

Springer raised his eyes. 'Yes, my friends, by you. You see, there is nobody else. You saw the girl, you saw the eels. You are the only ones who truly believe. You were brought together by the will of Ashapola, believe me. By design, rather than by accident. Your destiny was laid out for you this morning, when you found the girl lying on the sand. You have to find the beast, and find it quickly. You have to destroy it.'

Henry's lower lip wouldn't stop juddering, but he managed to say, 'What if we refuse? What if we just go about our business and refuse? What if we don't want to have anything to do with it?'

Springer slowly shook his head. 'You have no choice whatever, my dear sir. Because if you fail to find the beast, then the beast will almost certainly find *you*.'

Chapter Six

Nancy's eleven-year-old Cutlass had almost reached the turn-off at La Jolla Drive when the steering stiffened and the brakes went mushy and the oil warning light blinked on. The car rolled slower and slower, and it was only by wrenching the steering wheel violently to the right that she managed to manoeuvre it off the freeway. It stopped, and she applied the hand-brake. She said, 'Shit'

It had been the scrappy evening to end all scrappy evenings. Now she was stranded on the northbound freeway at eight o'clock in the evening, all dressed up in her best blue linen suit and her matching blue shoes, angry, frustrated, and unhappy.

It had been her second date with John Bream, who worked alongside her in the creative department at Sutton & Ramirez, the second-largest advertising agency in San Diego. John was advertising's answer to Richard Gere. At least, that was what Nancy had thought at first. He was athletic, argumentative, highly creative, and sullenly handsome; and when he had asked her out on a date two weeks ago, she had spent half a week's salary on a new silk dress from Capriccio and three hours at Young Attitude having her bright red hair cut and styled in a wave.

The first date had been wonderful. A Korean dinner at

the Seoul House, disco dancing and then a drive out to the seashore to watch the surf. They had kissed, and John had told her how vivacious she was. 'You're the most vivacious girl I ever met, bar none.'

Tonight, though, when she had called around to his apartment in the Old Town, he hadn't booked dinner and he hadn't planned on dancing. He had been wearing nothing but a bright green towelling bathrobe and what he must have thought was a seductive smile. When she had protested, he had lost his temper. 'Do you know how much money I've spent on you already? And now you're telling me you're not going to come across, because it's against your principles? Jesus, you women! Some feminist revolution! You're only independent when it happens to suit you!'

His crudeness had appalled her. She had read letters in *Cosmopolitan* about men who expect sex in direct repayment for money invested on dates, but she had never encountered it before – at least, not so blatantly. She had turned around and left. He had shouted at her down the staircase, 'You tight-assed bitch!'

She twisted the key again and again in the Cutlass's ignition. The starter-motor whinnied and whinnied, but then after a while it began to sound like a regurgitating horse, and finally it refused to do anything at all but click. Her previous boyfriend, an overbearing know all called Ned, had warned her several times that her alternator was on the way out. She climbed out of the car and stood glaring at it with her hands on her hips, as if there was a possibility that it might start up out of sheer embarrassment.

Although it was summer, there was a cool wind blowing up here, where the freeway cleaved between the grassy hills of La Jolla Village. The sky was the colour of pasque flowers, blue fading into violet, and southern swallows soared high above Nancy's head. Oh well, she thought wryly, at least they aren't vultures.

Traffic whizzed and whistled past her, orange lights glowing smugly, interiors dark and private, and even though she raised the Cutlass's bonnet, and switched on her emergency flashers, nobody wanted to stop. There had been too many rapes and too many muggings on the freeway lately. Too many motorists had stopped to assist stranded ladies, only to find themselves attacked by two or three hoodlums jumping out from the bushes.

Nancy began to feel shivery, and she rubbed her arms to keep herself warm. It was almost completely dark now, and she was beginning to think that she would have to leave the car and walk all the way to La Jolla Village, to see if she could get a taxi to take her home.

She reached into the car for her pocketbook, and was just about to lock the door when a white Lincoln slowed down and pulled off the freeway only twenty yards in front of her. It waited with its engine running, and with its brake lights still flaring bright, indicating that the driver was holding the car in gear. Nancy hesitated for a moment, and then began to walk towards the Lincoln, ducking her head a little so that she could make out what kind of a person was sitting inside.

She drew level with the passenger-door, and the driver wound down the window. She looked in, her hand shading her eyes from the glare of the traffic. White leather seating, expensive. The driver was wearing a black leather designer jacket and black pants. His face was thin, hollow cheeked, and swarthy, almost Mexican. The whites of his eyes sparkled in the darkness.

'Having trouble?' he asked her. Nancy could hear the soft tones of hymn-singing on the car tape-deck. O *Jesu, I have promised* ... Perhaps he was a priest, Nancy thought to herself. But then what kind of a priest wears a black leather designer jacket, and drives around in a white late-model Lincoln?

'My car died on me,' she said, anxiously. 'The battery's dead, I guess. Anyway it won't start.'

'Where are you headed?'

'La Jolla. Right at the top of Prospect Street.'

'Is that far?'

'If you take the next turn-off, it's about two miles towards the ocean.'

'Can I offer you a ride?'

Nancy bit her lip. She remembered her friend Carole, who had accepted a ride home from a Thanksgiving party in Leucadia last November, and had been robbed and raped by three teenage boys. She remembered a girl from the office, Linda, who had been attacked in Balboa Park in broad daylight and almost killed. Just because this man was good looking and well dressed and driving an expensive car, that didn't mean anything at all. Sex criminals came in every colour and size and every conceivable variety, with optional extras.

The young man waited, with unusual patience, while Nancy tried to make up her mind. At last she said, 'Okay Thank you. That's very kind of you.'

The young man released the central locking system, and Nancy opened the passenger-door and climbed in. Before he started off, the young man looked at her appraisingly, without any pretence at discretion, and said, 'You're a pretty girl. You ought to be careful, out on the freeway.'

Nancy tried to smile. 'I was scared at first that nobody was going to stop. Then I was scared that somebody might.'

The young man glanced in his rear-view mirror, and then steered the Lincoln out into the traffic. 'You're not scared of me, are you?'

'Do I have any reason to be?' Nancy asked him.

The young man pulled a face. 'I don't think so. But you never can tell, can you, what evil lurks in the hearts of men?'

He paused, steering the car with one hand. Then he added, 'Only The Shadow knows, ho-ho-ho.'

'That dates you,' said Nancy. 'My father used to know all those radio catchphrases.'

'Like "Nobody home, I hope, I hope, I hope,"' the young man suggested.

'That's right! How did you know that?'

'That was Elmer Blurt, out of *Al Pearce and his Gang*.'

Nancy shook her head in amusement. 'You know, I never met anybody who knew all those catchphrases, except for my father.'

The young man looked in his mirror again. 'Should I turn off here?'

'That's right. Just where it says La Jolla Village Drive.'

The young man piloted the Lincoln off the freeway and up the La Jolla exit ramp. At the top of the ramp, he took a left, and headed uphill towards La Jolla itself.

'I should introduce myself,' he told Nancy. 'My name's Ronald DeVries. 'I'm Nancy Busch,' said Nancy.

'You might have gathered that I don't actually live around here,' Ronald told her. 'As a matter of fact, I just came up from Mexico. I was living in San Hipolito for quite some time.'

'I don't know San Hipolito,' Nancy confessed. 'Is that a nice place?'

Ronald lifted a hand, as if to say, San Hipolito? What can I tell you?

'You didn't like it too much, then?' asked Nancy.

'It's okay, if you don't *have to* stay there. I *had to*.'

'I love La Jolla,' Nancy told him. 'I've lived here for eleven years now. It's much more commercialised than it used to be, but it still has charm. You can sit right out on the rocks in the winter, when there's nobody around, and you might just as well be the only person in the whole darn world.'

'You'll have to direct me,' said Ronald, as they reached the top of a La Jolla Drive.

'A left here. A left.'

As he steered the car around the corner with exaggerated care, Ronald said, 'You look as if you were going out someplace tonight.'

'I was. I had a slight disagreement with my boyfriend. Well, ex-boyfriend, from now on.'

'That's too bad,' said Ronald, and lapsed into silence.

Nancy said, 'Are you a priest, or anything like that?'

'A priest?' Ronald laughed.

'Well, those are hymns, aren't they, on your tape-deck?'

Ronald reached over and immediately switched the tape-deck off. 'It was just something I was listening to, to pass the time.'

'Are you going far?'

'I was planning on getting to Santa Barbara.'

'That's a real long drive. I hope I haven't delayed you.'

Ronald overtook a toiling cement-truck, and then pulled over to the inside lane again to let a red Porsche blare past them. 'As a matter of fact, I was thinking of giving up on Santa Barbara and inviting you out for dinner.'

Nancy immediately shook her head vigorously. 'Oh, no, I can't expect you to do that, not after giving me a ride and everything. Besides, I have to arrange for somebody to go collect my car. I don't want to wind up with no wheels and no engine.'

'Listen,' said Ronald, 'Call the emergency services and arrange for them to collect your car. They won't need your keys. Then come out to dinner.'

'I'm sorry, Ronald,' Nancy told him. 'That's real generous of you, I mean it. But I hardly know you, and I'm not at all sure that I feel in the mood for it any more.'

Ronald turned the Lincoln into Prospect Street, without Nancy directing him, and then parked on the slope outside her house.

'How did you know I lived here?' she asked him, in amazement.

'You told me. Right at the top of Prospect Street, that's what you said. Now, how about dinner? I've really gone cold on the idea of driving all the way to Santa Barbara, and I'm going to have to eat somewhere.'

'But you're right *here*, right outside the exact house.'

'Coincidence,' Ronald told her, off-handedly. Then, 'Come on, Nancy, how about it? A friendly *diner a deux*, no strings attached, no complications. All I'm looking for is company. I hate to eat alone.'

'Well ... all right,' said Nancy. 'But I'm going to have to call the tow-truck first. Do you want to come inside?'

'I'll wait in the car, if you want me to.'

'Of course not. Come along in.'

The house in which Nancy lived was large and secluded. It had been built in 1936 in the red-brick style of an English country villa, although it was difficult to see much of the brickwork now because of the thickly overhanging ivy. Fifteen years ago, the owner of the house had gone back East, and ordered that the property should be divided into apartments, for long-term lets. Nancy had sub-let the second-floor apartment at the back of the house, from an oceanologist who had been sent to work in Kyoto for four years.

Nancy opened the front door and led the way inside. The hallway was gloomy and smelled of lavender-polish and Chinese cooking. There was a dark long-case clock opposite the stairs, which ticked with infinite weariness, and whose half-seen pendulum always reminded Nancy of something written by Edgar Allen Poe.

She climbed the stairs, Ronald following her. 'Do you know who to call to pick up your car?' asked Ronald, as she unlocked the front door of her apartment.

'Don't worry, it's happened before,' she told him, as she switched on the lights. Ronald came in, and looked around her living-room with approval. It was sparsely but tastefully

GRAHAM MASTERTON

furnished with plain modern furniture, glass-topped tables, Italian lamps with necks like futuristic giraffes, and Red Indian blankets on the walls. While Nancy went to the phone, Ronald walked over to the window, and drew back the plain woven curtains.

'You have an excellent view of the neighbours,' he complimented her. 'Are those two having a fight over there? They certainly look like they're shouting.'

There was a painting on the wall beside the telephone. It was a nude, in oils, and at first glance it was obviously Nancy. Ronald came closer, and made a deliberate play of comparing the portrait and the model, turning his head from one to the other as if he were watching tennis. The likeness was unmistakable: the pale-skinned, slightly squarish face, with the short straight nose and the sudden splash of freckles, the bright red hair; the tall, angular figure, with small but well-rounded breasts.

Nancy watched him as he made his comparison, the phone still held to her ear.

'One of my boyfriends was an art student,' she commented.

'He was good,' Ronald acknowledged.

She looked round at the portrait. 'You're the first man who's ever said that. Usually, they say that they prefer the original. You know, flattery, and jealousy, too, that some other man has seen me with nothing on. My girlfriends don't like it, either. They think it's an upwardly mobile way of streaking.'

Ronald shrugged. 'I'm not like other men. Do you mind if I smoke?'

'Go ahead. There's a Sheraton ashtray over on the bookcase.'

122

Ronald went over to the other side of the room and picked up the ashtray. As he did so, he inspected Nancy's collection of books. *Advertising Art. The 100 Greatest Advertisements. The Techniques of Persuasion.* Then he came back across the room, tucking a Russian *papirosi* cigarette between his lips, and lighting it one-handed with a folded-over matchbook. The tricky technique of a man who thinks that appearances are all-important. The kind of a man who can toss peanuts up into the air and catch them in his mouth.

'So, you're in advertising?' he asked, as Nancy completed her call to the tow-truck company, and put down the phone. 'The second-oldest profession.'

'I'm a designer,' said Nancy. 'I paste eentsy little bits of lettering on to slippery sheets of overlay, and draw a lot of lines, and get paid for it.'

She was obviously waiting for him to tell her what *he* did, but he stood there silent with his hands in his pockets, puffing at his cigarette and looking at her unblinkingly.

'Shall we have some dinner?' she suggested.

'Sure. What do you like to eat?'

'Could you bear Mexican?' Nancy asked him. 'Manuelo's is good.'

'I could bear Mexican,' said Ronald.

They drove down to Manuelo's, even though it wasn't more than five minutes' walk away, down on the tourist stretch of Prospect, with its fashionable boutiques and its high-priced restaurants and its art galleries and realty offices. The sidewalks were crowded with evening promenaders and there were no free parking spaces, so in the end Ronald parked the Lincoln outside La Galeria art gallery. As he locked the car, he nodded towards the art gallery window. 'How about that?' he asked Nancy.

They crossed the sidewalk and stood close to the window. On a blue hessian-covered stand, under a single spotlight, stood a bronze statuette of the Great God Pan, cloven-hoofed, goat's horned, dancing and playing his pipes. His face was sly and sharp and infinitely wicked.

'It's terrific,' said Nancy. 'A classic.' She was being sarcastic. She thought it was awful. She wouldn't have bought it even as a doorstop.

Ronald said nothing, but nodded, and stood staring at the statuette with his hands down by his sides, as if it somehow mesmerised him. Nancy waited patiently. She didn't like to urge him on too much, since he was buying.

Eventually, without explaining what it was about the statuette that had interested him so much, Ronald turned away from the art gallery window and offered Nancy his arm. They walked together along the noisy, brightly lit sidewalk, and Nancy found herself feeling unexpectedly cheerful. Perhaps fate had been taking care of her, after all, when she had argued with John, and when her car had broken down on the freeway. Perhaps at last (*please*, fate!) she had found herself someone special; because there was no doubt about it, Ronald DeVries was special.

They shared *guacamole* and *cuesadillas* smothered in Manuelo's thick secret sauce. They ate rich *chilli*, and washed it down with strong red wine. They talked about advertising and office affairs and cars that broke down and childhood embarrassments. They laughed and they held each other's hands across the tablecloth, their eyes sparkling in the light from the candles that flickered between them. Ronald ordered more wine and Nancy went to the restroom. She looked at her face in the mirror, and said, out loud, 'I hope you're not becoming infatuated, my dear.'

She came back to the table. Ronald had already poured her another glass of wine. He said, with amusement, 'You know something? You know what our Christian names are? Ronald and Nancy! Can you believe that? Isn't that too Presidential for words?'

'You were telling me all about those old WC Fields radio sketches,' Nancy reminded him.

'Oh, sure. They were terrific. There was one where he says he always collapsed at the sound of the word "work". In his family, they wouldn't say it out loud, they always referred to it as "W". Otherwise, he would pass out, and the only remedy was a deep dipper of dogberry brandy diluted with straight gin.'

Ronald did a passable WC Fields impression. 'I remember the first drink of it ... I turned a little pale.'

Nancy laughed. She hadn't felt so incredibly happy for months. She took hold of Ronald's hand again, and said, 'How do you *know* all this stuff?'

He shrugged. 'I guess I always enjoyed the radio.'

'But they don't have that kind of programme on the radio these days, do they?'

Ronald made a disinterested face, and took out a cigarette.

'Do you have tapes?' asked Nancy. 'I mean, could I listen to some of them?'

Ronald shook his head. 'I just heard it, that's all.'

It was clear that he didn't feel like talking about it any

longer, so Nancy tried to change the subject. 'You haven't told me anything about Mexico, what you were doing down there.'

He looked at her as if he was surprised that she had asked him. 'I wasn't doing anything down there,' he replied, after a short pause.

'I'm sorry,' she said. 'I didn't mean to be nosey. I was interested, that's all.'

'Well, don't be. It wasn't interesting at all.'

'Okay, I'm sorry,' said Nancy, rather put out. She couldn't understand why the mention of Mexico should have made Ronald so unsettled all of a sudden, and so sour. He had enjoyed his Mexican meal, but it seemed as if the country of Mexico itself was a platinum-plated downer. He puffed quickly at his cigarette, and then crushed it out, half smoked. 'Well, let's talk about something else,' Nancy suggested. 'We don't have to talk about Mexico.'

Ronald stared at her sharply. 'Look – what is it with you? I said I didn't want to talk about Mexico. I thought I made it perfectly clear that I didn't want to talk about Mexico. And all I'm getting is Mexico, Mexico, Mexico.'

'For goodness sake –' Nancy put in, trying to calm him down. 'I asked you in all innocence. I didn't know that it was going to upset you so much. Listen, I don't care what you did or didn't do, down in Mexico. I was only making polite conversation, and if you don't want to talk about it –'

Ronald's face was expressionless, unreadable, as blank of information as a headstone.

'*Ronald?*' she queried, reaching out for his hand.

At that moment, the waiter came bustling over. 'Is there anything else, *senor?* Did you enjoy your meal, *senorita?*'

'Just bring me the bill,' said Ronald, shortly.

The waiter glanced worriedly at Nancy. 'Is everything to your satisfaction, *senor*? *Senorita*?'

'Everything's fine, just bring me the damned bill!'

Nancy said nothing until they were walking back to the car. 'Did you have to talk to the waiter like that? I was embarrassed.'

Ronald was tossing his car keys up in the air and catching them again, over and over with an irritating slap-jingle, slap-jingle. He didn't answer straight away, but it was plain that his mood had drastically changed to one of unrelenting coldness.

'What happened in Mexico, that upset you so much?' Nancy persisted. 'I mean – whatever happened, you don't have to take it out on the rest of us. It wasn't *my* fault. And it certainly wasn't that waiter's fault.'

'You don't think so?' asked Ronald. 'It's been your fault all along, people like you and people like him.'

'I don't understand you at all,' Nancy retaliated. 'A half-hour ago, I thought you were fantastic, the nicest, funniest guy I'd ever met. A half-hour ago, if you can believe it, I even thought that I was going slightly crazy over you. But the way you're acting now, what can I say? What are you blaming me for? Something that happened in Mexico that I don't even know anything about? I never saw you before tonight, how *could* I be responsible? And the way you're going on now, I don't think I ever *want* to see you again.'

Ronald stopped beside his car, and regarded Nancy over the top of the white vinyl roof with an expression that had altered yet again. The coldness had gone. In its place was self-satisfaction, and patronising smugness.

'You *will* see me again, whether you want to or not.'

'I don't think so,' said Nancy. 'Now, I think I'll walk home, thank you very much. Do you want me to pay for my share of the dinner?'

Ronald unlocked his car. 'Forget it. The condemned lady ate a hearty meal.'

'What in hell is *that* supposed to mean? Are you trying to frighten me, or what?'

'Nobody – ever – has accused me of trying to frighten them,' said Ronald.

Nancy stood where she was. Ronald climbed into his car, and slammed the door. His last reply hung in the evening air like a complex carillon of bells. He had placed unusual and provocative emphasis on the word *ever*, and on the word *trying*. He had sounded to Nancy as if he had really meant *ever*. Not just a human lifetime, but hundreds of years, even thousands of years, even eternity. And he had emphasised *trying* as if he had meant that it was unnecessary for him to try: that he frightened people without any effort whatsoever.

As he leaned forward to insert his ignition keys, she caught a glimpse of his face, and the bright street-light seemed to catch him at an unusual angle, so that he appeared suddenly drawn and old and inexplicably unpleasant. He looked up again, and the old expression vanished, but in that brief moment of – what was it? insight? revelation? – she felt that she had seen him as he really was, and she was unhappily glad of it. All right, so fate hadn't been good to her, after all. Ronald had turned out to be just as much of a macho bastard as John Bream, and all the rest of them. But at least he had revealed himself quickly, before she became entangled. Fate may have been playing around with her, but at least it had spared her the long-drawn-out waiting and hoping that she usually had to suffer.

She swung her bag over her shoulder, and started to walk north along Prospect. It was only five minutes back to her house. She didn't wave; she didn't turn around. She had encountered Ronald by chance, she was going to part with him the same way. Casually, like two people who have talked together on a plane, and then go their separate ways. She heard his engine start up behind her, and the squealing of his tyres as he pulled away from the kerb but she kept on walking as steadily as before. Ronald turned the Lincoln around in the middle of the road, suspension bucking, and then he drove past her at high speed, without looking at her.

Goodbye, she said to herself, knight in shining armour thou never went. Still, she was grateful to be back in La Jolla, instead of marooned on Interstate-5. She owed him that much, whatever his complexes were; and for the Mexican dinner. She wondered why he was so incredibly sensitive about Mexico. What could have happened to him there that was so appalling that he blamed practically the whole world for it?

She thought about something else, too, as she followed the curve of Prospect Street north-eastwards, her hair blown by the cool sea wind. She thought about Ronald standing in front of La Galeria window, for minutes on end, staring at that statuette of Pan. On reflection, his behaviour seemed really strange, although it hadn't struck her as particularly peculiar at the time. He had stared and stared at it and she could just picture his expression. Contempt, but fascination, too, as if he couldn't tear himself away from it, no matter how incompetent a piece of sculpture it was.

She reached her house, and walked up the driveway to the front door. There were no lights in any of the front windows. Most of the other tenants were out for the evening. The woman who lived directly below Nancy had found herself a wealthy Indian petrogeologist (married, of course) and he had taken her away to an oil seminar in Phoenix.

She took out her keys, but as she stepped up to the front door, she was surprised to find that it was slightly open. She hesitated, for a very long time. Nobody ever left the front door open. It was not that they didn't trust their neighbours, or the local inhabitants. Out of the tourist season, La Jolla was as peaceable a community as you could find anywhere in Southern California. Boondocks-On-Sea, one of her friends called it. But the summer brought casual theft, purse-snatching, and spasmodic outbursts of aggravated assault, and rape.

At length, Nancy pushed the door open a little wider. The hallway was dark and silent. She could just make out the lower part of the staircase, faintly illuminated by the stained-glass window at the bend in the stairs. She called, 'Hallo? Is there anybody there?'

Silence. She waited a moment longer, and then she pushed the door open as wide as it would go. She could hear the long-case clock ticking now, wearily, wearily, and see the intermittent reflection of its pendulum. She remembered Ronald's curious warning: *You* will *see me again, whether you want to or not* – and she had an irrational fear that he was waiting for her under the stairs, ready to pounce on her and stab her.

'Ronald?' she called, although she felt foolish.

There was no answer. Holding her breath, she slid sideways into the hallway and reached for the light switch.

The lights flicked on. The hallway was deserted. Drab, and shabby, and smelling as it always did, of cooking.

There was a note on the hallstand. She walked quickly across and picked it up. It was addressed to her, from the Tecolote Road Wrecking Company, Inc. It was written in a quick, scrawled hand, and advised her that her vehicle had been towed as she had instructed to their downtown auto-repair shop, where it would be fixed and ready for collection in approximately four days. She tucked the note back in its envelope, and looked around. The tow-truck crew must have called here; somebody had answered the door to them, and then failed to close it properly. She could hear, faintly, the sounds of *Matt Houston* from old Mrs. Oestreicher's television, first floor back. It had probably been her.

Nancy closed the door behind her and climbed the stairs to her apartment. She opened it up and went inside, throwing her bag on to the sofa. Kicking off her shoes, she went through to the kitchen, and took a bottle of white wine out of the fridge. There were three neatly washed wine-glasses on the drainer, the only three wine-glasses she had. She filled one up with Paul Masson's best, and went back through to the living-room.

She kept thinking about Ronald DeVries, and how his mood had swung so violently. One minute he had been infinitely charming, the next he had seemed capable of strangling her. Oh well, her mother had always warned her about accepting rides from strange men. 'The white slave trade's still thriving, Nancy – and don't let anyone tell you different.' Nancy finished her glass of wine in three thirsty swallows, then refilled it.

She tried to watch television for twenty minutes or so, but she was tired and restless and woozy with wine, so in the end she went through to the bedroom, tugged down the raffia blinds, and undressed. She hung her blue suit up carefully in her closet, and parked her blue shoes neatly side by side beneath it. She had a fragment of music on her brain, the introduction to Bob Dylan's song *What's a Nice Girl Like You Doing In a Dump Like This?* She hummed it again and again as she ran herself a bath, and went backwards and forwards from the bathroom to the bedroom, cleaning off her nail polish, clipping up her hair, wiping off her lipstick.

She spent ten dreamy minutes in the bath, watching the drips from the leaky tap, and the steam rising up to the ceiling, a succession of embryonic ghosts. She found herself thinking again and again of the statuette of Pan, with its hoofs and its beard and its wicked slanting eyes. She seemed to have an image of it caught in her mind, like the shuddering frame of a video film on pause; an image that wouldn't go away, no matter how hard she tried to dismiss it.

She dried herself, and sat at her dressing-table naked, dusting herself with iris-scented talc, and smoothing her face with Clinique cream. Look at me, she said to herself. Twenty-six years old, fashionable, good looking, intelligent. Big green eyes, sensual lips, a model-girl figure. What is it about me that proves irresistible to all the wrong men? Why am I sleeping alone tonight, for the one-hundred-and-fifty-seventh time this year? I don't even know why I bother to take the pill.

She cupped one hand over her left breast. If you touch me, am I not aroused? If you kiss me, do I not respond? I'm a woman, a fully equipped highly emotional woman, with all the passions of a fully equipped highly emotional woman, and more. Yet I expect to be treated like a human being, too, not the way that John Bream tried to treat me. Not the way that Ronald DeVries treated me, either. Why do men blame me for everything? John, for being sexually ungrateful for a Carte Blanche bill of $78.25, including gratuity. Ronald, for some inexplicable hardship he had suffered down in San Hipolito, Mexico.

She tied a scarf around her hair, and went to the closet to take out a clean shirt. She always slept in men's shirts; partly because they made comfortable nightwear, and partly because she liked to go into Sears' menswear department and buy them, as if she had a husband, or a steady boyfriend. She climbed into bed with the book she had been reading for the past seven months, never progressing more than two or three pages a night, *An Analysis of Contemporary Advertising*. She wound her Minnie Mouse alarm-clock, and then tugged the cord which switched off the ceiling light.

'Ogilvy's 1958 advertisement for imported Rolls-Royces contained nothing but facts, without adjectives ...' she began to read. But then she thought about the statuette of Pan, and Ronald's voice saying, 'Nobody – ever – has accused me of trying to frighten them. Of *trying* to frighten them.' She tried to concentrate harder on her book. 'The agency was faced with an antiquated public image of Rolls-Royce as a box-like car that sold for $20,000 and over, and required a chauffeur to drive it ...'

'Nobody – *ever* –'

She read about a page and a half, and then she yawned and put the book aside on the night table. She switched off her bedside lamp, and wriggled herself down beneath the covers. She lay on her side for a while, watching the patterns of light dancing on the wall. They danced there every night: the streetlights shining through the yuccas in the back yard. On stormy nights they flickered wildly, but tonight was temperate and calm and only slightly breezy, and their dance was more sedate. Nancy's eyes closed. She jerked once, and frowned, but then she slept.

Her sleep was dreamless at first, but then she found herself somewhere on a windy hill, miles from anywhere. In the distance, she could see the red-and-white lights of traffic, flowing along the freeway, but something told her that it was the wrong freeway, and that she was walking in the wrong direction. She tried not to panic, but she knew that she was lost, and that it would take her hours to find her way back home.

She reached an old-fashioned house, standing on its own, silent and derelict. She glided up the steps, and found that the door was open. Glancing to the side, she saw that there was a wicker-seated rocking-chair lying on its side on the derelict verandah, and that grey rats were tugging at the wicker seat with their teeth. 'Someone has died,' she thought to herself; and a thick feeling of darkness and claustrophobia came over her. She knew she would have to enter the house, and try to find a telephone.

She opened the door. The interior of the house was gloomy and suffocating. There was a tall display cabinet standing by the side of the stairs. Its glass windows were obscured with grease and dust and the patina of hundreds of neglected years. She glided towards it and tried to peer inside. She could make out dark and twisted shapes, but even when she wiped her hand across the greasy glass it was impossible to see what they were. For some reason, she found them frightening.

'Nobody – ever –' whispered a voice. A voice as cold as the drip of a tap, in a long-abandoned bathroom. 'Nobody – *ever* – has accused me of trying –'

She ascended the staircase without even moving her legs. She passed a lighted window, halfway up, in which a bronze statuette of the Great God Pan was dancing. The statue remained motionless, but she was sure that it would pursue her, once she had turned her back on it. It seemed for some reason to be poisonously evil, the essence of corruption and terror.

'To frighten them – *to frighten* them –'

She rose to the second-floor landing. She tried to turn around to make sure that the Great God Pan wasn't following her, but she found it impossible to turn her neck around. She felt as if all her muscles had seized up, and that she was powerless to prevent herself from gliding across the landing, not quickly, but steadily and silently and irresistibly – towards the door of her own apartment.

The apartment door dissolved, like brown fog, and she passed through it into the living-room. She suddenly thought of the naked portrait of herself, by the telephone. Supposing somebody saw it and was scandalised? Supposing somebody saw it and thought that she was immoral, and that she would have sex with any man who asked her? She tried to turn around to see if the portrait was still there, but her neck remained locked in a painful muscular cramp. She forgot that she was supposed to be looking for a phone.

She went gliding into the bedroom. It was dark in there, impenetrably dark, and the door closed behind her, soft and airtight. She strained her eyes to see where her bed was, but the darkness was complete, and she had to make her way cautiously across the room with her hands outstretched, feeling her way. She found it at last, and climbed into it; but she had the strangest sensation now that this was no longer a dream, that what she felt was real. She reached across the bed and she could feel the wrinkled sheets. She could hear the alarm-clock ticking. All that was missing was the streetlight, dancing on the wall.

Then she heard a sound. It was a scraping, rustling sound – very faint, but sufficient to convince her that there was somebody or something in the room with her. She lay stock-still, her eyes wide, her ears straining to listen, her breath caught tight. Was that somebody breathing, down at the foot of the bed? Or was it simply the echo of her own breath?

She waited. The hands of the clock crept towards half-past eleven.

Silence, except for the rushing of her own blood.

Then there was another scraping noise, louder this time. She held her breath again, and lifted her head off the pillow, holding it up so that her neck ached, peering and peering into the darkness to see what was there.

I'm dreaming, she thought. This is a dream. All I have to do is wake up.

But then supposing I wake up and find out that it's real, that it's still happening, that there's something in the room with me?

A wind began to blow, very softly, lifting one of the raffia blinds away from the window, so that the very faintest of lights penetrated the room. It was so dim that Nancy couldn't see anything she recognised. Either that, or the room was completely different, completely changed. She propped herself cautiously up on her elbows. Was that a mirror, where the door should have been? Was that a chair, standing in the corner? And next to the chair, that curving shape looked like the side of a large terracotta vase.

Scrape, rustle.

Nancy jerked her head around, to the other side of the bed, to the side where the shadows were. And suddenly he was standing there, right next to her, white and naked as a corpse, his eyes glowing dull red in the darkness, his teeth catching the light: Ronald DeVries, or a creature that looked like Ronald DeVries. The wind died down, the blind fell back, the room was buried in darkness again. Nancy clutched herself close, pulled her legs up under her, squeezed her eyes tight shut and screamed, '*No!*'

Something clawed for her, in the blackness. She felt fingernails lacerate her thigh. She tried to twist over, out of the way, but two powerful hands gripped her wrists, and forced her on to her back. She felt a sharp knee, forcing itself between her thighs; then one of the hands that was gripping her wrists adjusted itself, so that her upper arm was pinned against the bed by an elbow, and the hand snatched an agonising, eye-watering handful of hair. She screamed, or thought she screamed; but how could anybody hear her screaming, if this was a dream?

Her shirt was pulled open at the front, the buttons twisted off. Then she felt a heavy, cold, bristly body lying on top of hers; a body like a dead pig. She tried to scream again, but she didn't seem to have the breath for it, and when she looked up into the darkness she could see those two dimly glowing eyes, like torches shining through a thick blanket, and she could smell winey breath and some other unutterable odour that tightened her throat and knotted up her stomach and made it almost impossible for her to speak.

'*Don't*,' she begged, in a strangled whisper. '*Don't!*'

The creature on top of her dragged at her hair even harder, and said something deep in its throat. Strange, guttural words that she was unable to understand, but which sounded obscene. She thought of John Bream, shouting at her down the stairwell. She thought of all the men who had turned and looked at her, a thousand pairs of eyes, all of them calculating, all of them remorseless, all of them wanting nothing at all but to relieve the urgency of their lust inside her.

'Oh no,' she whimpered, as the creature's calloused hands began to twist her breasts. She tried one last furious struggle, throwing herself from side to side, tossing her body backwards and forwards, clutching and tugging at everything she could reach. But the creature was far too heavy, and far too strong. It loomed above her, chilly and rank, its eyes hovering only inches away from her face, and it pronounced those incomprehensible words again, and she could feel them reverberate against its hairy ribcage.

'Please let me wake up,' she cried. 'Please, dear God, *please* let me wake up!'

But now the creature was leaning forward on to her shoulders, and she could feel its tangled beard scratching against her neck and her cheek. She could feet it pushing itself against her vulva, as if somebody was forcing a clenched fist up between her legs.

'Please, it's too big,' she wept. 'Please, you're going to kill me. Please!'

She felt pain so intense that she thought that her pelvis had broken apart. Her head jerked upward involuntarily, and her spine arched. She was hurt too badly to do anything but shudder and gasp, and she had to cling on to the creature's shoulders to prevent it from thrusting itself too far inside her.

There was nothing she could do to save herself, she was powerless. She couldn't even wake herself up. All she could do was hold on tight to the very creature that was hurting her so much, and keep her legs stretched as wide apart as she possibly could, and pray, and pray, and pray.

The creature suddenly cried out '*Sabazius!*' and roared, and she felt its muscles bunch and wriggle like snakes smothered in cold lard. It cried out again, and then again; and then immediately it drew itself out of her, with a noise that she would never forget, liquid and viscous.

She lay where she was, in the same position, as the creature climbed up off the bed. She heard the mattress springs crunching together under its weight. She said a silent prayer to the Lord Almighty that it wouldn't take it into its head to kill her.

Oh God, oh God, please don't let it kill me. Please let it go away now. Please, God, let me wake up. She babbled and babbled like a mad and penitent nun.

It seemed as if she remained hunched up on her bed for hours. She opened and closed her eyes, never knowing for sure whether she was asleep or awake. Gradually, the raffia blinds began to lighten, and after a while the sun was filling the room. She sat up, and tugged her hands through her hair. Had it been a dream? She looked down at herself. Her shirt was unbuttoned, but not torn, and when she turned her hands this way and that, there were no scratches on them, no bruises, nothing to bear witness to a furious struggle with a sharp-nailed beast. She stood up, and walked through to the bathroom, and looked at herself in the mirror. Her eyes were a little puffy, as if she hadn't slept very well, but apart from that, she looked quite well.

Just to make certain, she reached one tentative hand down between her legs. She was moist, as she usually was when she had been dreaming about sex. But there was no trace of the spurting liquid flood with which the creature had filled her. Nor was she sore.

She stared at herself in the mirror. 'A dream,' she said, out loud. 'It was nothing but a dream. Can you *believe* it?'

She stepped into the tub, drew the pink vinyl shower-curtain around herself, and turned on the faucet, hot and hard. Although there was no evidence that what had happened to her was anything but a vivid nightmare, she made sure that she washed herself thoroughly. She felt polluted by what she had imagined about Ronald DeVries.

She also felt frightened.

She towelled herself, and dressed, choosing light beige slacks and a white short-sleeved blouse. She brushed her hair, but didn't blow it dry. It was only seven o'clock, and by the time she had called a taxi to take her to work and made herself some coffee, it would be practically dry anyway. She switched on her radio and went through to the kitchen. She hummed along with 'We Are The World'.

The telephone rang. She went back through to the living-room to answer it. 'Hallo?' she said. She was a single girl living on her own. She never gave her name until she knew who was calling.

'Nancy? Is this Nancy?' The voice sounded very far away.

'Who is this?' asked Nancy.

'Don't you recognise my voice? This is Ronald, Ronald DeVries.'

Nancy felt a cold prickling, all the way across her back. 'Ronald? What do you want?'

'I just wanted to know whether you enjoyed yourself, Nancy.'

Nancy pressed her hand against her forehead. 'Well, yes, as a matter of fact, I *did* enjoy myself. That is, until you decided to lose your temper, and accuse me of all kinds of things I hadn't even done.'

'No, Nancy, not then. I wasn't talking about *then*. I was talking about afterwards.'

'Afterwards? What do you mean, afterwards? There wasn't any afterwards. I went home to bed.'

'And you dreamed, Nancy, didn't you? You dreamed!'

A sensation of pure, slow dread began to crawl through Nancy's veins, branching gradually towards her heart.

'How do you know that?' she demanded, shakily. 'How do you know that I dreamed?'

'Most people *dream*, Nancy.'

'But how did you know that *I* dreamed?'

Ronald was silent for a long time. Nancy could hear the long-distance wires crooning and warbling.

'Ronald,' she repeated, frightened and impatient, 'How did you know that *I* dreamed?'

Ronald laughed. For an instant, she could have sworn that his laugh turned into a snarl. Then he said, 'I know that you dreamed, Nancy, because you dreamed about me. That's how I know that you dreamed.'

Chapter Seven

Two days later, Henry was sitting in his living-room listening to Beethoven and drinking chilled vodkatinis when there was a buzz at the door. He closed his eyes in long-suffering martyrdom, and let the buzzer go five or six times before he finally heaved himself out of his chair, and walked with dragging footsteps into the hall.

'Who is it?' he bellowed, swaying on his slippered feet.

'It's me, Gil Miller.'

'Ah, the redoubtable Gil Miller. Hold on for just a moment, and I shall furnish access.'

Henry unchained the door, and opened it. Gil hesitated for a moment when he saw him, unshaven, wearing a fraying blue bathrobe, with a large glass of vodka in his hand, but Henry said, 'Don't mind me. It's Friday morning, and I'm having fun.' He led the way into the living-room, leaving Gil to close the door, and he waved his arms expansively, so that he sent a neat splash of vodka right down the back of one of the sofa cushions. 'Beethoven! Ludwig van Beethoven!' he proclaimed.

Gil nodded towards the frosted jug of vodkatinis. 'How many of those have you had?' he asked, but not critically.

'I don't count my drinks,' said Henry. He sat down

abruptly, spilling more vodka on his bathrobe. 'Drink cannot be measured like days of the week, or like linoleum, or socks. Drink is an endless river, flowing majestically towards the sea. From mountain-top to ocean, via the kidneys of a million million devotees. And when I fall, exhausted by my pleasurable duties, there will always be another to take my place.'

Gil said, 'I've been thinking about Springer.' 'Ah' Henry replied, with alcoholic sagacity. 'You've been thinking about Springer. Well, I too have been thinking about Springer! In fact I have hardly been able to think about anything or anyone else ... apart from bloody Springer.'

He touched Gil's chest very lightly with the flat of his hand, and burped a deeply suppressed burp, and then said, 'Sit down, please. I implore you.'

'You're drunk,' said Gil.

'I know,' said Henry.

'Maybe I should call back tomorrow morning, when you're sober.'

'Don't! You won't get any sense out of me then.'

Gil blew out his cheeks, and thought about it, and then reluctantly agreed to sit down. Henry lifted the jug and waved it so wildly in the air that Gil was sure that he was going to spill it all. 'Would you care for a ... libation, m'dear boy?'

'I'm fine. I have to drive.'

'Ah, well,' said Henry. 'Driving is a chore that I have long since abandoned. I have a car though, you know. A Mercury, 1971 vintage. Nine thousand miles on the odometer, that's all. It's in the garage, draped in tarpaulin, waiting for the day when I finally make up my mind that I have drunk sufficient for one lifetime.'

Gil said, 'Has Springer called on you?'

Henry looked truculent. 'Springer never stops calling on me. And each damn time he looks different. Three visits in two days. First, he looked like a nun, all dressed up in white. Then he looked like the Dalai Lama on his day off. All saffron-yellow robes. He called again this morning ... about an hour ago ... wearing some black apparatus. Well, I say "he," but he isn't really a "he", is he? He's more of an "it". He could even be a *"she"*.'

Gil sat down, crossing his bare, tanned legs. 'And each time he called on you, he asked you the same question?'

'That's right. Just that one question. *"Have you made your mind up yet?"* And then, when I told him no, to wait a little longer, he left. No argument, no bother. No oratory. But each time he left me feeling guiltier than I had the time before. So now I'm feeling *very* guilty. And I expect to feel even more guilty as the day wears on.'

Gil said, 'Do you think we ought to do it?'

Henry shrugged, and drank, and made six or seven different faces. 'How should I know? Chase some mythical beast? It doesn't even sound *sane*, let alone logical. It doesn't even sound *real*.'

'Then why do you feel guilty when Springer asks you if you've made up your mind?'

'Because –' Henry began harshly, and then stopped himself, and pouted. 'Because – I don't know. I don't know what he is, or what he represents, or what he's doing here, or why. He simply has that way of making me feel guilty.

You have to understand that it doesn't take very much to make me feel guilty. My ex-wife makes me feel guilty. *You* make me feel guilty.'

He drained his glass, and burped again, and said, 'Drink, the endless river ... flowing with awful majesty ... towards the sea. Taking a detour, of course, through the human kidney. That's what they call ... a pleasant diversion.'

Gil watched him for a while, as the music came to a mighty crescendo and then died away. Quite casually, he said, 'Springer's been round to see me, too. He asked me the same question. I guess he's talked to Susan, as well.'

'I see,' said Henry. 'And what did you tell him? Or her! Or it? Do you know what *I* told him? Or her? Or it? I told him that everyone has their own path to follow. Everyone has their own duty to perform. And that *my* path did not wend its way anywhere near mythical beasts, nor killer eels; and that my duty was certainly not to search for invisible rapists.'

'I told him I'd do it,' said Gil.

Henry stared at him, blearily. 'You did *what?*'

'I told him I'd do it,' Gil repeated.

Henry opened and closed his mouth, as if he were stupefied. But then he said, 'My dear young man ... you don't even know what hunting this beast *entails!* Remember that policeman, on the beach, the one who lost half of his face! Remember the girl! Believe you me, this beast, whatever it is, is no mean opponent. Come on, we're not hunting for rabbits here! We're hunting for something that as far as I can determine is supernatural. Like a poltergeist! Or a vampire! Or – or, or, the Devil himself!'

Gil uncrossed his legs and sat up straight. 'You've agreed

to do it, too, haven't you? That's why you're drunk, and listening to all this music.'

Henry slitted his eyes.

Gil said, 'I bet you agreed to do it before I did. You went away and you thought about it, the same way I did, and in the end you couldn't think of a single decent reason for saying no.' Gil looked around him. 'I mean, Henry, what do you have to lose?'

Henry came over and laid a trembling hand on Gil's tee-shirted shoulder. He looked down at Gil with watering eyes. Somewhere beneath those heaped-up blankets of alcoholism that were smothering his emotions, he felt genuinely touched by Gil, the son he should have had and never did. He had always been too selfish to have children, too preoccupied with Marx and Engels and Russell and Kant.

He quoted Kant now, as one of his justifications for having agreed to do what Springer demanded. 'Two things fill my mind with ever-increasing wonderment and awe ... the starry heavens above me, and the moral law within me.'

'What's that?' asked Gil. Henry had been speaking very indistinctly.

Henry said, 'My reason, I suppose, for saying yes. That, and the fact that I believe what Springer says, although don't ask me why.'

'And this – Ashapola?' asked Gil. 'What do you think about that?'

Henry shook his head. 'You can call God whatever you like. You can think of Him in any way you want. He's still God.' He paused for a moment, and then he said, 'We're still talking about the never-ending struggle between good and evil, Gil. That's why I told him yes. Whatever Ashapola happens to be, He obviously stands for enlightenment, and kindness, and protecting the innocent. That girl on the beach was an innocent, and look what happened. If nothing else, other young girls should be protected, and she – well, she should be revenged.'

He sighed, and then he added, 'You're right, of course, my dear young boy, I have nothing at all to lose. A few books, most of which don't really belong to me. A few heaps of paper. A good pen, and about forty bottles of vodka. No life any more, nothing worth worrying about, anyway. I couldn't ever kill myself, don't think that, but I'm no longer afraid of dying.'

Gil said, 'I agreed to do it because I'll never get the chance to do it again. And because of that girl. And – well, *because*, that's all.'

Henry sat down next to Gil, and the two of them were silent. Then, at last, Henry suggested, 'We ought to call him. Or her. Or it. We ought to meet him, now that we're both decided.'

'What about Susan?' asked Gil.

Henry said, 'No. She's too vulnerable. She wouldn't make a very good beast-hunter, believe me. I was taken caribou-hunting once, you know, in Canada, and there were two women with us, and they were an appalling liability. They did nothing but chatter and complain about how far they had to walk.'

'I don't think hunting for this beast is going to be very much like a caribou-hunt,' said Gil, trying not to sound facetious. He didn't quite know why, but he was beginning to like Henry, even to feel protective towards him. He had never come across anybody like Henry before, somebody who could spout philosophy and reel off tines of poetry and smart remarks without even hesitating, and at the same time act with such lack of reverence for anything and everything, including himself. He didn't necessarily *admire* Henry. But he would have liked very much to count him as a friend.

'It could be *very* dangerous, you know,' said Henry.

'Maybe so. But Springer wants Susan to help us, doesn't he? And he must have a reason. He wouldn't have suggested that she should get involved if he didn't think that she could take it.'

Henry stood where he was, thinking, tilting now and then from side to side, as if he were standing on the deck of an ocean liner in a mild swell. 'Has it occurred to you what Springer actually is?' he asked Gil, changing the subject.

'Well, no, I don't know. Just some kind of sexless kind of a guy, that's all. Like a Buddhist monk or something.'

Henry raised his eyebrows. 'I think he's more than a Buddhist monk, you know. And I don't think he's sexless. I think he's a mixture of all sexes, known and unknown. I think he's a microcosm of everything you ever wanted, an encyclopaedia rather than a book.'

Henry came very close to Gil, and clasped his shoulder. Gil could smell the drink on his breath, and examine the tracery of bloodshot capillaries in his eyes. 'I think that Springer is what, in medieval times, they used to call an angel.'

'You're kidding,' said Gil, pulling himself away. He turned around on his heel, and then stared at Henry again. 'You're kidding, right?'

Henry slowly and emphatically shook his head. 'Springer is an angel. You look up angel, in your dictionary, and see how angel is defined. A messenger from God. And that is exactly what Springer is. A messenger from Ashapola, who to all intents and purposes is God. So, my friend, when you are talking to Springer, you are talking only one stage removed with the Supreme Being, the Creator of the Universe. You should tremble! This is like Moses and the Burning Bush!'

'You're kidding me,' Gil repeated. Henry was being so theatrical, flinging his arms around and shouting out like Laurence Olivier, that it would have been hard to believe him even if he had been reading out the nutritional information on the side of a box of Granola.

'Well, you can think what you like,' said Henry. 'The only way to find out is to confront Springer himself.' He put down his drink, and looked around the room, patting his shirt-pockets in an imitation of jungle drums. 'Now, where are my spectacles?'

'I'll call Susan,' Gil suggested.

'You really think that's wise?'

'We have to, Henry.'

Henry sighed. 'Very well,' he agreed. 'But I will tell Springer this – and I will tell him loud and clear – Susan is not to come along with us if there is the slightest risk. I am not having the life of a young girl on my conscience. Especially one so personable.'

'You like her, don't you?' smiled Gil.

Henry frowned at him. 'Yes,' he said, pugnaciously. 'What's it to you?'

While Henry rummaged around for his spectacles and his

shoes and his crumpled linen coat, Gil telephoned Susan. Her grandmother answered and wanted to know who it was.

'A friend, that's all.'

'A boy?'

'The last time I looked, ma'am.'

'Don't you be fresh with me. Susan's out right now. She's having lunch with the Morgensterns. You can call back later if you want to, but I'm not giving you any guarantees that she'll be here.'

'Okay, ma'am. Thank you.'

Henry said, 'Not in? Oh well – it's probably all for the best, you know. I wouldn't like to see her get hurt.'

He thought about what he had said, and then he added, 'I wouldn't like to see *me* get hurt, either, come to that.'

They drove down to Camino del Mar in Gil's yellow Mustang, parking right outside the house where Springer had showed them the recreated memory of the girl they had discovered on the beach. They climbed out of the car, and stared at the dark-windowed, run-down facade. For the first time, they asked themselves whether Springer was going to be here. In fact, Henry was asking himself if Springer had existed at all.

They walked up the weedy front pathway and rang at the corroded doorbell. They could hear no sound from within the house, no bell jangling, no chimes. The day was hot and bright and humid, with a layer of high cirrocumulus, warning of unsettled weather to come. Henry was sweating, and took out a balled-up handkerchief to dab at his forehead. He loosened his necktie with his finger.

'Don't know what you're wearing a tie for,' Gil remarked.

'I'm a professor,' said Henry, with mock pomposity. 'A necktie is my symbol of respectability. Besides, if I follow it upwards it enables me to find my head.'

They waited and waited and there was no reply. 'Ring again,' Henry suggested, but just as he was about to do so, the front door swung open and Springer was standing in the hallway, white faced, dressed in black.

'You are early,' he smiled.

Henry lifted his left wrist and frowned at it. He had forgotten to put on his watch. 'How can we be early if we didn't have an appointment?'

'What I mean is, I didn't expect you so soon.'

They stepped inside. There was a dusty, lingering smell of patchouli. The banisters were draped with sheets, as if the house was being closed up for the summer.

'You knew we would come, then?' asked Henry.

Springer nodded. 'Your friend is here as well, she came even earlier than you. She is waiting for you upstairs.'

Gil and Henry exchanged glances of surprise. Springer smiled at them, with all the mechanical humour of a clown, and led the way upstairs to the large back room where he had shown them the death agonies of the girl they had found on the beach. Susan was standing by the window, looking out over the overgrown yard. She wore a white tee-shirt and a simple white skirt, and her hair was tied up with ribbons. As they came in, she turned around.

'Hello. Springer said that you would come.'

Henry briskly rubbed his hands. He found his own predictability rather upsetting; especially since he had originally planned to do nothing more today than sit in a chair and listen to Beethoven and get astonishingly drunk.

Susan came over and kissed Gil on the cheek, almost ceremonially, and then Henry. 'Excuse my ...' Henry said, rubbing his unshaven chin. 'Prickles.'

Springer closed the door. 'You have come because it is your chosen destiny to come. You have come because there is something within each of you that demands it. Susan, you have lost your parents. Your mind is still asking for explanations, and you have a strong feeling that if you embark on this adventure you will have many of your questions answered. In some ways, this may be so.'

Springer approached Henry, and stood looking at him benignly. 'You, Henry, are afraid that your life may have been wasted, that all your learning and all your intellect may have gone for nothing. To track down this beast would be an achievement. And, apart from that, you are glad of the company of these two young people. You would have had children if your marriage had been happier. These two are quite an acceptable substitute.'

Henry said nothing. He was too good a philosopher to know that it was useless arguing against the absolute truth. Springer moved on to Gil, and laid a hand on his shoulder.

'You seem to have a far more contented life than Henry and Susan. You have parents who love you, a stable home, and you are working hard at your schooling. But still, you are discontented. Unlike your father, you will never be satisfied with anything as mundane and restricting as a store. You expect more. You expect excitement, and danger! What did your father say, before you came to meet me? What did he advise you to do?'

Gil flushed in embarrassment. 'Guess he didn't realise how you were going to turn out. Guess *I* didn't, either.'

Springer smiled. 'Your father has always told you to take precautions. Not just sexually, of course, but in everything you do. Now you are tired of playing it safe. You want to test yourself. Hunting this beast, you think, will be a worthy test.' Springer raised his hands. His face was as smooth as a pebble, expressionless but peaceful. 'Now you see why you were chosen, why your footsteps were directed that morning towards the beach. Now you see why you have all agreed to help me.' Henry thrust his hands in to his pockets, and rocked backwards and forwards on his heels. 'I was surmising earlier this morning, that you were a messenger, of sorts. A *divine* messenger.'

Springer looked back at him with interest. 'Go on,' he said.

'Well, this may be preposterous. In fact, it sounds completely lunatic now that I'm saying it directly to your face. But I surmise that you are an angel.'

Springer seemed to take this remark quite seriously, and in good part. He considered it for a moment or two, and then he nodded, as if he quite liked it. 'Not an angel perhaps in the sense that you understand it. No wings, no robes, no trumpets. More like a collection of projected information, a living hologram. But if you wish to use the word angel ... then I would be flattered.'

Susan said, 'What I want to know is, if Ashapola is so powerful, why can't *He* find this beast Himself? Why do we have to do it for Him?'

'He is all powerful, but also powerless,' Springer explained. 'He created the world and everything in it, but for the most part He allowed His creation to have freedom of choice. If humans choose to believe in Him, then He is pleased. But He has allowed them *not* to believe in Him, to believe instead in other gods, if that is what they find most comforting. Ashapola is a god who does not intervene, as a rule, in the destiny of His creatures, and *cannot* intervene, any more than a parent can intervene in the life of His children.'

'He seems to have intervened quite considerably in this particular situation,' said Henry.

'Yes,' said Springer, 'because this situation is different. It is no exaggeration to say that this situation is a direct threat to Ashapola Himself, and to the future of this world, and everybody who lives in it. Without Ashapola's guidance, there was a considerable risk that you would not have discovered the nature of this threat until it was far too late. Ashapola cannot grapple directly with the beast itself, but through me he can give you the power that will enable you to do so, and, with luck, to overcome it.'

'The beast,' said Susan, quietly. 'Is the beast the same as the Devil?'

'There has never been one single Devil,' Springer explained. 'As it says in the Bible, the Devil is legion. But today, most of the scores of demonic manifestations which used to plague this earth have been destroyed, or somehow contained, and up until this poor girl's body was discovered, the only active Devil we knew of was Asmodeus, who has been causing havoc in Israel and the Middle East for years now, in spite of the efforts of the Hebrew exorcists to track him down and contain him.'

Springer's face seemed to alter subtly, from masculine to feminine. He walked gracefully over to the window, and when he spoke his voice was much more high pitched and precise, although neither Henry nor Gil nor Susan found his sudden change to be at all disconcerting. They had accepted her for what she was, a living image, rather than a real person.

Springer said, 'It appears that a Devil whom we usually call Yaomauitl has reappeared in Southern California. Every Devil has his own way of spreading his evil. Yaomauitl is the emperor of nightmares. By day, he is as ordinary as you or I. By night, when people are sleeping, he can enter their nightmares and do to them whatever he desires. He can kill them in their sleep, he can infect them with terrible sicknesses, he can blind them. He can also impregnate them with his own seed, and that is what happened to the young girl you found on the beach. The seeds devour the womb which nourished them, and make their escape. If they can find a hiding-place, they grow, and after six months or so, they emerge as fully grown as their parent.'

'And then what happens?' asked Gil.

'The same process is repeated, through nightmare after nightmare, until there are sufficient Devils to dominate the dreams of an entire nation. That is what happened in Iran. That is what happened in Hitler's Germany. Whoever holds a nation's dreams, holds that nation's power. That is why Yaomauitl is so called: his name means Dreaded Enemy.'

Susan asked, 'How do we find Yaomauitl? Especially since he's so ordinary during the day.'

'I have no idea,' Springer confessed. 'You will have to be detectives.'

'Well, that's up-front for you,' Gil admitted.

Susan said, 'What do we do with him, once we find him? *If* we find him?'

'There I can help you,' Springer told them. 'Through me, you will be invested with the traditional powers of the Night Warriors.'

'The Night Warriors,' Henry repeated. He liked the sound of that. There was a magnificent warring darkness to it; like black plumed horses and black-painted shields, and thunderous rides across midnight fields.

Springer came away from the window. 'Once, there were many Night Warriors. There were enough of them to have a secret society of their own – their own rules, their own legends, their own particular chivalry. Of course, when Yaomauitl was finally defeated, there was no longer any need for them – and although much of their secret lore was passed down from one family to another, the Night Warriors themselves died out.'

She paused for a while, and then she said, 'Another reason you three were chosen was because all of you have ancestors who were Night Warriors. Henry, your paternal great-grandfather was Kasyx, the charge-keeper, one of the greatest of the Night Warriors. Gil, your great-great-great-grandfather on your mother's side was Tebulot, the machine-carrier. And Susan, your great-great-grandmother was one of the last of the Night Warriors, Samena, the finger-archer.'

Henry, in spite of himself, laughed out loud at Springer's seriousness. 'I'm sorry,' he said, 'I'm sorry. You're really stretching my credulity here. I feel like any moment now the whole of the philosophy faculty is going to come bursting into the room, and they're all going to shout out April Fool I'm sorry. 'Well,' smiled Springer, 'Your scepticism is understandable. Your mind has been educated to challenge everything. But if I can ask you to suspend your disbelief for a little while longer you can judge what I am saying from a practical demonstration.'

'A practical demonstration?' asked Gil. He had kept quiet and listened so far, but Springer was rapidly losing him. Tebulot, the machine-carrier? He was beginning to think, like Henry, that somebody somewhere was taking them all for a long and ultimately hilarious ride.

But Springer glanced at Gil, sharp and amused, almost as if she could read what Gil was thinking, and then she said, unabashed, 'Kasyx the charge-keeper is the power-centre of the trio. It is Kasyx who draws power from Ashapola, at any one of the nine hundred power sources, of which this house is one, and keeps it ready for his comrades to use in their battle against Yaomauitl. If you like, Kasyx is the battery, which Tebulot and Samena use to charge up their night-weaponry.'

'So, Kasyx ... has no weapon of his own?' asked Henry.

'His power can be used as a weapon,' said Springer, 'but only in the last resort. This is because it can only be discharged in one total blast, leaving all three of you powerless. So, if the discharge fails to have the desired effect, you are left without any means of defending yourselves. Also, the release of energy is tremendous – and it is usually far too powerful for normal combat. It can demolish a building. There are several famous explosions in the past which were explained as natural phenomena, but which were charge-keepers fighting a last battle with the Devil.'

'What about Tebulot?' asked Gil.

'Yes, the machine-carrier. The machine is a weapon but also a tool. It uses power from Kasyx to cut through walls and doors, if that ever becomes necessary; to make welds and repairs; but also to fire controlled bursts of pure energy. The machine, if you like, is a power-controller, but it cannot be carried by Kasyx himself because any attempt by him to use it would result in the instant discharge of all of his power.'

Gil folded his arms. He was finding everything that Springer was telling them quite impossible to believe. His excitement of only a few minutes ago had flattened out completely, and he could quite happily have gone home. He should have gone bowling with Bradley.

Susan didn't believe any of it, either; but unlike Gil she wanted to stay and listen. Springer's stories of Kasyx and Tebulot and Samena were almost like fairy-tales, and she found them fascinating. She smiled at Springer as she approached, and kept on smiling as Springer laid her hands on her shoulders.

'Samena is the quickest of eye; the fastest runner, the athlete. Where Tebulot is a heavyweight destroyer, Samena is a lightweight sniper. She, too, draws her energy from Kasyx. But her weapon is her finger.'

Springer held her arms straight out in front of her, and crossed her right wrist over her left wrist, keeping her left hand loosely held in a fist. She pointed her right index finger rigidly, and took a sight along her right arm.

'That is how Samena uses her weapon, but it is better to demonstrate it for real.'

She took hold of Henry's arm, and led him to the centre of the room. He stood beside her, his hands on his hips, embarrassed. I'll bet you dinner at Anthony's that nothing happens,' said Henry.

Springer stepped lithely around, and drew Gil and Susan closer to Henry, one on each side of him.

'Now you are ready,' she said. 'You must understand that you will normally be dreaming when this happens. Your physical body will be lying asleep in your bed, while your Night Warrior manifestation goes out into the darkness, looking for the Devil. Your power will be greater when you have left your physical body, because the energy will not have to pass through the resistance of solid flesh and bone. But this will give you some idea of what you will be able to do.'

She came forward and touched Henry's forehead. 'When I have trained you, you will be able to build up your power by yourself. Right now, I am having to do it for you. It might help you if you closed your eyes.' Henry hesitated at first, but then he closed his eyes. Well, he thought, I might as well get this over and done with. When I open them up again, the whole of my freshman philosophy class is going to be standing around, laughing at me. But I think I'm still drunk enough not to mind.

Charge-keeper, he thought to himself, with mounting scepticism. The only things that he got a charge out of were vodka and beautiful women and Beethoven, and not always in that order. Still, he had come here, he had listened to what Springer had said to him, and so there must be some part of his mind that was still open to argument, no matter how eccentric that argument happened to be.

Springer's fingers against his forehead began to vibrate and irritate him. He could almost imagine that high-voltage electrical current was running through them, and coursing into his brain. He had to admit it, Springer was a genius at stirring up illusion and self-suggestion. He could almost have believed that he was growing, that he was straightening up, that his body was glittering with thousands of volts of stored-up energy.

He slowly opened his eyes. Springer took her hand away. There was a burned, metallic odour of lightning, and gunpowder, and cauterised copper. Gil and Susan were staring at him in astonishment. He had never seen faces look like theirs before. They could have been hit in the face with a plank, they looked so dumbstruck.

'Come,' said Springer, and beckoned Henry over to the far wall of the room. She opened a white built-in closet, empty of clothes, and showed him the full-length mirror on the back of the door.

'This is you – Kasyx, the greatest of the Night Warriors,' she told him.

Henry stared at himself. Slowly, slowly, he lifted his hand towards his head, and the figure in the mirror lifted his hand, too. It was actually him. Henry Watkins, threadbare professor of even more threadbare philosophy, alcoholic and far-too-frequently frustrated genius, as Kasyx, the Night Warrior. Not taller – although he was standing much straighter, with his shoulders held back. No more muscular, although his expression was somehow much more determined, and there was a look of power about him, the look of a man who could handle himself in a fight. What was really extraordinary about him, however, was the semi-translucent armour which covered him from head to foot, including a wedge-shaped helmet. The armour looked heavy and elaborate, with a slab-sided breastplate, jointed hips like lobster-tails, and scores of power-points and cables and racks and hooks.

He could scarcely see the armour, and he certainly couldn't feel any weight. Yet, when he moved, the armour moved with him, as if he were really wearing it. He turned to Springer, and said, 'This suit ... it's as if it doesn't exist.'

'It exists only in dreams,' said Springer. 'What you can see of it now is nothing but my memory of it, just as the girl I showed you was only a memory, too.'

Henry stared at himself. 'It's true, then,' he said, with great simplicity. 'The Night Warriors actually existed.'

'Yes, Henry, they did; and they will again. Kasyx, Tebulot, and Samena.'

Springer beckoned Gil to come forward. Gil hesitated at first, but then stood beside Henry, glancing at his armour from time to time with fascination. This was absolutely amazing. This beat burning up Interstate-5 at 120 mph, riding his dirt-bike all around the Del Mar fairgrounds, Montezuma's Revenge at Knott's Berry Farm, and any other thrill he could think of. This beat *everything*.

'Kneel down beside him, on one knee,' Springer instructed Gil. Gil did as he was told, looking up at Henry with his eyes wide with excitement.

'Now, Henry,' said Springer, 'lay your left hand on Gil's right shoulder.'

Henry did as he was told. Gil immediately felt a tide of energy tingling through Henry's fingers, and surging through his nervous system with all the urgency of flood-water pouring into a complicated network of irrigation ditches. He felt as if Henry's hand had given him an electric shock. He opened his mouth, and blue sparks crawled around his teeth like crackling caterpillars. His hair stood up on end.

'This is you: Tebulot, the machine-carrier,' Springer announced, and Gil stared at himself in the mirror. He seemed lither and stronger, and there was a deadly look of conviction in his eyes that almost made him smile. He wore a helmet similar to Henry's, but white, with two triangular wing-plates on each side of it. His breastplate was white and decorated with tactically placed triangles, but he wore no leg-armour, just clinging white tights, for quickness of movement, and a pair of wedge-soled shoes that looked like the most fantastic pair of Nikes ever designed.

In his hands, he carried a massive piece of shining machinery, shaped like a machine-gun, but larger and longer, with one T-shaped lever like a gear-shift on top of it, and all kinds of slots and bolted-on clips and slides and switches.

He tried to heft the machinery in his hands, but like Henry's armour, it weighed nothing, it was hardly even visible.

'Raise it up, and aim it,' said Springer. 'It will fire a weak charge, if you pull the trigger.'

Gil cautiously lifted the machine, and squinted along the sights. Springer stood directly behind him, and said, 'Pull back the T-bar, that charges it. You can see a linear charge-scale, along the side there, glowing gold. That tells you how much charge you've got. All right – aim it at the wall there, and fire it.'

With trembling hands, Gil tugged back the T-bar, until he felt it lock. The charge-scale glowed dimly, and registered only about a tenth, but that was enough for a demonstration. He touched the trigger. There was a sharp, soft *zzafff!* and a bullet of bright yellow light zipped across the room, and exploded against the wall, punching a two-inch hole through to the brick.

'In a dream, the charge will be very much more powerful,' said Springer. 'You will also discover that the machine has many different functions. It was created in a dream, and therefore its capabilities are only as limited as a dream is limited, which is hardly at all.' Gil turned the machine from one side to the other, admiring it.

'Quite a weapon!' Henry remarked.

'Unbelievable,' said Gil.

Springer now brought Susan forward. Susan had been watching the other two cautiously. She sensed the newly born comradeship between them, but she had not yet understood the fatherly concern that Henry felt for her, nor the fact that Gil thought she was pretty and cute – and that if Springer hadn't appeared, and turned the routine of his daily life totally upside-down, he probably would have wanted to date her. She caught his smile, however, as she came to stand on Henry's other side, and she realised that he was trying hard to show her that he cared about her.

Without needing Springer to tell him, Henry laid his right hand on Susan's left shoulder. Susan watched herself closely in the mirror as the power with which Springer had charged Henry began to flow through to her. Her eyes sparkled as she blinked; a shower of tiny white sparks cascaded from her hair.

Gradually, faintly, her own costume of Samena the finger-archer began to appear. She wore a triangular cocked hat that was laden with ostrich feathers, eagle feathers, and peacock plumes. She was fitted with a tight leather bodice, decorated with sequins and studs and oddly shaped pieces of metal, and laced across her cleavage with tight leather thongs. She also wore a high-cut pair of tight leather briefs, around the waistband of which were clipped twenty or thirty different types of arrowhead – hooked, barbed, triangular, flared, and smooth. A broad scabbard also hung at her waist, containing a double-bladed knife with a velvet cord attached to its handle. Her legs were bare, except for a small pair of soft leather boots with turn-down tops.

'Samena,' said Springer, with undisguised pride.

Susan asked, breathlessly, 'Could I try shooting? Is there enough power left?'

Springer touched Henry's forehead, and then nodded. 'One shot. Use an arrowhead; see if you can hit the wall where Gil hit it.'

Susan unclipped a sharp triangular arrowhead. Its body was hollow, so that she could fit her index finger into it, making it appear as if she had a long metallic fingernail. As Springer had instructed her, she crossed her wrists, using her left arm to steady her right. She pointed her arrowhead finger at the wall, directly at the spot where Gil had blasted a scar in the plaster, and concentrated.

Nothing happened at first. 'What do I do now?' she asked Springer, in disappointment. 'How do I fire it?'

Springer smiled. 'You have to *think* it, that's all. It isn't difficult, and after a while it will come so easily to you that you will be amazed to remember that you ever had any trouble.'

Susan aimed her finger again. Again nothing happened.

But Henry suddenly pressed his hand against her shoulder as forcefully as he could, and shouted '*Fire!*'

Instantly, with an ear-piercing whistle like a Fourth of July rocket, the arrowhead flashed across the room, followed by a three-foot shaft of golden light. It buried itself in the wall only two or three inches away from the hole that Gil had made, at which point the light immediately vanished, leaving the arrowhead deep inside the plaster.

'Yeah!' shouted Gil, and applauded. Susan skipped and danced and jumped up and down. 'I did it! I did it!'

Springer said, 'You needn't necessarily use an arrowhead. The shaft of light alone – depending on how much charge you put into it – will kill or stun or frighten people away. But, you must train very hard. To take the part of Samena, you must be highly skilled, highly sensitive, and so quick that nobody can catch you. Samena is the most emotional of all the Night Warriors, the one whose nerves have to be stretched to the tautest pitch. But she is also the most deadly.'

Henry closed his hands together, as if in prayer, and what was left of the charge that Springer had given him began to flow upwards towards the ceiling from between his fingers, crackling and spitting and bright blue. Eventually it had all been discharged.

'Springer,' he said, 'if I ever doubted you, which I did, then please forgive me. This is all quite astonishing. This is like a child's fantasy come true.'

'I regret that the ultimate purpose is far from childish,' said Springer. Her voice had become deeper again now, and there were barely discernible changes in her face which made her appear much more masculine. 'Yaomauitl is by far the most malevolent of all the Devils. He is the Devil of madness and greed and genocide. He came over to the New World with Cortes in 1519. There are some stories which say that Cortes himself was the Devil, walking the earth in the guise of a man. Certainly, Cortes was responsible for the murder of countless thousands of Aztecs; and even if he was not the Devil himself, then he took the Devil along with him when he discovered Baja California in 1530.'

Henry said, 'Why has he reappeared now?'

'There is no telling,' said Springer. 'The ways of the Devil are masked from the eyes of Ashapola. That is why only you, the Night Warriors, can discover how he has returned, and what his evil intentions are; and that is why only you can destroy him.'

Henry laid his hands on Gil's and Susan's shoulders. 'You have given the three of us a terrible responsibility. You know that, don't you?'

'I do not think that you will fail me,' said Springer.

Susan said, 'How do we start? I mean, what do we actually do? You've said that we're Night Warriors now, and that we can leave our bodies when we're asleep. But how do we do that? And how can we meet each other when we're asleep?'

Springer said, 'You will use this house as your rendezvous. When you retire to bed each night, you will repeat to yourself the time-honoured battle-hymn of the Night Warriors, and the influence of that hymn will make sure that your dreaming presences meet at the nearest point of sacred power, which is here. From then on, you will journey through the dreams of others, to seek out Yaomauitl and any of his minions which may have already been spawned.'

Gil said, 'I think I'm dreaming already.'

Springer smiled. 'You will soon grow used to the landscapes of the night. You will come here, every night for the next two months, and I will train you in the mental and physical skills of the Night Warriors. I will teach you their history, their traditions, and their lore. I will tell you of their greatest victories, and their most terrible defeats. By the time you have completed your training with me, you will feel that your real self is the self which exists in dreams, and that your waking personality is nothing but a flesh-bound parody of what you really are. Your concept of *awake* and *asleep* will be completely reversed. At the end of the night, when you have to return to your earthly body, you will be doing so to rest; and many times you will feel that this resting is a chore. There is so much more inside your mind than the intelligence necessary to carry your body through the waking day. Your mind is a powerhouse, a limitless store of talent and skill and inspiration. Asleep – as a Night Warrior – you will begin to realise that power. No matter how much you have failed during the day, no matter how meanly other people regard you, you will be heroes and heroines in your dreams. Understand this, my friends: you are the people of legends – just as every human being can be, once they have understood the strength and the majesty inside their own heads.'

Gil asked, 'This strength – this skill – once we've achieved it, will it affect our everyday lives?'

'Of course,' said Springer. 'Once you have learned to have confidence and power in the dream world, your abilities will not be forgotten during the day. Your life will change immeasurably, whether you want it to or not. But you will find that the success you achieve during the day will count little compared to the success you achieve during the night. The greatest of adventures awaits you, my friend, as soon as the sun begins to set.'

'That first time you came to see me,' Gil said to Springer, 'that time when you looked like a girl ... you mentioned that book *De What's-its-name –*'

'*De Sortilegio*,' Springer nodded. 'Yes, I did. That was to trigger inside your mind the memories that you have inherited from your great-great-great-grandfather. I did not mean to trigger them violently, but you went to your Mexican friend Santos, didn't you, and smoked a drug, and that of course heightened your inherited memory to the point of immediacy and violence.'

Springer paused for a moment, and then said, '*De Sortilegio* was written by Paul Grilland in 1533, after the return of some of Cortes's men from Baja California to Europe. His tract takes into account the frightening stories that some of the Spaniards told him about devilish Sabbats that took place on the West Coast of America in those early times. Although some refused to say exactly what happened, it appears that Cortes initiated Black Sabbatical rites, and that he summoned a manifestation of the Devil, or himself became such a manifestation, and that during the course of those Sabbats native women were forced to have sex with him.'

'Sixteenth-century theologians were always arguing amongst themselves how it was possible for a Devil to have sex with human women. But Paul Grilland said that there was irrefutable evidence of it, from stories that he had been told, and William of Paris, the confessor of Philip le Bel, supported him. So did the Salmanticenses, the lecturers of the theological college of the Discalced Carmelites at Salamanca, in their *Theologia Moralis*. And Dom Dominic Schram said that he had personally known several persons who had been compelled against their will to endure the foul assaults of Satan.' Springer smiled sadly. 'St Augustine himself said that anybody who did not believe that the Devil could appear in the night and have carnal relations with a woman was deluding themselves. The evidence of history is overwhelming. When the Devil is free, and able to travel abroad, no woman is safe from his desires.'

Susan said, 'When do we start? Do we start tonight?'

'Do you *want* to start tonight?'

Susan said, 'Yes.' She had never felt so motivated. She had never felt so inspired. She had suddenly been shown that there was something above and beyond her grandparents' upbringing, that there was something far more rewarding and exciting than school, and hanging out with Daffy, and sitting on the beach hoping to be noticed by Tad Summers and Gene Overmeyer. She felt that Springer had lifted her up and shown her a distant vista that lay beyond the rooftops of Del Mar; a vista of mountains and clouds and great achievements. It was intoxicating, dizzying; and Daffy had talked about 'really getting her life together' with aerobic dance!

Gil nodded. 'I'd start now, if I could get to sleep.'

'Henry?' asked Springer, his eyes watchful, guarded.

Henry said, 'It seems that I'm in a minority, whatever I think.'

'Don't you want to do it tonight?' asked Susan.

Henry cleared his throat. 'If you want to know the God's honest truth, I'm frightened.'

Gil said, 'So am I, Henry. But it's something we've got to do. It's a chance in a million-grillion. Henry – supposing they said you could go to the moon?'

'The moon?' said Henry. He shook his head. 'I wouldn't go to the moon. Believe me, Gil, the best view of the moon is through the bottom of an upturned glass of vodka.'

Springer said, 'You'll start tonight, though, won't you?'

Henry thrust his hands into his pockets. 'Of course I will. It's wonderful. It's amazing. But don't forget that I'm frightened, as well as impressed.'

Springer touched his hand in a strange, furtive way, that for some reason put Henry in mind of an early Christian, secretly passing him a Communion wafer. 'You will have no fear tonight, my friend. Kasyx the charge-keeper is fearless.'

Henry said, 'That's what I'm afraid of.'

Chapter Eight

Henry just managed to unlock the front door of his cottage in time to catch the phone, which had been ringing ever since he turned the corner by the promenade. He left his keys hanging in the front door, and scrabbled across the back of the sofa to hook the receiver up into his hand.

'Henry? Is that you, Henry? I almost hung up.'

'Andrea! I was out. I only just this second dived in through the door.'

'You *dived!* I wish I could have seen it.'

'Let me close the front door,' Henry asked her. 'There's somebody outside using a power-saw. I can't hear you too good.'

He laid down the receiver, went to the front door and closed it, and then crossed over to the liquor cabinet, lifting out a bottle of vodka and a moderately clean glass. Picking up the receiver again, he opened the bottle and half filled the glass one-handed in mid-air, without spilling a drop.

'Got your drink?' asked Andrea, sharply.

Henry ignored her. 'Did you find out anything about the eel?'

'That's why I was calling. You don't think I would have called you to make small-talk, do you?'

Henry swallowed vodka, and shivered. Don't let her intimidate you, he thought. Tonight, when she was asleep (black lurex-decorated eyeshade over her eyes, which every morning had prompted him to stare in mock bafflement at the bathroom mirror, and say to himself, 'Who *was* that masked woman?') he would take on the form of Kasyx, the charge-keeper, the central core of the newly resurrected Night Warriors; and everything that Andrea had done to hurt him would be meaningless.

'I promised to tell you about the eel,' said Andrea.

'Yes,' agreed Henry. 'You did.' He drank more vodka, then put his glass down.

He could hear her shuffling papers. 'First of all,' she said, 'it *wasn't* an eel. That is, it wasn't a member of the teleost order *Anguilliformes*, like conger eels or moray eels or freshwater eels. Neither was it a gulpen-eel, of the order *Saccopharyngiformes*, or a spiny-eel, of the order *Mastacembaliformes*, or a cuchia, of the order *Symbranchi-formes*.'

'Was it a hagfish?' Henry suggested.

'No, it wasn't a hagfish, either.'

'Well, now you know what it *wasn't*, do you have any idea what it was?'

'Nothing positive, no. It isn't a species that any of us have come across before.'

Henry waited for her to say something else. When she remained silent, he said, 'Is that it? You don't know what it is, and that's it?'

'Let me put it this way, Henry, it has well-known physical and developmental characteristics. It has a skull, with jaws, and it possesses an internal skeleton, and a digestive system. It is an amphibian, rather than a pure fish, in the sense that it possesses lungs, and rudimentary limbs that would enable it to balance itself on land, like a eusthenopteron.'

'A what?'

'Oh, Henry, you're still as ignorant as ever. A eusthenopteron, an advanced fish of the late Devonian period, about three hundred and sixty million years ago. They were capable of crossing stretches of land from one lake to another during droughts.'

'And that's what this so-called eel has turned out to be?'

'No,' said Andrea. 'It simply happens to have rudimentary limbs like a eusthenopteron. The rest of it is quite different.'

Henry was silent for a moment. He, of course, knew what the eel actually was. Or at least he knew what Springer had said that it was. One of the seeds of the Devil, already part grown. And what had Springer told them? *If they can find a hiding-place, they grow, and after six months or so, they emerge as fully grown as their parent.*

'You had some people digging on the beach,' said Henry.

'That's right,' Andrea replied. 'So far, though, they haven't found any more of the eels. They're going to dig a little further, but they don't hold out much hope. It seems as if the eels have managed to escape very deep into the sand.'

'I thought you said they weren't eels at all.'

'They're not, but that's what everybody calls them. Here in the laboratory we've christened them plourdeostus, because they have skull similarities with some of the first fish that evolved with jaws, in the Silurian period.'

'Well, that all sounds very much like your usual scientific mumbo-jumbo to me,' said Henry, amiably. 'But then, you always were way ahead of me, weren't you, in the department of applied tomfoolery?'

'Now you're being rude again,' said Andrea. 'You're drunk, aren't you?'

'Not at all,' Henry replied. 'Not *enough*, anyway. It just struck me that you people at Scripps can never bear to admit that you don't know what something is. So to make up for that shortcoming, you always call it by some mystifying name. Plourdeostus!

Why don't you just call them biters? Or vicious bastards, which is what anybody with any sense would call them?'

'You're being rude again,' Andrea repeated.

'Well, you always drive me to it,' said Henry. 'I'm a paragon of courtesy until I start talking to you. Then, I don't know. I don't know what it is that you do to me. Perhaps I should christen you dentireversioptus, because you always set my teeth on edge.'

'Goodbye, Henry,' Andrea warned him.

Henry took a deep breath. 'I'm sorry,' he told her. 'Thanks for keeping your promise. Just forget you ever knew me.'

'I did that a long time ago,' Andrea retorted, and put down the phone.

Henry sighed. He put down the phone, and sat on the sofa and stared at the framed poster for Lucky Strike cigarettes on the opposite wall. He wished he hadn't drunk so much today. On the other hand, there wasn't much point in stopping now. He had reached that middle-to-advanced state of inebriation when to stop suddenly would be to guarantee a pounding headache by six o'clock this evening. Better to go on drinking and to ward off the hangover until tomorrow morning. It would be far worse tomorrow, there was no question about that, but at least it wouldn't interfere with tonight's bit of business.

Gil, meanwhile, was walking with Susan along The Boardwalk at Solana Beach. He had taken her along to the Taco Auctioneer for lunch, and now he wanted her to meet his family. Susan was chattier and happier than she had been for months, and Gil hardly had to say anything. She talked enough for the two of them.

'I just can't wait for tonight,' she kept telling him. 'Did you see my costume?'

Gil lifted an eyebrow. 'Pretty sexy, I thought.'

She pushed him into the road. 'Well, what if it is?'

'Terrific,' Gil joked. 'I'm not complaining. The sexier the better.'

'What do you think you look like in those tights of yours?' Susan retaliated. 'The Rudolf Nureyev of Solana Beach!'

'Hey listen, lady, that's the last time you get a taco out of me!'

They kidded along for a while, until Susan suddenly went serious. 'Do you think Henry's going to be all right?'

'In what way?' Gil asked her. There was chili-sauce on his tee-shirt, and he was trying to rub it off with spit.

'Well, it seems like he's drunk all the time.'

'He had a bad divorce or something, that's all.'

Susan brushed her hair out of her eyes. 'I'm not saying I don't like him, because I do. I'm not saying I don't trust him, either. But you heard what Springer said, about all this being so dangerous. Do you think he's going to be able to handle it if he's drunk?'

'I don't know. I get the feeling that Springer's going to get him off the sauce during training. I mean, the reason he drinks is because he's bored, right, and because he doesn't feel he's worth anything to anybody, and because he doesn't have any companionship. What else is there to do except sit at home and get drunk? But now Springer's offered him a challenge – I mean, like he's offered the challenge to all of us, hasn't he? We've agreed to go hunt this Devil or whatever because we want something more out of our lives than what we already have. We want some answers. We want some questions, too, questions we never even thought about. Have you ever sat down and thought to yourself, is this it? Is this what my life adds up to? Isn't there any more? That's the question that Springer's given us, right? And that's the question we want to answer.'

Susan reached out and unselfconsciously took hold of Gil's hand. 'You know something,' she said, 'ever since my parents died in that car-crash, I've never really thought about anything but how to be normal. When you don't have any parents, people are either much too sympathetic, or else they treat you like you're slightly weird, mentally backward or something. Either way, you constantly get treated like you're some kind of abnormal person. I've been to senior citizens' meetings with my grandmother, and one of these strawberry-rinsed old ladies used to introduce me to another strawberry-rinsed old lady, and say, right in front of me, 'This is Susan, both her parents were killed in a car-crash, poor lamb, but she's taken it so well you wouldn't credit it.' Right in front of me! As if I constantly needed reminding that they had died. As if I needed to feel anything but *normal*. I've been reading normal books, wearing normal clothes, watching normal TV programmes, and hanging out with normal friends. I'm so normal I'm practically a Federal statistic on normality. But now that all of *this* has happened – Springer and everything – now that I know about the Night Warriors, I don't want to be normal any more. I want to find out what I can do if I really stretch myself.'

Gil said, 'You may have been trying to be normal, but you sure didn't succeed. I don't think you're normal at all.'

She squeezed his hand. 'Is that a compliment?'

He grinned. 'Maybe. Not your *normal* kind of compliment.'

They reached the Mini-Market. Phil Miller was behind the cash-desk, checking a week's groceries for Mrs. Lim, who ran the Tian Dan Chinese restaurant along the strip. Mrs. Lim was watching Phil narrowly, counting up the groceries in her head. She didn't believe in electric adding-machines.

'Hi, Gil,' his father greeted him, looking at once at Susan.

'Hi, Dad. This is Susan Sczaniecka.'

'How're you doing, Susan?'

'Fine, thank you, sir. Gil just took me out for a taco.'

Phil said, 'A taco? Is he getting serious already?'

'Don't take any notice,' said Gil. 'That's just my old man being my old man. He thinks he's the natural successor to Don Rickles.'

'Little Middles is one dollar sixty-nine cents,' Mrs. Lim corrected Phil.

'Oh, I'm sorry,' Phil apologised. 'That'll teach me to concentrate. Help yourself to an ice, if you want to, Gil.'

'Thanks, Dad.'

Susan looked around. 'It must be really fantastic, owning a store.'

Gil shook his head. 'You'd better believe it. You should

come down here one Sunday afternoon, when we're checking the stock.'

They took an orange ice-lolly each, and then went out through the back yard, which was crowded with wooden crates and empty cardboard boxes, and through the gate which led out to the back alley. This alley took them down to the beach.

It was bright and hot down on the shoreline. Scores of kids were out surfing in wet-suits, and scores more lay on beach-towels under the sandy-coloured rocks, listening to ghetto-blasters or throwing peanuts to the squirrels or simply lying on their backs and baking their bodies. Every few minutes, Gil saw somebody he knew. Being brought up by the ocean, the son of a store-owner, he knew a whole lot of people, and Susan was amused by his constant waving and nodding and calling hallo.

'Seems like you're the local celebrity,' she said. The sea-breeze whipped fine blonde hair across her face.

'We're all local celebrities around here,' Gil told her, sucking his ice-lolly until one side of it was colourless ice. 'We used to have a gang when we were younger. The Solana Sharks, if you can believe it. I think the worst thing we ever did was have a pitched battle with a whole lot of kids from San Elijo, using seaweed instead of car antennae. Mind you, I don't know if you've ever been hit in the face with a seaweed bullwhip. It *hurts!*'

They walked for over a mile along the beach. The surf seethed and roared, and every now and then the water tumbled up as far as their feet, and then slid away again. They held hands as they walked, and the feeling was friendly and good, not only because they liked each other, but because they shared a secret, too; a huge and exciting and dangerous secret.

It wasn't long before they reached the police trestles which barred off the beach at Del Mar. Two officers in sunglasses were passing the time with two high-school girls in very small bikinis, but they kept their eyes on Gil and Susan as they approached.

'Sorry folks, the beach is still off limits.'

'Jellyfish, huh?' asked Gil, leaning on the trestle. He knew one of the girls in the very small bikinis, and said, 'Hi, Candice.' Susan, without really wanting to, stood a little bit closer to him. She didn't know why, but she felt possessive.

Not far off, three researchers from the Scripps Institute, white coated, were probing the sand, accompanied by John Belli the medical examiner, Salvador Ortega, and two bored-looking detectives with their coats slung over their shoulders.

Salvador Ortega noticed Gil and Susan standing by the barrier, and shaded his eyes with his hand. Then he excused himself from the rest of his party, and came over, 'Mr Miller,' he said, nodding to Gil, 'and Miss Sczaniecka.'

'You pronounced my name right,' said Susan. 'You're about the first person who ever has.'

'My sister married a Pole,' said Salvador. 'Now, her name is Carmen Krzysztofowicz. If I don't pronounce Polish names right, she gives me a hard time.'

'How are the jellyfish?' asked Gil, nodding towards the party of researchers.

'We've turned this beach Into Swiss cheese. We still haven't located a single one.'

'Do you think you will?'

Salvador shook his head. 'Those sons-of-bitches are born survivors, if you ask my opinion. They've probably dug their way to Mexico by now.'

Gil looked up. 'I don't know,' he said, with disquiet. 'I've got a funny feeling. Like, we didn't walk down this way by accident. Do you feel that, Susan?'

'I'm not sure,' she said. She touched her fingertips to her temples, and concentrated. 'There's something ... I don't know what it is. I can't describe it.'

Salvador watched them with interest. 'You sense something?' he asked them, looking from one to the other. 'What do you think it is?'

'I'm not certain,' said Susan. 'It's like the beach is moving under my feet. You know that feeling you get during an earth tremor?'

'Well, we've had enough of those over the past six months,' said Salvador. 'Maybe you just felt one that I didn't.'

It was then that they felt another sensation – an extraordinary sensation, as if an invisible door had suddenly been opened in mid-air, and someone had stepped through. They both turned their heads and looked up the beach towards the promenade, and there in the distance was Henry, in an open-necked turquoise shirt and large flapping white Bermuda shorts. He looked like a senior citizen on his annual vacation.

'Did you *arrange to* meet Professor Watkins here?' asked Salvador, nodding toward Henry inquiringly.

Gil said, 'No, sir.'

'You're sure about that?'

'Yes, sir.'

Salvador beckoned to the two uniformed officers. 'Would

you let these people through the line for me? Yes – and this gentleman walking down the beach. Professor Watkins! Henry! Would you come this way, please?'

The cops shifted the trestle aside, and Gil and Susan walked through, closely followed by Henry. 'Well, well,' Henry said, 'what a surprise. What are you two doing here?'

'I'm not sure,' Gil told him. 'It just occurred to us to take a walk.'

'Me, too,' said Henry. As the officers dragged the trestle back into place, he stepped forward and shook Salvador's hand. 'Well, Salvador, it seems as if something summoned us here. Something imperceptible, like a dog-whistle.'

'Come and take a look over here,' Salvador invited them, and they followed him over to the small party of police and researchers, who were digging a large circular hole in the black, damp sand, and looking tired and bored.

'You know John Belli, don't you?' said Salvador. The medical examiner gave them a tight, unwelcoming smile. 'And these three gentlemen are all from the marine biology department at the Scripps Institute.'

Three faces, one Caucasian, two black, all three bespectacled, greeted Henry and Gil and Susan with a high degree of disinterest. Henry came forward and peered down the hole, his hair rising up on end in the afternoon wind.

'We'd appreciate it if you didn't stand too close to the edge,' said one of the researchers, nasally. 'The sides, you know, have a tendency to slide inwards.'

Henry nodded. 'Of course. Don't want to make your work any more tedious for you than it is already. No sign of plourdeostus then?'

The three researchers stared at him with immediate hostility. 'What do you know about plourdeostus?'

Henry beamed. 'What I know about plourdeostus is that it's a pretty darned silly name. Oh, come on, stop looking so amazed. My name is Henry Watkins, department of philosophy at UC San Diego. My wife – or *ex-wife*, rather – is Andrea Steinway. Yes, *that* Andrea Steinway. I was talking to her on the telephone only about an hour and a half ago.'

'Professor Watkins was here when the cadaver was discovered on the shore,' put in Salvador, by way of additional explanation.

The three researchers appeared to be slightly reassured, but not particularly happy. 'We'd appreciate it if non-expert observers could be kept well out of the way,' said one of them, haughtily.

'Oh, come on, we're *all* non-expert observers, yourselves included,' said Henry, with tremendous cheerfulness. 'Andrea told me that she had never seen anything like this eel before, anywhere, and she knows more about the ocean's more disgusting denizens than anybody alive. We're all in the dark together.'

Salvador waited for a moment while digging resumed, and then came over and took hold of Henry's arm, leading him aside. 'Perhaps you're right, Henry. Perhaps we are all in the dark together. But it seems to me that you three who found the cadaver are slightly less in the dark than the rest of us. Tell me – what made you come down here, just at this particular moment?'

Henry glanced at Gil and Susan. They both nodded, so slightly that nobody else would have noticed. 'Well ...' said

Henry, slowly, 'it was just a feeling, that's all ... It's difficult to know how to describe it.'

'Try,' Salvador urged him. 'I'm not sure whether I can,' said Henry. 'It was simply a feeling that I had to be here.'

Salvador said, quietly, 'Mr Belli here is convinced from his examination of the girl's body that she was already dead when she entered the water. He thinks the eels were nothing to do with her death at all. The only problem he has is that he cannot establish any other cause of death. There is no indication of strangulation, or battering the head with a blunt instrument, or shooting, or stabbing. Of course, much of the abdomen was missing, and it is possible that she was killed by a severe trauma to the abdominal region, but most of the girl's blood remained in her veins and arteries, which suggests that her heart stopped beating before any wounds were inflicted on her.'

Salvador waited for a moment, to see what impression this information would have on Henry, and then he added, very quietly, 'Mr Belli is extremely angry and frustrated.'

At that moment, one of the Scripps researchers threw down his shovel and said, 'That's it. There's nothing here. Let's call it a day.'

Susan stepped forward with one hand raised. 'Wait!' she said, in a clear, high voice – a voice that they could all hear over the constant grumbling of the surf. 'Wait – don't stop yet. Dig a little deeper.'

The Scripps researcher looked at Salvador with an expression on his face which could clearly be interpreted as, 'Get this girl out of here, would you, please?'

But Salvador turned on his heel, with his hands clasped

behind his back, and said, 'Gil? Henry? What do you think? Should they carry on digging?'

Gil said, 'Susan's right. They should carry on.'

'Who are these people?' the Scripps researcher wanted to know.

'They found the body of the girl,' said Salvador.

'And that gives them some kind of expertise?' the researcher demanded, climbing out of the hole.

Salvador took out his handkerchief and wiped his nose. 'Sir,' he said 'if you don't continue to excavate this hole, then I shall ask my officers to do so. Of course, if there is anything here my officers will not perhaps be so delicate in their handling of it as you might be, but that is a risk I shall have to take. I am interested in the biology of this matter, of course; but I am also investigating a person's death, and that to me is the first priority.'

The researcher stared pugnaciously at Henry and Gil and Susan, and then said, 'Very well, have it your way. We'll dig for another half-hour; then we're calling it quits.'

They all waited on the beach while the sun gradually burned its way down towards the western horizon, turning the ocean into dazzling gold. The Scripps researchers dug slowly and systematically, stopping every time they struck a stone or a fragment of buried wood. Salvador came close to Henry, and said, 'How about you? Do you think there's something down there?'

'I don't know,' said Henry, thickly. He was beginning to feel the tight band of a headache around his forehead, and the sun's glaring reflection on the ocean wasn't helping him at all. He should have brought a hip-flask, to keep his hangover away, but it was too late now. The membranes around his brain were beginning to tighten and throb, and his optic nerves felt as if they were made out of chewed string.

John Belli checked his watch. 'There's nothing down there, Sal, let's face it. Those eels were totally incidental to the primary cause of death. I vote we forget this whole digging operation altogether.'

'Five more minutes,' Salvador insisted.

Three minutes passed, four. Then without understanding why, Susan found herself stepping nearer to the excavation; when she looked around, Henry and Gil had followed her, and were standing close behind. Salvador noticed their move forward, and watched them closely.

In the black wet sand at the very bottom of the excavation, something shifted. The researcher touched it with his shovel, and it shifted again.

'I've found something,' he said, not loudly, his voice cracking in the middle. 'It's moving.' Salvador immediately came forward, reaching into his waistband for his .38 revolver, and cocking it. 'Take a whole lot of care,' he instructed the researcher. 'The last one of those things we tried to capture, it took off half of one of my officers' face.'

'Thanks for the warning,' said the researcher sarcastically. One of his colleagues slid down into the excavation beside him, and together they began to clear the sand away from the shape at the very bottom.

'It's alive,' said the second researcher. 'There's no doubt about it. It feels like it's warm blooded, and I can feel it moving.'

'Does it feel like an eel?' asked Salvador.

'No way,' said the first researcher. 'This is big, much bigger than that eel you brought in to the Institute. I can feel a ... spine of sorts. Kind of a knobby spine. And ribs.'

'Just be careful,' Salvador repeated.

Henry thought, again and again and again, *If they can find a hiding-place, they grow, and after six months or so, they emerge as fully grown as their parent.* He didn't have to look at Gil or Susan to know that they were thinking the same thing. They had already developed that much mental rapport.

Cautiously, the two researchers exposed the shape they had found in the sand. A spinal column, gristly and black. A curved ribcage, each rib separated from the one next to it by dark, semi-transparent cartilage. Then a pelvic girdle, attenuated and narrow, and a long jointed coccyx that almost formed a tail, and bony legs, drawn up underneath the body in the position of a developing foetus.

Henry could see the creature's heart beating through the thin gristle of its ribcage. He had a feeling of terrible dread, and found himself praying under his breath. He prayed that the creature might die when they brought it out of the sand. He prayed that he wouldn't have to look at it. He prayed that it was the only one, and that all the others had suffocated in the sand. *'Our Father, which art in Heaven; hallowed be Thy name.'*

The two researchers, working side by side, cleared the sand away from the back of the creature's head. In all, the creature looked as if it would measure about three feet from head to toe, if it were stretched out.

One of the researchers ran his hand along the creature's spine, and then suddenly said, 'Look at this.' An envelope of papery, scaly skin had fallen away from the coccyx. He gently handed it up to his colleague, who was kneeling by the brink of the pit. His colleague held it up, so that the last of the sunlight shone through it. It rustled in the sea-breeze as faintly as tissue-paper.

'What is that?' asked Salvador.

'It looks like the discarded skin of an eel to me,' said the researcher.

'So this is it? This is what we're looking for? And in only two days it's developed as much as this?'

The researcher reached behind him for his rucksack. He unbuckled it, and took out a long specimen envelope, into which he carefully folded the eel skin. 'It sure looks like it, doesn't it?'

'But what kind of a creature can do that? And what kind of creature can gestate right underneath the sand?'

The researcher gave him a grim smile. 'That's what we're here to find out, Lieutenant.'

Salvador looked across at John Belli, but John Belli stood there with his hands folded uncommunicatively across his chest, his lower lip jutting out, and said nothing.

'All right,' said Salvador. 'You want to lift the creature out of there? Duncan – go get that stretcher from the trunk of my car, blankets, too. Keith – there's some canvas webbing in the squad car, go get that. We should be able to run it under the creature's body and lift it out real gentle.'

Susan whispered, 'You *can't* lift it out.'

Salvador said, 'We sure as hell can't leave it where it is.'

'Now you've found it, you must kill it,' Susan insisted. 'You must bring wires, with high voltage, and electrocute it. It's the only way. Electrocute it, and then bury it again.'

The Scripps researchers shook their heads. One of them said, with mock weariness, 'First of all she insists we go on digging, so that we locate it. Now she wants us to kill it, and cover it up again. Are you sure she's ...?' He pointed to his head, and spun his finger around, to suggest that Susan was mentally touched.

'You've got to do what she says,' Gil insisted, in a harsh, loud voice.

'Oh, we do?' retorted the researcher. 'Well, you listen here, this is our show, and we run it the way we want to, and we certainly don't take orders from every wandering beach-bum who happens to be passing. Do we have that clear?'

Henry touched Salvador on the shoulder. 'They're quite right, you know. It's imperative that you destroy this creature at once.'

'Now, why is that?' asked Salvador. 'I'm not saying that you are wrong, my friend, but before I decide on any course of action, I want to know *why*.'

'I can't tell you why. I don't even know why myself. But the urgency is great. This creature must not be allowed to live for one second longer than you can possibly help.'

'My dear Henry,' said Salvador, quietly, 'I cannot order it to be killed without a sensible reason. It is an integral part of a full-scale homicide investigation; it is a living creature of considerable scientific interest, for all that it has devoured the body of a young girl, and mutilated one of my officers. It may be the only one there is, or at least the only one we'll ever find. What will I say to my superiors, if I electrocute it and bury it again? That I was instructed to do so by a seventeen-year-old girl and a nineteen-year-old boy and a professor of philosophy at the university? That you three insisted on it, as a matter of urgency, and that I then decided that it was wise to obey?'

Salvador said nothing more for a moment or two, but put his head on one side, questioningly, asking Henry to understand why there could be no question of destroying the creature where it lay. 'You understand me?' Salvador asked at last. 'You see what I mean?'

Henry felt terrible. He was sweating and shaking and chilled, all at the same time. He wiped his greasy forehead with the back of his arm.

'I don't know what to say to you, Salvador. The danger is extreme. If you don't kill this creature now, then believe me, you will regret it for the rest of your life.'

Salvador's eyes began to darken. 'That is not a threat, I hope.'

'A threat?' Henry expostulated, in disbelief. 'My dear Salvador, I don't have the power or the means to make any threats, not even to my ex-wife, and certainly not to you. I am talking about that, that thing down there in that excavation. What do you think it is, Salvador? What do you honestly think it is? You saw what it did to your officer, when it was scarcely grown. What do you think it can do now? Look at it! It's the spawn of a Devil, that's what it is! And you must kill it!'

John Belli came over and said, very brusquely to Henry, 'You – you and your two playmates. I want you out of here. That creature down there is evidence, and it has to be pathologically examined. I don't want any of you anywhere near it, do you understand me? You're a potential threat to that creature, in my opinion, and I want you back beyond that barrier, out of my way.'

Gil said, 'Mister, we're no threat to that creature; but that creature is a threat to humankind.'

'He's right,' Susan added. 'That creature is the spawn of a Devil.'

John Belli sighed, and rubbed his chin. 'Salvador,' he appealed, with badly concealed impatience.

Salvador said, 'He's right, I'm afraid, you three. You're going to have to back off. It's plain regulations, as much as anything else. Just go back behind the barrier, you can see quite a lot from there. But, you know, keep quiet, or else I'm going to have to move you further, or even take you downtown for obstruction.' Henry looked at Salvador steadily. 'One last appeal,' he said, with a dry mouth.

Salvador said, 'I'm sorry, but no.'

Henry and Gil and Susan reluctantly backed away from the excavation, and Salvador escorted them to the police line. 'These people are allowed to stay here,' Salvador told the officers. 'But no nearer, you understand me?'

The three of them waited behind the line while the Scripps researchers carried on with their careful clearing away of the damp black sand. John Belli walked off after a while, and then drove back on to the beach in his station-wagon, backing up towards the excavation until he was only fifteen feet away from it. He climbed out of the wagon and let down the tailgate.

'Let's just pray that the creature can't survive, once they've taken it out of the sand,' said Henry.

'It'll survive,' said Gil, tersely.

Susan said, 'We can still pray.'

'Who to?' Gil asked. 'God? Or Ashapola? Or the San Diego Police Department? To Serve and Protect?'

John Belli took blankets out of his station-wagon and shook them out. He handed them down to the researchers; and even though Henry couldn't see what they were doing, he guessed that they were wrapping the creature up now, so that they could lift it out of the hole. After a lengthy pause and a long inaudible discussion, one of the officers went off to Salvador's car to fetch a coil of canvas webbing, and this was lowered down to the researchers.

Eventually, just as the sun touched the edge of the sea and began to flatten across the horizon, the blanket-covered creature was lifted out of the hole by the combined efforts of the three Scripps researchers, two police officers, John Belli, and Salvador Ortega. From the way that they lowered the creature immediately on to the stretcher, Henry could see that it was enormously heavy in proportion to its size.

'That looks like it really weighs something,' Gil remarked.

Henry nodded, biting at his lip.

There was another conference between the police and the researchers, and then they gathered around the creature and carried it over towards John Belli's station-wagon, sliding it carefully into the back. John Belli closed the door. Henry saw Salvador say something to him before locking the door. Henry also noted how deeply the rear suspension of the station-wagon had subsided.

It took another ten minutes for John Belli to drive off the beach. His rear wheels sank so far down into the sand that the police officers had to go looking for pieces of driftwood to wedge under them, to give him some traction. At last, with a spray of sand, his station-wagon whinnied off up the beach, and jounced on to the road.

Salvador walked over to the police line with his hands in his pockets. 'Well, my friends,' he said, 'that is all there is to see, for today.'

'Where is Belli taking it?' Henry asked him.

'He'll take it downtown, first of all. But the Scripps people have a claim on it, too. Once Belli has examined it in relation to the death of the girl, he will transfer it to La Jolla. There, they will be able to analyse it biologically, and tell us something about its life-cycle.'

He smiled. 'I am sorry you were asked to come back here, but John Belli is very sensitive when it comes to interference, of any kind.'

Gil said, 'We weren't interfering, sir, believe me. If anybody's been interfering, it's those Scripps people and your friend Belli. This creature isn't a joke, sir. It's a living epidemic.'

Salvador looked at him sternly. 'Nobody suggested that it was a joke, my boy. There are no jokes when it comes to the death of a human being, believe me.'

'I'm sorry,' said Gil. 'But you should have listened. We know what we're talking about.'

'You don't know anything,' said Salvador. 'And just remember that you are only permitted to stay as close as this through my good offices.'

Henry put in, quietly, 'Was the creature still alive when you lifted it out of the hole?' 'As far as I could tell,' Salvador told him. 'Its heart was still beating.'

Susan said, 'its face – did you get a look at its face?'

Salvador shook his head. 'It was all wrapped up in blankets. They soaked the blankets that covered its face with water, and then bundled them tight around its head. I guess they supposed that this would simulate the effect of having wet sand all around it.'

'Well,' said Henry, in resignation, 'I suppose you have done what you consider to be your legal duty. But please may I ask you to make sure that the creature is kept firmly locked up, and that there is always somebody there to guard it.'

Salvador stared at him narrowly. 'What *do* you know, Henry?'

'I know nothing, except that this creature is destructive and malevolent, and that it will very quickly grow into something that neither you nor I nor anybody else is capable of handling.'

'And who told you this, that you're so certain about it?'

'I can't tell you that. I promised not to. But, believe me, it came direct from the highest possible authority.'

Salvador said, 'I recognise only two authorities, Henry. The San Diego Police Department, and God. If it wasn't either of those, then I'm really not interested.'

Henry said, 'It wasn't the San Diego Police Department.'

Salvador laughed. His driver had started up his car, and the Scripps men were tidying up their equipment. 'I have to go now,' he said, and waved. 'But I am sure that I will bump into you again. Thank you for all your frightening warnings! I am sure that you annoyed John Belli no end.'

When he had gone, Henry and Gil and Susan walked back up the beach to the promenade.

'Would you like a drink?' Henry asked them.

Susan said, 'No, thanks. And you should stay off it, too. We' re going to be Night Warriors tonight.'

'That's all very well for you to say,' Henry protested, 'but I have the ancient ancestor of all the hangovers that ever were.'

'You won't get rid of it by drinking.' 'I won't get rid of it by not drinking, either. So I might just as well drink.'

Susan took hold of his arm, and walked along the promenade with him towards his cottage. It was growing dark now. Up above their heads the glow of sunset was gradually fading away, and the gulls were turning against the breeze in their last search for insects. Susan said, 'Just for me, as a personal favour, will you not have any more to drink tonight?'

Henry made a face. 'I'm not at all sure that I could cope with being a Night Warrior without a drink.'

'Don't tell me you're that much of an alcoholic.'

'Did I ever say that I was an alcoholic? Of course I'm not an alcoholic. I didn't drink at all last Tuesday, not one drink all day. I'm a heavy drinker, sure, but I drink because I like it. It makes me feel good. I'm not furtive about it. I don't hide bottles of vodka down the back of the sofa. And I don't drink anything that I don't like. I had a bottle of Malmsey in the house for months, and never even touched it. Now, your genuine alcoholic, he'll drink anything.'

Susan squeezed him closer. 'The trouble is, Henry, we're really going to have to depend on you tonight. You're the centre of the whole thing, the charge-keeper. Supposing something goes wrong because you've had one too many drinks?'

Henry said, 'I promise you, I can handle it. There are some people who can, and there are some people who can't. But I happen to be one of the people who can handle it.'

Susan said, 'You know that I lost my parents?'

They had reached the corner by Henry's cottage now. Gil had been walking a little way behind them, and he kept his distance, pretending to be looking out to sea, where a dark curling cloud hung in the shape of a question-mark.

Henry said nothing, but looked back at Susan, serious faced.

'They were in a car-crash,' said Susan. 'They were coming back from a dinner-party at Escondido, and they went off the road by Lake Hodges.'

'I'm truly sorry,' Henry told her. Susan lifted her head and looked Henry straight in the eye. 'The medical examiner said that my father had twice as much alcohol in his blood as the legal limit.'

Henry laid a hand on her shoulder. He attempted a smile, but it didn't come out very convincingly. 'Well,' he said. 'I guess there isn't any answer to that.'

Gil came forward, and held up his left arm, showing his wristwatch. 'We have to arrange a time,' he said. 'How about ten o'clock?'

'That's a little early for me,' said Henry. 'Let's make it eleven, shall we? Otherwise there won't be a hope of my being asleep, and you two will be left on your own.'

'Eleven's okay with me,' said Susan. 'My grandparents go to bed at ten-thirty, and that's when the television gets switched off. There isn't a hope in hell of getting to sleep before then.'

Henry said, 'Eleven it is, then,' and quoted from *Macbeth*: 'When shall we three meet again – in thunder, lightning, or in rain?'

Susan quoted back at him, 'When the hurly-burly's done – when the battle's lost and won.'

Henry took his hand away from her shoulder. 'I'm afraid that you might be right.'

He watched Gil and Susan walk back along the promenade toward Solana Beach. It was still light enough for them to be able to make their way along the shoreline, and the tide was well out. Romantic, he thought, on a warm night like this, a night full of expectations and promises.

But also a night of fear, he thought, as he unlocked his front door, and stepped into his silent living-room. All that was gleaming was the curve of the television screen, and the half-empty vodka bottle on the table. *They shine*, he thought, as he closed the front door behind him; *the two placebos for every sickness known to man, physical or mental*. A fifth of vodka and half an hour of *The Pyramid Game*, and insensibility will supervene, guaranteed.

He switched on the lamps beside the sofa. His wristwatch was lying where he had left it last night, next to a dog-eared copy of Spinoza's *Ethics*. He picked up the book first. For some reason that he couldn't remember, he had underlined the words 'We feel and know that we are eternal". Then he picked up his watch. Seven-eighteen. Nearly four hours to go. How was he going to occupy himself for four hours?

He could finish his thesis. He could read more of Spinoza. He could take a shower and wash his hair. He sat down, and slowly unlaced his sneakers. He looked up, and there was the vodka bottle shining at him.

Chapter Nine

She was pushing her shopping-cart through Ralph's when the young man came around the corner pushing his shopping-cart and collided with her.

'Oh, I'm real sorry,' he told her. He was tall and curly headed and he put her in mind almost straightaway of Elliot Gould. 'I guess I'm not much of a driver. Did I hurt you at all?'

'I'll live,' she smiled.

She went on pushing her cart along by the herb and spice shelves. She was giving a small dinner-party tomorrow – not that she particularly felt like it. Paul had been away for a week in Las Vegas, negotiating a new lighting contract with the Desert Hotel Group, and he would be bringing back three of his clients so that they could inspect the full range of his latest fixtures, out at his engineering works at Burbank.

She hated business dinners. The clients were either short and fat and Jewish, or short and fat and Italian, or short and fat and Japanese. They all drank too much and smoked too much and tried to grab her behind. Afterwards, she always felt that she and her house had been gang-banged. She had begged Paul to take his clients to restaurants – 'They'll be so much more impressed with a restaurant' – but Paul believed implicity in the personal, family touch. When men were away from home on business, he argued, they saw far too many restaurants. They wanted to feel comfortable and relaxed. They wanted to feel they were *friends* rather than business clients.

So it was that two or three times a month, Jennifer was expected to prepare a four-or five-course dinner of *boeufcarbonnade*, or glazed duck with baby vegetables, or roast rack of lamb Provencale. She had Inez to help her, of course, but even if she had run a kitchen staff of twenty, her feelings about business dinners still wouldn't have changed. It was the loud laughter, the crass remarks, the blue jokes, and the sub-Rabelaisian table-manners. Whenever she thought of business dinners, she thought of the president of Northern Frate, and how he had crushed out his cigar in the Madeira sauce that he had left on his plate.

Jennifer thought that she probably deserved better. A better home, a better husband, a better life. When he wasn't making business-dinner demands on her, though, Paul was still amusing and gentlemanly and she believed that he still loved her, as much as he could love anybody. It was just the unrelenting sameness of every day that depressed her; the sameness of housework, and then the sameness, once the housework was finished, of wondering what on earth she could do to occupy her spare time. She often tried to spin out a small embroidery project for days on end, unpicking it unless it was absolutely perfect. She had plenty of friends, but they were all caught up in the same predicament as she. Their children were all away at school, their husbands were all away at work, and let's face it, not every woman could write *Scruples* or head up Twentieth-Century Fox or play championship tennis.

She used to look out of the window of the plane whenever she flew back from seeing her sister Nesta in San Francisco, and try to count all of the bright turquoise swimming-pools that studded the Valley, thinking to herself as she did so: by each of those pools there stands a house, and in each of those houses there sits a woman, waiting out the rest of her life in emptiness.

Jennifer stopped beside one of the mirrored pillars and deliberately looked at herself. Brunette, dark eyed, with excellent bone structure, seeks amusement. Dresses tastefully, talks intelligently, makes love with enthusiasm when required. Will not consider embroidery or business catering. Prefers hunting rhinoceros, sailing uncharted oceans, dancing until well past dawn, and running naked through breeze-blown fields of golden poppies.

She focused her eyes. The young man who had collided with her only a few minutes before was standing behind her, watching her. She blushed suddenly, and turned around, hoping that she hadn't been making her usual faces.

'I'm sorry,' he said. 'I was thinking how attractive you were.'

'What?' she asked him, as if he were mad. God, he probably was.

'I have to cook this meal tonight,' he told her, and he said it in such a way that she wasn't at all sure what he had said to start with. Her memory had been getting worse, as forty gradually approached. Forty, like the exit gate from Disneyland. Once you were through, there was no going back, and there was nobody there to stamp your hand.

'It's lamb,' he added, distractedly.

She stared at him. 'What is?'

'This meal that I have to cook tonight. My fiancée's folks are coming over. I can't afford to take them out to a restaurant, so I thought I'd cook.'

'And you were going to cook them lamb?'

'I have this recipe, look. I cut it out of last Friday's food section.'

He held out a well-folded cutting from the *Times*. She took it, but she couldn't read it because she wasn't wearing her glasses. She fumbled in her bag and finally managed to find them. 'Now then,' she said, peering at the cutting. 'What is this?'

She read it quickly. It was *lamb en croute*, boned leg of lamb smothered in pate and herbs, wrapped in pastry, and then baked in the oven. She gave the recipe back to him. 'Do you cook much?' she asked.

'Only burgers.'

'Don't you think *lamb en croute* is rather ambitious for somebody who only cooks burgers?'

'I guess. But I thought that if I followed the instructions carefully, and used frozen pastry instead of trying to make my own ... well, it would probably turn out okay.'

'Well, I suppose so, with lots of luck,' smiled Jennifer. The young man amused her. He was gentle and earnest and good looking and he spoke to her as if he respected her advice as a person, not the way that Paul did, as if she were lucky that he was wonderful enough to share his priceless conversation with her.

The young man scratched the back of his neck, thinking hard. 'It's just that this meal is real important, and if I cook something dumb then what are her parents going to think of me?'

'You don't have to cook anything so complicated,' said Jennifer. 'Most people really prefer plain food, anyway. I give dozens of dinner-parties, and the most successful ones are always the simplest ones. Ham, or tenderloin of pork, or –'

'They're Jewish,' the young man interrupted.

'Well, in that case, you can always do something simple with beef or fish.'

The young man looked down wistfully at the recipe he held in his hand. 'You're right,' he said. 'Maybe I should cook something real simple. Broiled ribs of beef or something.'

Jennifer watched him for a moment. In the bottom of his shopping-cart, he had already collected liver-pate, *herbes de Provence*, and frozen shortcrust pastry, as well as snow peas, baby carrots, and russet potatoes.

'Let me make a suggestion,' she heard herself saying. 'Why don't you come back to my house this afternoon, and I'll prepare the *lamb en croute* for you. You have to partly cook the lamb in any case, before you wrap it in the pate and the herbs and the pastry. I'll do all that, and decorate it for you, and then all you have to do tonight is take it home and put it straight into the oven.'

The young man stared at her. 'You'd do that?'

'Why not? I don't have anything else to do this afternoon. It should be fun.'

'Well, that's terrific,' the young man said. 'But you don't even know me. I could be the Hollywood Hatchetman, or somebody like that.'

'Oh, sure,' said Jennifer briskly, pushing her shopping-cart ahead of her. 'The Hollywood Hatchetman wanders around Ralph's, wondering how to cook *lamb en croute* for his Jewish parents-in-law-to-be.'

The young man followed Jennifer along the aisle. 'Even Charles Manson used to shop,' he said, breathlessly.

Jennifer stopped, and their carts collided again. 'You're not a friend of Charles Manson, are you?' she asked, only half seriously.

The young man clapped his hand against his chest in horror. 'Me? No, of course not!'

'Listen,' said Jennifer, 'we'd be better off with just one shopping-cart. Otherwise there could be a serious traffic accident before we've finished.'

It took them ten minutes to finish their marketing, then the young man pushed the shopping-cart out to Jennifer's car, a metallic green Eldorado, six months old.

'Where's your car?' asked Jennifer.

The young man flapped one hand diffidently toward a scabrous Le Sabre, twelve years old, with collapsed suspension. Jennifer smiled. 'You want to leave it here and come back in mine?' she asked.

'No, that's okay, I'll follow you. Not too close. I wouldn't want to embarrass you.'

Jennifer said, 'I really ought to know your name. And I guess you ought to know mine. I'm Jennifer Shepheard.'

They shook hands. 'Bernard Muldoon,' the young man told her. 'I'm a business studies student at UC San Diego. Training to be a captain of industry.'

'Good to know you, Bernard.'

They drove out of Ralph's on to Hollywood Boulevard, heading west. Jennifer kept her eye on Bernard's limping car, making sure that she didn't leave him behind as she turned up La Brea. She didn't live far away: just up the canyon on Paseo del Serra. But by the blue smoke that was blowing out of the back of Bernard's car, she thought she ought to keep the pace sedate. In five minutes, however, they were parking on the sharply sloping driveway outside Jennifer's split-level ranch-style house, and Bernard was helping Jennifer to carry the groceries around the back to the kitchen.

Bernard glanced around as Jennifer opened the door for him. 'The neighbours won't gossip, will they?' he queried.

'You're not bent on giving them anything to gossip about, are you?' Jennifer smiled.

Bernard flushed red, from the neck up. 'Well, no, of course not. But I know what some of these suburban neighbourhoods are like. They live entirely on gossip and Stouffer's candies.'

'You think I'm like that?' asked Jennifer, thinking of the afternoon last week when she had put her feet up and read *Lace 2* and eaten a whole box of violet creams. She didn't binge like that very often; she wanted to keep her figure as well as her mind. But she swore now that she would never let herself do it again.

The kitchen was tiled in Thanksgiving Brown, with glazed pictures of golden poppies beside the sink (the poppies through which she sometimes imagined herself dancing naked). There was a cookie jar with a silty rabbit's face on it, and an egg rack with ten brown eggs in it, and a Currier & Ives calendar which Sammi her favourite niece had given her, in a frustrated teenage attempt to teach her aunt some taste. Jennifer unpacked the groceries on to the tiled central island, and told Bernard where to put things away.

'Would you like a glass of wine?' she asked him. 'There's some Chablis in the icebox. Or else there's a beer, if you'd prefer it. The glasses are in that cupboard next to the scales. That's it. And could you pour one for me, please?'

They spent the whole afternoon in the kitchen, preparing the *lamb en croute* and chatting about everything and nothing. Politics, art, television, how good Raquel Welch looked for her age, what about contraception for under-age girls, atomic energy, Greenpeace, the meaning of other people's lives, the meaning of their own lives. Jennifer could hardly believe it when she looked up at the reproduction early-American wall clock and saw that it was well past five. Bernard had kept her continuously interested, continuously amused. *If only* – but then '*if only*' was as far as a married woman was allowed to think, as far as Jennifer's upbringing was concerned, anyway. Beyond 'if only' there was excitement and pleasure; but there was insecurity and danger as well.

'What time is your dinner?' Jennifer asked Bernard, as she glazed the pastry with egg. 'You should put this in the oven at least an hour beforehand, 220 degrees.'

Bernard stood with his hands tucked into his back pants pockets and looked down at the lamb for a long while, saying nothing. Jennifer stopped brushing it with egg, and asked him, 'Is anything wrong?'

'Well ...' he began.

'Well what? Is there something wrong with the lamb? You don't like the way it looks? Maybe those pastry flowers are too fussy. It was supposed to have been cooked by a man, after all. We don't want your fiancée's parents thinking there's anything limp-wristed about you, do we? You know what these Jewish people are like when it comes to carrying on the good old family tree.'

'Nothing like that,' said Bernard. 'The truth is, I have a confession to make.'

'A confession?' asked Jennifer. She went over to the sink and washed her hands. Then she untied her apron strings, and said, 'You don't owe me anything, you know. Not even the truth.'

'The truth is,' Bernard told her, with great simplicity, 'that I have no fiancée.'

Jennifer said, 'Oh,' and looked at the lamb. 'But if you have no fiancée, that means your fiancée's parents aren't coming to dinner.'

'That's right,' Bernard admitted.

'But if your non-existent fiancée's non-existent parents aren't coming to dinner, then who is?' 'I was hoping that I was, with you.'

Jennifer stared at Bernard open mouthed. 'You were hoping that ... You mean you – I don't *believe* it! You picked me up in that supermarket and got me to invite you home to dinner! You even got me to cook it! I just don't believe it!'

'I told you that you were beautiful. At least I was honest about that.'

Jennifer shook her head. 'I really can't believe it. I thought I was hearing things, when you said that. I couldn't believe that a total stranger – I *still* can't believe it! I need a drink! Pour me another glass of wine, before I pass out!'

Bernard hurriedly splashed out another glass of Chablis, and handed it to her, 'I'm real sorry,' he said. 'I didn't know how else I was going to approach you. You can throw me out of here if you like. You can even keep the lamb. I'm sorry. You just attracted me, I thought you were so fantastic looking, and I didn't know what else to do.'

Jennifer perched herself on the edge of one of the kitchen stools, still shaking her head. 'I have to admit that you succeeded. What a line! But how did you know that I was going to be able to invite you home? I guess you must realise that I'm married.'

'Oh, sure,' said Bernard. 'I was in the drugstore yesterday, you know the drugstore on Sunset, and I saw you talking to a friend. I came up close and I heard you saying that your husband was away until Saturday. That decided me, I guess. I only had one day, and I had to think of something pretty darn fast. So that's what I thought of.'

'Well, now,' Jennifer told him, 'what are we going to do? Morally, I guess I should take you upon your offer and throw you out. Immorally, of course, I should say to hell with everything and since I've spent all afternoon preparing this damn lamb, I may as well cook it and invite you to share it with me, which is not as generous as it sounds because you bought it in the first place. On the other hand, what will the neighbours think? Those feeders on gossip and Stouffer's candies? On the other hand again, who gives a damn what they think?'

'It's your choice,' said Bernard, a little sadly.

Jennifer said, 'You've thrown me. You've really thrown me. Nothing like this has ever happened to me before in my whole life. Listen, stay. Let's cook the lamb, let's have some more wine, let's talk a whole lot more, I haven't talked so much in three years. There's only one thing I'll ask you to do, if you don't mind doing it, and that is to drive your car away from here and maybe park it in Orchid Avenue, you know where that is? At least then the gossip will be kept to a reasonable minimum.'

Bernard said, 'You're some lady. I mean that. I knew when I very first saw you that I wasn't going to be disappointed.'

They ate dinner in the dining-room, with a fresh white linen tablecloth embroidered at the edges with columbine. The lamb was far too much for the two of them, but Jennifer assured Bernard that her husband would be quite happy with curried lamb next week.

'Three nights running?' asked Bernard.

Afterwards, they sat on the curved custom-built sofa in the living-room, which overlooked the pool patio, and Jennifer played Frank Sinatra records and offered Bernard a glass of Paul's Courvoisier brandy. She sat on the floor quite close to Bernard, humming along with *My Way*. Bernard sipped his brandy, and told her about his business studies.

'You have to grow, when you're in business. You know what Roger Falk said.'

'No,' smiled Jennifer. 'What did Roger Falk say?'

'Roger Falk said that many executives think they have ten years' experience, whereas in fact they simply have one year's experience ten times over.'

'Well, I think that's true,' said Jennifer. 'I mean, take Paul, for instance.'

'Do we have to talk about Paul?'

Jennifer turned and looked up at him. 'What does that mean?' she asked him. The lamp-light was shining in her eyes and she knew that she was looking attractive. Bernard shrugged. 'It means that I don't particularly want to talk about Paul, that's all.'

Jennifer laid her hand on his knee. 'Paul is a long way away,' she said.

Bernard laid his hand on top of hers. But quite unexpectedly, he said, 'It's late, anyway. I'd better be going.'

Jennifer said, in undisguised bewilderment, 'It's only eleven o'clock.'

'Sure, but I have to get all the way back to Venice.'

'Bernard,' Jennifer protested. 'Eleven o'clock is *early*.'

'Well, I know, but I have an early class tomorrow, and you know how it is.'

'No, I *don't* know how it is. You've gone to all the trouble of tricking your way into having dinner with me; we're alone together; there's music, and wine; my husband isn't due home until tomorrow; and you're *leaving*?'

Bernard finished his brandy, and set the glass down on the table beside the sofa. 'I'm sorry. I enjoyed every minute of it. But I really have to go.'

Jennifer turned around, so that she was kneeling, clutching his hand. 'What are you trying to do?' she demanded. 'Are you trying to get me to *beg* you to stay?'

Bernard slowly shook his head. 'I have to go, and that's it. I didn't mean to upset you.'

Jennifer took in a long, deep, steadying breath. Then she said, 'You haven't upset me. As a matter of fact, you haven't upset me at all. Go on, you'd better go. And don't forget to put on your sneakers. I'd hate any of the neighbours to see you leaving the house with your shoes in your hand. Then they would definitely get the wrong idea.'

She stood up, flustered. She had to face up to the fact now that Bernard had aroused her to the point where she was quite ready to go to bed with him; that she had been mentally and physically prepared for adultery. She felt guilty and cheated and unutterably relieved, all at once.

Bernard hopped around on one foot, trying to lace up his sneakers. 'I'm sorry,' he said. 'I've made you angry and I didn't mean to.'

'You haven't made me angry at all,' Jennifer told him, tightly.

'You're married,' he said. 'I didn't expect –'

'I don't care what you didn't expect or what you did expect. Just go. You can take that lamb with you if you want. I'll get you a doggie bag out of the kitchen.'

At the back door, with his doggie bag clutched in his hand, Bernard turned around and said, 'I guess I'm not very good when it comes to seduction.'

'No,' said Jennifer, 'you're not.'

'I'll go, then. Thanks for everything. Thanks for the dinner.'

Jennifer began to feel less frustrated, less punitive. She had at least spent a cheerful and talkative afternoon with Bernard. For the first time in years, she had been able to think about something else apart from her own isolation and her own boredom. She should be grateful to him for that.

'Goodbye, Bernard,' she said, softly, and kissed his cheek. 'And – you know, don't be a stranger.'

'I won't,' he told her, and kissed her back. Then, without even a wave, he was gone, and she heard the wrought-iron gate at the side of the house clanging shut behind him.

She closed the door, and locked it, and put on the security chain. Frank Sinatra was still singing in the living-room. She cleared away the dishes with a lump in her throat, then switched off all the lights, and went through to the bedroom with a large glass, and what was left of the wine. The bedroom was white, with a white fluffy carpet and a white frilly bed-cover and white seersucker drapes. She switched on the television, and then went across to her dressing-table, where a white poodle with a red felt tongue and a zipper in its belly was jealously guarding her nightdress.

She undressed, watching herself in the mirror. How many business wives are doing the same, she thought to herself. All over Hollywood, all through the canyons, all across the Valley, a hundred thousand women stepping tired and lonely out of their clothes, and watching themselves in their mirrors as they did so.

She tied up her hair in a pink chiffon scarf, and walked through to the en-suite bathroom. She showered, standing in the steam thinking at first of nothing at all. But when she washed herself between her legs, she held her hand there for an extra moment, and closed her eyes, and thought of Bernard. She should have known when she first saw him that he wasn't dashing enough to make her a new lover.

She dried herself, and went back to the bedroom. She disembowelled the white poodle, taking out the pink transparent baby-doll nightie that Paul liked most of all. Her nipples showed through the nylon like cherries on top of two white ice-cream sundaes. There were matching briefs with the nightie but she very rarely wore them.

She climbed into bed, and reached into the bedside table for a *magazine*. She flicked through *Western Living* and *Los Angeles* and *Cosmopolitan*, her spectacles perched on the end of her nose; then she tossed them aside and watched television for a while. It was almost midnight. They were showing See *Here, Private Hargrove* on 11; and *Horror*

Hospital on 9. She watched both movies for five or ten minutes, flicking with her remote control from one to the other; then she changed over to the news.

She wasn't quite sure when she fell asleep, or even if she had. She felt herself dozing, felt her head sliding sideways on the pillow, then she recovered and blinked and tried to focus on the television screen. A newsman was saying, '... given the rich diversity of Asian immigrants' backgrounds, it is impossible to generalise about their experiences in becoming Americans ...'

She drank a little more wine, but it tasted vinegary. She listened to the news a little longer, then her head began to slide again. She slept, but she wasn't sure for how long. She dreamed that she was crossing a wide polished floor, and that she could hear her footsteps echoing all around her. On all sides, tiers of balconies rose up around her, balconies draped with gaily coloured blankets and bedding, and hanging plants. She heard music, Italian music like her father used to play when she was a child.

She reached the end of the polished floor, and opened a door. Inside, her family was sitting down to lunch. She looked around the room and realised that she had never been away, that she had always been a child, and that she had never grown up and left the Astoria neighbourhood, had never moved West and married. Her father was sitting where he always used to sit, with his back to the door, his shirt bunching out of the triangles made by his criss-cross suspenders, his bald patch shining because it was hot. On the dresser, the same yellow-and-blue plates were propped up, and the porcelain Madonna stood where she had always stood, her holy baby in her arms.

Her sister Grace and her brother Michael were there, too, waiting at their places. Only Momma was missing. Jennifer moved through the room, and heard herself saying, 'Where's Momma? Isn't Momma here? It's lunchtime.'

She looked down at their plates. They were all empty, cold, and the vegetable tureens were empty, too. 'Where's the food?' she asked. Her father raised his head and told her in a reverberating voice, 'It's lamb.'

She thought to herself, 'My God, he's sick, I can hear the sickness in his throat. Doesn't he realise that he has to eat, or else he's going to die?'

She ran to the door. Her black dress rose up and down with every step, making a slow thundering sound. She snatched at the door-handle, and the door swung wide. She found herself running along a narrow tunnel, her shoes splashing through ice-cold puddles, her footsteps echoing and echoing. She was panicking now, there was somebody after her. She could hear them close behind, but she didn't dare to turn around in case they were really there, closer than she had feared.

She reached the end of the tunnel. Her eyes were blinded by a sudden dazzling whiteness, and she had to press her hands over them to protect them. She slid backwards, stumbling over something white and furry, like the body of a Polar bear. She opened her eyes, and she was lying in her own bed, in her own bedroom, but she was sure that she was still dreaming, for outside the window the landscape was blood red. Blood-red sky, blood-red garden, blood-red palm trees. Even the swimming-pool was blood red.

Someone's been killed, she thought. Someone's been killed, and their blood has splashed everywhere, over the sky, over the houses, over the ocean, too. Someone has died and their death has coloured the world red.

She wondered if there was anything about the killing on the news. She slowly turned her head towards the television. The screen was flickering blue-grey, and all she could hear was the muffled sound of waltz music.

As she stared at the television, however, freckles and speckles of coloured light began to fly off the screen, into the room. Gradually, they assembled themselves into a blurred shape, standing in the centre of the white fluffy carpet. A body, a ribcage, a pelvis, a head, two muscular legs, all slowly created out of flying particles of light. The waltz music went on and on, dim and crackly, like a shellac record from the 1930s.

Jennifer sat up in fascination and terror. The shape that was slowly manifesting itself in front of her was tall, at least eight feet tall. Its head almost touched the ceiling. It was broad-shouldered, and as it became more distinct, she could see that it was muscular and lean, with skin as purplish brown as if it had been stained with dogberries. Its face was pointed and malevolent, with slitted eyes that gleamed the same blood red as the landscape outside the window, and two horns slanted back from the top of its head. Its thighs were thick with fur, and out from between them reared a huge reddened phallus below which hung two purple testicles as big as oranges.

The creature stank. It stank of sweat and greasy fur and foul breath and sex; an odour so overwhelming that Jennifer retched. She thought, in mounting horror, how can I smell this smell, when I'm supposed to be dreaming?

How can I see this creature so clearly? It's so clear! I can see every hair of its beard; I can make out every wrinkle around its eyes! My God, it's just like the Devil out of fairy-stories, but it came out of the television and it's here in front of me and it's *real*.

She heard a voice inside her head coax, '*Jennifer. This is what you wanted, isn't it? This is what you were longing for, all today? You wanted to take him to bed, didn't you, Jennifer? You wanted him on top of you! You wanted sweat and pain and the feel of another man's body! This is what you wanted, you whore! This is what you wanted, you slatternly bitch!*'

Jennifer clutched at the sheets and screamed. But the scream didn't seem to come out of her mouth at all. She felt as if her face had been smothered by a pillow, and that it was impossible for her to breathe or to say anything. The creature approached the bed, and it was so grotesque that she kept on screaming, even though no sound was coming out.

It sat down on the edge of the bed. It must be real, I can feel the comforter pinned under it. I can feel its weight. Then it slowly pulled back the top part of the covers, revealing Jennifer in her baby-doll nightdress.

'Don't kill me!' she begged. Her screaming had stopped now; her voice was hurried and low and erratic, like water tumbling down a dry creek bed for the very first time. 'I beg you in the name of the Holy Mother, please don't kill me.'

The creature's eyes appeared to flare a little as Jennifer mentioned the name of the Blessed Virgin. It reached out its hand and touched her cheek with its left hand. The skin on its fingers felt as hard and shiny as the skin on the paws of a dog.

'*Silence,*' said the voice, inside her head. '*I am your Master One and your Master Many. You will do whatever I say. I have come to you today in two guises, the guise of your friend and the guise of the goat, but I have as many different faces as the ocean has waves, and each one changes as the waves change.*' For one liquid second, Jennifer thought that she could see Bernard's features flowing across the creature's face. Then it returned to its narrow, pointed, ill-intentioned self, with its eyes that were filled up with blood.

'*You see the Devil you believe in, my love,*' the voice continued. '*Did you not wish today that you could lie with the Devil, rather than your husband? Well, this, my filthy dear, is what you can do.*'

The creature took hold of her just behind the knees, gripping her with bruising strength, and spreading her legs so wide apart that she heard the ligaments crack. Then it reared up over her, heavy and huge and evil smelling, and glared down at her with a face that was so old and so wicked that she found herself unable to speak, unable to cry out, unable to do anything but lie on the bed and shiver.

'*Now, you will be my little mother,*' the voice whispered; and Jennifer stared down at herself in freezing disbelief as the creature's massive member slid into her, right up to the shaggy fur which clung to the lower part of its protuberant stomach.

She closed her eyes. It was pain, solid pain, wall-to-wall agony, but it was also something else. Deep down underneath the pain there was a dark-running rivulet of pleasure; a rivulet that trickled through the forbidden recesses of

Jennifer's mind, and down her spinal column, and into the nerves which were feeling the size and the power of the creature's penis.

The creature began to thrust in and out of her, slowly at first, but then faster and faster, and even more brutally, like a mindless mechanical piston. The dark rivulet flooded the lower chambers of her brain, and then began to rise up from beneath, flooding chamber after chamber, until all of her body and all of her brain seemed to be darkness. The creature let out a guttural, indistinct shout, and held itself rigidly still for a moment, pumping itself deep inside her. Jennifer was a hair's-breadth away from a climax, clinging to the very edge of it, her eyes tight shut, her face clenched, her chest flushed. Her nipples protruded, and the muscles in her pelvis were tightly bunched in readiness for her final release.

But the final release never came. She opened her eyes, and the creature was gone. Slowly, inch by inch, as she looked around her in mystification, her muscles began to relax. But she was still shaking, and her mind was still contracted for that ultimate moment of orgasm, and at first she couldn't understand what had happened, or even if anything had happened at all. The television was tuned to *The Rose Tattoo*. Her drink remained untouched on the night-table. Outside, in the darkness, a dog was barking, endlessly and hopelessly.

Jennifer touched her body. The covers had been dragged back, and her baby-doll nightie had been pulled up to bare her breasts, but had there really been anything here? A creature? A Devil, with horns and hair? It didn't seem possible. She sniffed, once or twice, but the rancorous smell, if it had ever been there, had completely vanished. She touched herself tentatively, between her legs. She was wet, and a little sore, but no wetter and no sorer than she would have been if she had been urgently masturbating.

She pulled down her nightie, and covered herself up again. Dreaming, she thought, I must have been dreaming. I *was* dreaming. The house is locked, nobody could have been inside. And there is nothing and nobody in this whole wide world which can manifest itself from out of a television. Not seriously, not for real.

She thought of the dream about her father. Somehow, that must have got all mixed up with a dream about Bernard. She had wanted to take Bernard to bed, and so her unconscious mind must have created the Devil for her, the real live hairy Devil, to express what she really felt about adultery. Pleasurable, exciting, dangerous, frightening – and wrong. In the old days, adulterers had been stoned. These days, God sent them bad dreams and nervous breakdowns.

Jennifer went to the bathroom, took two Valium, and washed them down with warm Perrier. Then she switched off the television, turned off the lights, and climbed into bed. She lay with her head against her pillow for a long time, not sleeping, listening to the dog.

Had that Devil really been a nightmare? God, it must have been. Even if the Devil actually existed, which she knew that it didn't, it certainly wouldn't have horns and fur and eyes that gleamed red in the dark. Not unless it appeared to people the way that they had always expected it to look. No, that was ridiculous; it hadn't appeared at all.

Nonetheless, she switched on her light again, and sat

up in bed, and wondered whether she ought to call Father O'Hare. She looked at the time. Two-twenty-five. Too late to call anyone and try to explain that she thought she had been raped by Satan.

And apart from that, she felt more than a little guilty about what had happened – or what she had dreamed had happened. It was one thing to explain to Father O'Hare that the Devil had appeared in her bedroom and forced her to have sex. It was quite another to say that although she had been frightened, although she had been shocked, she had taken out of it some wild and perverse pleasure; a pleasure that was as urgent as the human appetite for self-destruction, and as deep as sin itself.

She turned out the light again. She slept, but didn't dream.

Chapter Ten

Susan told her grandmother that she was feeling nauseous, and went to bed early. She was too excited about what was going to happen tonight to stay in the living-room watching television and listening to her grandfather's interminable drolleries about every single programme that came on. He was a devotee of that kind of humour they used to call 'ribbing', the sort of pointless dead-pan tall-story humour favoured by those old men who sit in rockers outside of small-town general stores.

'That Jack Lord, do you know how he-keeps his hair so thick? He insists as a condition of their contract that every guest star who appears on *Hawaii Five-O* gives him a plug of their scalp, to add to his hair transplant.'

Susan closed her bedroom door behind her, and wondered whether she ought to lock it. She didn't know what would happen if her grandmother came in to see her when she was asleep, and her Samena personality was away somewhere, out in the night. She knew that it was supposed to be dangerous to wake a sleep-walker, but she wasn't at all sure if waking a Night Warrior amounted to the same kind of thing.

Perhaps she wouldn't wake up at all, and then her grandmother would panic and call an ambulance. On the other hand, if she locked her door, her grandmother would almost certainly start banging on it, and if Susan failed to reply she would almost certainly try to force it open.

It was probably better to leave it unlocked, and hope that her grandmother didn't disturb her while she slept, or that it wouldn't affect her Night Warrior personality if she did.

She tugged off her tee-shirt, and was just about to take off her shorts when her grandmother knocked at the door and came straight in.

'How are you feeling?' she wanted to know. 'Would you like some Pepto-Bismol? Is it that kind of nauseous? You haven't been eating those chili-dogs again, have you, the ones that made you sick the last time?'

'It's not that, grandma,' said Susan. 'I think it's just my period coming on.'

'You ought to see the doctor, if you're feeling nauseous.'

'I'm okay, grandma. It's just my period, that's all.'

'So long as it *is* your period.'

'I'm not pregnant,' Susan smiled.

Her grandmother was flustered. 'I do try to look after you the best I can.'

'Grandma, I know you do, you're wonderful. Don't worry about it.'

Her grandmother blinked behind her spectacles. It had been a long time since Susan had said she was wonderful. Pleased, disarmed, she retreated to the door, and gave Susan a little finger-wave. 'You can have some tea later, if you'd care to.'

'I don't think so, grandma. I'll just get some sleep.'

'Okay, then. I'll see you in the morning.'

Susan finished undressing, rummaged around in her drawer for a clean tee-shirt, put it on, and jumped into bed. It was twenty after ten. In ten minutes or so, her grandfather would reach over and lay his hand on her grandmother's knee, and say, 'Well, then, Dolly, I think it's time to strangle the chickens.' That was what he always said, when he was suggesting that they turn off the television and retire to bed. Why going to bed should have anything to do with strangling chickens, Susan never found out, but then she never asked, either, just in case it referred to something personal, like the noise that her grandmother made, once or twice a month, when her grandfather fulfilled his conjugal duties.

Susan lay in bed with the light on for a while, her hands clasped behind her head. Then she switched off the light, and lay in the dark. She could hear the traffic along Camino del Mar, and the cicadas chirping, and the steady blowing of the air-conditioning through the vent in the celling. After a while, the television in the living-room was switched off, and she heard her grandmother and grandfather walking past her door. They were murmuring something about doctors, and hepatitis, and how Hispanics never washed their hands after going to the bathroom.

'One hamburger out of every ten will make you ill. An old friend of mine proved that. He ate nine hamburgers and he was perfectly okay, but when he tried to eat the tenth, he was violently sick.'

'You and your silly stories,' Susan's grandmother complained.

The old couple took a long time getting to bed. There were teeth to be taken out, corns to be planed, curls to be wound up in heated rollers. By the time the toilet had flushed for the very last time, it was almost quarter of eleven, and Susan was growing anxious that she would miss the rendezvous with Henry and Gil.

At last, however, the house was silent and dark. She lay back on the pillow, looking up at the ceiling, and she repeated the words that Springer had given her to memorise. They were strange and simple words. Springer had said that they were translated from Latin and carried to the New World in 1601 by the first of the Night Warriors.

'Now when the face of the world is hidden in darkness, let us be conveyed to the place of our meeting, armed and armoured; and let us be nourished by the power that is dedicated to the cleaving of darkness, the settling of all black matters, and the dissipation of all evil, so be it.'

Susan repeated the words three times, as Springer had told her to, and then she closed her eyes and lay perfectly still on her bed. I'll never get to sleep in time, she thought to herself. I'm going to be late, and then the others will go off without me. The luminous hands of her bedside clock said six minutes of eleven. How can I possibly get to sleep in six minutes? Curiously, though, her eyes began to close, and even when she wanted to open them again to look at the clock, she found that she couldn't. Her body slowly began to relax, all the way through, as if it were a building in which all the lights were being extinguished, floor by floor. Her heartbeat slowed, her respiration became flat and shallow, and she began to feel as if she were slowly moving backward, inside her head, backward into the darkness that all of us carry inside of ourselves. She went back faster and faster, deeper into inner space, and she heard a high-pitched metallic singing sound, an inanimate choir.

She rose now, dark and invisible, through the ceiling of her room, through the attic, and up into the night above Del Mar. To the south, she could see the dim surf gleaming as far as La Jolla, and the lights of San Diego sparkling beyond. To the north, she could see the long curve of Cardiff and San Elijo Lagoon and Encinitas. The traffic poured along I–5 like streams of fireflies. Beyond the highway, the inland hills were wrapped in shadows, and crowned with condominiums.

Susan didn't feel as if she were flying. The sensation was more like being *absorbed* through the evening air, as if she were no more substantial than ink that was quickly being absorbed by blotting-paper. She felt as if the molecules of her personality were mingling with the molecules of the night through which she was passing; as if nobody could tell where the night ended and Susan began, a girt of shadows. But she could see the landscape below her quite clearly and as she spun slowly down towards the house on Camino del Mar, and passed through its roof-shingles and into the upstairs room, she was aware of an extraordinary friction.

The room was lit by a single naked bulb, which threw stark shadows in all directions, as if a black box had exploded in the centre of the room. Springer was already there, in his male manifestation, dressed in a plain black suit. Gil had arrived, too, but as yet there was no sign of Henry.

Susan went straight to the mirror and looked at herself. She had not yet taken on the guise of Samena: she was still wearing her tee-shirt. But she was delighted and frightened and fascinated to see that she was *transparent*, that she could see the opposite side of the room right through the outlines of her body. Gil was the same. Substantial enough to recognise and to talk to, but unreal. A dream-figure, a living memory of himself.

Springer said, with a small nod of his head, 'You are both to be congratulated. It is not easy to leave one's body for the first time.'

'Will we be safe?' asked Susan. 'Our actual bodies, I mean. I was worried that my grandmother might try to wake me up.'

Springer smiled. 'All you need worry about is someone destroying your body. That would give you nowhere to go back to. But I don't think your grandmother is likely to do that, do you?'

'I feel like I'm dreaming,' said Susan.

'You *are* dreaming,' Springer told her, coming up behind her and laying a hand on her semi-transparent shoulder. 'Your mind is here, your spirit is here, but your material substance remains at home, sleeping.'

Gil said, 'There's no sign of Henry yet.'

'Henry will be here,' Springer assured her.

'I hope he wasn't doing any more – you know,' Susan remarked, making a drinking gesture with her hand.

Springer ignored what she had said, and held out his hands to the two of them. 'Now is the time for you to prepare yourselves, Tebulot and Samena, for your first training as Night Warriors. Come here, both of you, and kneel in front of me.'

A little hesitantly they knelt side by side. Springer raised both of his hands, with the palms facing outwards, and chanted the ancient words of the Night Warriors. 'Now, when the face of the world is covered in darkness, let us prepare ourselves here at this place of our meeting, let us arm and armour ourselves; and let us be nourished by the power that is dedicated to the cleaving of darkness, the settling of all black matters, and the dissipation of evil. So be it.'

'So be it,' Gil and Susan repeated.

'You are Night Warriors now,' said Springer. 'You are members of that great and glorious host who captured and chained all nine hundred and ninety-nine manifestations of the Devil, and who earned for all time the gratitude of Ashapola and of the Council of Messengers. You have dedicated your dream selves to the extinction of evil, and in particular to the pursuit and capture of Yaomauitl, the Deadly Enemy.'

Springer circled his hands in the air, and over their heads two golden circles of light appeared, then slowly faded.

'Tebulot! Stand,' Springer instructed Gil, and Gil rose to his feet and found as he did so that he was mantled in the hard gleaming white armour of the machine-carrier, and that in his arms he was carrying the huge weapon with which he would protect himself from harm, and which he would use to track down Yaomauitl. This time, the armour felt solid, although it wasn't excessively heavy: it was fashioned out of a thick, lightweight alloy, and brightly enamelled. The machine, though, was a different matter. It weighed at least thirty pounds, and even though its odd horn-shaped handles made it easy to hold, it was not the most manoeuvrable of devices.

'Whoever dreamed this up, could have dreamed it up lighter,' complained Tebulot.

'Its weight is necessary, in order to stabilise it when it fires,' Springer explained. 'At full strength, it can vaporise the walls of a fortress.'

He turned now to Susan, and said, 'Samena! Stand,' and

Susan rose to her feet to assume the identity of Samena, the finger-archer. Her plumed hat gleamed in the light of the naked bulb, and the arrowheads hooked around her briefs jangled as she turned around.

Now that her costume had materialised fully, she could see that the soft leather had been perfectly tailored to fit her snugly, and that it was elaborately decorated with semi-precious stones, opals and turquoises and jet.

Springer said, 'The design of these costumes and armour stretches back hundreds of years. They are the combination of many men's dreams, and many women's dreams, too. Parts of Tebulot's armour can be seen in the drawings of Leonardo da Vinci; some of Samena's jewelled decorations are exactly the same as decorations seen at the Kandariya Mahadeva temple at Khajuraho, in Bundelkhand, dating from one thousand AD.'

Tebulot said, 'What time is it now? Henry's late.'

'Give him the chance to leave his body,' said Springer. 'Remember that he is older than you, and much more set in his attitudes. It is not at all easy for a man of his age and his demeanour to leave his body while he sleeps. There are many chains which have to be broken first. Chains of habit, chains of doubt, chains of apprehension. The mind argues, why should I take the risk of facing the Devil, when I would much rather stay asleep, in the safety of my own bed?'

But Springer had hardly finished speaking when there was a soft noise like someone dragging the hem of a silk cape along a polished wooden floor; and Henry slid into the room through the ceiling, wearing a pair of pale blue pyjamas.

'I couldn't get to sleep,' he told them, apologetically. 'I tried and I tried, but my brain was free-wheeling so fast I thought I was going to burn out my cortex. Even after I repeated the incantation, I stayed awake. I'm sorry.'

Springer said, 'It was not your fault, my friend. Your difficulty was quite understandable. But, we should hurry now. The quicker we prepare, the longer we will have to train you. Kneel, please, Henry, and I will recite the words which will transform you into Kasyx.'

Samena touched Henry's arm. Under her plumed hat, her eyes were bright and serious. 'Henry?' she said. 'Are you all right?'

Henry shook his head. 'If you mean, am I *drunk*, the answer is no. I spent the whole evening staring at a bottle of vodka, but I didn't open it once. I remembered what you told me about your parents. Then I looked around my house and remembered what Gil had told me when we first decided to be Night Warriors. He said that I had nothing to lose, and he was right. So I thought to myself this evening, I've been alive for nearly half a century, and to have nothing to lose at the age of fifty is not much of an achievement. In fact, it's a pretty miserable thing to have to admit. So – even if I have no real duty to you two, or to that girl who died on the beach – at least I have a duty to myself.'

Springer was waiting patiently, so Henry said, 'That's all of it,' and knelt down where Springer had told him to.

Springer repeated the ancient words of the Night Warriors. He swept his hand around, and drew the golden halo over Henry's head. 'Stand, Kasyx,' he said, more quietly than he had before; and Henry stood up in the full armoured paraphernalia of the charge-keeper, the source of all righteous energy. Kasyx's armour was a dull metallic crimson, and fingers of electrical energy played repeatedly across his chest and around his shoulders, crackling fire-creatures of sheer hair-raising voltage.

Instinctively, Kasyx laid his left hand on Tebulot's right shoulder; and his right hand on Samena's left shoulder, and for a moment they stood in silence as the vast amounts of power which Kasyx had been given by the god-of-gods Ashapola coursed through their bodies. At last, the charging was complete, and the three of them saw now that they were no longer transparent, that their flesh and muscle was as real as any waking human's.

Springer said, 'I will take you first into a nightmare, so that you may see and feel and hear for yourselves what the landscape of dreams can often be like. I have scanned the sleeping minds of thousands of people in Del Mar – children and old people, blacks and whites – and I have found for you a nightmare which will challenge your abilities, but which will not be too dangerous.'

'We're going to do that *now?*' asked Samena, nervously. 'I thought we were just going to train. You know – like learning to use our weapons.' 'In the landscape of dreams,' smiled Springer, 'the only useful training is through practical experience. I can tell you anything you like. I can tell you about nightmares in which terrible monsters appear, and absolutely refuse to die, no matter what you do to them. I can tell you about nightmares in which you can be torn apart, or in which you *think* that you've been torn apart. I can tell you about tortures and spiders and drowning and fire. But I can never recreate for you in words what you would ultimately have to face in the real world of dreams.'

Springer walked around them, and showed them how to grip their hands together, so that as they passed from dream to dream, they would be inseparable.

'The night is full of dreams; it is like a huge invisible palace, of a million rooms, one room for every dream. It is not difficult to lose one of your warriors as you move from one dream to another. Sometimes, this can be perilous. Occasionally, it can be fatal. It takes a long time to trace your way through to any one particular dream, and by the time you have returned to where you left your stray warrior ... well, dreams change and many dreams are more frightful than you can possibly imagine.'

He faced them one last time, and said, 'I have asked you to take up the task of being Night Warriors because each of you has inherited something of those mystic qualities which make you a natural hunter of Devils. But, you may still choose not to take up your dream identity; you may still return to your sleeping body, even now, and never again wear this armour and never again carry these weapons. It is yours to decide. There is much terror ahead of you, and much struggle. But, if you succeed in your adventures, you will know the ecstasy of great achievement, and you will become exalted.'

Kasyx raised the visor of his helmet, and said, 'I'm going to continue, thanks. I didn't spend the whole evening staring at a bottle to back out now.'

Samena said, 'I want to go on.'

There was a pause. They all turned and looked at Tebulot. 'You have the most to lose, Tebulot,' said Springer, gently.

'Yes,' replied Tebulot. 'But also the most to gain. I'm coming.'

They stood close together and clasped hands. Only Springer stayed apart. He looked at the three of them, one by one; his eyes were frightening and remarkable, as dark as windows which looked out into infinite space. Beyond his eyes there were galaxies, and spinning star systems, and light-years of impossible distance.

'Follow me,' Springer said, simply. 'Be wary, trust nothing – for nothing will be as it seems.'

Springer began to rise into the air and to fade. For a moment, the three Night Warriors hesitated, uncertain how they were going to follow him. But then Kasyx heard the clear words inside his head, words as bright and sharp as slices of fresh-cut lemon: *Rise up, Kasyx! Use your power and rise up!*

Kasyx closed his eyes, and concentrated on rising up. His concentration was far more Intense than it needed to be; the Night Warriors rocketed up through the roof of the house and soared high into the night, hundreds of feet up above Del Mar, spinning off to the right as they did so because Samena was so much lighter than the other two.

Springer came looping up to join them. Kasyx noticed that as Springer passed through the air he seemed to leave behind him a trail of absolute darkness, which took several seconds to dissipate. The thought occurred to him for one jagged half-second that they had not yet been given any proof that Springer was actually what he or she claimed to be; that for all they knew, Ashapola could be the Lord of Darkness, instead of the Lord of Light. Quite innocently, all three of them could have been recruited to help the Devil, instead of fighting against him.

But the words of Springer cut into his mind again, this

time speaking in the lighter tones of a woman. You will always question; you will always doubt. Ashapola expects you to. Faith should never be blind, as it is in Christianity and so many other religions. Faith should come through questioning and criticism, through the proof of intellect and the proof of experience. Gods should be tested, as well as men. The moment of religious ecstasy comes when you know for certain that your God is infallible.

They hung high in the air, like four dark kites. Below them, traffic twinkled, surf gleamed, and Southern California edged closer to midnight.

Springer said, 'To enter a dream, you must first encounter the dreamer. Follow close behind me. I am going down now to that apartment block on 101. You see it? The one with the roof-garden. On the fourth floor of that apartment block, a man is sleeping. He is exhausted. He has been working hard to keep his business from bankruptcy. Two years ago, his wife divorced him because of his adultery with his secretary. He has a son, whom he sees only twice a month. He is haunted again and again by guilt and by responsibilities which are not even his.'

They sank slowly through the warm evening wind. Kasyx found that he was able to control the movements of all three of them quite easily, with only a minimal consumption of power. Together, they soared and circled, descending all the time, until at last they faded through the walls of the apartment block, and into the bedroom of the man whose dreams they were going to penetrate.

His room was in darkness. The windows were closed and the air-conditioning was set to sixty-five degrees, so that after the warmth of the night outside, it felt distinctly chilly. The man lay on his back on a crumpled and twisted sheet, wearing nothing but jockey shorts. He was dark, with a bald patch that shone white in the darkness, and a dark hairy body. By the side of the bed there was a copy of *Reader's Digest*, a bottle of Nytol sleeping tablets and a glass of mineral water.

Springer leaned over the man and touched his eyelids with his fingertips. 'He is experiencing the worst of his nightmares even now. You can see by his eye movements that he is dreaming. This is what they call REM sleep – for Rapid Eye Movement.' 'How do we get into his nightmare?' asked Tebulot, shifting the weight of his weapon.

'More important, what do we do once we get in there?' Kasyx wanted to know.

Samena said, 'Will he know that we're there – will he be able to see us in his dream?'

Springer said, 'He will see you in his nightmare as clearly as everything else that he can see. As for what you may and may not do, once you have penetrated his sleeping mind, the rules are quite simple. You may explore the dream in the same way that you can explore the waking world. If you are threatened in the dream, you may defend yourselves and fight back. There are virtually no limitations, except one, and that is that you may not and must not hurt the dreamer himself, if he happens to appear in his own dream as a separate personality. You must be very wary of this, for sometimes the dreamer will appear in his own dream as a child, or as somebody of the opposite sex, or in some kind of disguise.'

'What happens if we hurt the dreamer?' asked Tebulot.

Springer looked at him through the darkness of the

bedroom. For a moment, Springer was neither he nor she, but something quite ethereal. 'If you hurt or kill the dreamer, then the dream will collapse in on itself – with you inside it. In the early days, before the symbolism of dreams was fully understood, many inexperienced Night Warriors were lost that way. Today, of course, even untrained people like yourselves are aware that much of what appears in dreams and nightmares is metaphorical, rather than literal.'

They looked down at the sleeping man. He groaned, and turned, and whispered to himself.

'Shall we go?' asked Kasyx.

Springer nodded.

'You, Kasyx, will use your power now to create a nexus, between your dream and his. All you have to do is draw an octagon in the air, with both hands, the hands separating at the top of the octagon and joining at the bottom. Then, place your hands back to back in front of you, and slowly prize them apart.' Kasyx did as Springer instructed. Allowing a steady current of power to flow out of his hands, he described a large eight-sided figure in the darkness. His fingers crackled and danced with bright blue sparks, and as he drew the octagon it remained suspended in the middle of the room, flickering like illuminated barbed-wire.

Then, he held his arms out in front of him, thrusting his hands into the centre of the octagon, and gradually parting them. He felt extraordinary resistance, and he had to use almost double the power, just to keep his hands from being pushed back together again. As he opened them out, however, he suddenly saw what he was doing. He was tugging the substance of the waking world apart, as if it were a heavy but invisible curtain; because beyond the octagon, where his hands had drawn the molecules of reality aside, he could glimpse a grim rainy landscape of rocks and mountains, and wind-lashed trees.

'Now,' said Springer, 'you must enter. I shall not be coming with you; I am forbidden. But I shall follow you with my thoughts, and I shall advise you and instruct you whenever it is necessary. Remember – all you are doing now is familiarising yourselves with the world of nightmares. Take no risks, and use no weaponry unless you are forced to do so for your own protection.'

Kasyx and Tebulot and Samena now linked arms again, and stood in front of the glimmering octagon.

'By the will of Ashapola, enter the world of dreams,' Springer intoned. The octagon rose slowly and turned itself sideways, until it was over their heads. Then it gradually sank down towards the floor, encircling them, as if a conjuror had passed a hoop over them, to show that there were no strings, no mirrors, no tricks whatsoever.

The instant the octagon touched the floor, the screaming of the wind exploded in their ears and they were hit by a solid wall of pelting rain. Still clinging together, ducking their heads, they looked around them, trying to orient themselves. The rain drummed against their armour, and the wind blew the plumes of Samena's hat into a fury of boiling feathers. Above their heads, the sky was the colour of rusted iron, and clouds tumbled and rolled across it helplessly. The ground beneath their feet was bare brown granite, slick with rain and riven with cracks. In the distance, there were broken crags and louring mountains, with a whitish building that looked like some kind of fortress or monastery standing just to the right of them, at the head of a valley.

'What do we do?' Susan shouted, against the wind.

'Head for that building, if you ask me,' Kasyx shouted back. 'That seems to be the core of what he's dreaming about.'

They released each other's hands, but stayed as close together as they could. Slowly, trying to acclimatise themselves to walking through the uncompromising terrain of somebody else's nightmare, they made their way across the sharply sloping granite foothills, until they reached a wind-blasted promontory, from which they could look down at the wide valley which led up to the building. They could distinctly hear a bell tolling from the building's tower, a soulful, melancholy bell, which uncomfortably reminded Kasyx of Edgar Allan Poe's lines on 'iron bells – what a world of solemn thought their monody compels – for every sound that floats – from within their rusted throats – is a groan'.

Tebulot touched Kasyx's shoulder, and shouted. 'Look, down there!'

Kasyx wiped the rain away from his visor, and strained his eyes to see down into the valley. In the shadows, in the slanting sheets of rain, he could make out a slow procession of figures. They were dressed in long white robes, and hooded; ten or eleven of them, gradually climbing the valley floor. The two leading figures dragged behind them a large wooden cross, and on the cross a naked man was spreadeagled.

Kasyx held his left hand against the side of his helmet, and his vision was altered immediately to close-up. He could now see the hooded figures as clearly as if he were standing only a few feet away from them. They seemed tall, much taller than ordinary men; and no matter how narrowly Kasyx adjusted his vision, he was unable to see anything inside their hoods except absolute blackness. He thought once that he caught sight of something like a black curling lock of hair, or tentacle, but as quickly as he adjusted his focus on it, it disappeared.

Now he turned his attention to the wooden crucifix, and the man who was stretched across it. The two leading figures were dragging the crucifix with its top bumping on the ground so that the man's head was lower than his feet. He had been nailed to the cross through his forearms and through his feet, and there were diagonal marks on his body, as if he had been whipped. His eyes stared wide in agony. Every jolt along the rocky ground must have been a punishment in itself. Kasyx recognised him at once as the dreamer himself.

Samena said, 'They seem like they're heading towards that building, too.'

'They'll reach it before we do,' Tebulot commented.

'Are we supposed to save him, or something?' Samena asked. 'I mean, it seems as if Springer's put us into this dream for a reason, to see what we do.'

Kasyx shook his head. 'We're not supposed to intervene unless our own safety is threatened.'

'Sure,' argued Tebulot. 'But what are the Night Warriors for? Isn't their whole reason for existence to go into dreams and save people?'

'I don't know,' said Kasyx. 'That man down there on the cross, he's the man who's dreaming this dream. Maybe he *needs* to have dreams like this, to express his sense of guilt. Maybe if he didn't have them, he'd wind up a head-case.

Look at what's happening to him down there: he's being punished. You heard what Springer said, things in dreams aren't always what they appear to be. Maybe those hooded figure are nothing more than his feelings of guilt.'

'So meanwhile we stay here and let them drag him across those rocks? Is that it?'

'We're not supposed to interfere,' Kasyx insisted. 'Well, I still think the whole *purpose* of our being here is to interfere,' Tebulot told him.

'Let's get to the building first,' Samena suggested. 'Then we can make up our minds what we're going to do next, whether we're going to help him or not.'

'They're going to get to the building way ahead of us,' said Kasyx. 'Supposing they don't let us in?'

Tebulot lifted his heavy weapon. 'You heard what Springer said. This thing can vaporise the walls of a fortress. We can get in there, whether they want us to or not.'

Bent against the wind and the rain, they scrambled noisily down from the rocky promontory, and headed towards the building along a narrow spine of grey granite. Below them, and to their left, the procession with the crucifix was now quite close to the head of the valley, and when the wind dropped from time to time the Night Warriors could hear them chanting in Latin. The bell still tolled from the building's tower, dolorously, over and over and over again.

At last, more than two hundred and fifty yards ahead of the Night Warriors, the procession reached the outer walls of the building, and crossed an extraordinary suspension bridge to reach its high main gate. In fact, as the three of them drew closer they could see that the entire building was extraordinary. It was constructed of granite, the same granite as the mountains around it, but highly finished, so that it glistened wetly in the rain. Its walls were smooth and unscalable up to about seventy feet from its foundations, but above that height there were hundreds of openings, on dozens of different levels, and these openings were connected by external stone staircases, without railings or supports. Up and down the staircases, in a never-ending stream, climbed men and women in sackcloth robes, chained and shackled and crowned with thorns.

At the very top of the walls, there were battlements, on which more of the hooded figures came and went, and from which wet black flags bellowed and snapped in the wind.

'I told you,' said Kasyx, as the three of them crouched down behind the last protective jumble of rocks. 'This man is punishing himself. That's what this nightmare is all about. We don't have to save him at all. Look at this place. Punishment Palace.

I've seen the symptoms a hundred times. He probably likes to wear ladies' garter-belts, and have his fingers trodden on with stiletto heels.'

'I don't know,' frowned Samena. 'I think there's more to this nightmare than that. I can sense something, I don't quite know what it is.'

Kasyx said, 'Believe me, Samena, he's probably loving every minute of it.'

But Tebulot put in, 'Don't dismiss Samena out of hand, Henry – I mean, Kasyx. Just remember what Springer said, that Samena Is the most sensitive of all of us. She could be picking up something that's out of our range.'

Kasyx looked at Samena, and Samena smiled. Kasyx had to admit she looked more than becoming in that plumed hat and that tight, decorated bodice and briefs. 'All right,' he admitted, 'maybe I should stop being so much of a lecturer, and start being more of a listener.'

Samena said, 'I can't describe it to you, but I get the feeling that there's some other presence inside that building, apart from the dreamer himself. Something that's stronger than the dreamer. Something that's taken over his dream.'

Kasyx said, uneasily, 'Maybe that's why Springer brought us here. Maybe Yaomauitl's hiding in this dream.'

'He said we had to train first,' Tebulot protested. 'He wouldn't send us out against Yaomauitl, not on our very first night.'

'Well, I'm not so sure about that,' said Kasyx. 'In fact, I'm not so sure about Springer. We don't know who or what he really is, do we? And we've all allowed ourselves to be beguiled into this incredible adventure, haven't we, without checking his credentials at all.'

Tebulot held out his armoured hands. 'He can do *this*, he can practically turn us into super-heroes, and we have to check his credentials? Come on, Kasyx, why are you doubting him all of a sudden? Don't you feet fitter, don't you feel better? Don't you feel that you could do absolutely *anything* you wanted to?'

Kasyx lifted his visor. He looked at Tebulot with steady eyes, while the rain dripped persistently from the rim of his crimson helmet. 'I guess you're right. I do feel better, guess that's why I found that I was volunteering to be a Night Warrior all the way along the line, without even asking myself why. Have you realised how calmly we've accepted all this, and yet how incredible it actually is? We've been calm because we all feel that this is something we've been waiting for; this is our chance to break free.' He paused, and then he said, 'I don't think I'll ever stop doubting. It's part of my nature, and it's most of what my job's all about. But, all right, I'll accept what Springer has done for me, and I'll go along with all of this until someone shows me that I'm making a dangerous idiot out of myself. Just one thing, though: don't ever ask me to lay down my life for Springer or Ashapola, not as a one-to-one choice, because the answer will always be, forget it.'

'Nobody asked you,' said Tebulot.

'No,' Kasyx replied. 'But there's always a chance that somebody might.'

Samena touched her fingers to her forehead. 'That feeling ... it's very powerful. It's very evil, too.'

'What do you mean, evil? –' asked Kasyx.

'I mean it's frightening. It's very cold, and it's very vicious. It's like the feeling you get when you're walking along a sidewalk and you suddenly realise that you have to go close to a really mad-looking dog. I mean, you're scared, but you can't run away.'

'Well,' said Kasyx, 'the question is, what do we do about it?'

'Didn't Springer say that he was going to keep in touch?' said Tebulot. 'Maybe you should try to ask him.'

Kasyx closed his eyes, and tried to concentrate on communicating with Springer. But even after two or three minutes he could hear nothing but silence, a silence as empty as the infinite look he had last seen in Springer's eyes.

'He's not there,' said Kasyx. 'At least, he's not keeping in touch.'

'In that case, I vote we go into the building and see what's going on,' Tebulot urged. 'Come on – we may not have very much longer. This guy might wake up soon, or turn over and start dreaming about hootchie-cootchie girls.'

Kasyx lifted his head, and narrowed his eyes against the wind. 'I'm not at all sure that I'd object to that.'

Nevertheless, Kasyx laid his hands on their shoulders and gave them as much of his charge as he felt was safe. Naked electricity wriggled across his chest, and sizzled in the driving rain. Tebulot checked the glowing charge-scale, and saw that it registered one hundred per cent full. Samena unhooked an arrowhead from her waistband, a simple triangular point, and fitted it over the end of her right index finger.

'Very well, then, let's go see what we can find in the way of evil influences,' said Kasyx.

They rose up from behind the shelter of the rocks, and headed diagonally across the valley floor towards the strange suspension bridge at the front of the building. They ran quickly, keeping their heads hunched down, but that was all they could do to minimise detection. Kasyx was thankful that the rain was coming down even harder than before, in thundering sheets, though he slipped once or twice on the rocks.

They reached the bridge without being seen, at least as far as they could tell. They ran across it without hesitation, their feet slapping on wet stone. The bridge spanned a deep, artificially cut ravine, in which lay stagnant water, black with slime. The surface of the water was circle patterned with raindrops, and occasionally furrowed, as if something were swimming deep below its surface.

The Night Warriors found themselves approaching a narrow, curved gateway. Kasyx was aware of the Freudian symbolism of gateways in dreams, and noted to himself that this one was remarkably similar in shape to the female vulva, but he said nothing, and led his two companions through to a long dark corridor. At the far end of the corridor, they could see an inner courtyard, cobbled and puddly, and two or three of the hooded figures, apparently standing guard.

'What do we do now?' asked Tebulot, nervously lifting his weapon.

Kasyx said, 'We approach them, that's all. But we keep ourselves right on edge. Any hostile movements, let them have it.'

'That sounds like good basic American thinking,' commented Samena, with noticeable sharpness.

'Well, what do you suggest we do? Go right up and shake hands? As far as we can make out, those jokers crucified the man who's dreaming this dream, and for all we know they might be quite happy to do the same to us.'

Cautiously, they walked the remaining few yards along the tunnel and emerged into the rainy courtyard. Tebulot glanced up. On the walls that surrounded the courtyard, there were twenty or thirty small balconies, and on each of those balconies stood a hooded figure with a weapon that looked similar to a crossbow.

'I think this is what they call a trap,' he said, nudging Kasyx's armoured elbow.

'You're probably right,' said Kasyx. But by now they were less than ten feet away from the two hooded figures who stood in the centre of the courtyard, and the option of turning back seemed very much more dangerous than the option of going on.

Kasyx stopped and raised his hand.

'They're not Red Indians,' Tebulot protested.

'For God's sake, this is a universally recognised gesture of greeting,' Kasyx snapped back.

The hooded figures regarded the three Night Warriors from the black emptiness of their hoods without revealing their faces, without making a sound. The wind spiralled down inside the courtyard, and raised leaves and litter and ruffled the hems of their pilgrim's robes. Kasyx said loudly, 'We wish to see the dreamer. We wish to ensure that he is safe.'

Still the hooded figures said nothing. But one of them raised its sleeve, and made a beckoning gesture; and then both of them turned and began to walk away across the courtyard, towards another tunnel on the far side.

'Do we follow?' asked Kasyx.

Samena glanced up at the hooded figures with their crossbows, all around them.

'I think we ought to,' she suggested.

Tebulot nodded. 'Springer talked about practical experience, didn't he? This is obviously it.'

Kasyx said, 'Keep a lookout behind us. I don't want us to get boxed in.'

The hooded figures glided faster and faster, and disappeared into the tunnel. Kasyx touched Tebulot's shoulder and said, 'Keep that weapon of yours ready. This could be an ambush.'

They hesitated at the mouth of the tunnel, but then without any further discussion, they entered it, knowing that whatever their destiny was, it lay somewhere beyond, and that they would have to follow it regardless of their fears.

Chapter Eleven

The interior walls of the tunnel were soft and slimy, with a distinctive aroma that reminded Kasyx even more strongly of the female vagina. Whatever the dreamer's obsessions were, they were obviously sexual as well as financial. In fact, the further the three of them penetrated the dream, the more urgent the erotic atmosphere became. Somewhere deep within the building, there was a rhythmic pounding sound, more like a human heart than anything mechanical, and Kasyx was aware that the building was gradually transmogrifying into a giant body.

At the end of the tunnel, they emerged into a vast enclosed gallery, with a dark domed roof that was laced with pipework that looked like veins and arteries. Dominating the gallery was an elaborate machine constructed of wood and metal, fifty or sixty feet high, with gears and cogs and pulleys and winches, and massive black greasy pistons which churned backwards and forwards on eccentric wheels. The machinery set up a low rumbling noise as it operated, overlaid with a higher-pitched sizzling of lubricated steel sliding against lubricated steel.

'Where did those two jokers in hoods get to?' asked Tebulot, keeping his weapon raised high.

'There,' said Samena, pointing across to the other side of the gallery. On a balcony supported by spindly staircases of iron and brass, the two hooded figures watched them dispassionately.

'Where's the dreamer, that's what I want to know,' said Tebulot, looking quickly around.

Kasyx lifted his head and scrutinised the machinery. 'I see him,' he said, at last. Tebulot and Samena followed his gaze. At the very top of the machinery, there was a jointed wooden track, which rattled over rows of revolving wheels. Into this track, the dreamer's wooden cross fitted, like an automobile axle on a production line, and the dreamer was still nailed to it, as far as they could see from the floor of the gallery. Gradually, the cross and its human burden was carried along to the end of the wooden track, where it was lifted so that it was standing upright, and then carried downward on an endless toothed belt, into the very heart of the machinery.

As he was transported through the huge device by tracks and pulleys and gears, the dreamer suffered continuous punishment. The cross was passed through a tunnel of lashing leather whips, which were attached to endlessly revolving wheels. Then he was repeatedly stabbed by flailing arms that looked like hairbrushes, except that they were fitted with spikes instead of bristles.

Kasyx watched the cross descend through the framework of the machinery level by level. Then he turned to Tebulot and Samena and said, 'That's enough. This guy doesn't need saving. Not by us, anyway. Maybe a shrink would do him some good.'

'So, what do we do, split?' asked Tebulot. He was almost disappointed that the dream hadn't turned out to require a rescue mission after all.

But Samena said, 'There's still something evil here, I can feel it. It's close now. Much closer. Maybe it's not in this dream ... but it's very near.'

Kasyx said, 'My vote is that we leave it for now. Come on, we don't have any real experience yet. If Yaomauitl turns up in this dream, then what the hell are any of us going to do?'

Samena touched her fingers to her forehead and closed her eyes. She could sense the evil almost as distinctly as the heartbeat which pounded through the building. It was like an intense black coldness inside the front of her brain; the blackness of diseased skin, the coldness of death. She could almost see grotesque faces, somewhere just out of focus; faces that whispered and conferred with each other, speaking of blasphemies and tortures and cruelties beyond human imagination.

Yet – there was some curiously *alluring* quality about all this darkness, all this evil. It promised sensations of intense pleasure, of delirious self-indulgence, of nakedness and passion and danger. The voices whispered of the 'little death'; and of moments of humiliation so extreme that the pleasure-centres of the brain craved for extinction, to make the humiliation complete.

Kasyx reached out for Samena, and drew her towards him. 'What is it?' he asked her. 'Is it really strong?'

She nodded. 'I don't know whether it's good or whether it's bad. It seemed like it was evil at first ... but now I'm not so sure.'

'Maybe we should check it out,' Tebulot suggested.

Kasyx shook his head. 'Enough for one night, okay? Let's get back to Springer. I want to know why he hasn't been keeping in touch.'

They turned back towards the tunnel; but as they did so, the two hooded figures stepped out of it, and barred their way – although how they had managed to get behind the Night Warriors without their noticing, none of the three could even begin to work out. But this was a dream, after all – and anything could happen in a dream.

The Night Warriors cautiously approached the hooded figures, and then stopped. It was clear that they were not going to move out of the way.

'Do you want to stand aside?' Kasyx asked them.

One of the hooded figures raised its arm and pointed across to the opposite side of the gallery. There was another tunnel entrance there, slightly narrower, but just as dark.

You will go that way, the hooded figure commanded.

'Sorry, pal,' Kasyx replied. 'We're going back the way we came in.'

You will go where you have been told, the figure insisted.

'And if we refuse?' asked Tebulot.

The two hooded figures, already tall, began to stretch taller and taller, and the shadowy mouths of their hoods widened, until they were leaning over the Night Warriors like blind man-eating worms. They swayed as they came nearer, and Kasyx again glimpsed those writhing black tentacles where their faces should have been.

Tebulot didn't wait for any orders. He wrenched back the T-bar on his heavy machine, lifted it up to his shoulder, and fired it at the nearer of the two figures. There was a soft, sharp *zzaffff* and a bright white bolt of pure energy was swallowed up by the darkness inside the figure's hood.

For one moment, Tebulot thought that the figure had absorbed his shot without injury; but then suddenly the tall hooded cloak began to tumble and collapse. It fell to the ground as if it had been completely empty, a magical trick; but at the very last second there was a nauseating wriggling from under the robes, and something emerged, something gristly and black and tangled. Tebulot tugged back the weapon's T-bar and fired again, and another bolt of white energy scored a direct hit. There was a crackle, and a sickening odour of burned fat, and a shriek that penetrated the Night Warriors' ears like the scraping of metal on glass.

The second figure had hesitated when its companion was attacked, but now it swayed ominously over Samena, and score after score of greasy tentacles began to unroll out of the front of its hood, as if it were vomiting snakes. Samena screamed out loud, but lifted her arms, and stiffly crossed her wrists, aiming her right index finger directly at the heart of the tentacles.

She let fly with almost all the energy that Kasyx had given her – far more than she needed – but then she was inexperienced and terrified, and the creature was almost on top of her. There was an explosion of power from the tip of her finger, and the arrowhead which she had fitted earlier lanced into the creature's body, followed by a six-foot shaft of pure dazzling light.

The arrowhead tore into the creature's flesh, opening up a path for the concentrated energy to follow. The energy zapped out of sight, burying itself beneath the surface of the creature's skin, then instantly detonated. With an ear-splitting crack, pieces of unravelled tentacle were spattered in all directions. Some of them struck Kasyx's helmet, making a slapping sound like fragments of wet wash-leather.

'Come on now!' shouted Tebulot, and the three of them ran into the tunnel.

It was very dark inside the tunnel, and it seemed narrower and moister than before. Their feet slipped on the ribbed, muscular floor, and several times they had to put their hands out sideways to prevent themselves from overbalancing. All that Kasyx could see was a jumble of light and shadows, and the back of Tebulot's helmet as he struggled along in front of him.

At last they reached the end of the tunnel, and were back at the cobbled courtyard. It was still raining, a torrential downpour that filled the courtyard with a rising mist of spray. Kasyx reached out and held Tebulot's shoulder to caution him not to go any further, and then he clasped his hand over the brow of his helmet. In this way, his vision switched to infra-red, for detecting enemies by heat rather than light.

Kasyx scanned the brightly-coloured green-and-yellow courtyard that the infra-red facility displayed in front of his eyes. There was nothing anywhere near that gave off calorific energy although Kasyx was aware that because they were nothing more than monsters in a dream the hooded figures might radiate no body heat at all. In which case they could be waiting outside in the rain, ready to devour them.

'I can't detect any of those tentacle creatures out there,' he told Tebulot and Samena. 'But we ought to come out of the tunnel ready for anything. Remember those figures up on the balconies? They might try firing down at us, or stretching down and trying to grab us. So we've got to sprint across that courtyard like goddamned ostriches, you understand, and set up as much attacking fire as we can.'

Tebulot cocked his weapon, and frowned in concentration as he set it for rapid side-to-side fire. There were no instructions on any of the switches or levers, but Tebulot seemed to know intuitively how to operate it. The weapon was partly mechanical and partly imaginary; it was capable of doing whatever its carrier could think up. If Tebulot had wanted his energy bolts to fire out forwards and then U-turn and hit a target somewhere behind him, it was quite capable of carrying out his command.

Samena, who had been alertly protecting their backs as they made their way through the tunnel, fitted her finger with a multiple arrowhead which would burst apart in mid-flight and send a dozen wicked barbs hurtling in a deadly hemispherical spray.

'All right,' said Kasyx, tensely. 'Now, *go!*'

They threw themselves out into the driving rain, and they were instantly met by a flying forest of thick black arrows, fired from the balconies above their heads. The arrows zipped through the rain with such velocity that they were invisible until they struck their targets; each one set up a hair-raising screech as it flew towards them. Thirty or forty of them flying together sounded like all the banshees of hell let loose at once. And they were so powerful that they penetrated the cobbles of the courtyard floor, up to three feet in depth.

Tebulot's machine was defensive as well as offensive.

Dropping on to one knee, he lifted it up and fired a spray of energy bolts which intercepted almost all of the next shower of arrows, so that they came clattering down harmlessly. For the first time, Samena showed her speed and skill in movement, dodging and ducking between hurtling arrows to reach the middle of the courtyard, lift her stiffened arms, and let loose a multiple burst of arrowheads up at the overhanging balconies.

There were cries and screams from above them, and four empty robes came floating down through the rain, to settle wetly on the cobbles. Tebulot adjusted his weapon and fired a short but punishing burst of energy at each of them. There were searing sizzles, and eternally echoing shrieks. Only one of the tentacled creatures managed to escape him, dragging itself like a deformed, tortured octopus across the courtyard and into the shadows.

Kasyx deflected two or three arrows by raising his arm in front of his face and discharging power. With a violent snapping of static electricity, the arrows lost their atomic integrity and vanished. But the drain on Kasyx's charges was too high for him to defend himself very much longer, and he took advantage of Samena's next flurry of arrowheads to run for the tunnel which would take them out of the building.

Once in the shelter of the tunnel, he looked back. Tebulot had almost reached shelter, pausing now and again to fire off a tremendous fusillade of dazzling white energy at the hooded figures who clustered on the balconies. Samena was further away, but she was so light and agile that Kasyx felt sure she could reach the tunnel without any difficulty.

The courtyard flashed and crackled and flickered with

blinding lights. The pouring raindrops were caught by the flashes in mid-air, as if they were being picked out by strobes, so that Tebulot and Samena appeared to be fighting in a cage of silver needles. There was a strong smell of burning linen, and some indescribable odour which the tentacled creatures gave off when Tebulot hit them, like scorched snail.

More arrows screeched down into the courtyard. More robes tumbled and billowed down from the balconies. But Tebulot checked his charge-scale now and saw that it was glowing only faintly, which meant that he had used up practically all the energy which Kasyx had given him before they had entered the dream. He loosed off one final flash of energy, and then came running towards Kasyx with his head down and his arm held up to protect himself from random arrows. One arrow hurtled close and crunched deep into the cobbles next to his running foot, but he managed to make a final football-tackle leap into the tunnel, his weapon clattering down next to him.

'Power!' he said, breathlessly. 'I'm right out of power!'

Kasyx said, 'Hold on. I don't have very much left. I'm going to need quite a dose of it to get out of this dream; I don't want to use that.'

They both anxiously watched Samena, who was almost halfway across the courtyard now, skipping and weaving and dodging every one of the swarms of arrows that the hooded figures were firing at her. She made her defensive movements look like a complicated dance, her perfectly co-ordinated muscles acting with speed and power and always with grace. She was unable to see the arrows that were aimed at her, but her sensitivity was such that she could pick up the tiny surges of emotion that came from the hooded figures just as they released their crossbows – they were like tiny pellets of ice, dropped down from the balconies – and she could also sense the hustling of the air molecules in front of the speeding arrows, as they were pushed out of the way by the arrow's 300 mph flight.

Kasyx and Tebulot were mesmerised for a moment by Samena's stunning ballet; but then Kasyx realised that she was not firing her arrowheads any more. Like Tebulot, she must be out of charge.

'Samena!' he shouted. 'Samena! You have to run for it!' Samena glanced at him quickly, and her face was tight with tension. He could see her judging in that same flick of the eye the distance from where she was standing to the tunnel, trying to decide which was the best way to make her escape.

'Now, Samena!' Kasyx bellowed at her. '*Now!*' Then, however, the courtyard began to change – and change dramatically. The balconies withdrew into the walls, like closing eyelids, and the hooded figures vanished with them. The tops of the walls high above their heads began to lean towards each other and close in, until at last they joined up together to form a vaulted roof. Beneath their feet, the heartbeat-drumming grew louder, and more insistent, and all the time the courtyard grew darker and darker, until Kasyx and Tebulot could only make out the whiteness of Samena's arms and legs, as she came struggling slowly towards them.

Kasyx called, 'Samena! One last effort!' But now the floor of the courtyard began to drop, and curve, so that Samena was having to climb her way uphill to reach the entrance to the tunnel. The cobbles rumbled up into soft, fleshy folds, slippery with mucus; after only two or three steps upward, Samena lost her grip and slid back down again. Kasyx leaned forward, and looked down into the deep curved reaches of the courtyard, but Samena seemed to have dropped right out of sight.

Tebulot shouted to Kasyx, 'Give me some charge! Just a little! I have to go get her!'

Kasyx lifted the visor of his helmet. 'Supposing we don't have enough charge to get us out of this dream? What then?'

'I have to go get Samena!' Tebulot yelled. 'For Christ's sake, give me some charge!'

Kasyx hesitated, but Tebulot said fiercely, 'We're in this together, Kasyx, like the Three Musketeers. One for all and all for one. If we don't take Samena with us then we don't go. We're Night Warriors, don't you understand that? Not just three people playing a game! This is us, this is real! Night Warriors!'

With a nod of acceptance, Kasyx held out his hand. Tebulot took it and placed it directly against his breastplate. 'Now,' said Tebulot, and Kasyx allowed a subdued flow of power to leave his body and pour into the machine-carrier's energy system.

'*More*,' Tebulot urged him.

Kasyx took a sharp breath, but gave him more, even though he could feel the power shrinking out of his own body with every passing second.

Tebulot checked the charge-scale on his weapon. It glowed up to the halfway mark, and so he took Kasyx's hand away. 'That's enough. Now I'm going after her.'

All around them the walls and ceiling of the building were closing in, heavy and suffocating and dark. Kasyx touched the centre of his forehead, and a bright beam of light shone out from the rim of his visor, narrow, but spreading out 180 degrees. It lit up redness, and wetness, and ridges of soft flesh.

The courtyard had now been completely transformed. Between Kasyx and Tebulot and the place where Samena had disappeared, the tunnel was gradually tightening, closer and closer together, like a muscular sphincter. As Tebulot struggled towards it, knee-deep in scarlet flesh, it drew itself together until the aperture was only two feet across.

'It's closing!' Kasyx shouted at him.

Tebulot yanked back the T-bar of his weapon with a slippery hand. He fired a brief burst of energy at the sphincter, and momentarily it recoiled, and shuddered, as if it were alive. But then it tightened even harder, until the tunnel was completely occluded.

'One more burst!' Kasyx called.

Tebulot fired again, but even though the sphincter winced, it kept itself tightly closed.

Now Kasyx came running forward, breathing heavily, panicking at the thought that Samena might be lost. He was charge-keeper, she was his responsibility; and what would happen to her earthly body if her soul was irretrievably lost in some strange man's nightmare?

He had sufficient power left to take Tebulot and himself out of the dream, but that was not what he was going to use it for. He was going to release it all – all of it at once – and hope that it would open the tunnel sufficiently wide for them to be able to rescue Samena. After that – well, he didn't know what would happen after that. But he had understood what Tebulot had said about what it meant to be Night Warriors. Loyalty was more important than

survival. The cause was greater than those who fought for
it. They were champions; and they would not only have to
live like champions, but die like champions, too.

He had never been so excited in his life. He had never been so
frightened. He reached the tightened-up knot of muscle,
slithering up against the slippery flesh which surrounded it
so that he could lay both hands against it. Tebulot shouted,
'What are you doing? *Kasyx!*' But Kasyx was now too scared
and exhilarated to answer. He was going to discharge all of
his energy in one shattering explosion: not only the energy
which Ashapola had given him, but the stored-up energy of
his own intellect and his own personality. If he was going to
go, then by God he was going to go spectacularly. Nothing
left but the smoking soles of his shoes.

He closed his eyes, and said a prayer under his breath.
But, just as he began to summon up all of the power inside
him, he felt the muscular sphincter relax, and open.

Tebulot scrambled up beside him, and together they stared
into the widening cavern that was gradually revealed to them.
It was dark red, almost black, and so hot that steam was
issuing from the complicated intaglios of flesh. As they looked
however, it began to alter again. The dark claustrophobic
walls began to fade into night sky, with millions of winking
stars. A cool wind blew the steam away, and covered the
folds of flesh with dust and grit, and then petrified them, so
that they looked like the edges of fossilised clam-shells. It
was night, out on some unknown desert, some prehistoric
sea-bed from which the ocean had long since crept away,
leaving its plants and its molluscs to bake to death under the
sun, and to lie lonely and forgotten under the moon.

In the distance, over the irregular crusted desert surface,

knelt Samena. Kasyx touched his hand to the side of his helmet and focused on her in close-up. She was bound with ropes, her hands behind her back, and there was a slip-knot around her neck.

Behind her, the air began to waver and thicken, and gradually to take on the shape of a standing figure. Kasyx focused more sharply, and saw that it was a young boy, not much older than twelve or thirteen, dressed in grey. The boy had a curiously unformed face, as if a sculptor had not yet decided what expression he should mould into his clay, or what meaning his creation should have. One meaning, however, was unmistakable: the boy's left hand held the end of the rope which was fastened in a slip-knot around Samena's neck.

Tebulot said, 'What the hell is that?'

'A boy, of a sort,' Kasyx replied.

'Sure, but *what* sort?' asked Tebulot, peering through the night.

'Let's go find out,' Kasyx suggested, and they began to walk towards him.

The boy watched them approach with complete calmness. When they were a little less than twenty feet away, however, he lifted one hand, and at the same time tugged on the rope around Samena's neck. The implication was unequivocal, and both Kasyx and Tebulot stopped where they were.

'Samena!' called Kasyx. 'Are you all right?'

Samena stayed where she was, silent, with her head bowed. The boy said, in an oddly gruff voice, 'She is well, for the time being, but she cannot speak. She cannot hear, either, nor see.'

'What have you done to her?' Kasyx demanded.

'You looking to have your brains blown out or something?' Tebulot put in, with undisguised aggression, lifting his machine.

The boy smiled, almost wistfully. 'Those must have been great days, when the dreams of whole nations were guarded by Night Warriors, and the Devils were free; and mighty battles were fought through all the landscapes of the human imagination. Sad that I should have no more than three adversaries, and all of those three inexperienced and weak.' 'Inexperienced, perhaps,' said Kasyx. 'But not so weak.' The boy shook his head. 'I know how little power you have left, old man. You have barely enough to return to the waking world. Even if you were to unleash all of it, here and now, I would deflect it as easily as you deflected those arrows from the Monks of Shame.'

He tugged at Samena's rope, and then he added, 'You would be powerless; I would be able to snuff you out like a candle.' 'Who are you?' Kasyx asked him. 'What do you want with Samena?'

'You know me quite well,' the boy replied. 'You saw me on the beach at Del Mar. Not as I appear to you now, but like this.'

For one single photographic instant, they saw what the boy really was. They saw the face of a demon, with flaring eyes; they saw a skeletal ribcage, with a half-developed heart that beat against the translucent skin like an embryo chick throbbing in its albumen; they saw clawed hands, and curved thighbones. Then the image of the boy blotted it out, the demon was gone, and they were standing on this dream desert with the wind blowing as sorrowful and soft as a funeral lament, wondering if they had gone to hell, or if hell instead had come to them.

'You are the spawn of Yaomauitl,' said Kasyx, thickly.

'Well, well, my inexperienced friend, you are more knowledgeable than I thought,' the boy replied. 'In that case, the contest between us will be keener, and much more exciting. There is no pleasure in destroying the dull witted, or the uninformed.'

'What are you doing here?' Tebulot challenged the demon. 'What are you doing in this dream?'

'You really don't know? You have no idea who the dreamer is? Why, you are innocents! Ask your friend called Springer, that's what I say! Ask your friend called Springer whose dream this is!'

'*You* tell us,' urged Tebulot.

The boy shook his head. 'That would spoil the pleasure.'

Kasyx said, 'What are you going to do with Samena?'

'I intend to keep her for a while, until I am fully grown. A hostage, you might say, to allow me to finish my gestation, and to reach the height of my powers.'

'Then you are not as powerful as you pretend to be,' said Kasyx, slowly.

The demon's eyes burned bright in the boy's expressionless face. 'I could still destroy you, old man!'

'Perhaps you could, but you are not powerful enough to destroy all three of us. If you were, you would do it. We do nothing but stand in your way. That is why you need one of us for a hostage, to keep the other two at bay.'

'Well, you are perceptive as well as knowledgeable,' said the boy.

Kasyx said, 'I want you to let go of that rope now, and release Samena. Otherwise, I'm going to give you the energy flash to end all energy flashes.'

The boy looked up at the night sky. The stars were beginning to whirl away, as if they were dandelion plumes being blown off a creosote-painted fence. The desert was beginning to shift and tilt beneath their feet.

'You feel that?' said the boy. 'The dreamer is waking up. His deepest sleep is almost over.'

'I'm still going to burn you,' said Kasyx, and took two or three steps forward.

But it was Tebulot who said, 'No, Kasyx. Not now.' Kasyx turned. 'Wasn't it you who said that we were the Three Musketeers? If one goes, we all go?'

'That's exactly why you can't use your energy flash now,' Tebulot told him. 'If he deflects it, which he says he can – he'll kill you and he'll probably manage to kill me. But what's he going to do with Samena?'

Kasyx slowly lifted the clear visor of his helmet, and turned back for a moment to look at Samena and the demonic boy. Tebulot said, 'It's too risky. It's too unpredictable.' 'But he has her as his hostage!' Kasyx exploded. 'I know ... but as long as he keeps her as his hostage, she's safe. We can always try to get her back tomorrow night, in another dream. Come on, Kasyx, it's too dangerous. You can see that it's too dangerous. Back off. You just can't tell what's going to happen.' Kasyx slowly stepped back. 'This is unlike you, Tebulot,' he said.

Tebulot didn't look at him. 'Maybe it is,' he replied, quietly. 'But before, I thought that Samena was dead. Now,

I can see she's alive; and as long as she's alive, she has a chance.'

Kasyx nodded. He understood. The passions of the young were often wildly uneven, but they were strong; and he admired strength, even in the pursuit of impossibilities. He had never had very much strength himself, and he had never tried to pursue the impossible. Not before tonight, anyway.

Kasyx said, clearly, 'We are forced to leave you here, Samena. For your own safety, as well as ours, we are going to have to go back to the waking world without you. But I make you this promise, and I make this same promise to all of the worlds both dreaming and waking, and all of the inhabitants of those worlds. I will come back, and Tebulot will be standing by my side, and we shall free you from Yaomauitl's bastard offspring, *in the dark and holy name of the Night Warriors!*'

The boy lightly applauded, patting the fingers of his right hand into the palm of his left, which was the hand in which he held the rope. 'Believe me, she didn't hear a word of that, my poor old man. But a fine speech, all the same.'

Then, still smiling, he folded his hands against his chest, and both he and Samena immediately began to recede into the middle distance. They shrank, faster and faster and faster, until they reached the desert's far horizon, and were gone.

Kasyx watched the horizon for a long time, and then turned back to Tebulot. 'I've lost her,' he said, and he was desolate.

Tebulot said, 'Not you, Kasyx. Us. *We've* lost her. But

we're darn well going to get her back. You can promise yourself that.'

The floor of the desert began to ripple and waver, like the ocean. 'It's time we left,' said Kasyx. 'I just hope to God that Devil does nothing to harm her.'

'I don't think it will,' said Tebulot. 'Not until it's fully grown, and not while you and I are still around. If you ask me, it was a whole lot more worried about us than it tried to make out.'

Kasyx formed the octagon in the air, using his penultimate reserves of power. The octagon hung in the air like an eidetic image, and then raised itself over their heads, and encircled them. As it touched the ground, the desert vanished, the sky vanished, and they were back in the dreamer's bedroom. The dreamer himself had tossed and turned so that he was sleeping on his left side now, his mouth open, his eyelids flickering in the last vivid dreams of the night. Outside his window, the sky was beginning to grow pale.

'Let's go, before he wakes up,' said Tebulot.

'No,' Kasyx replied. 'First of all, we're going to find out who he is.'

'But he's going to wake up in a minute. Supposing he finds us here?'

'Then we can vanish,' said Kasyx, impatiently. He walked across to the dreamer's closet, opened it up, and began to rummage through his clothes.

'Nothing here, no name-tags,' he said, closing the closet doors, and moving across to the bureau. He opened one drawer after another, lifting up socks, shorts, and tee-shirts. On the bed, the dreamer began to snuffle and snore, and tug at his pillow.

'Hurry up, Kasyx, for God's sake,' Tebulot urged him.

'I don't see you helping,' Kasyx retorted. He opened the topmost drawer of the bureau and found what he wanted. 'Eureka! Here we are, wallet, ID card, Social Security card, credit cards, everything.'

He lifted one of the ID cards out of the wallet and peered at it. Tebulot could see his lips moving as he read out the words on it. Then, very slowly, he tucked it back into its plastic holder, folded up the wallet, and returned it to the drawer. When he looked across at Tebulot, his face was very serious.

'Who is he?' asked Tebulot.

'His name's Lemuel F Shapiro, and that card identifies him as a senior medical examiner for the San Diego County coroner's office.'

'What?' Tebulot whispered. 'I thought that Springer said he was a businessman, a bankrupt –'

'That's what Springer said, sure. But Springer was spinning us a yarn, wasn't he? And it makes me wonder just how many other yarns he's been spinning us. You see what he did, don't you? He guided us into the dream of one of the few people who were likely to have nightmares about that embryo-devil they dug up from the beach today. He knew that we were bound to come up against it sooner or later, and he didn't give a damn what happened to us. He didn't warn us; he didn't give us enough power to fight back.'

Lemuel F Shapiro opened one eye, and lay on his bed listening, like a man who can't be quite sure if he can hear voices. Kasyx immediately beckoned to Tebulot to clasp his hand. Together the two of them rose slowly through the wall, their molecular structure disassembling to let them through, and then sailed almost invisibly over the dawn streets of Del Mar. The sky was the colour of iced tea. The ocean splashed listlessly against the shore, its surface wrinkled like the skin of a very old woman.

Kasyx and Tebulot descended, scarcely stirring the morning air as they vanished through the tiled roof of Springer's house on Camino del Mar, through the ceiling of the upstairs room, and materialised side by side, their arms upraised.

There was no sign of Springer. They looked all through the house, vanishing through ceilings and walls and doors, and reappearing in every room. The house was quite empty. A thin film of undisturbed dust lay everywhere, as if to give them proof that nobody human had passed that way.

'We'd better get back to our beds,' said Kasyx. 'But – as soon as you can – I want you to go up to Susan's place, and check out what's happening to her body. If there's any problem at all, call me. They may think she's gone into some kind of coma, if she doesn't wake up. I just don't want them to think that she's dead, and try to cremate her or something stupid. You heard what Springer said – she won't be in any danger unless they destroy her physical body.'

'Can we believe anything that Springer said?' asked Tebulot, taking off his helmet and wearily running his hand through his hair.

'I don't know,' said Kasyx. 'But I sure want to ask him some questions. Now, you won't forget to call me about Susan, will you? In fact – call me anyway.'

Tebulot raised one hand until it was level with his eyes, the back of it facing towards Kasyx. Although Kasyx had never seen such a gesture before, he knew what it was. The farewell salute of the Night Warriors; the salute that is always given as day breaks and the adventures of the night come to an end. It means, may you be taken safely through the hours of the sun, to preserve you and keep you for the hours of the moon.

Kasyx made the same gesture, and then the two Night Warriors rose and faded through the roof of the house, wheeling over it for a moment, and then each returning to his own bed. Kasyx sank into his physical body with both relief and regret, just as his alarm-clock began to bleep. He reached out with an unexpectedly heavy and clumsy hand, and switched it off.

Chapter Twelve

Henry sat up in bed, licking his lips because they were dry. The sun fell in zig-zag patterns across the rumpled comforter, and on to the framed print of *Fragrance of Love* by Christine Nasser. He washed his face all over with his hands, surprised at how thick and coarse his skin felt, as if it were a latex mask of himself that he was wearing over his real face.

He went to the bathroom and stared at himself in the mirror. He was still the same Henry from yesterday evening, the same man who had sat staring at a bottle of vodka and defying himself not to pick it up and turn the screw cap and give himself all the courage and confidence that lay distilled within it. But during the night, he had found a different courage and a different confidence. During the night he had penetrated the nightmares of Lemuel F Shapiro, and fought against the worst that his imagination could offer. During the night he had faced the Devil.

He showered, soaping himself slowly and evenly. Then, wrapped in a towel, he walked through to the kitchen to make himself some coffee. Just as he was spooning it into the filter paper, the door buzzer went, like a disconcerted wasp. He went to the door and called out, 'Who is it?'

'Lieutenant Ortega. Do you mind if I come in?'

Henry drew back the security chain and unlocked the door. Lieutenant Ortega looked more summery today, in a pale blue seersucker coat and a dark blue pair of permanent-press pants. He wore mirror-lensed sunglasses, and a folded handkerchief in his breast pocket, both of which were tell-tale signs of his age.

'I was passing close by, on my way to headquarters. I thought I would drop by to see how you were.'

'Oh, yes?' asked Henry, a little suspiciously. He let Salvador pass by him, Into the living-room, and closed the front door. 'You'll have to excuse the way I'm dressed.'

Salvador's eyes darted around the room, as if he were checking for clues that would tell him how Henry had spent yesterday evening. Henry said, 'I'm making some coffee. Do you want to join me?'

'Sure, that would be nice.'

Henry went back to his bedroom, and dressed quickly in a short-sleeved shirt and banana-yellow slacks. He came back into the living-room, combing his hair. 'Did the coroner get the chance to look at that creature you dug out of the beach yesterday?' he asked.

'They're starting on tests this morning, so I understand.'

'Do they have any idea what it is?'

Salvador lifted his head slightly. 'Why did you ask it like that?'

'Why did I ask it like what?'

'You asked me, do they have any idea what it is, as though you yourself *knew*.'

Henry pulled a face. 'Did I? I didn't mean to.'

'There was an intonation in your voice,' Salvador persisted.

Henry paused by the kitchen door. He said nothing. But Salvador sat where he could watch him as he made the coffee, his legs crossed, and Henry could tell by the expression on his face that he was still expecting an answer.

Henry brought the coffee in, and sat down opposite the detective.

'Whatever it was, it looked as if it grew out of one of those eels,' Henry said, trying to sound conversational.

Salvador nodded. 'John Belli is quite convinced of that, too. The eel had obviously secreted itself in the sand, down where it was damp, and then sloughed its skin. Of course, John Belli's only problem is to find out what kind of a creature goes through such a life-cycle. He is beginning to wonder if the eels found their way into the body of the girl not as predators, attacking her flesh from the outside, but from inside, as growing elvers. Children, as it were, who had an insatiable appetite for their mother.'

Henry said, 'That's impossible. A woman can't be impregnated with eels.'

'Nevertheless, there are indications on the girl's remains that she was devoured from the inside of her abdomen outwards, rather than the other way round. The pattern of the teeth-marks, for instance, and – if your stomach can bear it at this time of the morning – the amount of waste material which the eels excreted *within* the abdominal cavity rather than outside it.'

'Why are you telling me this?' asked Henry.

Salvador looked at him steadily. 'I am telling you this because your interest in what has happened here has been unusual. I keep asking myself, why does Professor Watkins wish to come down to the beach and inspect the evidence for himself? What does Professor Watkins know about these creatures that he is declining to share with his friendly neighbourhood detective?'

'I used to be married to an oceanologist, that's all,' said Henry. 'I guess I have a taste for the aquatic.'

Salvador put down his coffee cup. 'I am not a fool, Henry. I want to know why you and those two young friends of yours are showing such a keen interest in following this investigation.'

Henry tugged at the wet hair at the back of his neck. 'This creature ... what are you going to do with it once you've finished examining it?'

'As I told you, it will be taken to the Scripps laboratories for full biological tests.'

'Are you going to kill it?'

Salvador's eyes flickered. 'How do you know that it is still alive?'

'I just assumed. You didn't tell me that it was dead.'

'You would like to see it dead, though?'

Henry said nothing. Salvador leaned forward, and repeated, 'You would like to see it dead. On the beach, you begged me to destroy it. Destroy it, destroy it, that's what you said. It's the spawn of the Devil. Now, don't you think you owe me some kind of an explanation for that? The spawn of the Devil?'

Henry said, 'I was ... rather the worse for wear. You know, more vodka martinis than was good for me. I was just – well, letting my imagination run away with me.'

Salvador very slowly shook his head from side to side. Henry noticed how neatly clipped his fingernails were. 'I don't think you were drunk, Henry,' said Salvador. 'And

I certainly don't think that Ms Sczaniecka was drunk. Yet she said the same thing. Destroy it. It's the spawn of the Devil. Now, what did you both mean by that?'

'Well, spawn of the Devil, that's a figure of speech. Just like calling somebody an s. o. b. I guess we both felt that what that creature had done to that poor dead girl on the beach – well, you know. I guess we both felt disgusted. We wanted to see it destroyed, the same way that anybody would want to see a mad dog destroyed, if it killed a child.'

Salvador leaned back on the sofa and laced his hands behind his head. 'Really, Henry, this is very weak. You are the kind of man who always says what he means. If you say spawn of the Devil, you mean spawn of the Devil. What I want from you now is some kind of a clear explanation of what that means. You said it loud. You *shouted it*. Why won't you talk about it now?'

'If I told you, Salvador, you wouldn't believe me.'

'You can always try me.'

Henry stood up, and went across to the window. He drew back the curtains and stood staring at the ocean. It was glittering again now; it had lost the ageing wrinkles that it had revealed at dawn.

Henry said, 'There's a legend about the Devil. It goes back hundreds of years. Apparently, if the Devil wants to reproduce, it appears to young women in the night and impregnates them. The Devil's sperm grow like eels. They eat the mother, and then they escape into the outside world, where they find themselves a burrow or a hidey-hole, and grow.' 'And you believe that what we have discovered on the beach is a Devil ... a growing Devil?'

Henry didn't answer, but kept on staring at the sea.

'Who told you this legend?' asked Salvador.

'I looked it up,' Henry told him. 'I was interested in finding out something about those eels, that's all.'

'And you believe it?' Salvador repeated.

'I didn't say that I did, and I didn't say that I didn't. So far, though, it's the only independent explanation that I've come across that fits all the circumstantial facts.'

'But Devils ...?' Salvador smiled, incredulously.

'What else?' asked Henry. 'Only Mr Belli and the people at Scripps can tell us any different.'

Salvador stood up, and brushed his pants with his hand. 'Well,' he said. 'It seems that you have given me something to think about, if nothing else. Do you have the reference to the Devil here, so that I could look at it?'

'I'm sorry, it was in a library book at the university,' Henry lied.

'Perhaps you could give me the title.'

Henry came over and patted Salvador in a friendly, paternal manner on the shoulder. 'It escapes me for the moment. But I'll check it today, and have somebody call you.'

'Better still, perhaps the university could photocopy the reference for me,' Salvador suggested.

'Dollar-fifty a copy,' said Henry, opening the front door for him.

'I think the police department budget can stretch to that.'

Salvador hesitated in the doorway. Then he said, 'We have managed to identify the girl, you know.'

'Oh, yes?'

'Her name was Sylvia Stoner. She was twenty-two, and a photographic model. She came from Houston, Texas.'

'Do you have any idea what she was doing in Southern California?'

'Oh, yes. She was on vacation, visiting friends in San Diego.' Salvador took out his spring-bound notebook, and wetted the tip of his finger, so that he could flick quickly through the pages. 'She stayed with them for a couple of months, and then disappeared. They didn't alert the police because they thought she'd simply gone freewheeling around for a day or two. According to them, she was something of a fun girl.'

'It was no fun, the way she ended up,' said Henry. As Salvador lowered his notebook, he caught a glimpse of the name Esbjerg, underlined twice, and part of an address that started with the name Market. Salvador flipped his notebook shut so that Henry couldn't read any more.

'Are you releasing all of this to the media?' Henry asked.

'Not so far. Not until we know what that creature actually is. If we go public on what we know so far, we're going to look like the loony tunes department. We had enough sardonic laughter over that Ramirez business last month.'

'Oh, I remember,' smiled Henry. 'The bordello bust.'

'Don't remind me,' said Salvador. Then, with a brief wave of his hand, he walked off down the path. Henry closed the door, and went immediately over to the bookcase, to take down his San Diego telephone directory. He took it into the kitchen with him while he filtered some fresh coffee. His finger ran up scores of Espinosas and Esmeraldas, until at the top of the page it peaked in Esbjerg, K, 603 Market St. There were two other Esbjergs, but one was out on 44th St by the Holy Cross Cemetery, and the other was on Gamma at 39th.

He picked up his telephone and dialled Gil Miller's number, at the Solana Mini-Market.

Gil had arrived back in his body this morning to find his mother worriedly shaking him, and saying, 'Gil? Gil? Are you all right?'

He opened his eyes, and blinked, and yawned. 'Sure, sure I'm all right. What's the matter?'

'I've been calling you for ages. Your father wants you to help him unload the van. I thought you were sick or something.'

Gil sat up. He had a tight headache, unlike any other headache he had experienced before. It felt as if somebody was gripping his head in their hands and squeezing it. He frowned at his watch, and saw that it had stopped.

'What time is it?' he asked his mother, as she tugged back the curtains.

'A quarter after six. I'll make you some breakfast while you help your father.'

Gil drew back his sheets and stood up. He had a small but brightly lit bedroom, with a large window facing south and a much smaller window facing east. The walls were painted pale yellow, and there was a large cork-faced notice board running the length of the bed, with school pennants and pictures of Lamborghinis and Maseratis and postcards from friends, as well as a poster of Karen Velez, *Playboy's* Playmate 1984.

Mrs. Miller went downstairs, while Gil dressed in a clean pair of shorts, yesterday's sawn-off denims, and a brown-and-orange Padres tee-shirt. Walking out through the kitchen, he poured himself a large glass of Minute Maid grapefruit juice, and drank it in three long gulps.

Phil Miller was in the back yard, stacking vegetables. 'You sleep good?' he asked Gil. 'There's ten boxes of lettuce to come out next.'

Gil climbed up into the back of the van, and began shifting boxes. He kept thinking about the nightmare from which he had just returned, and about Susan, who was still trapped in that nightmare somehow. In the light of the morning, in the back of his father's van, it all seemed so far away, and so bizarre, that he could have quite easily convinced himself that it hadn't happened at all.

'You're quiet,' said his father, after a while.

'Something on my mind, that's all,' he replied, passing down a boxful of radishes.

Phil Miller looked at his son narrowly. 'Anything a father ought to know about?'

Gil shook his head. How could he possibly explain to his father that only a couple of hours ago he had been Tebulot, the machine-carrier, and that he had been killing creatures in a torrential rainstorm, in a castle that didn't exist? How could he tell him that he was worried about a girl whose dreaming personality had been taken hostage by an embryo Devil? His father's imagination was capable of encompassing price changes and new grocery products and baseball scores, and occasionally a random episode of *V*; but that was about as weird as it went.

'You're not sick?' his father asked him.

'No, no. I'm fine. Listen – do you need me in the store today?'

'I was hoping you might help out with the deli counter.'

'If I got Lisa to do it?'

'Then, sure. If you get Lisa to do it.'

Lisa Dalwick was a school friend of Gil's, whose father was one of the most successful of the local realtors. Lisa's father didn't particularly approve of her mixing with Gil; but Lisa thought that the sun shone out of Gil's every available aperture, and so there wasn't a lot that Dalwick *pere* could do about it. Gil drove around to Lisa's house after breakfast and promised her a whole afternoon's swimming together if she helped out at the market. Lisa was okay. She was cute and petite and her figure turned heads, but right now her mouth was crowded with more braces than the Coronado Bay Bridge.

Once the problem of the deli counter had been settled, Gil drove up to Del Mar Heights, and parked outside Susan's house. He jogged up the steeply angled driveway, and rang the doorbell, still jiggling from foot to foot.

After a long wait, Susan's grandfather came to the door. 'Is Susan there?' asked Gil.

The old man shook his head. He was carrying a copy of the *National Enquirer* in one hand, folded over. 'She's in hospital,' he said. 'They took her away about an hour ago.'

Gil felt a sensation of dread slide right through him, as if he had swallowed a mouthful of mercury. 'Hospital?' he asked. 'What, is she sick or something?'

'They don't know,' the old man told him. 'They can't work it out at all. She just wouldn't wake up this morning, that's all. She's breathing all right. Her blood pressure and all the-rest of it, they're okay. But it's just like she went into some kind of a coma, when she was asleep.'

'God, that's terrible,' said Gil, thinking to himself, if only this poor old man knew just *how* terrible.

'They, er, took her to the Soledad Park Clinic,' said Susan's grandfather. He took off his spectacles and stared at Gil with bleary, widely cast eyes. 'They said that any friends of hers would be welcome to visit. You know – like a familiar voice might snap her out of her coma.'

'Sure,' said Gil. He touched the old man's arm. 'I'll call up, you know, and see what time visiting hours are. I'm real sorry this has happened. Can I keep in touch? You know, call you now and again, to see how she is?'

Susan's grandfather nodded. 'You're welcome to. Do I know your name?'

'Gil,' said Gil. 'Gil Miller.' He was almost tempted to say Tebulot.

It was nearly eleven o'clock by the time he reached Henry's cottage and buzzed at the door. Henry opened the door with relief when he knew it was him. 'I've been trying to call you. Your mother said you were out.' 'I went up to Susan's place.' 'And?'

Gil lifted both hands in resignation. 'She's in hospital already. Her grandparents couldn't wake her up this morning so they called a doctor. She's okay, as far as I can make out. She's still alive, and all her vital signs are normal. But she's – what do you call it? – comatose. Her personality hasn't come back yet, which means that Devil's still keeping her hostage.'

Henry didn't say anything for a while. Then he slowly nodded, and sat down, and said to Gil in the bleakest of voices, 'All we can do is hope that it keeps her hostage until nightfall.'

'What I want to know is, where is it keeping her?' said Gil. 'It took her out of that desert dream, but where did it go from there?' 'Into another dream, maybe,' Henry suggested.

'There's always somebody asleep, somewhere, even during the day. Shift-workers, nightclub staff, prostitutes.'

'Another question is, how to find what dream she's in, even when it does get dark?' Gil asked him.

Henry said, 'I don't know. But there must be a way. I mean, surely the original Night Warriors must have had some system for detecting where the Devils were. After all, how many millions of dreams do you think there are, just in a single night? It would take you a lifetime to search through them all, even if you were sensitive, the way Susan is.'

'I'm glad you said is, and not was,' Gil remarked.

'We very much need to talk to Springer, don't we?' said Henry. 'I vote we go to the house to see if he's there. But there's something else I want to follow up, too. Lieutenant Ortega was here this morning, poking and prying as usual; but this time I think that I got more out of him than he got out of me. He's found out who the girl was, the girl we discovered on the beach. And I've found out where her friends live, down in San Diego. When we've been to talk to Springer, maybe you could drive us down there. I have a feeling we may be able to get a little more out of them than the police obviously did. After all, you and I know what this business is really all about, don't we?'

'Speak for yourself,' said Gil, unhappily. 'I think I'm about as "oh-fay" with what's going down here as a blindfolded gopher down a six-foot hole.'

Henry went across to his desk, took his wallet out of the top drawer, and counted the money in it. Then he pushed it into his back pants pocket. 'I feet agonised about Susan,' he said. 'I feel like I mismanaged the whole thing. We should never have gone into that building to begin with.'

'You didn't mismanage anything,' said Gil. 'For starters, you're not in charge. Just because you're older, and just because you're a professor, you feel you're responsible for everything we do. But this is different. Whatever we decide, we decide together; and that makes us all responsible for what happened, including Susan herself.' 'Well, I guess you're right,' Henry told him. 'But it doesn't make me feel very much better.'

They drove in Gil's Mustang down to Camino del Mar. They parked across the street from Springer's house, and went across to knock at the door. They waited and waited, and knocked again, but there was no reply. The door, when they tried the handle, was firmly locked. Traffic passed them noisily. Above their heads, two hot-air balloons sailed silently north-eastwards.

Gil said, 'Looks like Springer's left us out on our own.'

'Maybe that was his whole plan, right from the beginning,' suggested Henry. 'Not to train us at all, but to throw us in at the deep end. Sink or swim.'

They left the house, and headed across to 1-5 so that they could drive south to San Diego. As usual, the interstate was teeming with traffic.

Gil said, as they passed by the Mission Bay exits, 'Aren't you drinking any more?'

Henry shrugged. 'I haven't made any conscious decisions about it. But, no, I haven't had a drink.'

'You should stick it out,' Gil told him. 'I like you better when you're sober.'

'I think I'm dull when I'm sober,' Henry replied. 'God knows how I'm going to lecture to my philosophy classes without the jolly old verbal lubricant. Do you know what sheer unadulterated torture it is, having to explain Straw-son's *Individuals* and the shortcomings of linguistic philosophy to two dozen dozey twenty-year-olds? Even when you're smashed?'

'What *are* the shortcomings of linguistic philosophy?' Gil asked, overtaking a huge tractor-trailer from Toys R Us.

'Well, the main criticisms are that it falls to address the serious and traditional problems of mainstream philosophy,' said Henry. 'In fact, some of the questions it attempts to answer are not just trivial but completely factitious.'

He stopped, and stared at Gil, with the slipstream blowing his hair. 'You don't want to know all this, do you?' Gil smiled, and shook his head. 'I just love to hear people sound off about their favourite subject, even when I don't understand it. You should hear my dad talking about retail price maintenance and bar codes. You wouldn't understand that any more than I can understand philosophy. But he sure gets complicated, and mad.'

Henry smiled. 'You get on well with your parents?'

'Sure. I'm not going to run a market, though, when I leave school.'

'After what we've been through already, I don't think any of our lives is going to be the same again,' said Henry. 'You can't blast nightmare monks by night, and sell Danishes by day.'

They left the freeway at the Tecolote Road exit, and drove into San Diego on the Pacific Highway. The streets were hot and dusty and run down. A black man in a grubby Hawaiian shirt was standing by the side of the road, hopelessly holding out his thumb for a ride. Henry said, 'Given all the sociological factors, the proportion of blacks to whites, the local history of crime, political attitudes, etcetera, I wonder what the mathematical probability of that poor fellow being offered a ride actually is?'

'Henry,' said Gil, 'You've got a strange mind.'

They drove along the harbour front, passing the tuna docks and the *Star of India* sailing ship. They took a left just before they reached Seaport Village, turning into Market Street. The 600 block was right on the corner of Kettner. Number 603 was a narrow, flaking building with a second hand auto-parts store at street level; a decaying remnant of the old San Diego. Gil U-turned his Mustang and parked outside.

Inside the auto-parts store it smelled of grease and exhaust and sweat. A thin young man with spiky blond hair sat behind the counter wearing greasy jeans and a greasy tee-shirt, listening to Bruce Springsteen on the radio and reading Aquaman. He was surrounded, like an Arabian thief, by all of his riches: differentials and steering-linkages and engine-blocks. Steering wheels and mufflers hung from the ceiling, and a smeary glass cabinet was crowded with side-mirrors and decorative hubcaps.

'Help you gentlemen?' the young man asked, tossing his comic-book on to the counter.

'I hope so,' said Henry. 'We're looking for somebody by the name of Esbjerg.'

'Tommi or Ericka?' the young man wanted to know.

'Either. Both. We're friends of Sylvia's.'

'Ah ...' The young man nodded. 'Requiescat in par-chay.'

'Yes,' said Henry. 'We were pretty cut up about it, too.' He looked around the store, and the young man followed his gaze with thinly concealed interest.

'That your Mustang out there?' he asked. 'I got an almost-new set of four anthracite steel low-profile wheels, make your Mustang look like a million dollars. Hold the pavement better, too. Grip like glue.'

Henry shook his head. 'I just wanted to talk to the Esbjergs, that's all.'

'Well, they're not here,' the young man said. 'They took off last night, after the cops came around. They took their camping gear, everything. They didn't say where they were going or when they'd be back. My guess is Yosemite, or maybe even Mazama, up at Crater Lake.'

'Oh, that's too bad,' said Henry. 'I was hoping to talk to them about Sylvia.'

'What about Sylvia?'

'Well – we hadn't seen her for quite a while. The cops won't tell us anything. We were wondering exactly what happened. She went off on vacation, and the next thing we knew she was dead.'

The young man sniffed, and arched his backside up off the moulded chair, so that he could chivvy two sticks of Juicy Fruit out of his back pants pocket. He unwrapped them, tossing the wrappers over his shoulder, and folded the sticks into his mouth.

Henry said, 'Was she here the day before she died?' The young man shook his head, with his mouth full. 'Can you tell us where she was?' Henry persisted.

The young man nodded. But then he said, 'I can, for sure. But I ain't about to.'

'Why not? We were friends of hers.'

'Oh yeah? From where?'

'From Houston.'

'From Houston, huh? Then of course you'd know what high school she went to, in Houston? And of course you'd know what street she lived on, and what her daddy did for a living?'

Henry was silent. The young man laughed, and chewed noisily, and said, 'I knew you for what you were, the moment you walked in here.'

'We're not police, if that's what you think. We're not private investigators, either. But we do have an interest in finding out what happened to her. You see – we have reason to think that a friend of ours is being threatened by the same person who was responsible for killing Sylvia.'

The young man sat and chewed thoughtfully. Then he said, 'How much do you think those wheels'd be worth? You know, current market value?'

Henry was no fool. 'How about a hundred?' he suggested.

The young man shook his head. 'They're worth two hundred and fifty, absolute minimum.'

'Two hundred,' Henry countered.

'Two hundred fifty.'

Henry reached into his wallet, and counted out one $100, two $50s three $10s, and a $1. He made up the difference with a handful of quarters and dimes. The young man scooped the money across the counter, and arranged it into neat piles, pressing the creases out of the bills with the side of his hand.

'Sylvia came here about three months ago, from Houston. She said she'd been having some kind of a long-running argument with her parents about going to school and snorting coke and stuff like that. Tommi and Ericka were always easy going, so they asked her to stay, and in any case Tommi had some kind of a mild thing going for Sylvia, you know, she was a pretty good-looking chick.'

'We know what she looked like,' put in Gil.

The young man paused for a moment as if interruptions annoyed him. But then he went on, counting up the loose change as he did so and arranging it into piles of $1 value. 'Anyway, soon after she got here Sylvia met some guy at one of those rock shows they hold up at the Planetarium; and the two of them – Sylvia and this guy – they both went to Mexico for the weekend. I don't know what happened to her in Mexico, because she wouldn't say, but I never saw the guy again that she went with, and she was kind of strange afterwards, like somebody who's had some kind of what do you call it, some kind of religious renovation.'

'Revelation,' said Henry.

'That's right, revelation.'

Henry said, 'Is that all? She went to Mexico for the weekend, and came back strange?'

'That's not exactly two hundred fifty bucks' worth,' said Gil, in a tone far more threatening than he had ever heard himself use before.

The young man glanced up shiftily, and then said, 'All I know about Mexico was that she went as far as a place called San Hipolito, you know? And apparently what happened was she met some other guy, apart from the guy she went with, and I don't know, there was some kind of an argument. Sylvia was never too clear about it. She was pretty doped up most of the time, you could never say when she was telling the truth and when she was fantasising. She used to tell all kinds of stories, how her father secretly bought himself a ride on one of the space-shuttle missions, that kind of stuff.'

Henry said, 'Is that all you know? Listen, I need everything, absolutely everything – even if it sounded like a fantasy.'

The young man shrugged. 'She stayed here for, what, a couple of months, but she kept talking about going back to Mexico. She said she had terrible nightmares all the time that she was pregnant. She kept having stomach cramps, but when Ericka told her to go to the doctor, she wouldn't, on account of being so high all the time. She was afraid the doctor would take her off the stuff.'

'Did she ever go back to Mexico?' asked Gil.

The young man said, 'Not as far as I know. But she lit out of here maybe two or three days before they found her dead, and she could have been anywhere during those two or three days. Mexico, L.A., who knows? She was always going places just on impulse.'

'What about the police?' asked Henry. 'Did you tell the police about any of this? About Sylvia going to Mexico, and having those nightmares?'

'No,' the young man told him. 'I just said that she stayed here, that's all. I don't tell the people nothing, not for free, anyway. I've got a living to make.'

'Sure you do,' said Henry. 'It's a pity you don't take Visa. I'd have bought those wheels, just for the hell of it.'

They left the auto-parts store and climbed back into Gil's Mustang.

'What do you think?' Gil asked Henry. 'It sounds to me like Sylvia could have gotten pregnant with those eels when she was down in Mexico.'

'My feelings exactly,' Henry agreed. He checked his watch. 'It's just after twelve now. Provided there isn't too much of a hold-up at the border, we could make it to San

Hipolito and back in maybe five hours. It's only seventy miles south-east of Tijuana, just past Ojos Negros.'

Gil said, 'I want to make sure that we get back in time to go looking for Susan tonight.'

'I don't think it matters where we are, Gil; our dream personalities can travel a whole lot faster than our waking bodies. Even if we get stuck in Tijuana tonight, we can still make it to Springer's house. And when we're flying, we don't need to go through border control.'

'Okay,' said Gil. 'Let's get back home. I have to tell my parents that I'm going to be late. Then we'll pick up everything we need, passports and stuff, and go straight through to Mexico.'

He started up the engine and steered the Mustang back towards the Pacific Highway and 1-5. It occurred to Henry as he sat in the passenger-seat, watching the dry summer hills flash past, that he had never worked so well with anybody in his life as he did with Gil, and as he had with Susan. The thirty-year disparity in their ages made no difference. They worked as one person, their minds and their actions interlocking, so that there were scarcely any wasted words.

All those years of teaching philosophy had given him such a narrow and distorted view of how young people thought and behaved; and he had never seen such a practical demonstration of how alert and wide ranging their thinking processes could be. Up until now, the only time he had been in contact with anyone under forty was when they were struggling to understand Heidegger and Kierkegaard. Faced with less speculative problems, however, they were quick and creative and instantly decisive.

'I should have had children, you know,' he told Gil,

as they sped over the bridge which took them across the Inland Freeway.

'Oh, really?' asked Gil, glancing behind him. 'What makes you say that?'

'Encroaching old age, I guess,' Henry replied.

Gil said, 'You're not old at night, are you?'

'Old? If I have to go through many more nights like last night, I'll wind up dead, not old.'

Gil gripped his shoulder for a moment. 'You're Kasyx, the charge-keeper, and don't you forget it.'

'Could I ever?' asked Henry.

Chapter Thirteen

'We have suffered many earthquakes here this year,' the priest told them, without expression. His English vocabulary was perfect; but he had not had enough conversational practice to be able to emphasise the right words. 'The earth has opened here, and here. A wall of the church fell here. And there, you see, we lost one complete row of houses. Four people were hurt. One was killed. Do you wish to look at his grave?'

Henry flapped his Panama hat in front of his face to cool himself down. Beside him, Gil was dressed in nothing but his sawn-off denim shorts, but his face was still scrunched up against the mid-afternoon glare, and his forehead was studded with sweat.

They had reached San Hipolito after a dusty, winding drive up into the Sierra de Juarez. The sky was as dark blue as concentrated copper-sulphate solution, and utterly cloudless. You could have driven through San Hipolito without even realising that it was there; two rows of adobe houses, a small dust-coloured church, a farm gate and a collection of rusted milk-churns. A monotonous bell rang far away across the hills, reminding Henry uncomfortably of the bell that had tolled in last night's dream.

Their first surprise had been that the soil around San

Hipolito had been so deeply riven with cracks. On the north-west side of the village, half a hillside had broken open and dropped away; and there were deep crevices running all the way across the main highway. In places, the tarmac was so cracked that it looked like a satellite map of the Mississippi delta. As the priest had explained, one of the end walls of the church had collapsed. A deserted wheel-barrow stood hopefully beside the rubble, waiting for the siesta to finish, so that it could once again be brought back into the service of the Lord.

The priest was short, only five feet five, but thickly built, with a large head, and penetrating eyes. His principal flock, he explained, were at Ojos Negros, but he had been born in San Hipolito, and the people here had known him all his life.

'We've been looking for a friend of ours, an American girl named Sylvia Stoner,' said Henry. 'We heard she might have come this way. Maybe a month ago, maybe longer.'

The priest said, 'Come inside' and led them through the churchyard, where stone crosses and blind-eyed angels baked in the hundred-degree sun, through the heavy dried-oak door, and into the church itself. Although a large rhomboid of sunlight fell across the nave from the half-collapsed wall, the church was very much cooler inside, and they sat down with relief on one of the polished pews.

'I wondered when somebody would come to find out what happened,' said the priest.

'Oh, yes?' asked Gil, looking around, at the single stained-glass window, at the simple altar, at the silent confessionals.

'Do not understand this wrongly,' the priest replied. He coughed, and cleared his throat. 'Everything was properly reported, to the church authorities, and to the police at Ensenada.'

'What was properly reported to the church authorities, and to the police at Ensenada?' Henry enquired.

'You came because of the girl, yes?' the priest replied, his thick eyebrows crowding together in perplexity.

'That's right, Sylvia Stoner. Pretty girl, blonde hair. Always wore a silver chain around her ankle.'

'And you do not know what happened here?' the priest asked them.

Henry shook his head. 'I think you'd better tell us.'

'Well ...' said the priest, licking his lips anxiously. 'If you do not already know ...'

'Father,' Henry put in, 'this information is vital. A friend of ours is in really serious danger. It could be that it has something to do with whatever happened here in San Hipolito.'

'I suppose it can do no harm, if I tell you,' the priest said, just as worriedly.

'It certainly won't do anybody any good if you don't,' Gil pointed out.

'Very well, then, come with me,' said the priest. He stood up, and beckoned, and they followed him along the nave to the very end of the church, where the wall had collapsed. They could see that the ground had gaped open to a width of nearly fifteen feet, and that there was a sixty-foot crevice zig-zagging from the middle of the graveyard to the foot of the very front pew. It looked as if part of the crevice had once been a vault of sorts because six or seven feet of the wall was lined with terracotta tiles, salt-glazed so that they were shiny black.

'Of course you know how bad the earth tremors have been,' said the Priest, standing right at the very edge of the crevice. 'You have probably felt them in San Diego.'

'I had no idea they were as strong as this,' said Henry.

'Well, they have been less frequent lately, and not so powerful. But the night when this wall collapsed, there was quite a severe tremor, three point four, and many houses and outbuildings were destroyed, all around this district. When I felt the tremor in my house at Ojos Negros, I had a strange feeling that something terrible had happened, and sure enough I was telephoned to come at once.'

'There's no damage here that can't be repaired,' Henry commented, shading his eyes so that he could look out of the church and into the sun. 'A couple of truckloads of concrete should put you right.'

The priest rubbed his hands together, slowly and nervously. 'I am afraid that something happened here which all of the concrete in the world could not put right. In this vault, there rested a box, a long wooden box, carved and sealed. I still have it, but it has been taken to my house at Ojos Negros for safekeeping. Up until the night of the earth tremor, the box was hidden below the ground, and covered with an iron trap, three inches thick, and tiled over so that it was indistinguishable from the remainder of the church floor. But, crack! when the earth shifted, the iron trap was broken in half, and the wooden box was exposed to view. My church curator, Miguel Estovar, ran here to the church as quick as he could, but he was too late. The trap had been broken, the seals had been damaged, and the wooden box was empty.'

Henry said, in a quiet voice, 'Tell me, Father, what was *inside* the wooden box?'

The priest stopped wringing his hands, and instead chivvied his fingertips anxiously against his sleeve.

Even more quietly, Henry asked, 'Was it Yaomauitl?'

The priest stared. 'You know about Yaomauitl?'

Henry nodded. 'We are Night Warriors. When the sun sets, I am Kasyx, and this is Tebulot.'

Immediately, without any further questions, and without any ceremony at all, the priest went down on one knee, and clasped Henry's hands. Then he clasped Gil's hands, and kissed them. As softly and quickly as if he were reciting his rosary, he said, 'The legends always said that the Night Warriors would come, if ever Yaomauitl was freed, but I never believed them.' He looked up at both of them, the sunlight shining around their heads like haloes, and he said, with the deepest of emotion, 'You have restored my faith. It is like a miracle.'

'We're not *that* miraculous,' said Gil. 'We only started training last night.'

The priest stood up, and gripped them both by the shoulder. 'I know that you will defend us. God be praised.'

'Tell us something about Yaomauitl,' said Henry. Was he buried here for very long?'

The priest said, 'He was buried here in 1687. It happened after a dream battle in which it is said that sixty of the finest Night Warriors lost their lives. He was placed inside a box of elm wood, through which evil manifestations may not pass, and the box was sealed with the nine holy seals of God. The iron trap was then lowered over his tomb, and the iron trap was blessed by nine priests and crossed ninety-nine times with holy water. The church of San Hipolito was built on top of the tomb, to further sanctify this place.

Yaomauitl has lain here ever since – until he was freed by that earth tremor.'

'Do you know what he looks like?' asked Henry.

'Come with me,' said the priest. 'I have a contemporary woodcut of the entombing of Yaomauitl in my study. It shows the Devil quite clearly. It also shows the nine seals, and the Night Warriors who entrapped Yaomauitl at last.'

They left the church and walked across the glaring courtyard at the back, until they reached a small adobe house shaded by scrub trees. A Mexican woman was outside on the verandah, cleaning moths off the oil-lamps with white spirit. She watched Henry and Gil in suspicious silence as the priest took them into the house.

'Maria is like most of the people of San Hipolito,' the priest explained. 'She doesn't take to strangers very readily.'

'You still haven't explained what any of this has to do with Sylvia,' said Gil.

'Well,' said the priest, ushering them into his house, and then leading them through to the living-room, 'this is because you have to understand the background of what occurred before you can come to the same conclusion as I. There are no easily explained facts. There are no reliable witnesses, either. But everything indicates that my assumption is correct, and I have to say that Monsignor Del Parral in Ensenada concurs with my opinion.'

The inside of the small adobe house was cool and musty. The furniture was simple: rushwork chairs and plain wooden sofas. The walls were painted white, and hung with brightly coloured native paintings of Biblical scenes – Joseph and his coat of many colours, Moses in the bulrushes, the

Pieta. The floors were tiled dark brown, and there was a basket of eucalyptus logs beside the hearth. Henry and Gil waited for a minute or two while the priest went through to his study. He came back with a red cardboard folder, which he laid on the low table in the middle of the room, and opened. Inside was a sheet of thick art paper, yellow at the edges and badly discoloured, but printed with the most richly detailed woodcut that Henry had ever seen. It was in the style of Diirer's *Apocalypse*, and although it was not nearly as accomplished as a work by Diirer, it clearly showed the Devil Yaomauitl being imprisoned in his elm-wood box.

'How old is this?' asked Gil, quietly.

'The print is relatively new, 1880 or thereabouts. But the original woodcut from which it was taken – which is now in the Museum of Religious Art in Mexico City – that was dated 1687. The artist was Paolo Placido SJ.'

Henry and Gil examined the woodcut with gradually increasing dread. It depicted a long coffin-shaped box, richly and fantastically carved with ivy and mistletoe and other holy plants, as well as the faces of angels and saints, being lowered by derricks into a tile-lined crevice in the ground. There were twenty or thirty people standing around the box, some of whom were dressed in elaborate armour and winged helmets. Henry and Gil both recognised a very much earlier form of Tebulot's armour, and a weapon that was primitive by the standards of the weapon that Tebulot carried now, but which must at the time have been the most powerful machine that anybody could have dreamed of.

It was the illustration of Yaomauitl which disturbed them

the most, however. He was tall, with dark slanted eyes that even after three hundred years still seemed to stare out at them with glistening malevolence. His body was gristly, with protruding ribs, and a grotesque pelvic girdle, from which depended a long sinewy penis. His hands and his feet were like claws, with curved razor-sharp nails – the kind of nails that could take your eyes out with one scratch.

Both Henry and Gil recognised the Devil at once. He was older, and more battle scarred, but he was indisputably the parent of the creature that had taken Susan hostage; the 'boy' who for one split-second had revealed to them the real shape of his body and the real wickedness of his soul.

Henry said, 'Yes,' gently, and handed the woodcut back.

'You recognise him, then?' the priest asked them.

Gil nodded. 'We saw one of his kids, if that's what you can call them.'

The priest stared at the woodcut with an expression of solemn apprehension. 'Then it has already started, the spreading of his seed.'

'Yes, Father,' said Henry. 'That was how Sylvia Stoner died.'

The priest looked up at him. '*Night Warriors*,' he whispered, with reverence. 'Perhaps you won't believe this, but I have been dreaming that you would come. It says in *De Daemonialitate* that the Night Warriors would always rise in response to a reappearance of the Devil, in any one of his manifestations. And here you are. You will forgive me if you are no surprise to me.'

'It's more helpful that we're not,' Henry smiled, and grasped the priest's shoulder. Perhaps there was still some residue of Ashapola's power in Henry's hand, for the priest glanced at it quickly, and smiled the smile of the reassured.

'Now then,' the priest said, 'You wish to know what connection was formed between Yaomauitl and your friend Sylvia Stoner. Let me tell you what happened as far as I know it; then I will take you to see Ludovico, who is the only person in the village who knowingly encountered Yaomauitl after the box was broken open.' He asked, 'Would you care for some wine? We cultivate our own vines here, you know. I cannot guarantee that it is as smooth as anything from Napa Valley, but it is quite refreshing.'

He poured each of them a glass of dark red pinot wine, fruity and aromatic, and then he sat back and said, 'Your friend Sylvia and her male companion arrived here in the last week of February. I remember that. They came in a wagon – you know, four-wheel drive – and they said they were touring Baja California on vacation. They asked me if I knew of any place they could stay for a day or two, and I directed them to Senora Rosario's house. Her two boys left home to work in America, her husband died, and so she has many spare rooms.'

'What did Sylvia's male companion look like?' asked Henry.

'Well, you could say that he looked like a tennis player who has let his training go by the way,' said the priest. 'Curly hair, not too tall, handsome but very untidy. Unshaven, crumpled clothes.'

'Did you catch his name?'

The priest shook his head. 'All the time she called him "baby". They came to take pictures of the church, and of the village, but they took no care with their pictures, and they spoke too loudly of what they were going to do on their vacation.'

'What are you trying to imply?' Henry asked him.

'Simply that they were not genuinely here on vacation. They came, like a few other Americanos have come before them, because they had heard that some of the villagers have another crop, apart from grapevines.'

'You mean – ?'

'Yes, my friends. Marijuana. The fragrant strain known amongst connoisseurs as San Juarez Paradise Number One. Very difficult to find, very expensive. And not many Americans know that it is grown in the hills around San Hipolito.'

Neither Henry nor Gil said a word about the priest's apparent approval of the marijuana crop, but the priest himself sipped his wine and smiled at them over the rim of his glass.

'I can see that you are surprised that I condone the sale of narcotics. Well – I do not condone it, but I do turn a blind eye to it. There is no money in San Hipolito, my friends. Most of the soil is stony and barren, so conventional farming produces little reward. Without the sale of San Juarez Paradise Number One, this village would die. The people who live here would be dispossessed, and the church would fall into ruin. I have to make a practical choice between a trade which transgresses the laws of men and a state of poverty and suffering which would transgress the laws of God.'

'So Sylvia and her companion were here for grass?' asked Henry.

'Of course. There is nothing else here that would entice

an American tourist, no matter how eccentric, to stay in San Hipolito for even a few minutes.'

'Then what happened?' asked Gil.

The priest spread his hands. 'They stayed for two days, maybe three, and I heard from one of the little birds who tell me such things that they were negotiating with the Perez family to buy two thousand dollars' worth of marijuana, first quality. Perez of course was holding out for more money, and Sylvia and her companion were constantly telephoning to America to see if they could drum up more promises of sales.'

He paused for a moment, and then he said, much more gravely, 'There came then the day of the earth tremor. The ground split, and everybody in the village rushed into the surrounding fields in case their houses fell on them. When they returned, they found that the church wall had fallen, and that Yaomauitl had escaped from his elm-wood box. They sent out dogs, and men with shotguns, but there was no trace of the Devil, or even of his passing.'

'Sylvia and her companion were still in the village?'

The priest nodded. 'They stayed for one more night and one more day. But certain things about them were strange. The night after Yaomauitl had escaped, Seftora Rosario heard them upstairs in their bedroom. They seemed to be arguing, or at least the girl Sylvia seemed to be arguing. Senora Rosario did not recognise the other voice. It was a man's voice, but very harsh and loud, and it sounded as if it was coming from everywhere at once. She said that it frightened her to hear it. However, it did not last for very long, because the argument finished with great abruptness, and then Senora Rosario – well, she usually does not listen to such things – but she heard Sylvia and her companion on the bed. She said that it sounded very violent, like rape. She could hear Sylvia crying out, in a muffled voice, as if she had a hand or a pillow over her mouth. She could hear the man cursing her, in the same harsh voice. And of course she could hear the frame of the bed shaking, as if they were trying to break it to pieces. The next morning she went upstairs and told them that they must go.'

'Sylvia's boyfriend was still with her?' asked Henry. 'In spite of the way that he had sounded the night before?'

'Ah, you are quick, Mr Watkins,' said the priest. 'Yes, her companion was still with her – but when they left Senora Rosario's to drive back to America, they made one mistake. One serious mistake.' 'What was that, Father?'

'Come,' said the priest. 'Now is the time for us to talk to Ludovico.'

They finished up their wine, and then the priest led them out of his house and across the highway. He pointed out Senora Rosario's house, a large secluded adobe at the very end of one of the two rows which made up the village, trailing with creeper and surrounded by a high wall. Although it was well past siesta time now, there didn't seem to be anyone around, only a small bare-bottomed boy playing in the dust, and a thin mangy-looking dog which kept prowling and barking around one of the houses. The priest waved a fly away from his face, and then pointed down the street, close to where Gil had parked his Mustang.

An old man was sitting in a shadowy doorway. His face was withered, and his eyeballs were as white and vacant as hard-boiled eggs. He wore a freshly pressed suit of pale beige linen, and his shoes had been highly polished, even though they now bore a thin film of dust. His hands rested on the gleaming brass knob of a walking-cane.

'This is Ludovico,' said the priest. 'Ludovico, these two gentlemen are special friends of mine from El Norte. I would like to introduce them to you. 'Ludovico blindly shook hands with Henry and Gil, and then said, 'What are they looking for, these special friends of yours, Father?'

'They have been asking about the girl who came here, the American. The girl who was here when the earthquake damaged the church.'

Ludovico licked his deeply lined lips, and said, 'You said that somebody would come one day to ask about her, didn't you, Father?'

'Yes, Ludovico, I did.'

'Can you trust this pair, Father? I sense something unusual about them. I sense something to do with electricity.'

Henry smiled. 'You're right, sir. Is there anything else you can sense?'

The old man touched his own face, as if to reassure himself that it was still there. 'I sense many strange things. Strange duties, strange ambitions. I sense danger, too.'

'Did you sense something the day that the earthquake damaged the church?' asked Henry.

'Not then, not then,' said Ludovico. 'But, the day after, when they left, that was when I sensed something. You see, they had passed by me several times during their stay in the village, and I had come to know them quite well. Their voices, their footsteps, the sound of their clothes.'

'And?' asked Gil, when the old man seemed to hesitate.

'And, they made the mistake of passing close by me when they left the village for the last time. Because I heard them, both of them, quite distinctly; and I sensed something which I never wish to sense again. It was the same girl, of that there was no question. Perhaps not in soul, but certainly in body. The man, however, was completely different. Other people say that he looked just the same. But when he passed me by, I heard hard skin rubbing on hard skin; I heard the sharp clicking of claws on the road. I heard hissing breathing, and a terrible rustling sound which filled me with fear. Worst of all I felt a dead coldness, as if somebody had opened an icebox door right in front of my face, and then closed it again. There was no doubt about it. That afternoon, whatever anybody else perceived with their eyes – I knew that a Devil had passed by.'

Henry turned to Gil. There was no need for either of them to speak. The pieces of the fateful puzzle were coming together now; and they had learned something new about their Deadly Enemy – something which Springer had either failed to tell them, or which Springer didn't know. He had admitted, after all, that even Ashapola was not always able to anticipate the ways of Devils.

That 'something' was that Yaomauitl could take on the form of a human being, so effectively, it seemed, that everybody who saw him was deceived. Only those who were unable to see him were not taken in. Only the blind could detect the distinctive sound of a demon from hell.

'So, Yaomauitl escaped from San Hipolito in the guise of Sylvia's boyfriend,' said Henry. 'And Sylvia's only crime was that she came here looking for high-quality grass.'

'At the wrong time, I regret,' said the priest. 'But if it had not been her it would have been somebody else. Yaomauitl is quite indiscriminate in his choice of familiars.'

'Did you find out what happened to the boyfriend?' asked Gil.

The priest said, 'That was the only time we did not involve the police. We ask you, too, not to pass this information on to any law enforcement agency, because it will only cause suspicion, and distress, and may even lead to a wrongful arrest. Victor Perez, you see, had many arguments with Sylvia's male companion about the price of his marijuana, and that could easily be misconstrued as a motive for his murder.'

'You found him dead, then?'

The priest said, 'Yes, we found him dead.'

'And you're certain that Yaomauitl did it?'

'No human being could have killed a man in this fashion, my friends.'

Henry said nothing, but it was obvious that he wanted to know how the Devil had destroyed Sylvia's travelling companion. The priest thanked Ludovico for his evidence, and they all shook hands with him. Then the priest led Henry and Gil further down the village street until they reached a stony side-turning that led down beside a vineyard. They walked alongside the vines under a baking sun, their feet crunching on the bone-dry soil, and occasional insects droning past them as they went.

'We haven't moved him yet,' said the priest, over his shoulder. 'Nobody will touch his remains, because they believe that they contain such evil; and in any case I didn't think it wise. If anybody did come asking questions about him, I wanted to be able to show them that it would have been impossible for Victor Perez or indeed for anyone else to have murdered him.'

They reached the end of the vineyard. Along the lower edge of it, for about a half-mile, the boundary had been marked out with staves, six or seven feet high and about fifteen feet apart. Halfway up the end stave, there was a large dry lump; a papery-looking excrescence that resembled a wasp's nest. They approached it with a mixture of mystification and alarm. But even on close inspection they couldn't make out exactly what it was. It was some sort of dessicated tissue, twisted and snarled with tendons, and there were some dark maroon lumps on the side of it, but it bore no resemblance to anything that Henry or Gil had ever seen before.

Henry stared at the priest in bafflement. But the priest beckoned him around to the other side of the pole, and pointed.

Squashed and distorted though it was, Henry could just make out the face of a man in the middle of all that dried-up flesh. His eyes were squeezed tight, like a newborn baby's, his nose was pressed into an indeterminate lump, and his mouth was dragged down sideways by the intrusion of five curled nodules that must have been his fingers.

The priest crossed himself, and said, 'He was found here three days after Sylvia and her companion had left San Hipolito. Yaomauitl could have hidden his remains, of course, but I believe that he left them here as a warning.' He looked away, out across the mountains. 'Now you know what a man looks like when every single ounce of moisture is taken out of him. We don't amount to much, do we, for all of our pride?'

They walked back up the hill again. Only Gil turned back to look. Tonight, they were going to have to face the offspring of the creature that was capable of doing that to a man, and he just wanted to keep the image sharp in his mind. It would ensure that he didn't hesitate, when it came to pulling the trigger of his machine.

The priest invited them back for more wine, but it was growing late now, and they wanted to return to San Diego as soon as possible.

'I will pray for you,' the priest told them. Gil started up the Mustang. Henry said, 'Thank you, Father. We appreciate your prayers.'

'There is one thing,' the priest added. 'Wait here for just a moment, and I will bring it for you.'

He hurried off towards his house. Gil and Henry sat in silence while they waited for him to return. Both of them were thinking about the dried-up remains of Sylvia's friend. And both of them were thinking of the Deadly Enemy Yaomauitl, and how he had stared at them out of that woodcut picture from so many years and years ago. That woodcut alone was proof of the longevity of utter evil. Evil could be contained; evil could be banished; but evil could never be destroyed.

The priest returned, perspiring and out of breath. He handed Henry a brown felt satchel, fastened at the front with a fraying cord.

'Take these,' he said. 'These are the nine seals which the Night Warriors placed on the elm-wood box, to keep Yaomauitl from breaking out of it. They were brought over to Mexico by Jesuits who had heard how the Devil was causing havoc in the New World. They are beyond price, my friends, so please guard them well.' Henry untied the cord, and looked into the satchel. Inside, there was a collection of small tissue-paper packages. He took one out, and carefully opened it. The priest watched him anxiously as he laid the seal across the palm of his hand.

It looked like nothing more than a blob of black, cracked sealing-wax, stuck on to an old piece of twisted fabric. The priest said, 'They were found in Jerusalem, in the year nine hundred. They were said to be fragments of the robes of nine of the twelve disciples, one from each, taken from their hems on the night of the Last Supper. Three are missing: that of Judas, that of Peter, and that of John.'

Henry touched the seal with his fingertip, and turned it over. 'What happened to the other three?'

The priest said, 'Nobody knows. But the saying is that if anybody could get all twelve together, he would be able to exile the Devil for ever.'

'Perhaps God has the other three,' said Henry. 'Perhaps he doesn't want us to exile the Devil for ever. Perhaps, from time to time, we need to be reminded of the ultimate evil, so that we can appreciate the ultimate good.'

'You should have taken the cloth,' smiled the priest.

Henry wrapped up the seal, and dropped it back into the satchel. 'I think, in a peculiar sort of a way, that I just did.'

They drove back down through the San Juarez mountains, their sun-visors lowered against the burning sun. They reached Mexican Highway 1 at Ensenada, and drove north to Tijuana. It was dark when they reached the border, and they had to wait an hour before they could get through, but at last they were back on I-5 and heading for Del Mar and Solana Beach.

'Those seals,' said Gil, 'what do you think of them?'

'Phoney, probably,' Henry replied. 'Have you ever come across a religious relic that isn't? If they joined together all the pieces of the so-called True Cross, they'd have themselves a crucifix as tall as the Sears Building. And as for fragments of cloth from Jesus's robe, you'd have thought that Jesus owned a seamless-robe warehouse.'

'You believe in Yaomauitl, though, don't you?'

'Do I? I don't know what to think. I know that something terrible's been prowling around, and that something killed Sylvia and Sylvia's boyfriend. But don't let's be too naive about it. Don't let's jump to hasty conclusions. Springer set us up once, and he could be doing it again.'

'You really don't trust anybody, do you?' Gil asked him.

'Yes, I do. I trust you, and I trust Susan, and I also happen to trust myself. But that's about as far as it goes. Don't think I'm getting all cynical on you. I'm not. The more I see, the stronger my belief becomes. I believe in the Night Warriors, and the task that the Night Warriors have to perform. I believe in them, implicitly. But if I can have so much supernatural stuff proved to me so unequivocally, why should I accept any other supernatural stuff that isn't proved so well? It would certainly make life easier for us if everything that priest said was one hundred per cent – but supposing it isn't? Supposing he's left out one or two absolutely crucial facts? Supposing he's lying, to protect a real murderer? Supposing none of it ever happened, and you and me were being suckered from beginning to end?'

Gil said, 'Henry – somewhere along the line we have to take one or two things for granted, otherwise we're not going to get anywhere.'

'Well, you're right,' Henry agreed. 'But let's not

automatically take everything at its face value, okay? Especially not priests, and men who seem to be messengers from God.'

They reached Henry's cottage, and Gil parked outside. Henry said, 'I have an idea. Why don't you call your folks and tell them you're staying over tonight with friends? I hardly ever get disturbed here, so there isn't so much chance of somebody bursting in on us and thinking we've gone into a coma.'

'That sounds like good thinking,' said Gil.

Henry unlocked the front door, and reached around to switch on the lights. 'The phone's at the back of the sofa. When you've finished, maybe we could go out and get ourselves an egg foo-yung to go.'

The lights blinked on – and there he was, or rather *she*, because this evening she was wearing a plain white costume that was more like a dress than a suit, and her face was more finely featured than usual. She was sitting in Henry's favourite chair, her legs crossed, watching and waiting as if she had been watching and waiting for hours.

'Well, well,' she said. 'The return of the Night Warriors.' Henry was taken off guard. 'Springer,' he said. 'I thought we'd seen the last of you.'

'The last? What on earth made you think that?' 'What on earth do you *think* made me think that?' Henry retorted. 'You abandoned us last night, left us tangled up in some goddamned nightmare with no power and no way out – and, thanks to you, Samena's been captured and held hostage by that Devil they dug up on the beach. You *knew*, didn't you? You knew, right from the very beginning, that we were going to come face-to-face with that Devil. I mean, you lied about it, you went out and tracked down one of the pathologists who was working on that Devil, and of course he was bound to have a dream about it – and now look what the hell's happened!'

Springer listened to all of this patiently, her hands pressed together in simulation of prayer.

'Is that all you have to say?' she asked Henry, at last. 'There could be more,' snapped Henry. 'It depends on the quality of your explanation.'

'My explanation is very simple,' said Springer. She rose from her chair and walked towards Henry and Gil with an effortless glide. 'Please, Gil,' she said, 'do call your parents. They would like to know that you are safe; and it would be a good idea if you were to spend the night here.' 'Well?' Henry demanded.

Springer smiled. In her utterly asexual way, she was really very attractive. She had a beauty that no human being can ever achieve. Faultless, pale, and perfect.

'I confess that I deceived you, and that I took you into Mr Shapiro's dream in the full knowledge that you would encounter the creature from the beach. I didn't tell you because I didn't want you to over-react. I believed, you see, that you would be able to cope quite easily with a Devil who is still only an embryo – or, what do they call the off-spring of kangaroos? – a joey.'

'Maybe we could have coped with it, with some forewarning, and a little more power,' Henry protested.

Gil said, fiercely, 'We were completely fucked. There was nothing we could do. We had to make up our minds whether we wanted to kill ourselves for no reason, or come back here to safety and leave Susan behind. That was some kind of choice, huh?'

'Well, that part of it I regret,' said Springer. 'But even *I* cannot be in two places at one time, no matter how many different faces I wear. I had to leave you because I had located the descendant of yet another Night Warrior, and it was essential that I recruited him as quickly as possible. He will join you tonight. His name is Xaxxa, the slide-boxer.'

'What is the point of recruiting another Warrior when it costs you one that you've already got?' Henry asked, bitterly.

Springer said, with a touch of sharpness, 'I am your trainer, Kasyx, not your nurse-maid. I fully expected the three of you to be able to deal with that nightmare, and to be able to overcome the creature, too.'

'Whatever you expected, Springer, the simple fact of the matter is that I don't trust you any more,' Henry told him.

'Me neither,' said Gil.

Springer thought about that for a moment, and then said, 'Do you consider it essential for your task that you trust me?'

Henry said, 'Not essential, no. I've only been a Night Warrior for one night, but I get the feeling that it's a very much bigger thing than both of us.'

Springer nodded. 'In that case, you will give me the opportunity to prove to you that I *am* trustworthy. You will go out tonight, with Xaxxa, and you will rescue Samena from the spawn of the Devil. I will guide you to the right dream, and this time I will advise you in advance of the true identity of the dreamer.' 'It's not our leather-and-lashes friend Lemuel Shapiro again, is it?' asked Henry.

Springer said, 'No. The creature was moved today from the coroner's laboratories to the Scripps laboratories. Your dreamer will be one of the people who is studying it there. Most probably, Doctor Steinway.'

Henry stared at Springer in disbelief. 'Doctor Andrea Steinway?' 'You know her?' asked Springer, mildly surprised at Henry's reaction.

'I should think so. She was my wife for four years. And now you want me to go into one of her nightmares?'

Gil slapped Henry on the back. 'Jeez, who knows, Henry, you might even come face-to-face with the monster she thinks you are!'

Chapter Fourteen

They went to bed at ten-thirty, after a quick Chinese supper that Gil had brought back from Chung King Loh. Henry took the bed and Gil bunked down on the sofa. Gil was happy to stay over at Henry's cottage: it made him feel more relaxed, even though he suspected that part of the reason Henry had invited him was to act as watchdog, in case Henry felt tempted to take a drink. Henry was fighting his alcoholism hard: he even regretted having accepted the priest's offer of red wine. As he told Gil, 'Once you've taken that first drink, it's ten times more difficult to say no to the next.'

Springer had left them with nothing more than a promise to meet them at the house on Camino del Mar at eleven. She would say nothing further about that night's assignment, nor about their new Night Warrior, Xaxxa. She wouldn't even explain what a 'slide-boxer' was. 'When you come tonight, you will see for yourself.'

In the darkness of their separate rooms, Henry and Gil said the words that would transport their dreaming personalities out of their earthbound bodies.

'Now when the face of the world is hidden in darkness, let us be conveyed to the place of our meeting, armed and armoured; and let us be nourished by the power that is

dedicated to the cleaving of darkness, the settling of all black matters, and the dissipation of evil. So be it.'

They closed their eyes, and felt the tides of sleep steadily overwhelming them, just as the Pacific steadily overwhelmed the shore. They rose, silent and transparent as ghosts, leaving their bodies lying in the cottage, and sailed high above Del Mar, darker tonight because of cloud cover, following the bright needlework of traffic towards the house where Springer would be waiting for them.

They were absorbed through the roof of the house, and sank into the second-floor room.

Springer, as promised, was already there, looking even more feminine than she had this afternoon. She had combed out her hair into impossible waves, and she wore an extraordinary white knee-length jacket with wide shoulders and a loosely tied belt, and nothing underneath but a white garter-belt and white stockings.

'You're early,' she said, with pleasure. 'That will give you time to meet your new warrior, Xaxxa.'

She turned, and ushered forward a tall, well-muscled black boy, dressed at the moment in nothing but pale blue shorts. His hair was cropped short, which emphasised the thickness of his neck. His face was flat, short nosed, one of those highly photogenic faces, like Muhammad Ali's. But although he was obviously athletic, and intensely fit, there was a cautious expression of humour somewhere around his mouth; an expression that contradicted the idea that anyone with this kind of physique had to be serious and dull.

'Xaxxa,' said Springer, nodding her head. 'Xaxxa – this is Kasyx, the charge-keeper, and Tebulot, the machine-carrier.'

'You didn't tell me they was white,' said Xaxxa, suspiciously.

'I didn't tell you they were black, either.'

'Well, Night Warriors, I guess I kind of assumed they was all black.'

'The Night Riders were white,' said Henry, and then wished that he hadn't.

Gil said, 'Does it matter – us being white?'

'That depend,' said Xaxxa. 'I mean, like that depend entirely on your attitude. I mean, for instance if you think that because you white you can start giving me orders, then you can forget it. You can forget this whole Night Warrior thing completely. My father was in Vietnam, and believe me, man, he took nothing but three years of shit from white men, and he always said to me never go joining nothing where there's a white man in charge because you going to be sweeping the floor even if you some kind of genius.'

'*Are* you a genius?' asked Henry, pertinently.

Xaxxa said, 'No, but that's if I was.'

'Do you have a name, apart from your Night Warrior name?'

'Sure. My name's Lloyd Curran.'

'I'm Henry,' said Henry, 'and this is Gil. I'm a teacher and Gil's a student and neither of us are geniuses either. The only other thing I can say is that the Night Warriors aren't like the army. We don't have officers and we don't have rank. We work together whatever our age and experience, and – now that you've joined us – whatever our colour. What do you do, Lloyd?'

'Trainee photographer,' said Lloyd, still suspicious. Henry didn't know what kind of recruiting spiel Springer had given him to persuade him to take Ashapola's shilling, but it was obvious that he had been expecting something rather different. Certainly not a skinny-looking storekeeper's son from Solana Beach and a blotchy-faced philosophy professor in creased pyjamas.

'Springer said you were a slide-boxer,' put in Gil. 'Did you try it out yet? The suit? The slide-boxing?'

'Kind of,' said Lloyd.

'Can we have a demonstration?' asked Henry. 'We don't even know what slide-boxing is.'

Springer walked around and touched Henry's arm. 'If you charge up, Henry, you'll all be able to show each other what you can do.'

Henry knelt down, and Gil and Lloyd knelt down beside him. Springer stood over them, and recited the words that would transform them into Night Warriors. Three golden haloes shone over their heads, and then faded. At last they stood up.

Kasyx's crimson armour crackled with even more static power than it had before. Springer said, 'I have given you the maximum charge this time. You have two powerful combatants to supply, and you will need it. The only reason I gave you less last time was because I did not expect you to have to fight so violently; and also because there is always a risk with an inexperienced charge-keeper of accidental discharge, which can not only kill you and your warriors, but the dreamer, too.'

Kasyx laid his hand on Tebulot's shoulder and Tebulot's weapon immediately hummed with full power, its golden charge-scale glowing bright. Now they turned to Xaxxa, the slide-boxer.

Xaxxa seemed even more muscular and well developed than he had before. His chest bulged and gleamed, and his stomach was flat and hard. He wore a white domed helmet which flashed and sparkled with bursts of silver light, as if it had been lacquered with flakes of chrome. There was a curved white bar around the brow of the helmet, and around this bar teemed dozens of tiny coloured lights.

On his shoulders, Xaxxa wore white protective pads, overleaved like the scales of a dragon. His torso was bare and all he wore around his loins was a tight white protective codpiece, of the same sparkling substance as his helmet. It was fastened in place by a thin leather waistband and a thin leather strap which cleaved deep between his muscular buttocks. His calves were clad in white boots, the sides of which were clustered with complicated insets of silver and copper, in patterns which reminded Kasyx of micro-circuits.

'The boots are the key to Xaxxa's talent,' said Springer. 'If you will charge him up, Kasyx, he will show you something of what he can do.'

Kasyx laid his hand on Xaxxa's shoulder. Xaxxa watched him closely as the power of Ashapola thrummed into his body. 'I always got to depend on you for power?' he asked Kasyx.

Kasyx nodded. 'Just as I, in my turn, have to depend on Springer's god-of-gods, Ashapola. In the Night Warriors, old buddy, we are all dependent on each other.' As Xaxxa's body was infused with power, the metallic patterns on his boots began to sparkle and glow. At last, Springer said, 'Enough,' and Kasyx drew away. Springer stepped forward and lowered the white bar from the brow of Xaxxa's helmet to the level of his chin. Over his face, there appeared a curved visor of absolute energy, which from the outside was an optically perfect mirror. Whenever an opponent faced Xaxxa, he would see nothing but his own face.

'Now, watch,' said Springer. 'I will pretend to be Xaxxa's opponent. Xaxxa will defend himself, and then attack me in his turn.'

Springer poised herself in an attacking position, her knees bent, her hands raised. Xaxxa crouched down, too, gradually moving away from her in a diagonal, his open hands tensely circling in the air.

There was a split-second of total tension. Then Springer flashed in towards Xaxxa, her hands flying in a style that looked like hyper-complicated kung fu. But there was a sharp *veeeowwfff!* and Xaxxa slid instantly to one side, on a shining two-foot-wide strip of pure golden power. Then, with a longer whistle, curving and higher pitched, a strip of power zipped across the room, twisting itself into a corkscrew loop, and Xaxxa slid along it at high speed, like a two-hundred-mile-an-hour surfer. He actually turned upside down at the top of the loop, then came hurtling back towards Springer on a streaking strip of power that brought him right up behind her, poised to drop-kick her in the back, even before she had recovered herself enough to turn around.

He allowed the power-strip to fade, and came to a standstill. He lifted his visor, grinning widely. 'Slide-boxing,' he announced. Then, '*Wow!*'

'That's something,' said Kasyx. He was impressed.

Tebulot was almost envious. 'Here you've got me lugging this damned great machine around with me, and look at him *go!*'

Springer touched each of them on the forehead. 'Each Night Warrior has his part to play. You are several, but you are one.'

'Well, then,' said Kasyx. 'Isn't it time we went looking for Samena?'

'Yes,' said Springer.

'Whose dream?' asked Kasyx, looking at Springer meaningfully.

'Your ex-wife's, I'm afraid. Out of all of those who have been studying the creature at Scripps, hers is the most vivid response. She was tired tonight; she went to bed at nine-thirty, and is already asleep.'

'We going into his ex-wife's nightmare?' asked Xaxxa.
Springer nodded.

'You said we were going into black dreams, as well as white. How come the very first dream I get has to be white?'

'You'll have a really good time,' said Tebulot. 'White people dream about other white people, so you'll have plenty of crackers to knock around.'

'Are you trying to be funny?' asked Xaxxa.

'What are you going to do?' Tebulot challenged him. 'Loop-de-loop and smack me in the back of the head? This weapon fires backwards, in case you're interested.'

'Jive ass,' Xaxxa retorted.

Kasyx said, 'For Christ's sake, Xaxxa, stop trying to act like Mr T.'

'Mr T?' Xaxxa yelped. 'Where's this man been?'

'He's a philosophy professor,' said Tebulot. 'That is,

during the day. But tonight he's Kasyx, your charge-keeper, and you need him; just like you need me and I need you. So let's go find Samena.'

Xaxxa made no more complaints. Tebulot recognised that in any case he was only playing the part of the aggressive black because he was nervous and excited and unsure of himself, the same way that Tebulot had been, just yesterday – and to a great extent, still was. He saw strength in Xaxxa, and resilience, and humour, and all of those qualities would make him a good man to rely on in case of a crisis. The three Night Warriors gathered close together, and clasped hands. There was no animosity on Xaxxa's face as he interlaced his fingers with Kasyx and Tebulot; only anticipation and excitement and a small measure of that feeling called fear. They rose up, through the ceiling of the room, through the rafters of the attic, through the shingles of the roof, and then they were out in the night, more than a hundred feet high, and turning southwards. This time, there was no need for Springer to direct them to the house of their dreamer. Kasyx had Andrea's address engraved on his bank balance.

'I keep thinking this can't be real,' Xaxxa whispered.

'Me too,' said Tebulot.

'I mean this is Peter Pan, right? This is real flying. I only wish I could bring my Pentax. The pictures you could get, you know? The shots!'

They followed the curve of the coastline southwards to La Jolla, perched on its headland overlooking La Jolla Bay. They turned inland when they reached the cove, flying over the glittering balconies of all the fashionable restaurants, over Prospect Street to Pearl Street, where they spiralled downwards at last towards a neat, small, whitewashed house with Spanish-style arches and a red-tiled roof. Andrea's Volkswagen Rabbit was parked in the exact centre of the well-swept driveway.

The three of them faded in through the red-tiled roof, into the main bedroom. Andrea was lying on her back on the Spanish carved double bed, her hair in curlers, her pale green nightdress rumpled up around her thighs. A paperback copy of Hardy's *World of Plankton* lay on the bedside table, next to a jar of cold cream and a small Cartier alarm-clock that had once belonged to Henry. The room smelled of Estee Lauder perfume, and it gave Kasyx something of a familiar shock. So did the sight of Andrea in her nightdress. Ever since their divorce, she had always been fully dressed when he met her, smart and neat and businesslike. To see her like this reminded him uncomfortably of the four years in which they had been married. 'Your ex?' Xaxxa whispered. 'Not bad looking, if you don't object to a second opinion.'

Kasyx looked at her curiously. He supposed, after all, that she wasn't all that bad looking. His impression of her face had been distorted by acrimony and alimony, so that if he had been asked to draw her, she probably would have turned out uglier than Yaomauitl.

'Let's get into the dream,' he suggested. 'How about you, Xaxxa? Are you ready for this?'

'Do your worstest,' said Xaxxa.

Kasyx lifted his hands, and across the darkness of the bedroom drew the crackling blue octagon of light. Then he pushed forward his hands, and divided the darkness inside the octagon like a curtain, stretching it apart. Slowly, a sunlit street-scene appeared, although none of the sunlight fell into the bedroom. Kasyx beckoned Tebulot and Xaxxa to stand close beside him, and then he raised the octagon over their heads. They held hands tightly as the light descended all around them, and gradually enveloped them in Andrea's dream.

Xaxxa breathed, 'Holy shit.'

The instant the octagon touched the floor, the three Night Warriors found themselves in a dusty, hot, brightly sunlit square, in what appeared to be a North African city like Tangiers or Marrakesh. A mosaic fountain splashed in the roasting wind and palm trees rattled above the white domed rooftops. They could hear the hoarse throaty tremolo of a bamboo *chebaba*; and the clamour of a street market not far away. Figures in green-and-white *jellabas* hurried through the square, every one of them wearing dark mask-like sunglasses. There was a smell of heat and sewage and roasted meat. Xaxxa looked around in awe. 'This is a dream? This is actually a dream?'

Kasyx said, 'That's right. And we're right inside it.' 'And we going to find this devil character inside this dream?' 'That's what Springer says.'

'*Fee-eew!*' said Xaxxa.

Tebulot suddenly pointed across the square, to a wide archway. 'There,' he said. 'Isn't that your wife?'

Kasyx pressed his hand to the left of his helmet, and his vision instantly jumped to close-up. He glimpsed a woman's back as she disappeared into the crowds of the *souk*; a woman in a solar topi and a white bush-shirt. He didn't see her face, but he saw the green feather in her hatband. Andrea's trademark colour had always been green.

'You're probably right,' he told Tebulot. 'I guess we'd better follow her, see where, she goes. But can you please remember that she's my *ex-wife*.'

Tebulot smiled, and beckoned to Xaxxa. Together, keeping shoulder-to-shoulder, the three of them crossed the square, and went through the archway, elbowing and pushing their way through crowds of Arabs. The sorrowful music of the *chebaba* grew louder, and was joined by the tremulous playing of pipes. Pan-pipes, from the Atlas mountains; magical pipes whose music could convey the listener into dreams beyond dreams. The crowds jostled even closer, and the Night Warriors found themselves forcing their way along a narrow market street, sheltered from the midday sun by layers of striped awnings and lined on each side by stalls selling bronze dishes and copper jugs, strange bead embroidery, leather shoes and intricate camel harnesses, caged birds which whistled and piped, and sweetmeats studded with flaked almonds and blowflies.

At the very end of this street they saw the white woman disappearing into the doorway of a shop. They followed her to the front of the shop, pushing aside dark-skinned children who danced around them for money. There was Arabic writing across the doorway; from inside, there was the sound of a radio playing Arab music, and the fragrance of *kif* resin, burning in a pipe.

'What do we do, go in?' asked Xaxxa.

Tebulot slung his weapon across his back. 'I don't see that we have any choice, Kasyx, do you?'

Kasyx shrugged. 'I just want to be careful. There's no telling what my ex-wife might do to me, if she finds that she's got me cold, right inside her own dream.'

'Just so long as she don't wake herself up,' said Xaxxa. Kasyx cautiously entered the shop doorway. 'Anybody there?' he called loudly.

Inside the shop, it was gloomy and hot, and smelled even more strongly of *kif*. The walls were lined with scores and scores of mahogany drawers, rather like an old-fashioned apothecary's, and each drawer was labelled in Arabic. A long flypaper hung from the centre of the ceiling, and dozens of flies buzzed and struggled on it fitfully. Some of the flies had white heads, and Kasyx realised that they were humans who had been genetically tangled up with insects in the same way as that scientist in *The Fly*. He remembered that Andrea and he had started to watch *The Fly* on late-night television once, after coming home from a dinner party, and Andrea had switched it off, saying how disgusting and puerile it was. Disgusting and puerile it may have been but she had obviously remembered it.

They poked around the shop but there was no sign of the white woman. Tebulot picked up a brass camel-bell from one of the shelves, and shook it. Almost at once, a door opened at the back of the shop, and two Arabs appeared, both wearing dark glasses. They were dressed in green *striped jellabas*, and one of them wore a fez.

'We're looking for a white woman who passed through here,' said Kasyx.

The Arab in the fez shook his head. 'No white woman has passed through here, lord.'

'There was a white woman. I saw her myself.'

'No white woman, lord. But there are many white women at the *Hotel Delirium*.'

'One special white woman, the dreamer of this dream,' Kasyx insisted.

'No, lord.'

'Tebulot, Xaxxa, look in the back,' said Kasyx.

'No, lord! You may not look there!' the Arab with the fez cried out, lifting both of his hands. 'Why not?' Kasyx demanded.

'*Mektoub*, it is written.'

Tebulot heaved his weapon off his back, and tugged back the T-bar. 'Sorry, buddy, but it's just been unwritten. Come on, Xaxxa, let's go take a look.'

The Arab stared at them in hostility. '*Eshkoon?* Who are you?'

'The dreamer of this dream knows who we are,' said Kasyx.

Tebulot and Xaxxa opened the door at the back of the shop and went through to the corridor behind it. Kasyx said to the Arabs, 'Stay where you are,' and followed them. Tebulot had already reached a large back room, windowless, lit only by *kinki* lamps which hung suspended at different levels from the ceiling. At the side of the room, almost in darkness, there was a bed, draped with a homespun woollen blanket. On this, still fully dressed, but with her baggy *sarouel* pants drawn over to one side, the white woman lay, her eyes closed. An Arab girl crouched between her legs, a tinker's wife, a prostitute, her tongue lapping furtively like a cat's. The white woman's solar topi rested on a wooden table in the middle of the room, on which there were plates of food, roasted spiced lamb and dates and *couscous*.

A thin boy sat on the opposite side of the room on a bright turquoise cushion, playing the full-bellied Arab lute called a *gimbri*. The music was hypnotic and repetitive, the same glissando over and over and over again, to accompany the barely audible licking. Around the boy's eyes, steadily feeding on the moisture which oozed out of them, flies clung like living mascara.

Now Kasyx knew why the Arabs had tried to prevent him from coming in here. They were the guardians of Andrea's innermost secret. No wonder his marriage had been so barren; no wonder he had suffered four years of coldness and isolation. Andrea had lived in Morocco for two years before she had taken up her appointment at Scripps. In Morocco she must have found the forbidden pleasure and the secret satisfaction which she was looking for; and she had never forgotten it.

Tebulot said uneasily, 'What are you going to do?'

But Kasyx had no time to reply. The white woman on the bed had opened her eyes, and was staring at them, and in an instant the room and the bed and the boy and the tinker's wife had folded up like figures in a child's pop-up book, and shrunk out of sight, a rectangle of patterned darkness flying in the wind. Instead of standing in the corridor at the back of a shop, they were out in the desert, under a glaring sun, and there was nothing but sand around them, wherever they looked.

'What happened?' asked Xaxxa.

'My wife suddenly realised we were there,' said Kasyx.

'Your ex-wife,' Tebulot corrected him.

Kasyx said,' Yes, my ex-wife. And judging by that, my wife that never really was.'

'You don't want to feel bad about it, man,' Xaxxa told him.

'I don't. I just feel embarrassed.'

They shielded their eyes against the throbbing brightness of the desert, wondering which way they should go. There were dunes upon dunes, ribbed by the wind and stretching for miles. And there was that extraordinary sound that the desert made, as if it were a huge distant dynamo, thrumming on and on and on. The sound of heat and distance and wind blowing through *the foggara*, the mysterious underground waterways that were built by the people of the Sahara in the centuries before the white imperialists began to criss-cross the sand.

Then, one by one, twenty or thirty horsemen appeared on the brow of a distant ridge, their outlines melted by the rising heat so that they looked like a frieze cut out of thin black tissue-paper. They paused for a minute or two, and while they did so, Kasyx pressed his hand against his helmet and examined them close-up.

'Can't see their faces,' he said. 'They're all draped around with muslin.'

'Are they armed?' asked Tebulot.

'Muskets, of a kind,' said Kasyx. 'Hard to tell what sort of firepower they've got, though. Andrea never did like guns. Maybe they're just decorative.'

In an extraordinary way, the sand-dunes in between the horsemen and the three Night Warriors began to move up and down, in a kind of carousel-motion; and as they did so the ridge on which the horsemen were standing was carried nearer and nearer, without the horsemen actually having to ride. Within a very short space of time, the horsemen were standing only fifteen feet away, silently, unmoving, their hands on their saddle-pommels, their heads completely wrapped in *tegelmousts*.

'*Allah akbar!*' the tallest of the horsemen proclaimed. 'There is no other god but Allah and Muhammad is his prophet!'

Kasyx stepped forward across the sand, closely followed by Tebulot and Xaxxa.

'We're looking for a white girl,' he said. In the dry desert air – air which could turn the inside of a man's nose and throat into glasspaper, his crimson armour crackled even more loudly with static electricity.

'You are unbelievers,' the horseman retorted. 'We have come to escort you away from the desert, and away from this land.'

'No way, Jose!' said Tebulot. 'We came to look for our friend Samena, and we're not leaving until we've got her.'

Without any further warning, the horseman reached into the folds *of his jellaba*, and whipped out a long curved sword. '*Bismillah!*' he cried, his voice as harsh as a hawk's, and spurred his horse forwards. Behind him, there was a teeth-grating ring of steel against steel, as twenty more swords were drawn from their scabbards. They flashed in the desert sun like pieces of exploding glass.

Tebulot lifted his machine, and fired a single heavy bolt of energy. There was a crack which echoed and re-echoed across the desert, and the horseman flared up into an incendiary ball of fire leaving nothing in the air but a smudge of black smoke. His horse reared, and whinnied, and then broke into a thousand tiny bricks, which scattered across the sand. '*Allah akbar! Allah akbar!*' shrieked the horsemen, and whipped their mounts towards the Night Warriors. But now Tebulot set his machine to fire a multiple spray, and with a deafening fusillade of pure power, a dozen horsemen burst into flames, and their horses shattered beneath them. As Tebulot reset his weapon, Xaxxa slid up and away to the left of the horsemen on a shining strip of energy, pulling down his protective visor as he went. He curved thirty feet up into the air, and then came streaking down towards the Arabs, his knees bent like a champion surfer, his body immaculately balanced, and as he flashed past them he punched and kicked in a flurry so fast that seven horsemen were hurtled off their horses before they could even take a swing at him with their swords.

'*Night Warriors!*' he crowed, as he rode his energy-strip up again, and turned a loop high in the desert air. Only three horsemen were left, and they were already yanking at their reins and turning their horses around to make their escape. Xaxxa whistled down on them as fast as a jet-fighter and drop-kicked the nearest of the three, so that he was hurled headlong into his two companions. All three of them collapsed on to the sand in a tangle of *jellabas* and flying limbs.

Tebulot methodically fired a single short shot at each of the fallen horsemen. Their robes flared up one by one, and they vanished. Puffs of smoke blew across the desert. Kasyx walked across the sand, occasionally kicking one of the bricks which had so recently been horses. From a hundred yards away, Xaxxa came slowly sailing back towards them, six inches off the ground, holding his hands up above his head like a boxing champion.

'Who were those dudes?' asked Xaxxa, as he came to rest beside Tebulot. 'Don't tell me your wife sent them.'

'*Ex-wife*,' said Kasyx. Then, 'No, I don't think she did. *Her* response to finding us inside her private dream was to hide, to run away. These horsemen were aggressive, and ready to cut our heads off. They were sent by the Devil, if you ask me. He may have used the Arabic vernacular of my ex-wife's dream, but I'm pretty sure that they were down to him.'

'So he's here somewhere,' said Tebulot. 'The question is, where?'

'He's back in that Arab city, in my opinion,' Kasyx replied. 'That's where my ex-wife's greatest guilt is located; that's the kind of place that a devil would find attractive.'

'Question is, where is it?' asked Xaxxa. 'I mean, she could even have stopped dreaming about it, in which case it won't even be there any more.'

But, strangely, they turned around and the city was only a half-mile behind them. Their thoughts about it must have drawn it closer; which made Kasyx realise that no matter how substantial anything appeared to be in a dream, it was really no more than a creation of the dreamer's imagination, and as such it could be moved and shifted and switched on and off as easily as the image from a movie camera. Tebulot glanced at him in surprise, but Kasyx said, 'Come on, while we still have the chance.'

They entered the city by a wide gate, at which crowds of leprous beggars sat and shook their wooden bowls for *dirhams*. Again they plunged into the twisting alleyways, pushing their way through children, and merchants, and hunched-up creatures in long *woollen jellabas* that may not even have been human. They were almost about to give up the search as hopeless, when a high, clear voice called out, 'Lords! Are you seeking someone?'

They looked to their left. There was a narrow alley between two buildings, cluttered with broken pottery and discarded bedding. At the end of the alley, a stone staircase rose to a green-painted door, and outside the door stood a pale, handsome boy in a simple white robe and a white head-dress, beckoning them.

Kasyx stepped forward. 'We seek a white girl called Samena.'

'She is here,' the boy acknowledged. He turned and glanced inside the half-open door, and then he beckoned.

'Could be a trap,' Tebulot suggested, 'don't see that we have any alternative,' said Kasyx.

'Come on, man, they give us any jive, we can always beat the shit out of them,' added Xaxxa, enthusiastically.

'This guy definitely thinks we're the A-Team,' Tebulot complained.

Walking in Indian file, they went down the alley and climbed the stairs. The boy held the door open for them, and they could smell the strong cheap perfume that drenched his hair and his clothes, a favourite in the Sahara, *Bint es Sudan*. Inside the house, it was stuffy and gloomy. Decorative shutters had been closed over the windows, so that only a few thin flower-patterns of sunlight shone on the blue-and-yellow mosaic floor, and on the figures who sat on heaps of dusty cushions around the walls.

One of the figures they recognised immediately, and Kasyx felt a surge of sheer relief. It was Samena – blindfolded and gagged, with her hands bound behind her back, but apparently safe and well. The other two figures were unknown to him. A fat European, unshaved, in a grimy white suit; a young man, with his face covered in a muslin *tegelmoust*; and an older man, thin and elegant, who could have been either Moroccan or European, wearing a combination of tailored grey Savile Row jacket and baggy *sarouel* trousers. He was smoking a thin clay-headed *sebsi*, a *kif* pipe, and the stony blankness of his eyes showed that his mind had already retreated into the dream within a dream.

Kasyx stepped down into the room, and faced the three men. 'I am Kasyx,' he said. 'I have come to demand the release of my fellow warrior Samena. Which one of you is the spawn of Yaomauitl?'

The European cleared phlegm out of his throat, and gave Kasyx a buttery smile. 'You have extraordinary bravado, my friend Kasyx. Are you not aware that any child of Yaomauitl is always closely watched by his father, and that anything you do to the child, the father will repay seven hundredfold?'

'We are Night Warriors,' said Kasyx. 'We have no fear of Yaomauitl, or of anything that Yaomauitl can do.'

'Then that tells me that you are very *inexperienced* Night Warriors, my friend Kasyx. A Night Warrior who knew Yaomauitl well would take far more care than you. Turn around, and see for yourself.'

'*Kasyx*,' Tebulot muttered, and Kasyx turned.

The door through which they had entered had been locked. The handsome youth stood beside it, jangling the keys in his hand. Worse than that – between the Night Warriors and the door stood four tall creatures dressed in close-fitting black hoods and suits, with eyes that gleamed yellow and malevolent, like the eyes of panthers.

'The Black Ones, the Afreets from the desert,' the fat European explained, quite nonchalantly. 'They are the stuff of Arabian nightmares; the beings which wake up even the most Westernised of Moroccans in the middle of the night, sweating and trembling.'

The thin man with the *kif* pipe began to repeat over and over again a *zikr*, a magic phrase that, endlessly chanted, would eventually take the *kif*-smoker into a state of magical trance. Behind them, the Afreets began to move forward, their feet utterly silent on the mosaic floor. The fat European smiled, and began to waggle his foot in time to the *zikr*.

'The Afreets destroy their victims by twisting their heads around and around, until they are facing behind them. You can always tell the victim of an Afreet, because his head is around the wrong way.'

'Tebulot,' Kasyx advised him. 'Get ready to hit them, and make sure you're quick.'

'Give me a little more power,' said Tebulot; and Kasyx reached over and grasped the machine-carrier's shoulder for a moment. The deep energy of Ashapola poured through his fingers into Tebulot's body. The charge-scale on Tebulot's machine glowed golden, and he slowly pulled back the T-bar until it clicked into the fully armed position.

'It is a pity that the new generation of Night Warriors should die thus,' smiled the fat European. He shook a cigarette out of an untidy paper package, and scratched a match on the sole of his shoe, so that it burst noisily into flame. 'However, it is always the least principled who survive.'

'*Kaluakaluakalua!*' the thin man suddenly cried out, in a high penetrating voice.

The Afreets pounced forward, bounding noiselessly through the air as if they were shadows of some invisible creatures in another room. Tebulot swung round, and let fly a dazzling burst of energy, a squib-like shower of detonating sparks and lancing fire. One of the Afreets screeched and tumbled over, his body ripped into cinders and tatters of fabric. Xaxxa swung up off the floor, sliding his feet upwards until they were on the same level as his head, then hurtled himself around like a propeller. His feet caught a second Afreet in the back of the head, audibly snapping his neck. The yellow-eyed creature twisted and collapsed to the floor as if he were a marionette whose strings had been abruptly cut.

A third Afreet leaped on Kasyx, seizing hold of his upper arms with hands that gripped like metallic pincers. Kasyx heard his crimson armour buckle, and felt the supernatural pressure of the Afreet's fingers against his muscles. But then he discharged a controlled burst of energy; and his armour suddenly jumped alive with blue snakes of electricity. The Afreet juddered and shook and dropped to his knees, his hands burned and smoking. Tebulot turned and fired from the hip with his heavy machine, blasting the Afreet's head from its shoulders in a spray of ashes, and leaving a neck stump like a tree-trunk that had been incinerated by lightning.

'Get that last one!' Kasyx shouted; but as Xaxxa twisted himself around on a corkscrew of glowing energy, and Tebulot swung his weapon around, the last surviving Afreet lithely rolled over behind Samena, and seized hold of her head.

'*Stop!*' roared Kasyx, as the Afreet started to twist her head to one side.

The thin man said something quickly in Arabic, and the Afreet stopped, its eyes smouldering like *kinki* lamps. The fat European drew in a leisurely fashion at his cigarette, and then slowly blew out smoke so that it issued from his mouth and disappeared up his nostrils. 'I see that you are not prepared to sacrifice the life of even one of your fellow warriors,' he said. 'This makes you very vulnerable, does it not?'

'Tebulot,' Kasyx instructed, 'point your weapon at the one in the middle, the one with the scarves wrapped around his head.'

Tebulot did as he was told.

'Full charge?' asked Kasyx.

'Ninety per cent,' said Tebulot. 'Enough to wipe out everything standing in my line of fire for three kilometers. Including, of course, our pal here.'

'Xaxxa,' said Kasyx, and indicated the fat European and the thin man with the *kif* pipe.

Xaxxa poised himself ready, and said, 'I can take 'em out before you can blink, man.'

Kasyx now approached the young Arab in the *tegelmoust*. 'Can I speak to you directly, spawn of Yaomauitl?' he asked. 'Or are you going to persist in using these two interpreters?'

The young man raised his head slightly. Behind the veils of muslin, Kasyx could make out the chilling slanted eyes of the Devil himself.

'We have been to San Hipolito, and seen your father's tomb,' said Kasyx, unsteadily. 'We know who and what you are, and we also know how to defeat you. Before another week is out, we shall have cornered your father Yaomauitl, too; and believe me he's going back to that box and back to that vault, and this time he's going to stay there for ever.'

'You are accursed,' the young Arab said, in the coldest of voices. His breath fumed through the muslin as if the room were refrigerated. 'You are a dog of Ashapola, and my father and my many brothers shall have revenge on you.'

'Well, you can promise what you like,' said Kasyx, trying to sound confident. It wasn't easy, because he was badly afraid, and he knew that Tebulot and Xaxxa were too, for all of their nonchalance. 'But if you don't let Samena go, right this minute, we're going to evaporate you, and that's a promise.'

The young Arab said, 'Very well, my friend. The finger-archer will be released. But let me warn you, you have made a serious mistake. It is not for nothing that my father Yaomauitl is known as the Deadly Enemy. We shall have our revenge on you, believe me; and the pain that you shall suffer shall outweigh ten thousand times the pleasure you are feeling now that you have succeeded in having her freed. I promise you this, Kasyx, by all the torments of Hell.'

'Let her loose,' Kasyx insisted. Tebulot drew back the T-bar of his weapon, and lifted it up to his shoulder, so that he could aim it more accurately.

The young Arab raised one hand to the Afreet. At once, the Afreet released Samena's head, and stood back, an evil shadow. Then the young Arab spoke quickly in Arabic to the fat European, and the fat European in turn spoke to the thin man with the *kif* pipe. 'The girl is to be released *Inch 'Allah*; and the Afreet is to return to the world beyond dreams.'

Positioning his cigarette between his lips, the fat European climbed to his feet, and went over to Samena. He took a heavy clasp knife out of his pocket, and unfolded it, keeping one eye squinched up against the smoke that rose from his cigarette, as if he were winking. All the time, Tebulot's aim never wavered once from the young Arab in his enveloping robes, and Xaxxa remained poised to strike if necessary at the thin man with the *kif* pipe. The fat European cut methodically through the cords which tied Samena's wrists, and then untied her blindfold and her gag. She opened her eyes, and stared at Kasyx and Tebulot in agonised relief.

'Oh, thank God!' she said.

Kasyx said to the young Arab, 'Let's get rid of that Afreet, shall we?'

The young Arab nodded to the thin man with the *kif* pipe, and the thin man recited his *zikr* again, and the Afreet twisted and faded like smoke, as if it had never existed at all.

Kasyx went over to Samena and helped her up. Then he edged his way back behind Tebulot and Xaxxa, keeping his arm protectively around Samena's shoulders.

It was then that he felt the floor shifting and stirring beneath his feet. He knew what was happening. Morning was approaching, and Andrea was gradually beginning to wake up. The North African dream would soon fold and collapse, like imaginary *origami*, and be forgotten for ever in a blatant flood of Southern California daylight.

'Time for us to go, I'm afraid,' he told the young Arab.

The young Arab raised both of his hands. 'Revenge shall be mine. *Mektoub*, it is written.'

Tebulot said, out of the corner of his mouth, 'Do you want me to blast him?'

Kasyx nodded, and just as quietly, he said, 'I'm going to

draw the octagon now. Wait until it's right up above our heads, then let him have it. That way, if he tries to retaliate – if he *can* retaliate – we'll be well out of the dream before he can hit back.'

Kasyx raised his arms and began to describe the electrical blue octagon in the gloom of the room. The octagon reflected in the silvery face-mask of Xaxxa's fighting-helmet and lit Tebulot and Samena in an eerie supernatural light.

'Are you ready?' Kasyx asked Tebulot.

'*One thing!*' the young Arab called, as Kasyx prepared to lift the octagon over their heads. There was very little time left now. The integrity of the dream city was beginning to come apart. Dozing memories of other days in Andrea's life were beginning to intrude on the equilibrium of the building all around them: sudden flashes of walks along the San Francisco Embarcadero, flickers of Paris, lectures at UC San Diego. Faces, voices, snatches of music. The floor began to ripple like water, somewhere the wailing of panpipes rose up again, to warn them that morning had arrived, and that all through the Western time zones, in the minds of millions of sleeping people, whole imaginary landscapes were crumbling and vanishing, whole metropolises were collapsing. The Atlantis of the night was sinking down again to the seabed of the collective unconscious.

Tebulot lifted his weapon, and aimed it at the young Arab's head.

'Fire when I give the word,' Kasyx murmured.

But the young Arab said, in a strange, strong voice, 'You would not break the code of the Night Warriors, would you, *effendi*? The code of the Night Warriors honours a deal struck; and the deal that you struck was to give me my life in exchange for your finger-archer.'

He turned toward the door of the room, and beckoned, and the pale, handsome boy who had first admitted them appeared. He was nudging in front of him the woman in the white solar topi, the dream-personality of Andrea herself. In one hand, the boy held a large curved knife, and he was smiling.

'If you attempt to kill me, then this lady will die, too,' said the young Arab.

Kasyx turned to Tebulot, and then back to the Arab. 'If you so much as touch her,' Kasyx warned, 'this dream will collapse, with you in it.'

'Ah, yes, but at least I will take you with me.'

Xaxxa said, 'He's got us, man.'

'Your black friend speaks the truth,' the young Arab told Kasyx. 'You have got what you came for, the finger-archer Samena. Be satisfied with that.'

Kasyx said, 'If you so much as *touch* that woman ...'

But now the dream was falling apart on all sides. Kasyx quickly grasped the hands of his companions, and initiated the slow descent of the octagon, to take them out of the dream and back to the real world. Behind the young Arab, the wall of the room had disappeared altogether. There was a beach there now, a windswept shoreline, somewhere Andrea used to live when she was a child.

A split-second before the octagon descended in front of his eyes and blotted out his view of the young Arab altogether, Kasyx saw him unwinding the veils which covered his face, and for one heart-swallowing fraction of a moment, he glimpsed the hideous face of Yaomauitl's embryonic son as it really was. Bulbous, malevolent eyes; cheekbones and gristle and semi-transparent skin; and a mouth that was stretched with two layers of developing teeth.

Tebulot dropped to his knee, ready to snap in one last shot if Kasyx ordered him to; but then they heard a thin, high, and distinctive scream, and Kasyx shouted, 'No, Tebulot, leave it!'

'*Henry!*' Andrea shrieked. '*Henry, for God's sake, don't leave me!*'

Then the octagon touched the floor, and they were back in Andrea's bedroom, all four of them, looking at each other in shock and helplessness.

'Kasyx – there was nothing you could have done,' said Tebulot. 'Believe me, you did everything you could.'

But Kasyx turned at once to the bed. Andrea was still asleep, but she was mumbling and tossing and thrashing her legs.

'That bastard,' breathed Kasyx. 'That *bastard!*'

'Wait,' said Samena. 'She's waking up.'

Tebulot said, 'You're right, look. She's opening her eyes. She's okay. Yaomauitl hasn't kept her hostage, after all.'

Kasyx stood over Andrea's bed, watching her gradually wake. To Andrea, the Night Warriors appeared only as the faintest of ghosts, the subtlest of shifting outlines, in the air. She frowned at Kasyx, and tried to focus her eyes; but then Kasyx turned around and grasped the hands of his fellow Warriors, and they rose up together through the ceiling of the house like vanishing memories.

It was past dawn as they descended through the roof of the house on Camino del Mar. Springer was waiting for them, cross legged, meditating. His head was closely shaved

GRAHAM MASTERTON

now, revealing all the bumps of his angular skull, and he was wearing plain white cotton robes like a monk. 'Ah, you have brought back Samena,' he said, rising to his feet. 'Are you safe, Samena?'

Samena said, shakily, 'They scared me, but they didn't hurt me. I'm not sure where they kept me. They took me out of that desert in the first dream, and then they locked me up in some kind of room that looked as if it was made out of fog. I sat there for hours and hours, and then they came to get me again, and then I was taken to that room in Arabia somewhere.'

'It sounds as if you were imprisoned during the day in the dream of someone who was brain damaged, or in a coma,' said Springer. 'But, at least you are free now, and the Night Warriors are four again.'

Kasyx said,' They tried to take my ex-wife Andrea, too, but I don't think they succeeded. We saw her wake up normally.'

Springer frowned at him. 'You actually saw the Devil take her captive?'

Kasyx nodded. 'Yes – but if he'd held her – she wouldn't have woken up, would she? She would have stayed asleep the way that Samena did.'

'No,' said Springer, emphatically. 'There is a great difference between capturing someone's dream-personality when they are inside their own dream, and capturing them when they are inside somebody else's dream. When they are inside somebody else's dream – as Samena was – their dream-personality remains in the dream state, because they are unable to return to their waking body. But when they are inside their *own* dream, they appear to wake

340

up as normal, and to behave as normal. The only difference is that when they go back to sleep at the end of the day, their dream-personality is still in bondage to whoever captured them the previous night. Your ex-wife is as much at the mercy of the Devil as Samena was.'

'And he said he was going to get his revenge on you, too,' Xaxxa reminded him.

Kasyx looked at Springer anxiously. 'Is there any way I can tell for sure that her dream-personality is being held hostage – while she's still awake?'

'There are ways. Can you get to talk to your ex-wife this morning?'

'I can try.'

'If the Devil threatened revenge on you, then you must,' said Springer.' Yaomauitl was known throughout history for his callousness and his brutality. His offspring are just as cruel. When she sleeps tonight, believe me, he will torture or kill your wife's dream-personality, and that will have the effect of destroying her mind completely. Her body will live, but her imagination will be extinct.'

Kasyx said, 'How do I tell if she's been captured or not?'

'Go talk to her. It doesn't matter what excuse you make. Talk about anything you like. But in the middle of the conversation, make sure you ask this question: *What are the seven tests of Abrahel?*'

'What good will that do?' asked Kasyx.

Springer laid a hand on his shoulder. 'It is the first question of the Demonic Interrogation, which was devised by Catholic inquisitors to determine who was possessed by Satan and who wasn't. If her dream personality has been held hostage by the spawn of Yaomauitl, she will answer, *The seven tests of Abrahel are his and his alone.* And she will refuse to say any more about it.'

'But supposing she says something else altogether?'

'Then you will know that the spawn of Yaomauitl has failed to capture her. There are twelve questions in the Demonic Interrogation, and every person whose soul is possessed *must* answer them.'

'But what if she answers the way that proves she's been held hostage? What then?'

'Then you have several choices. Either to leave her to the Devil's devices, in which case she will more than likely be killed; or to wait until nightfall and go to rescue her, the same way that you did Samena; or to kill the spawn of the Devil himself, during the day, so that he may no longer dream that he has captured her.'

'The Devil's under police guard at Scripps laboratory,' put in Tebulot.' How are we possibly going to be able to kill him?' Kasyx said, 'I don't know. But we can try, can't we? Listen, Tebulot is staying at my place. He can come along to the laboratory with me, and see if we can get access to the Devil. Samena – you try to get some rest. You're going to have a difficult day today, going back into your body and trying to prove to your grandparents and your doctors that you're perfectly okay. Xaxxa – maybe I can call on you if I need you.'

'Anytime, man,' Xaxxa acknowledged.

The four Night Warriors talked for a little while longer before first Xaxxa and then Tebulot broke free from the room and floated out into the daylight. Kasyx and Samena were the last to leave, except of course for Springer, who prowled up and down at the far end of the room, thinking deeply.

Samena said, 'I haven't really had the chance to thank you.'

'What for?' asked Kasyx.

'For saving my life. That Devil was threatening to eat me alive. *Literally*, inch by inch.'

'I guess you shouldn't always believe what Devils tell you, should you?'

Samena reached out and held his hand. 'I was frightened, Kasyx. I was sure that they were going to do something terrible to me.'

'Did they talk to you?'

'They talked to each other all the time, but not very often to me. There were always at least three of them – the fat man with the dirty suit, the thin man with the pipe, and the Arab. But sometimes there were more, although I couldn't see who they were. Their faces were all masked behind those veils. The young Arab spoke to them in strange languages. I mean they weren't French and they weren't German and they weren't Italian.'

Kasyx said, 'None of them touched you?' It was the question that any father would ask his daughter after an assault, and both were aware of it.

Samena shook her head. 'They swore at me, some of them. One of them tried to touch me but the young Arab warned him off.'

Kasyx was thoughtful. 'He needed you, that's why. He isn't yet ready to fight us. He isn't strong enough.' He rubbed his hand against the side of his neck, and then said, 'How many others do you think you counted?'

'At least ten,' said Samena. 'They were just the same, all wrapped up in those veils.'

Springer put in, 'That means that at least ten of those original eels managed to dig themselves into the beach and survive. They must still be there now, gestating.'

'In that case, we'd better start digging them out,' said Kasyx.

'You won't find them easy to kill,' said Springer. 'They are arch-survivors, with a ten-thousand-year history of staying alive against all possible odds.'

'I'll find a way,' said Kasyx. 'Believe me, Springer; I'll find a way.'

Chapter Fifteen

Samena blew Kasyx a ghostly farewell kiss as they parted company over the rooftops of Del Mar. She would now return to her earthly body to recuperate after her ordeal as the Devil's hostage; Kasyx would go back to *his* earthly body, and attempt to find out if Andrea had been captured by the Devil.'

Samena turned towards La Jolla, and flew like a rippling wraith towards the University. The Sisters of Mercy Hospital was a large white building on the slope overlooking the freeway, with cedars of Lebanon standing around it, and windows that reflected the hills and the traffic and the morning sky. Samena could feel the tug of her own body, somewhere within the hospital, and she allowed that tugging to guide her down through the building's roof, down through its concrete floors, down through its electrical conduits and its air-conditioning pipes. At last she located the private room on the fourth floor in which her body lay comatose, her own white-faced body connected to a saline drip, and to scores of electrical contacts that measured her heartbeat, her respiration, her blood-pressure, and the electrical impulses that flickered within her brain.

Although it was only six-thirty in the morning, her grandmother was there, sitting beside the bed, watching her. There was a half-empty cup of coffee on the bedside table, which showed Samena that her grandmother must have been keeping a vigil all night. This fussy irritating woman who had built her whole life around television soap operas had been watching over her, praying for her, ever since she had failed to regain consciousness yesterday morning.

Samena hesitated for a moment, the scene was so poignant. Her grandmother said nothing but sat with her hands clasped together, her eyes red with tiredness and tears.

Slowly, silently, invisibly, Samena sank into Susan's body. Susan's skull encased her mind; Susan's flesh enrobed her limbs. She waited, with her eyes closed, feeling her muscles, feeling her nerves, feeling the blood that circulated around her arteries and veins; feeling the suppressed thumping of her heart. The sensation of returning to a physical body after so long as a dream-personality was extraordinary. It was like being dressed up in five overcoats, six pairs of gloves, fur-lined boots and a thick woollen face-mask. All of the agility and responsiveness which characterised her life as Samena was buried inside her flesh; all that spiritual buoyancy was now susceptible to the pull of gravity and the pressure of the atmosphere.

She opened her eyes. Her grandmother had her head bowed down, and was whispering something that sounded like the Lord's Prayer. Susan watched her for a little while, and then reached out her hand. 'Grandma?'

Her grandmother slowly lifted her head. At first, she couldn't believe that Susan had spoken. Then she said, 'Susan?' and clutched Susan's hand tightly, and burst into tears. 'Susan, thank God, you're awake! Nurse, she's awake! Oh, Susan, Thank God! Thank God!'

Susan and her grandmother clung together as close as they could, and in spite of herself Susan started sobbing too, releasing at last all the terror she had felt during her long day in the hands of Yaomauitl's bastard. She wept and wept uncontrollably, and it was only when her doctor came in to see her, and administered a sedative that she gradually settled down.

The doctor stood beside her bed and kept watch on her until she had stopped crying.

'You gave us quite a scare, young lady,' he remarked. 'We thought we might have lost you for good.'

'I was just as scared as you were,' said Susan.

The doctor gave her an uncertain smile. 'I'm not quite sure what you mean by that.'

'I just mean that I was scared, too.' 'You were *unconscious*, my dear. You can't actually be scared when you're unconscious.'

Susan realised that she was making things dangerously complicated. 'I was dreaming, that's all,' she told the doctor. 'I was dreaming, and I was scared in my dream.'

'I see. Like Dorothy, in Oz.'

'Yes,' said Susan, and she thought to herself; if only you knew how right you were, doctor. 'Just like Dorothy in Oz.'

Kasyx returned to his sleeping body just in time to be woken up by his alarm-clock. He sat up. There was a good smell of fresh coffee in the air, and he suddenly remembered that Gil had spent the night at his cottage, instead of going home. Henry stretched, and then pushed back his comforter and stood up. When he went through to the living-room, he found Gil sitting at the table eating a large bowl of muesli and reading the paper.

'Ah, you're back,' said Gil. 'There's coffee in the kitchen. I just made it.'

Henry poured himself a cup of coffee and then came back in. He sat down on the opposite side of the table, and said nothing for a while, watching Gil read.

'Anything interesting in the paper?' he asked, eventually.

'Padres licked hell out of the Braves.'

'Well, that's one bit of good news.'

Gil folded up the paper and tossed it aside. 'They've had more earth tremors down in Baja. Two winos were found dead in Balboa Park. Shamu the killer whale had been suffering from flatulence.'

'Thanks for the precis.'

Gil said, 'I'm real pleased we got Samena back. I'm sorry about your ex-wife, though.'

Henry shrugged. 'It had to be her, of all people. Still, I'm going up to the laboratory as soon as I'm dressed. Maybe she hasn't been taken over by that Devil after all. It happened pretty much in the very last second of that dream, didn't it?'

'The stuff about asking her that question,' said Gil. 'Do you think it's really going to work?' 'Don't ask me. But what else can I do?' Gil was silent for a long time, and then he said, 'You know something, Henry, this is all crazy. This whole thing is completely crazy. Here are you and land Susan – and now Lloyd Curran, too – all risking life and limb and sanity just to fight off some insane creature that only appears in people's dreams. I mean, why the hell should we?' 'You want to quit?' asked Henry, straightforwardly. 'I didn't say that.'

'Well, I don't want to quit,' said Henry. 'That creature

we were fighting last night, he's only one out of ten, maybe a dozen. He's only a fledgling, too. Imagine what kind of power he's going to have when he's fully grown. He's going to get inside people's heads while they sleep and he's going to make them think and feel anything he damn well wants them to think and feel. Come on, Gil, we spend one-third of our lives asleep. That creature and all his brothers are going to be able to dominate one-third of our existence – and probably the other two-thirds, too.' Henry stared at Gil steadily. 'Somewhere, Gil – somewhere not too far away – Yaomauitl *himself is* prowling around – and he's impregnating more women with Devils every day. God knows how many he's managed to fertilise already. Think about it each woman has a dozen eels, each eel becomes a fully grown Devil within only a couple of months ... how long, mathematically, before we have Devils in their *thousands*, and those Devils are dominating the minds of nearly everybody in the country? Let me tell you something, Gil, this is nothing short of an invasion.'

Gil said, 'But why *us*, that's what I want to know? Why does it have to be *us* who must try and stop it?'

Henry finished his coffee. He looked at Gil for a moment, and then turned his head and looked out of the window, towards the sea. It was a bright, sharp, glittery morning.

'I guess it has to be us because it was always written that it was going to be us. What did those Arabs say last night? *Mektoub*, it is written.'

'You really believe that? I didn't think philosophers believed that.'

'I don't think you want a long lecture on Determinism and historical inevitability, do you?' smiled Henry.

Gil shook his head. 'The point is, whether it's written or not, what are we going to do about it? I mean, what *can* we do about it?'

Henry said, 'Do you want to drive me up to La Jolla? We can start by trying to find out if this creature's got any kind of a hold on Andrea.'

Gil checked his watch. 'Let me call my mom and dad first. Then – okay, I'll drive you. If it's written, then I guess it's written, and there's nothing that any of us can do about it.'

They reached the Scripps Institute of Oceanography shortly after eight. There were three police cars in the parking-lot, which Henry took as a bad sign that they may not be able to get as close to the embryo Devil as they might have liked. Gil parked the Mustang, and heaved himself out without opening the door. Henry sat in the passenger-seat without moving for a while, and then awkwardly clambered out in the same way, showing his maroon socks as he did so.

'Hey!' Gil complimented him. '*The Dukes of Hazzard* strike again!'

They went inside the marine biology department. It was cool and air conditioned and almost silent. At the far side of a wide reception area, a Mexican security guard was talking to a newly arrived receptionist. She kept saying, over and over again, 'Well, they won't even *think* of changing the lunch break, I know that. They won't even *think* of it. I've tried, I've tried asking them, well, I've tried asking them, but they won't even *think* of it.'

Henry and Gil waited for a minute or two, and then Henry noisily cleared his throat.

'Yes?' asked the receptionist, plainly irritated by the interruption.

'We'd like to see Dr Andrea Steinway, please,' said Henry.

'Who shall I say wants her?'

'Her husband, if you don't mind.'

"Ex-husband,' put in Gil, and Henry dug him sharply in the ribs.

It was nearly ten minutes before Andrea appeared. She was wearing her white lab coat, with a row of pencils in the breast-pocket, and her hair was severely tied back with a green riband.

'Henry,' she said, in an odd tone of voice.

'Hello, Andrea.'

'What are you doing here? This is most peculiar.'

'What's peculiar about it?' asked Henry.

'I –' began Andrea, and then stopped herself. But Henry could see in her eyes the unspoken mystification that she was feeling. Last night, she had dreamed; and in her dreams she had seen Henry, in extraordinary armour, with an unfamiliar youth – who was now standing next to him, in real life, amongst the potted plants of the Scripps Institute's reception area.

Henry said, 'I wanted to know how the work was coming along.'

'Work?' asked Andrea, still a little dazed. 'Your investigations ... the creature they dug up on the beach.'

'Oh, that – well, we're waiting for two or three digestive experiments, as well as a full electro-encephalograph, and some skin and blood analyses.'

Henry thrust his hands into his pockets and tried to look

affable. 'I was wondering if you'd had any preliminary ideas – made any guesses about it.'

'Henry, you know very well that I simply don't work that way – and, listen, why on earth are you here at eight o'clock in the morning asking such peculiar questions? And who on earth is this?'

Henry turned around and looked at Gil as if he had never seen him before in his life. '*This?*'

'Yes, Henry, I –' She leaned forward a little, and peered at Gil quite closely. 'I'm sorry to sound rude,' she said, 'but have I met you somewhere before?'

Gil said, 'I'm Gil Miller. Your husband, your ex-husband and me, we were the ones who found the girl's body on the beach.' He put out his hand, and Andrea rather distractedly shook it.

Henry asked, nonchalantly, 'Is there any chance that we could take a look at the creature?'

'A *look?*' said Andrea. 'No, I'm sorry, that's out of the question. The police are here, guarding it. They've been here ever since it was brought over from the coroner's department.'

'Surely a look won't do any harm,' said Henry.

'I'm sorry, Henry, no, they won't allow it.'

'Oh, well,' said Henry, 'I guess that was a wasted journey.'

'Yes,' Andrea agreed, still baffled. 'I guess that it was.'

'You, er ... don't happen to know when the police might release some information?'

'Henry, I don't understand why you're asking me these peculiar questions.'

'You're right, they *are* peculiar,' Henry told her, suddenly smiling. 'Like – *what are the seven tests of Abrahel?*'

Andrea stared at Henry for what seemed like minutes on end. He could almost feel the world turning under his feet. Andrea didn't blink for the whole of that time; her eyes remained fixed on Henry as if she were trying to set fire to him with X-ray vision. He stared back at her, but it wasn't easy. There was such force in her eyes – or in whatever it was that was concealed behind her eyes – that he could scarcely prevent himself from looking away, and then turning around and hurrying out of that building as quickly as he could.

Gil sensed the tremendous tension between them, and stepped back a little way, a response that he suddenly realised was one that Tebulot would have made, rather than Gil as he once used to be.

Gil could sense the evil, too, the increasing coldness; and whether Andrea answered Henry's question from the Demonic Interrogation or not, he knew that the Devil was here and that the Devil had possessed her. 'I ...' began Andrea. Her voice was deep and thick and turgid, as if her throat was filled with frozen slush. 'The ...'

Henry tried to smile, but his face was rigid. 'The seven tests of Abrahel, Andrea? What are they? That's all I want to know.'

'You ... want to know –' Andrea said, hoarsely. 'If ...'

'If what, Andrea? Come on, you can say it. Don't be afraid. We used to be man and wife remember? We shouldn't have secrets, even now.'

Terrified as he was, Henry stepped closer, until he was no more than a foot away. Andrea still didn't take her eyes away from him, and now they were dark and glistening like the eyes of some predatory beast. He could feel the coldness pouring off her like liquid oxygen; the coldness which those who have come close to Devils always remember, *'uerie cold, like unto yce'*.

Andrea said, quickly and quietly, 'The seven tests of Abrahel are his and his alone. Now, go, both of you, and don't let me see you here again, do you understand?'

Henry rested his hand on Andrea's shoulder. She slowly turned her head sideways to stare at it, but she made no move to push it off.

'Andrea,' said Henry, 'I know all about your dream last night. I know what happened to you. I've come to help.'

She looked back at him. 'You *know* ... how can you know?'

Henry smiled. There was enough residual energy in his body for him to warm her up, to dissipate the coldness of Yaomauitl's bastard offspring. The Devil may have captured her dream-personality, but he had not yet captured her earthbound body, or her Christian soul.

'It's hard to explain,' Henry said, still smiling. 'But all you have to know is that I understand what's happened to you, and that I can help you.'

'You're lying,' she said. 'You're *mad*.'

'Remember Morocco?' asked Henry. 'Remember the back room of the shop?'

Andrea stiffened. She took hold of Henry's hand, and lifted it off her shoulder as if it were something inanimate that she had been carrying there – a hat, or a dead bird. Henry could tell that there were two distinct forces inside her, tumbling and turning and raging against each other. Her indecision was catastrophic. She turned around, and began to walk away; and then she turned again, and began to walk back again.

'You *can't* –' she said. 'You can't *possibly*-' It was then, however, that Lieutenant Salvador Ortega appeared from the direction of Andrea's laboratory. Today, he was wearing a green-and-yellow plaid sports jacket, and green slacks, and a green bow-tie. He came up to Andrea in a matter-of-fact way, not noticing her intense agitation, and linked her arm through his.

'Now then, Doctor, I'm going to start getting jealous. We were supposed to be running through these pathology tests, weren't we? And what do I find? You're out here, making time with your husband-as-was.'

Andrea stiffened, and then tugged her arm away. For the first time, Salvador realised that something was wrong. 'Dr Steinway?' he asked. But Andrea stalked away, back to her laboratory, leaving Salvador with Henry and Gil and his own perplexity.

'What did I say?' Salvador asked Henry. 'It was not what you said,' Henry told him. 'Well, then, what did *you* say? She was fine when she came in this morning. Now look at her.'

'Salvador,' said Henry, 'I want you for once in your career to stand logic and procedure right on their heads. I want you to believe that what you've got in there – that creature – has already had a serious effect on my ex-wife's mind, and that unless you destroy it – and I mean right away, *now* – it could very well kill her.'

Salvador turned and looked back toward the laboratory. Then he said, 'Do you have any evidence of this, Henry?' 'What kind of evidence do you want?' 'Concrete evidence, Henry. Something in black and white that I can show to the captain of detectives.'

'You know that's impossible.'

Salvador folded his arms tightly across his chest and gave Henry and Gil a brief, resigned smile. 'John Belli's in there, too. We're doing a complete forensic examination, and trying to come up with some kind of explanation for this creature's appearance that will satisfy the media and the public – and, most of all, *us*.'

'Salvador, I beg you to kill that creature before nightfall. Do you hear me? I'm begging you. Otherwise, Andrea will certainly die.'

'He's telling the truth, lieutenant,' Gil added.

Salvador said, 'I believe you. Can you understand that? I *believe you*. I don't know why, but I do. But there's nothing I can do without substantive evidence. My hands are tied.'

Henry ran his hand through his hair. 'Is that your last word?'

'I'm sorry, yes, that's my last word. I don't have any alternative.'

'All right,' said Henry, and reached out for Gil's arm. 'Let's go, Gil. We have other fish to fry.'

Salvador stood watching them as they left, his arms still folded. 'I'm sorry, you know?' he called after them, as they reached the revolving doors.

Henry nodded, without answering, and the two of them went back out into the sunlight.

'What are we going to do now?' asked Gil.

'For the moment, nothing. At least, not as far as *this* Devil is concerned.' He checked his watch. 'But I want to come back here before they close at six o'clock. We're going to destroy this creature tonight, you and I, and that's all there is to it.'

'You're going to break in to the laboratory?'

'If I have to.'

'Okay, then,' said Gil. 'I'm with you. I may be nuts, but I'm with you.'

'Let's drive down to Prospect Street,' said Henry. 'You know that little shell-store down by the cove? I want to talk to somebody down there.' They climbed back into the Mustang without opening the doors, and Gil swerved out of the parking-lot and back toward Torrey Pines Road. The morning was clear and two students were flying Japanese fighting-kites. The kites' tails swirled and corkscrewed in the warm breezy air; indecipherable messages of oriental peace and contentment.

Henry found the man he was looking for outside the La Jolla Shellerie, hanging a row of shiny pink conch shells from the store's front awning. A carousel of postcards whirled in the wind, making a clattering noise. The man was thin and rangy, with a bulbous nose and close-set eyes, and a neck that had as many folds as a matelot's concertina. He wore a striped fisherman's tee-shirt and a shapeless yachting cap.

'Good morning, Laurence,' said "Henry, climbing out of the Mustang.

'Good morning, Henry,' said Laurence, as if Henry visited him every single morning. He went on twisting wires around his conch shells.

'How's business?' Henry asked him. 'So-so,' replied Laurence. 'Had a coach-party of Episcopalian ministers here Thursday, so I sold out of sand-dollars.' Sand-dollars were white chalky shells which were supposed to be marked with symbols representing the Apostles and the life of Christ.

'Laurence,' said Henry, 'I was *thinking* this morning, and I remembered something you told me about digging up clams.'

Laurence narrowed his eyes and stared at Henry with some caution. 'Clams?' he asked, tying the last of his conchs, and propping his hands on his bony hips.

'You said that you could detect clams under the sand by tapping the beach in a certain way.'

'That's right. Clam-drumming, I call it. But it don't just apply to clams. Any creature under the sand you can detect the same way. Clams, crabs, mussels, lugworms, you name it.' Henry said, 'How much would you charge me for a day's detecting?'

Laurence shrugged. 'Hundred, maybe, hundred'n fifty.'

'All right, then,' said Henry. 'How about today?'

'*Today?* What in hell are you looking for today?'

'Will you help me?'

Laurence looked at Henry closely, and then at Gil, and then back again at Henry. 'What are you trying to dig up, Henry? Tell me that.'

'I'll show you when we dig it up, Laurence. Otherwise, you won't believe me.'

'You're not looking for buried treasure? I only do living creatures. You need a metal-detector for buried treasure.'

Henry said, 'We're looking for living creatures, Laurence. Hundred and fifty. And I'll throw in two bottles of Chivas Regal.'

Laurence took a long, deep, thoughtful breath, and then at last he nodded. 'Okay,' he said. 'Let me go get my stuff. Janie can take care of the store for today. She always makes more money than I do, anyway. She's hard bit. She won't never give no tender-hearted discounts to small kids with not enough pennies for a seahorse.'

Laurence collected a heavy shapeless kitbag from somewhere at the back of the store, as well as a six-pack of Michelob with one can already missing, and a thin salami sausage. 'Rations,' he remarked, laconically. He sprawled himself out on the Mustang's rear seats as Gil turned out of Prospect Street and back towards Del Mar.

'You and me haven't been fishing in a while,' Laurence remarked to Henry, as they roared down the long hill towards the beach.

'Been busy,' said Henry.

Laurence made a face. He knew what Henry meant by 'busy'. 'Drunk', that's what he meant by 'busy'. With his hand keeping his nautical hat on, Laurence leaned forward and said, 'Fishing in a small boat in a good strong surf is the world's A-number one cure for a hangover.'

They reached the beach where they had found Sylvia Stoner's body, and parked. It had been almost a week now, and no further eels had been discovered in the ocean, so the police barriers had been taken away. There were one or two joggers around, and a small gang of dedicated surfers, but as yet it was too early for the mother-and-baby crowd, and very much too early for the school lunch break brigade.

They walked across the beach leaving imprints on its immaculately smooth surface. The tide was well out, and still retreating. The clouds were reflected in the wet sand, like fragments of jigsaw.

'It would help to know what kind of a creature you're looking for,' said Laurence. 'Is it big, or small? A shellfish, or a worm?'

Henry shielded his eyes against the wind and the sun and looked around the beach, trying to remember where it was that the writhing eels had buried themselves.

'It's big,' he said. 'More like a kind of a lizard, I guess you could say.'

Laurence wrinkled up his nose. 'You're wasting your time, in that case. Ain't no lizards on these beaches.'

'You'd be surprised,' said Gil.

'*Lizards?*' Laurence demanded. 'You're putting me on.'

Henry pointed to the sand in front of him, and said, 'Try rousting them out here.'

Laurence lifted his kitbag off his shoulder. 'If you say so. You're paying the money. But I can promise you one thing. If it's lizards you're after, you're going to be real disappointed. I never did see no lizards on these beaches, not once in forty years.'

He hunkered down on the sand, and began drumming on the beach with the palms of his hands. Gil looked across at Henry and raised one questioning eyebrow, but Henry gave him a look which meant, this may seem ridiculous, but bide your time, and watch.

'Rousted some clams there already,' remarked Laurence, nodding towards a slight patterned disturbance in the surface of the sand. 'See, what this drumming does is simulate the sound of the sea coming in, and the clams get themselves all excited and prepare to come up. Least, that's the theory. Some people say that it don't do nothing but irritate them, like a snake-charmer tapping his foot irritates the snake, and makes it come out of the basket. Snakes is stone-deaf, same as clams. Never saw a clam with ears, anyhow.'

He kept up this long bantering commentary as he moved around in a wide semi-circle, crabwise, his left leg leading the way, his hands pattering on the sand in a light, insistent rhythm.

'Not everybody can do this. It's what you call an acquired skill. You remember Gene Krupa, the famous drummer? Well, he came down to San Diego once, and he wanted to know how to do it, but he couldn't work up that rhythm for anything.'

Gil suddenly touched Henry's arm. 'Look,' he said. 'Over there.'

Only twenty feet away, right in the centre of the sloping beach, the sand was beginning to shiver and crack. Whatever was causing the vibration, it was at least three feet long, maybe longer, and it was moving deep beneath the sand with a restless, spasmodic jerking.

Laurence peered at the movement, and said, 'Now that's something. I never saw nothing like that before.'

He walked over to the patch of disturbed sand, and prodded at it with the toe of his sneaker. 'Now that's really something.'

Out of his kitbag, he took a small metal shovel, which he usually used for digging up clams. He began quickly and methodically to dig a narrow, deep trench.

'What did you say this was? Some kind of lizard? It's sure buried itself way down deep.'

Henry and Gil waited by the side of Laurence's excavation, both of them shivering slightly in the sea-breeze. Their bodies may have been sleeping peacefully during their exploits in North Africa last night, but their minds were tired; and Gil would have done anything to go back to his own bed and sack out for the rest of the afternoon. But he was determined to stay by Henry. Between them, they were the core of the Night Warriors, and if they didn't hold together, then they might as well give up their fight against Yaomauitl, and his buried offspring.

After twenty minutes, Laurence suddenly said, 'I got something. There's something down here all right.'

'Laurence, be careful,' warned Henry.

'Feels like something *knobby*,' said Laurence. 'That's right, Jesus, you're right. It's like the back of some kind of a lizard or something.'

He swung himself out of the hole in the sand and then stared back down inside it. 'Jesus, you see that? Well, you can't see too much of it, but that mother's *big*. What is it, Henry? Jesus, that gave me a scare, when I realised the size of it.'

Henry said, diffidently, 'It's a kind of a lizard, that's all. Now, do you want to fill that hole in again? I just wanted to make sure that it was down there.'

Gil stared at Henry in surprise, but Henry lifted his hand to indicate that he knew what he was doing. Laurence sniffed, and wiped his nose with the back of his arm, and said, 'You want to fill it in again? What in hell for? That must be some kind of rarity, that lizard. Must be worth something. They pay good money for specimens at Scripps, and at the San Diego Zoo, too.'

'Laurence,' Henry insisted, 'I want you to bury it.'

'Could be a thousand dollars in a rare specimen like that,' Laurence protested.

'*Bury it*,' Henry repeated. Laurence huffed, but picked up his shovel and reluctantly obeyed.

Gil took Henry aside. 'Why are we covering it up again? I thought you wanted to dig them up and kill them.'

Henry nodded. 'I *do* want to kill them, but I've had a better idea than digging them all up. You stay here; I'm going to see a friend of mine in the chemistry department at the University. You don't mind if I borrow your Mustang, do you?'

Gil looked doubtful, but Henry said, 'Have you seen me take one single drink this morning?'

'No, I guess not,' said Gil, and handed him the keys.

'Keep an eye on our friend Laurence here,' Henry told him. 'As soon as he's finished covering this Devil up, get him to drum up some more. Cover the whole beach as far as the cliffs. When you find one of the Devils, mark it with stones or something. I'll be back well before the tide starts coming in again. You should be able to locate at least ten. That's about as many as I can remember, and it tallies with what Susan said about the creatures in her dream.'

Henry jogged off up the beach. Gil thrust his hands into his pockets and turned back to Laurence.

'You have any idea what the hell these critchers are?' asked Laurence.

'Search me,' said Gil. 'I'm only the chauffeur.'

'Strange guy, that Henry Watkins,' Laurence observed. 'Good fishing partner, because he fishes and drinks and keeps his mouth shut. Last thing I like is a gabby fishing partner. But very brainy. I mean, at least as brainy as somebody like Einstein, if you ask me. I reckon if he didn't drink, he could've been famous. Could have won a Nobel prize, or something like that.'

He finished filling up the excavation, dropped his shovel on to the sand, and went across to his kitbag to twist out a can of beer. He made no attempt to offer one to Gil. He popped the top and drank half the can in one long swallow.

'Want to roust out some more?' Gil asked him, after he had finished the can, pressed the flat of his hand against his belly, and loudly eructated.

'You're paying the money,' said Laurence.

Gil stood by and watched with his hands in his pockets as Laurence slapped away at the sand in gradually progressing semi-circles. Maybe Gil was just tired, but it occurred to him that the dream world of the night and the waking world of the day were beginning to overlap. It was almost as weird, pursuing the Devils out here on the beach, in the sunshine and the wind, as it was pursuing them through the labyrinths of people's nightmares. It was more frightening, too, in a way, because to go after them in the daytime meant that they were real flesh and blood, not just the fractured pieces of somebody else's imagination.

What's more, he was unarmed and unarmoured, and if any of those Devils decided that it objected to being disturbed by Laurence's drumming, there would be nothing he could do to protect himself except run like hell.

Laurence suddenly said, 'Here's another – and another.'

Gil stepped forward. There were two shivering disturbances in the sand, quite close to each other. They were unmistakably similar to the first one they had located. Gil made a pattern of stones over each one. A crucifix, as if he were hunting vampires.

'I wish you'd tell me what these darn things are,' Laurence grumbled. 'It's unnatural, to go clamming and not know what kind of a critcher you're after.'

Gil said nothing, but forced a smile. He was still smiling when Bradley appeared, weaving along the beach on his bicycle. He was wearing a tee-shirt with *Let My Fingers Do The Walking* printed on it. He whistled when he saw Gil, and whooped.

'Hey, Gil, haven't seen you for *days*, compadre. Where you been?'

'Hi, Bradley. How are things?'

'Well, they're okay, I guess. You didn't come to Donna's *party* last night. Everybody was asking where you were. And guess who was there? Shirleen! You remember Shirleen, she used to go to school with the Kaiser brothers. Really enormous cakes. She went off with Jay McDonald, of all people, what a smooth-ass. I swear to God he puts rolled-up socks in the front of his pants, just to give him profile.'

Bradley stopped for a moment, and then looked around at Laurence, and frowned. 'Is that guy with you?'

'Kind of,' said Gil.

Bradley leaned closer. His breath smelled of orange-flavoured Bubble-Yum. 'What's he doing, or is it impolite to ask?'

'He's drumming up clams. He slaps the sand, see, and the clams come up to the surface.'

'This isn't the season for clams, is it?' asked Bradley.

'Not really, but we're practising.'

'I see,' said Bradley, although clearly he didn't. He watched Laurence for a little while longer, and then he said, 'Where were you, anyway? Your dad said you were staying the night someplace. Not with some lady of ill repute, I trust?'

'I was just doing some studying,' said Gil, uncomfortably. He realised how far he had grown away from Bradley after his experiences as Night Warrior. He suddenly thought of firing his weapon up at those Monks of Shame, and the way they had come fluttering down through the rain. He thought of those Arab horsemen, flaring like magnesium.

'Hey,' said Bradley, 'did you hear the one about the guy who phones home from the office?'

'No, Bradley, I did not hear the one about the guy who phones home from the office.'

Unstoppable, Bradley said, 'This guy phones home from the office, and this unfamiliar woman answers and so he says, who's this? And she says, it's the maid, but he says what maid, we don't have a maid, but the woman says your wife hired me this morning. So the guy says where is my wife, and the maid says she's upstairs with her boyfriend, in bed. So the guy goes crazy, and he says to the maid, go to the closet in the den, and take out my shotgun, and blast the shit out of my whore of a wife and her boyfriend. So the maid puts down the phone and a couple of minutes later he hears two bangs, and then the maid comes back and says it's okay, they're dead, what shall I do with the bodies? And the guy says throw them in the swimming-pool. And the maid says, *what* swimming-pool? And the guy says, this *is* 689-2281?'

Gil stared at Bradley and Bradley stared back at Gil, bursting to laugh.

'You don't change, Bradley, do you?' said Gil.

'You didn't think that was funny?'

'It was okay.'

'Hey, you coming to Ken and Lilian's barbecue tonight?' Bradley wanted to know.

But Gil didn't answer. His yellow Mustang had reappeared, and Henry was making his way down the beach towards them, carrying a large glass carboy and a length of shiny glass tubing.

Bradley saw that Gil wasn't looking at him at all, but watching Henry, and suddenly he frowned. 'Gil? What the hell is going on here, Gil?'

Gil slapped Bradley on the back, and tried to look cheerful. 'Just a little experiment, that's all.'

Bradley looked back at Laurence, who was still slapping the sand. 'Experiment? What kind of experiment?'

'I'm sorry, I can't tell you. It's kind of secret.'

'Can I watch?'

Henry came struggling up to them, and set down the carboy on the sand. '*Whewf!*' he said. 'That's darn heavy. There are two more of them in the trunk.'

'Henry,' said Gil, 'this is my friend Bradley.'

'Pleased to know you, sir,' said Bradley, holding out his hand.

'Well, absolutely likewise,' Henry replied, tautly. 'But do you think you could make yourself scarce? What we're doing here is rather – well, you know, unorthodox.'

'You want me to leave?' asked Bradley, somewhat hurt.

Gil said, 'I'll tell you what, Bradley, go back to the store, help yourself to any magazine you like. Tell Dad that I said it was okay, and that I'll pay for it out of my allowance.'

'You mean *any* magazine? *Hustler* or something?'

'You got it.'

Bradley mounted his bicycle, waved, whooped, and went wavering off again. Henry said urgently to Gil, 'I want to be quick, before any lifeguard patrols come past and ask what the devil we're up to. How many embryos have you located?'

'Six so far. Laurence is still drumming away.'

'Okay, then, I want you to help me,' said Henry. 'This carboy contains concentrated sulphuric acid. I borrowed it on permanent unofficial loan from the chemistry department at the University, as payment for a favour I once did for one of the lecturers. A horrible man called Kinsky.'

'What are you going to do with it?' asked Gil.

'Very simple. Wherever Laurence has located an embryo, I'm going to push this glass tube down until it touches the Devil underneath. Then, with the aid of this funnel, I'm going to pour down a hefty beakerful of acid. Look – we might as well start here, where we dug up the first one.'

'Do you think it's actually going to work?' asked Gil, fearfully.

'My dear fellow, this stuff will burn its way through the trunk of a giant sequoia, from one side to the other. There isn't a creature alive that can withstand it.'

Henry handed the glass tube to Gil, and Gil hesitantly positioned it over the spot where they had found the first of the Devil's offspring. Slowly, he pushed it down into the soft sand, inch by inch, until he suddenly felt the resistance of something that felt like a body. The sand shifted, and cracked, and he knew that he had located the Devil.

'Is that it?' asked Henry, and Gil swallowed, and nodded.

'Very well,' said Henry, and he carefully filled up a half-litre chemical beaker with the fuming, straw-coloured acid. Gil watched him as he fitted a glass funnel into the top of the glass tube, and prepared to pour the acid down it.

'You're really sure this is a good idea?' he asked Henry.

'It's the quickest and the most effective way I could think of,' Henry replied. His face was very grim.

'Okay, then,' said Gil. 'You'd better do it.'

Keeping tight control over his trembling hands, Henry slowly emptied the beaker into the funnel. The funnel filled up for a moment, and then gradually emptied, as the acid drained down the tube and into the cavity where the Devil's embryo was concealed.

The last of the acid disappeared, and Henry said, 'All right, now. Take the tube out.' He was white with stress, and he accidentally dropped the beaker on to the sand.

'Found another one!' Laurence called them, from across the beach.

'Thank you, Laurence,' Henry replied. 'We'll be right there.'

Gil watched the patch of freshly dug sand. 'Is it working?' he asked Henry. 'What are we going to do if it doesn't work?'

But his answer came from the sand itself. Suddenly and frighteningly, it started to heave and boil, and to kick up in sprays. Henry and Gil stepped back, and watched the commotion with increasing dread; but the creature did not emerge from its hiding-place. Instead, it twisted and thrashed deep below the surface, invisibly, and there was no sign of its death agony but the sand furrowing and humping and rippling.

At the very last, though, as the disturbance began to die away, Henry and Gil heard a scream that was quite unlike anything that either of them had ever heard before. It was a purely mental scream, inside their heads, but it set Gil's teeth on edge, as if he had been biting limes, and it cut through

Henry's thinking-processes like a sharp cleaver through calves' liver. Both of them squeezed their eyes tight shut as the scream went on and on; and in those moments of blindness both of them saw hell itself, the real hell of degradation and disappointment and pain and despair, the hell of cancer and fire and love gone cold. In the instant before the creature died, there was something else, though, something that chilled them even more, something that wrapped their foreheads in wind-chilled sweat. It was a sensation of mockery; of bloodthirsty taunting – that by kitting the Devil's child they had achieved nothing whatsoever, only the bringing down on to their own heads of the fearful revenge of Satan and his nine hundred and ninety-eight evil associates. The Devil's children were also the children of death, and so they returned gladly to the charnel-house of hell. They could be tortured, they could be imprisoned, they could be burned into raw fats by concentrated sulphuric acid, but they could never be truly destroyed.

When the scream had at last died away, shrinking into the back of their occipital lobes, Gil wiped his face with both hands, and looked at Henry with undisguised fear and deep respect.

'Oh, boy. Yaomauitl is really going to go for us now, isn't he?' he asked.

Henry said, 'It would seem so, if you experienced the same kind of feeling as I did. But I had a pretty good idea that this would happen. These embryos are not real embryos – not in the sense that each one of them is a separate individual. At least, I don't think they are. They're more like replicas, endless copies of Yaomauitl, which are closely connected through their unconscious minds with the master himself, their father. If one of them dies, if one of them gets hurt, then Yaomauitl knows about it, just as surely as if it had happened to him.'

Gil looked around at Laurence, who was patiently standing beside another disturbance in the sand.

'That makes eight,' he called.

'Are we going to kill them all?' asked Gil.

'Yes,' said Henry. 'Help me.'

Chapter Sixteen

They left the beach when the tide came in. They had emptied two-and-a-half carboys of concentrated sulphuric acid, and burned eleven embryos beneath the sand. It was four-thirty in the afternoon as they climbed back into Gil's Mustang, and turned around for La Jolla, to take Laurence back to his shell store. The sky had clouded over, and a cooler wind was blowing off the sea.

They had twice been obliged to halt their acid-pouring when lifeguard patrols came past, and once during the lunch break, when a gang of school kids decided to make camp close by, and to horse around on top of the very places where the Devil's embryos lay concealed. But Henry had been patient. By four o'clock they had succeeded in destroying every one of the embryos they had located, and Laurence had drummed all-over the beach for a second time, just to make sure that they hadn't missed any.

Henry turned around in his seat and counted out Laurence's money. 'I'll bring you the Chivas Regal tomorrow,' he promised.

'That's okay by me,' said Laurence, licking his thumb and counting through the bills, tidying them up and turning them around whenever they were upside-down. 'Just glad to be of service.'

'There's one thing,' Henry added, as they turned down Prospect Street. 'I don't want you shooting your mouth off about what we did today. It wasn't exactly illegal, but it wouldn't please the police department if they happened to find out about it. What the police don't know, the police aren't going to grieve over, if you get me.'

'I get you,' nodded Laurence. 'Besides – to tell you the truth – I still don't have the first goddamned idea what you guys were actually doing.'

'Good, let it stay that way,' said Henry, as Gil brought the Mustang to a halt outside the shell-store. He climbed out of the car so that Laurence could struggle out of the back, heaving his kitbag over his shoulder.

'*Hasta la vista*,' said Laurence, and disappeared inside his store, leaving the conch shells swinging on the awning.

'What do you think?' asked Gil, as they drove back to Del Mar. 'Do you think you can trust him?'

'Laurence?' asked Henry. 'No, I don't think so. But find me somebody else who could have done what he did today.'

Gil said, 'There's just one thing ... you kind of thought all of that acid thing up on your own.'

Henry glanced at him. 'I know what you're going to say,' he answered. 'You're going to say that I should have involved you, right from the moment I first thought about it. You're going to say that two heads are better than one, and that four heads are better than two. You're also going to say that because I'm older, I seem to have taken charge of the Night Warriors, and that I expect all of you to do whatever I tell you.'

Gil thought about all that, and then nodded his head. 'Yeah, that's pretty much it.'

GRAHAM MASTERTON

'Well,' said Henry, 'I've been thinking about that as much as you have, and all I can say is that I'm sorry. I should have discussed the idea with you earlier. I should have discussed the idea with *all* of you. Being a teacher, I'm used to being in control, and I guess I expect to have things my own way automatically, without thinking. But from now on, I'll try to give the Night Warriors the benefit of my experience without the authoritarianism that seems to come along with it.'

'Henry,' Gil told him, 'I like you a lot. Don't misunderstand me.'

'Well, I'm pleased about that, because I like you, too.'

They returned to Henry's cottage, where Henry went through to the kitchen to make some bologna and pickle sandwiches, while Gil called Susan's house to see if she was back from the hospital.

'She's back,' said her grandmother, 'but the doctors say that she has to rest for at least a week, and in three days she has to go to the clinic for more tests.'

'I'm really pleased she recovered,' said Gil.

'Thank you, Gil,' said her grandmother, and Gil could hear that her tone had softened. 'We praise the Lord that she's well again.'

'Is it possible I could talk to her, just for a minute?'

'I'm sorry. Maybe tomorrow.'

'Okay, then. Could you please just tell her – *eleven.*'

'Eleven?'

'It's just a little joke between us, that's all.'

'All right, then. I'll tell her eleven, whatever that means.'

Henry came in with the sandwiches just as Gil put the phone down. 'Any luck?' he asked. 'How is she?'

'She's fine. She has to rest, but she should be able to join us tonight.'

'Excellent,' said Henry. He took a mouthful of sandwich, and passed the plate to Gil, saying, 'Help yourself,' with his cheeks crammed.

When he had eaten two sandwiches and drunk a large glass of milk, Henry checked the time. 'I want to get back to the Scripps Institute before it closes. I'm afraid we'll have to play this one by ear, since we don't know where they're keeping the creature, or how well it's guarded.'

'Do you have a gun?' asked Gil.

Henry shook his head. 'I used to have a Japanese sword that my brother brought back from Tinian.'

'My father has a gun, behind the counter in the Mini-Market. A .357 Python.'

Henry thought about this, and then slowly shook his head. 'It's too risky, carrying a gun. Far too risky.'

'Well, how else are you going to kill this creature? Chop its head off? An axe is going to be a whole lot more conspicuous than a gun.'

'Maybe you're right,' Henry agreed. 'But the question is, how are you going to get hold of it?'

'What's today? Thursday, right? Well, tonight's the night my father goes off early, to his sports club meeting. I can get in there and lift that gun and nobody will even notice.'

Henry picked up a slice of pickle that had escaped from one of his sandwiches and popped it into his mouth. 'Well ... very much against my better judgement –'

'There's something else,' said Gil. 'Why don't we get Lloyd in on this? He looks pretty athletic, and pretty bright. I think we ought to involve him, too.'

'Do we know where he lives?' asked Henry.

'Not far, somewhere on Lomas Santa Fe Drive, I think he said. I'll look it up in the telephone directory.'

So it was that a little after five they left Henry's cottage and drove to the Mini-Market at Solana Beach, where Gil handed over his Mustang to Henry, and went into the store. Henry then drove alone over to Lomas Santa Fe Drive, pulling up just past the fire station at a neat small white-painted house with a green roof and green shutters. He made sure that nobody was looking and then he hopped out of the Mustang without opening the door.

He walked up the short sloping driveway and rang the chimes. He waited two or three minutes before a black woman in a purple-and-white dress answered the door, and stared at him suspiciously. 'Yes?' she asked him.

'You're Mrs. Curran?' he smiled, straightening his necktie.

'That's right. What do you-all want?'

'I'm looking for Lloyd Curran. My name is Henry Watkins. I'm a professor at the University of California at San Diego.'

'What do you want with Lloyd?' Mrs. Curran demanded.

'I was talking to him yesterday. We were discussing educational prospects, university degrees, things of that kind. I have some information he asked for, on university curricula.'

Mrs. Curran stared at Henry for a very long time, without saying a word. Then she turned back into the house, and called, 'Lloyd! Some professor wants you!'

Lloyd came to the door wearing a bright red tee-shirt, and smacking his fist into a catcher's mitt. He didn't recognise Henry at first, but then Henry lifted his hand in the unique salute of the Night Warriors, his hand raised, palm facing behind him, and Lloyd suddenly understood that he was receiving a house call from Kasyx, the charge-keeper.

'Hey, come on in,' he said, but Henry could hear the sounds of television and rock music and arguing children inside, and so he shook his head. 'Just come out and sit in the car for a minute. We can talk there.'

'Well – okay,' Lloyd agreed, reluctantly. They walked down the path together and climbed into Gil's Mustang. Lloyd ran his fingers over the dashboard, cut out of machine-turned aluminium, and the special sport steering-wheel, and said, 'Are these *your* wheels, man?'

Henry shook his head. 'I haven't driven my own car in years. Up until the time I was initiated into the Night Warriors – well, I had a little drinking problem.'

Lloyd was obviously impressed by Henry's candour. He said, 'I smoke a little ganja now and again – but, you know, nothing heavy.'

'When you're a Night Warrior you don't need anything like that,' said Henry. 'The high comes with the power. Your slide-boxing is something special.'

Lloyd said, 'Can I tell you something?'

'Go ahead.'

'Last night, in that dream, I was scared. I mean I was really truly scared.'

'You had every right to be,' said Henry.

'Well, I know that, man, but the strange thing is, when I woke up this morning, I felt disappointed. I felt that I wanted to be back there, where the action was. I couldn't believe it, but that was the way I felt. I was scared, but I loved it. I felt like I was really somebody, doing something.'

Henry smiled, and nodded. 'You were,' he said. 'How about your ex-wife?' asked Lloyd. 'Are you going to try to rescue her tonight?'

'I'm going to try to rescue her now,' Henry told him. 'In a minute, Gil and I are driving up to the Scripps Institute to kill that creature we met in that dream last night. We were wondering if you would care to come with us.'

'You mean – without being a Night Warrior? Just as me? No armour, no slide-boxing?"

'Just as you,' said Henry. 'The only weapon we're going to take with us is a gun, and the sole purpose of carrying that is for executing the creature, nothing else.'

Lloyd blew out his cheeks, and rapidly drummed his fingers on his knee. 'You're talking about breaking the law, man.'

Henry said, 'Yes. But then again, no. We – you and me and Gil and Susan – we are the only people who truly understand the danger of what is going on here. For that reason, we have to think of *ourselves* as being the law. Vigilants, do you see, whose duty it is to protect the world from the Devil.'

Lloyd said, 'We're taking a gun?'

'That's right.'

'And we won't have none of the armour, none of those special skills?'

Henry shook his head.

'Okay then,' Lloyd agreed. 'You can count me in. Just let me go tell my ma I'm going to be late.'

Henry waited in the car. There was some argument between Lloyd and his mother, but eventually he came scuffling out, and climbed into the car again.

'Everything all right?' asked Henry, starting up the engine.

'Ma thinks I'm a kid still. She don't like spooks, neither.'

Henry U-turned the car, and headed back towards Solana Beach. 'I don't think anyone ever called me a spook before,' he said, with an odd sense of satisfaction.

They picked up Gil by the Santa Fe railroad crossing. He was carrying a brown paper sack full of groceries. He waved, and ran across the road to meet up with them.

'Did you get the gun?' asked Henry, heaving himself uncomfortably back into the driver's seat.

Gil lifted a box of Cheerios out of the sack. 'Right inside here,' he smiled, triumphantly. 'I told Mom I was staying around your place another night to revise some English Literature, and we needed some groceries.'

'She doesn't object to your staying?'

'Not at all,' said Gil, steering the Mustang across the highway. 'Once I convinced her that you weren't a faggot.'

'Thanks for nothing,' said Henry.

It took them another fifteen minutes to reach the Scripps Institute. One of the police cars was still parked in the lot, but apart from that the building and its grounds were almost completely deserted. Henry told Gil to park the Mustang at the very far end of the parking-lot, under the shadow of a cypress tree, where it would be out of sight of the main entrance to the marine biology department.

'I'll walk in, and ask to speak to my wife,' said Henry.

'Your ex-wife,' Gil corrected him.

'That's right,' said Henry. 'Then I'll walk through to the marine biology laboratory, and as I pass by I'll open that emergency exit right there – that brown door, you see it? – from the inside. As soon as you hear the door click open, you should get yourselves inside as fast as you can, but don't close it after you. I'll go back to the reception desk, say that I've finished talking to my ... ex-wife, and sign out. Then I'll come round to the emergency exit and let myself back in.'

'What do we do once we're in there?' asked Lloyd, apprehensively.

'To your right, about thirty feet along the corridor, there's a broom closet. Hide in there until I join you.'

'That emergency exit – it doesn't have an alarm on it, does it?' asked Gil.

'Not the last time I used it. Soon after we were divorced, I snuck into the laboratory to steal back my gold fountain-pen. Andrea never even realised it was me who took it. She was always complaining how dishonest the laboratory staff were.'

'What about the gun?' asked Gil.

'You're the gunner, you take it. Tuck it into your belt, at the back, and just make sure you don't sit down too quick. The last thing I want is an ass less Warrior.'

It was seven minutes to six, almost time for the marine biology department to close. Henry marched straight inside, and Gil and Lloyd watched him through the window as he spoke to the receptionist. At first, the receptionist seemed reluctant to let him through, but then they saw him sign the visitor's book and make his way back towards the laboratory. They loped over to the emergency exit, and waited beside it for Henry to open it up.

'Supposing he gets caught?' Lloyd wanted to know.

Gil turned back and looked at him. 'Then, my friend, we are well and truly fucked.'

But it was only a minute before the brown door abruptly clicked open Gil and Lloyd looked quickly all around them, and then dodged inside, pulling the door to behind them, but not quite closing it. Inside the corridor, it was white and fluorescent and smelled of institutional floor polish. There were framed photographs on the walls of dolphins and narwhals and squids.

Their sneakers squeaking on the polished floor, Gil and Lloyd hurried to the broom-cupboard, and let themselves in. Gil tripped over a bucket, and a mop slid sideways down the wall and clattered on to the tiles, but they held their breath for what seemed like minutes on end, and nobody came to investigate.

'Next time, why don't you just yell out, "we're over here!"' Lloyd whispered.

'It was an accident, for Christ's sake.'

They waited for only a few minutes more, and then the cupboard door suddenly opened again, and Henry came in, gasping and out of breath. He nearly knocked over the mop, but Gil managed to catch it before it fell.

'Security guard was taking a look around,' Henry panted. 'I had to jog around the building and come up behind him.'

'Man, you're not fit at all,' said Lloyd.

'You don't need to be an Olympic athlete to teach Kant,' Henry retorted, with a small show of bad temper. Exertion always made him bad tempered.

They stayed in the broom cupboard for almost half an hour. They heard doors being slammed and feet squeaking on the corridor floors and people calling goodnight. Eventually, the corridor lights were dimmed, and Henry eased open the door and looked out.

'It's all right now. It looks like just about everybody's gone home.'

The three of them walked as softly as they could along the corridor until they reached a short staircase on their left with a notice that read *Marine Biology Laboratory – Spectator Seating*.

'We'll go up there,' said Henry. He remembered Gil's words about always taking charge, and so he added, 'If you agree that it's a good idea, that is. There's a balcony there, overlooking the main laboratory. We'll be able to see exactly where the creature is being kept, and where the police guard is situated. Then we can discuss how we're going to take the creature out.'

'Sounds okay to me,' said Gil.

'Me too,' Lloyd agreed; and so the three of them crept up the stairs, until they reached the swing doors which led out on to the balcony. Through the small wired-glass windows in the top of the doors, they could see that the laboratory was still brightly lit. Henry held them back for a moment, and then eased one of the swing doors open, so that he could see the laboratory's main floor. Gil and Lloyd crowded closely behind him.

Below the railing of the balcony, the laboratory was about fifty feet square, white and tiled and gleaming. There were three long varnished benches, stocked with test-tubes and chemicals and pipettes and flickering bunsen burners. At the far end of the room an IBM computer terminal flickered and glowed, next to a microfiche retrieval display. To the right, up against the wall, there were rows of steel shelving on which stood scores of aquarium tanks. Most of the tanks were empty, but in some of them there were shoals of tropical fish swimming backwards and forwards like showers of brightly coloured needles, and turtles dipping and diving in search of food.

In the centre of the laboratory floor stood a large dissection table, flooded by bright overhead spotlights. On this table, face down, a sinewy black creature lay, its face turned towards Henry and Gil and Lloyd, its eyes closed, its scaly body shining in the lamplight. Andrea was standing over the creature, peering up at an X-ray transparency. She was wearing her spectacles, and looked tired and drawn. A little further away, sitting on the edge of a tilted laboratory stool, talking quietly to a uniformed police officer from the San Diego police department, sat Salvador Ortega.

Henry very carefully let the swing door close again. He turned to face Gil and Lloyd and said, 'Well? What do you think?'

Lloyd shook his head. 'We don't have a chance, the way things stand. If we came down that balcony, waving a gun, those cops would waste us before we could make it anywhere near enough to make sure of that beast.'

'I agree,' said Gil. 'We daren't risk using the gun until the police are out of the way.'

'That means a diversion,' said Henry. 'Something to get them out of the laboratory just long enough for one of us to nip in there and blow that creature's brains out.'

Lloyd said, 'I hate to raise this at a time like this, man, but what happens after we've blown that creature away? Those cops are going to run us in, right? I mean if we kill that thing, isn't that murder?'

'Not murder, no,' Henry assured him. 'The creature isn't

human, after all. The worst they can get us for is illegal possession of a firearm, and tampering with police evidence.'

'Those are still offences, right? They can still lock us up?'

'Well, yes,' said Henry, uncomfortably. 'I suppose they can.'

'In that case, I pass,' said Lloyd. 'I don't know about you guys, but I'm not going to be locked up in no cell for nobody, and especially not the ex-wife of somebody I don't hardly know.'

Gil said, 'Henry, he may be talking sense. This may not be the right way of doing it.'

Henry looked from one to the other, thoughtfully. 'We have to destroy that creature some way,' he said.

'Well, listen, I've got an idea,' said Lloyd. 'If you can get everybody out of that laboratory for just about a minute – your wife, the cops, everybody – then maybe I can jump down off the balcony and hit it with something, crack it on the head.'

'How about setting fire to it?' Gil suggested. 'There are bunsen burners down there, and bottles of methylated spirit. Maybe we could make it look like an accident.'

Henry went back to the window in the swing door, and angled his head so that he could peer down into the laboratory. 'You may have a good idea there, Gil,' he remarked. 'There are two bottles of pure alcohol on the actual examination table itself. All you would have to do is knock one of them over, make sure the creature was drenched with it, and set it alight. It may not seem a very *likely* accident but there's a good chance that nobody would be able to prove anything different,'

He turned around. 'It won't be as quick and as effective as a gun.'

Gil lowered his head. 'Well, I know; but I guess I wasn't too keen on using the gun anyway. I know that it was my idea, but if my dad found out that I'd borrowed it – well, he wouldn't trust me again, with anything. Especially if I used it to shoot somebody, or something.'

Henry nodded. 'I understand. Let's see if we can't burn it.'

Five minutes later, Henry knocked at the door of the laboratory. '*Andrea!*' he shouted. 'Andrea, are you in there? *Andrea!* 'The doors were opened immediately by Salvador Ortega. 'Professor Steinway – what are you doing here? This building is all closed up for the night.'

Henry tugged at his sleeve. 'I have to see Andrea – to warn her –'

'Come on, Henry,' Salvador cajoled him. 'This isn't the way to behave.'

Henry seized Salvador's lapels, and stared wildly into his face. 'Salvador, listen to me. You have to listen to me! Andrea's going to die! Andrea's going to die, do you understand me? You mustn't let her touch that creature any more! It's going to kill her!'

'Who's that?' called Andrea. 'Henry, is that you?'

'Oh, Andrea,' Henry babbled. 'Andrea! Andrea! I always loved you, didn't you know that? You mustn't touch that creature any more! You must run, flee! I loved you when I was married to you, Andrea, and I love you now!'

'You're drunk,' said Andrea, coldly.

'I'm not! I'm sober! I'm stone-cold sober! Smell my breath! Go on, smell my breath! Smell it! *Haahhhhhhhhh!* Did you smell that? *Haaaahhhhhh!* There you are, nothing but garlic, and that came from two baloney sandwiches.'

Andrea came out into the corridor with Salvador. 'Henry,

listen,' she said, 'I don't care whether you're drunk or not. I'm a very busy person, and I have four skin-tests to complete tonight before I go home. So would you please be good and go back to your cottage and submerge your senses in whatever brand of distilled grain you happen to be favouring this month.'

Henry gripped Andrea's lab coat, and wound his hands around it. 'Andrea, I love you! Haven't I always said so? You mustn't touch that creature any more! Promise me! Promise!'

Salvador opened the door of the laboratory, and called out. 'Officer, would you escort this gentleman out of the building? I think he's suffering from nervous strain, not to mention too many vodkatinis.' The uniformed officer came out of the laboratory with a grin, his thumbs tucked into his leather belt. 'Yes, sir,' he said to Salvador, and then to Henry, 'Come along, pal, I think you've overstayed your welcome.'

Henry glared at him. 'Pal? I'm no pal of yours, you uniformed chump! Did you hear that, Salvador? This police officer claimed that he was a pal of mine – or at least that I was a pal of his. Do you know what a serious offence that is? Referring to a member of the public in an overly amicable manner in an attempt to secure his co-operation to waive his rights under the Constitution.'

Salvador put an arm around Henry's shoulder. 'Come on, Henry, I don't know what this act is all about, but it's time to go. I don't want to have to take you down to the cooler, do I? It wouldn't look good in the papers. "Famous Philosophy Prof in Chokey".'

Henry melodramatically slapped one hand against his heart. He arched his head back and rolled his eyes. 'Aaagh!' he shouted. 'Aaagh!'

'Henry, what is it?' Andrea asked him, anxiously. 'Henry!'

Henry allowed his knees to buckle, and he took two or three steps around the corridor with his legs bent. As he came around for the second time, he glimpsed orange flames leaping up inside the laboratory, and he knew that his diversion had worked. Lloyd had managed to jump down from the spectator's balcony and splash the creature with alcohol.

'Henry –' said Andrea, but before she could say anything else she was interrupted by an ear-splitting screech. She and Salvador both whipped around, and the uniformed officer instantly pushed open the laboratory door.

'Oh my God!' Andrea cried. 'Oh my God, the poor thing's on fire!'

They burst into the laboratory. To Henry's horror, the Devil-creature was sitting up on the dissection table, with flames pouring out of it like a sacrificial Buddhist. Its slanted eyes were blazing crimson, its double layers of teeth were stretched back in agony, and it windmilled both arms around so that the flames made a terrible flaring, roaring noise. Henry glanced up towards the balcony, but Lloyd and Gil had both disappeared.

'Fire extinguisher, for Christ's sake!' yelled Salvador. He tore off his jacket and approached the blazing creature like a matador, trying to avoid its circling arms.

The creature screamed and screamed and screamed. In every scream, Henry could hear the clashing of hell, the fury of fire, the agony of torture. The screaming was so piercing that he wasn't sure whether it was audible or not; only that it was unwiring his nerves with the systematic insanity of a lunatic slashing at a telephone cable.

Salvador tried to dance in closer, but the heat from the burning creature was already unbearable. It was astonishing that it was still alive and able to scream. Its black flesh crinkled and crackled like paint being heated by a blowtorch. Flames gushed out of its chin, so that it grew a beard of fire. Greyish brains began to bubble and leak out of its ears, and its blood sizzled noisily as the fire burned its way down through its layers of skin.

'Where's that fire extinguisher?' Salvador roared. He made one pass at the creature, holding out his jacket and over the smell of charring flesh they could also smell the distinctive odour of scorched wool.

But before the uniformed officer could get back to the dissection table with the extinguisher, every fluorescent light in the laboratory abruptly exploded, showering them with broken glass. Ghostly flickers of blue light danced momentarily on the ceiling, and then the laboratory was drowned in darkness – apart from the fiery Devil itself. It rose up, blackened, on the dissection table, until it was standing on its hind legs, like a goat or a monkey. Its eyes were burned out, its bare bones gleamed through its incinerated flesh, but it stood there in front of them, still blazing, still mocking them, still defying them to come nearer.

With a succession of ear-splitting crashes, all the aquaria along the wall of the laboratory burst open. Henry heard water splashing on to the floor, and the desperate flapping of suffocating fish. Then, one by one, the bunsen burners flared with gas, and exploded; and immediately afterwards every single test-tube and every single pipette and every single bottle of chemicals smashed into thousands of pieces of hurtling glass. 'Out!' yelled Salvador. 'Out!'

Henry awkwardly pushed Andrea toward the door. But as she reached it, she turned and screamed at him, 'It's locked! I can't get out! Henry, it's locked!'

Henry looked desperately around him for something to beat the door open. He picked up a mahogany-seated lab stool, grasped hold of its legs, and bashed it at the wooden panelling once, twice, three times. At the third blow, the stool's seat flew off and he was left with nothing but a handful of sticks.

Salvador, his coat still lifted up in front of him, made a last effort to smother the creature's flames. The uniformed officer had managed to bring the fire extinguisher forward, but the mechanism seemed to be jammed, and he was hitting it again and again with the butt of his police revolver. The scene in the darkened laboratory was like some grotesque marionette show. A small screaming figure standing on a stage, gushing with flames, while nobody could do anything at all but stand around and helplessly watch. The room was filling up with thick black smoke now that choked their noses and filled up their throats with the sickening odour of burning bone.

Salvador turned in horror to Henry and shouted out, 'Can't you get that door open?'

'It's locked!' Henry shouted back. 'I've tried breaking it down but it's too solid!'

'We'll have to climb up on to the balcony!' said Salvador. But as he lowered his sports jacket, and took a step back towards them, there was a sudden roaring rush of flame, and the burning Devil leaped off the dissection table and clung on to him, like a child clinging on to its father. '*Madre mia!*' Salvador shouted, and frantically clawed at the burning Devil. But it had wrapped its arms tightly around his chest, and was digging its claws into him. His cotton shirt scorched and suddenly flared, and he staggered back three or four hysterical paces, with the Devil still hugging him tightly.

'*Help me!*' Salvador screamed. '*Help me, for God's sake, help me!*'

The uniformed officer circled warily around Salvador. Henry glimpsed his terrified face in the light of Salvador's burning shirt. But then the creature lashed out with one of its claws, so quickly that Henry saw nothing but a semicircular rush of fire. Its claws caught the flesh of the officer's face, and ripped off everything below his eyeballs, right down to the bones of his skull, with a sound like a tearing sack. The officer's hands jerked up to his face in a reflex of agony and utter horror, and then he collapsed into the darkness.

Salvador wrestled with the Devil, suddenly silent now in the depths of his unbearable pain. But the more he twisted, the more he struggled, the tighter the burning Devil clung on to him. Salvador's hair burst into flame, and Henry watched in morbid fascination as it curled and shrivelled, and his scalp turned patchy and red. Salvador didn't scream, even though the Devil's thigh-bones must have burned right through to his pelvic girdle, and its claws must have deeply penetrated his back.

It was then that the laboratory doors swung open, and Gil and Lloyd appeared, Gil holding his father's gun. Gil said, 'Christ Almighty.'

Henry turned to him, and shouted, 'Give me that!' His voice was almost hysterical. Gil handed him the gun without any argument, and Henry took it, cocked it, and walked up as close to Salvador and the Devil as he dared.

Over the Devil's hunched and blackened shoulder-blade, Salvador caught sight of Henry lifting the revolver. He nodded his mutilated head up and down, in silent supplication. Kill me, *por favor*. Henry held the heavy pistol in both hands, his aim wavering for a moment, and then fired. The recoil was terrific; the laboratory bellowed with echoes. The top of Salvador's head burst open like a pot of red chili that had suddenly boiled over, and he dropped backwards against one of the varnished benches, and then on to the floor, the Devil still clinging to his chest.

The blazing Devil turned, thwarted of Salvador's living soul, looked up at Henry and screamed again, a terrible carrion-crow scream that chilled Henry from the roots of his hair to the joints of his toes. Its claws released their hold on Salvador's body, and Henry heard them scratching on the tiles.

He fired once. His ears sang. The Devil's chest flew open, like an exploding birdcage, and blazing fragments tumbled in all directions. He fired again, and the Devil's skull was smashed. He fired twice more, and at last the creature was nothing more than pieces of burning bone.

A wind began to blow. Softly at first, stirring the ashes of what had once been Yaomauitl's bastard child. Then much more strongly, and much more loudly, a low doleful shriek like the mistral which blows down the Rhone-Saone valley in France, and eventually drives men mad with depression; or the sirocco which blows across the Sahara, its flying grit turning glass windows into blinded stones.

Henry lifted his head, his grey hair blown sideways by the wind, his eyes watering with heat and emotion.

'Yaomauitl!' he shouted. 'Yaomauitl!'

But then the wind died away, whispering into the corners of the laboratory, and Henry knew that Yaomauitl had gone. He turned around and looked at Gil and Lloyd and Andrea, and outside he could hear footsteps approaching along the corridor, and the sound of police sirens.

He laid his hand on Gil's shoulder. Gil stared at him in shock.

'It wasn't your fault,' Henry said, hoarsely. 'Nobody could have known what that creature was going to do.'

Gil pressed the back of his hand against his forehead. 'It was burning,' he said. 'It was burning and it wouldn't die.'

The uniformed officer whose face had been ripped off by the creature's claws started to moan and bubble, somewhere in the shadows.

Lloyd said, 'Oh my God. It's a real Devil, isn't it? I mean a real actual Devil.'

'Yes,' Henry replied. He was conscious that Andrea was looking at him fixedly, her glasses held close to her chest.

'Henry,' she said, in a trembling voice. 'Henry, what happened here?'

'You were examining that creature,' said Henry. 'You must have known what it was.'

'I had no idea, Henry. The tests that we managed to complete showed that it was nothing more than a kind of amphibian ... a kind of urodela, like a salamander or a siren. Very highly developed, of course, but –'

'A Devil,' Henry interrupted her.

'What?' asked Andrea, perplexed.

'What are the seven tests of Abrahel?' Henry asked her, his voice choking.

'The what? Henry, you asked me that before. I don't know. What on earth are you talking about?'

Henry said, 'You're saved, Andrea. You don't know it, but you're saved.'

At that moment, an arc-light suddenly flooded the laboratory, and Henry realised that the place was crowded with police and medics and firemen. A police officer came up to Henry and prized the gun out of his hand, and said, 'Okay, sir. I'll take that.'

Chapter Seventeen

Springer was a woman that night. She wore a complicated gown of white taffeta and white silk, with a high ruffled collar and a triangular bodice of pleated lace embroidered with white seed-pearls. It looked as if it had been created by the court dressmaker of Queen Elizabeth I in conjunction with the Emanuels.

She said, when they were all assembled, and all transformed into the arms and armour of the Night Warriors, 'You have been rash.'

'We have killed all of Yaomauitl's offspring,' said Kasyx, defiantly.

'You have killed all of those offspring which came from the body of Sylvia Stoner. But there will be others, just so long as Yaomauitl is free.'

'We know that,' said Gil. 'That's part of the reason we did it.'

Xaxxa put in, 'We could have spent years, hunting for Yaomauitl, without ever finding him. You know that. Dream after dream, with no luck at all. The only reason you found that Devil son of his last night was because you knew where to look.'

'Same as the night before,' said Samena. 'The night you sent us into Mr Lemuel Shapiro's nightmare, with no hint of a warning.'

'So, what we've done now is, we've made Yaomauitl mad,' said Xaxxa. 'We've made him *so* mad that he's going to come looking for us, instead of the other way around.'

Kasyx added, 'We plan to bushwhack Yaomauitl, if that's the right word.' Springer paced slowly around the assembled company of Night Warriors, her dark impenetrable eyes taking in the crimson electric armour of Kasyx, the white breastplate of Tebulot, the plumed tricorn hat of Samena, and the tight harness of Xaxxa. When she had walked around them in a complete circle, she said, in the sharpest of tones, 'Well ... we speak differently tonight. We speak with independence. We speak with accord.'

'Perhaps we're learning who we are, and what we can do,' Xaxxa replied.

'You killed one man and seriously disfigured another, in your new flourish of independence and accord,' said Springer.

'No,' said Kasyx, 'that's where you're absolutely wrong. *We* didn't hurt those men, Yaomauitl did. This is a war, Springer, not just a frolic for four people who want to do something more exciting at night. This is an invasion. Believe me, I regret the death of that detective more than anybody. He was the first detective with whom I was ever on first-name terms. But in wars, in invasions, people get hurt. You can never win unless you take that risk.'

Springer remained expressionless for a moment, and then smiled. 'You have spoken well, Kasyx,' she said. 'You have understood the gravity of what Yaomauitl is attempting to do. You have begun to act on your own initiative, too; and even though your attack on those buried Devils was hasty and ill prepared, you were lucky, and it worked, and you destroyed them. Whether it is owed to luck or not, there can be no serious criticism of success.'

Samena said, 'Were you planning on putting us into any particular dream tonight?'

Springer shook her head. 'You must go out on your own now, and choose whichever dream you will. You are not yet fully experienced Night Warriors, but you are ready to select a dream of your own. My task is almost finished.'

'You're leaving us?' asked Samena. Suddenly she found the prospect of being without Springer quite unsettling, like driving for the very first time without an instructor. Samena had spent a whole day in limbo, as a hostage to Yaomauitl's offspring, and she was still nervous about going back into dreams. She had not yet been able to explain to any of the others the total fear that she had felt; the deathly despair of sitting alone for hour after hour in a room whose walls were as intangible as fog, and yet as impenetrable as tempered steel. There had been no sound in that room, no feeling, no vibration. Nobody had visited her. And there had been nothing at all to suggest that she was not going to stay there for all eternity.

Springer produced a white peacock fan out of her sleeve and began to flutter her face to keep it cool. 'I am not exactly what you think I am, any more than Ashapola is exactly what you think *He* is. We are greater and at the same time lesser; yet greater because of our lessness.'

Kasyx, trained as he was in philosophy, was equal to that riddle. 'I see,' he said. 'Ashapola is the God of Human Possibilities, and you are his messenger.'

Springer said, 'You make a wise charge-keeper, Kasyx. One day, in years to come, they may remember your name with great admiration.'

Kasyx turned to Tebulot, Samena, and Xaxxa. 'I've learned something else,' he told Springer. 'I've learned that no charge-keeper can be greater than the Warriors he is appointed to serve. We are one. We are Night Warriors.'

Springer took hold of Kasyx's hand, and bowed her head. 'I wish you good fortune in your fight against Yaomauitl. I shall be watching you.'

Now, clasping hands, the four Night Warriors rose through the roof of the house and into the night. There was no moon. They rose high, scanning the sparkling landscape for any intimation that Yaomauitl was coming after them; listening and looking, and using their heightened psychic senses, too. They drifted northwards, following the luminous line of the coast, four dark shadows in a dark sky. They could feel beneath them the dreams and nightmares of the thousands of people who were already asleep. Collectively their dreams were like palaces and apartment blocks with invisible walls, in which the strangest events were acted out, in darkness and in daylight, in fear and in happiness, in passion and in agony. Clocks spun, clouds rushed across unimaginable skies, fields of corn waved like fire. There were voices and sobs and so much music that it sounded as if a great unseen orchestra were tuning up, cellos and piccolos and anguished violins. Shouts. Laughter. Muttering and weeping.

In dreams and nightmares, everything was possible. The dead could walk and talk as if they had never been away. The unborn could open their eyes and stare at their mothers who never were. Love could be consummated between passing strangers. Fortunes could be won by the poorest, and to the rich could come ruin and humility.

Over these dreams and nightmares, the Night Warriors passed, trailing their shadows behind them. Every dreamer who sensed them go by would frown in their sleep, and feel in the morning that something unusual had happened to them during the night.

It was Samena who first sensed the presence of Yaomauitl. They had almost reached Beverly Hills, and they were about to turn eastward and head out towards Glendale and Pasandena. But Samena suddenly lifted her head, and raised her hands, and said, 'He's here. I can feel it. He's very close.'

The Night Warriors slowed their shadowy journey through the night. Samena closed her eyes, and slowly sank to the west, following her emotions rather than her eyes. The other three Night Warriors stayed close, keeping up with her, looking around them as they descended into the darkness for any signs of an ambush. They had seen how ferocious Yaomauitl's offspring could be. Yaomauitl himself, the Deadly Enemy, was fully grown, and centuries old. They had every reason to be frightened of him.

'Left, left,' murmured Samena, and they spiralled down towards a large pale green stucco house on Lago Vista Drive, in Coldwater Canyon. There was a free-form swimming-pool at the back of the house, an orchid garden, and a Bentley Eight parked in the driveway. There were lights on all over the house, and the Night Warriors could hear the sounds of music and laughter.

'Are you sure this is the place?' Kasyx asked Samena. 'I can't imagine that anyone could be sleeping with this noise going on.'

'Follow me,' said Samena, gently, and led the way down through the green tiled roof, through the large attic studio, through the ceiling, and into a child's bedroom.

It was a pretty bedroom, decorated with floral print curtains and an ice-blue wall-to-wall carpet. In the middle of a large brass bed, on top of covers that matched the curtains, a boy of about eight was sleeping. He was blond headed, suntanned but delicate featured, with skinny wrists and skinny ankles. He wore pale blue pyjamas, with wrinkled-up trouser legs. On the pillow next to him a small blue teddy-bear stared up at the ceiling, as if it had been pole-axed. At the head of the bed there was a sentimental religious picture of the four Apostles standing around the cot of a sleeping child, with the words *'Matthew, Mark, Luke, and John, bless the bed that I lie on.'*

The four Night Warriors stood at the foot of the boy's bed and looked down at him.

'The Devil's here?' asked Xaxxa. 'In this kid's dream?'

Samena said, 'Can't you sense it?'

They were silent for a moment. Downstairs, they could hear the adults of the house laughing and talking. From the fragments of conversation that they could pick up, it sounded as if the house belonged to a motion-picture executive celebrating the success of a recent production. A woman with a penetrating high-pitched voice kept saying, 'Charlton was *wonderful* ... I was never a fan of his, but he was absolutely *wonderful*.'

Kasyx said, 'Very well. The longer we delay, the more chance the Devil will have to prepare himself.' He lifted his arms, and drew the fluorescent blue octagon in the air, while the other three Night Warriors came closer to him.

Kasyx parted the night inside the octagon; the Warriors glimpsed darkness and sinister shadows. Tebulot eased his weapon off his back, and held it ready in case they were attacked as soon as they penetrated the dream. Kasyx raised the octagon over their heads, and then commanded it to descend all around them.

As soon as the octagon touched the floor, the Night Warriors found themselves in a whirling, cavernous nightmare. They were standing in what appeared to be a cathedral, or a church, with a high domed roof and a wide floor of black and white tiles. The cathedral was filled with an endless howling noise, echoing and breathy, like the sound of a subway train rushing along a tunnel; shadows and objects hurtled through the air in a mad defiance of the normal laws of gravity.

As they looked around, a massive rocking-horse appeared, the size of a small building, with snarling lips and bared teeth and wild blind eyes. It rocked thunderously over their heads, and when they looked up into its belly they could see huge oily springs and groaning gears, and scores of small children clinging desperately to its stirrups.

'Some nightmare,' said Tebulot. 'I bet the poor kid's parents have been forcing him to have riding lessons.'

Kasyx asked Samena, 'Any idea which way?'

Samena touched her forehead with her fingertips and closed her eyes. 'He's outside somewhere. I don't quite know where. But he's keeping very still and very quiet. He probably knows we're here, and he's hiding.'

'Okay, then,' said Kasyx. 'Let's head for the door, shall we? But keep a look out for absolutely anything.'

A screaming jack-in-the-box flew past them, its mouth stretched wide in mechanical agony, followed by the running shadows of fierce dogs. Then a table came by, turning end over end, and four chairs, and a shower of cutlery, and a grown-up's voice was barking and shouting all around them just as fiercely as the dogs. '*Now look what you've done! Now look what you've done! Now look what you've done!*'

They reached the doorway and looked back inside the cathedral. There were objects flying everywhere, even as high as the domed ceiling: keys, candlesticks, chairs, scissors, toys, shoes; the walls echoed and re-echoed with the sound of hundreds of conflicting voices – adult voices, shouting and screeching and bullying and nagging.

'*Now look what you've done!*' '*Can't you be more –?*' '*How many times do I have to –?*' '*Look at the mess you've –!*' '*If you don't tidy up your –!*' '*Don't you be so –!*' '*If you talk back to me once more, I'll –!*'

They glanced at each other, and each of them recognised the pit-of-the-stomach smallness of being a child. None of them said a word. This was the first time they had been reminded of the real feelings of childhood since they passed adolescence. For Kasyx, that was nearly forty years ago; for Tebulot and Samena and Xaxxa, it was only five or six. But until now they had completely suppressed the fear and the anxiety and the sense of utter dependence on adults whose tempers could unpredictably change from friendly to sarcastic to nightmarishly violent, for no reason that a child could even begin to work out. It was all here, however, inside this nightmare; the chaos and the turmoil of childish uncertainty.

The Night Warriors left the cathedral, closing its doors behind them. All around the cathedral spread an unkempt cemetery. It was daytime, but the sky was slate grey with impending thunder, and a wind furrowed the dry grass between the headstones, like a bony hand. The tombs here were enormous, huge stone engines of exalted death, with angels and masks and scythes carved on them; and open stone books in which words were written in strange indecipherable languages. Somewhere, a branch or a gate intermittently tapped in the wind, *tak-tak, tak-tak*, and they all felt that Yaomauitl the Deadly Enemy was somewhere close.

As they passed through the cemetery, towards the crumbling lych-gate, they heard the hollow grating of stone on stone. Xaxxa was taking up the rear, and he suddenly looked around, and quietly said, 'Oh Jesus Christ, man.'

Kasyx halted, and turned. Tebulot lifted his weapon. But Xaxxa remained where he was, staring at the tombstone right beside him. The lid had slid off to one side, leaving a narrow triangular gap, and inside the triangular gap they could see a yellowish corpse in a winding-sheet, an old woman who glared at them with eyes that were bloodshot and bulbous.

Kasyx said, 'It's just part of the nightmare. Forget it.'

Xaxxa slowly stepped away, without taking his eyes off the open tomb. As he passed the next tomb, however, there was another grating noise, and that opened up, too, revealing a half-decayed man in a morning suit. Then another tomb opened, and another, and another, until the sliding of stone lids on top of stone catafalques sounded like the grinding of teeth. Over two hundred bodies lay open to the thunderous sky, unmoving but unquestionably alive in the tattered finery in which they had been entombed; wedding gowns and dinner-suits, evening dresses and frock-coats, a celebrating company with staring eyes and rotten flesh.

The branch went *tak-tak, tak-tak*, and the Night Warriors walked cautiously through the cemetery, glancing apprehensively from one side to the other, ready for anything.

Suddenly, lightning cracked from the clouds, a thick-trunked tree of solid electricity, and earthed itself on a distant hillside. The wind whipped up, and leaves rattled through the air all around them. There was a smell of ozone, ozone and death. The freshness of allotrope of oxygen, mingled with the sweetness of human disintegration.

The dead sat up in their tombs. Whether they had been galvanised into life by that devastating discharge of lightning, like Frankenstein's monster; or by nothing more than a random fantasy that had entered the mind of the sleeping boy, the Night Warriors couldn't tell. Anything was possible in a nightmare. But the dead sat up, stiffly, their dry skin audibly cracking, their flesh flaking from their faces like pieces of desiccated fish, and they turned towards the Night Warriors and screamed at them.

It was no ordinary scream. It was a hellish discordant clamour that lifted up the hair at the backs of their necks, and chilled their bladders with a sudden primitive urge to urinate and then to run. Kasyx had never heard anything like it; not even this afternoon, from the blazing Devil. This was a cry of utter despair, from those whose lives had already been lived out, and finished. This was the most elemental human terror of all, expressed in one hideous noise. The fear of dying; the horror of being dead.

'Come on, let's get out of here,' shouted Kasyx; and the Night Warriors quickly retreated from the cemetery with the dead still screaming at them. Beyond the cemetery was a grassy field – although the grass was deep crimson, and the trees around it were pungent yellow, like a photograph that had been printed with the wrong dyes. Together, they jogged through the grass, looking back from time to time to make sure that the dead from the cemetery weren't following them.

After a few minutes, the screaming died away into the distance. The crimson field began to rise, until at last they found themselves standing on a ridge overlooking a strange city. All of the city's buildings were towering and black, sparkling with tights, and walkways connected the upper levels, one to another. There were black flags flying in the wind, and small aircraft swarming around the city like hornets. The city ticked, with a regular tensile tick; Tebulot turned to his companions and said, 'Clockwork. Can you hear that? The whole place is clockwork.'

It was then, however, that Samena turned around, and touched Xaxxa's arm. Xaxxa turned around, too, and alerted Kasyx.

'They've followed us,' he said.

Kasyx looked back at the wind-blown field of crimson grass. Advancing across it in a single line that was strung out from one horizon to the other, came the dead. They were silent now, and they walked with their heads lifted in decaying defiance, their tattered robes and dresses dragging through the knee-deep grass.

'Tebulot,' said Kasyx. 'This isn't any figment of the boy's imagination; this is Yaomauitl's doing. Are you fully charged up?'

Tebulot checked his charge-scale, and then nodded. Samena unclpped a multiple arrowhead from her belt, and slipped it over her index finger. Xaxxa stepped to one side, and crouched, ready to attack.

Now, the distant thunder began to grumble, and lightning walked across the far horizon like the long-legged scissorman. As the dead came nearer, the rain began to fall, big fat widely spaced droplets that rustled in the grass. Kasyx heard a high-pitched clicking behind and above him, and almost immediately four small clockwork airplanes from the clockwork city came curving overhead, their propellers shining in the rain, their stubby black wings buffeted up and down by the wind.

There was another sound, too. The tearing of grass. They looked down, and saw that handfuls of crimson turf were being ripped away from underneath by skeletal fingers that were demanding access to the world above. Only fifteen feet away, a hand broke loose from under the grass, and then another, and then the rotting head of a corpse emerged from under the ground, grinning the grin of the long-dead, its teeth and its ears and its eye sockets clogged with soil. At last, it tore aside the turf as if it were opening the zipper of a sleeping-bag, and rose to its feet, blindly and unsteadily, its head lifted to seek out the scent of living flesh. Another hand tore through the earth, right by Samena's foot, and then another. Soon the whole grassy ridge was wriggling with decayed hands, as the dead struggled out of their burial-barrow.

Kasyx said, 'This is it. This is Yaomauitl's army. The dead! Look at them!'

Xaxxa wrinkled up his nose. 'Man, they got to smell like the *worst*.'

Tebulot raised his weapon, and aimed it.

'Are you ready?' asked Kasyx. 'They'll tear us to pieces, if they ever get their hands on us.'

Samena was lifting her arms into the firing position, when suddenly she stiffened, as if she had heard something, and turned around.

'What is it?' asked Kasyx. But then he looked for himself, and saw it.

The clockwork city was somehow reassembling itself, changing, interlocking, like a gigantic child's toy. With an amplified mechanical clicking and clanking, it was rising into the threatening sky, building upon building, chimney upon chimney, whole railroad yards turning on their sides and interlocking into bridges; pyramid-shaped office buildings grinding around on their axes and rumbling into diagonal slots in the side of parking-lots. It rose, the city, and it darkened a sky that was already dark; a huge construction of buildings and highways and bridges, still glittering with light, still teeming with traffic, but a humanoid now, a city in the shape of a man.

The Night Warriors stared up at the clockwork city's staggering bulk, and for the first time since Springer had first invested them with the power of Ashapola and the ancient armour that had protected their ancestors, they felt helpless.

Slowly, two gleaming yellow eyes opened in the head of

the clockwork city, and a voice thundered down at them like a succession of trucks being hurled off a cliff top.

'*You have dared to defy Yaomauitl, the Deadly Enemy, the Scourge of the Church! You have dared to destroy my beloved children! For this, there is no forgiveness; no mercy! For this, there is nothing but eternal punishment, and the tortures of hell!*'

With another piercing scream, the tattered dead came running up the crimson hill towards the Night Warriors. They were armed with baling-hooks and scythes and curves of broken glass, which they clattered above their heads as they screamed.

'*Hit them!*' Kasyx shouted; and Tebulot dropped to one knee and fired a blinding salvo of power, one charge after the other in a tight quarter-circle. One after the other, corpses screeched and exploded and burst into flames. One of them was detonated in all directions – hands and feet flying one way, skull tumbling into the air behind him. Another, blazing, cartwheeled away across the grass, a fiery crucifix.

Samena dodged and skipped between the grasping hands that were still rising up from the grass beneath their feet, trying wildly to clutch at their ankles. She crossed her arms, and fired her multiple arrowhead at nearly a dozen corpses which had broken into an epileptic run and were heading up the slope towards Kasyx. The arrowhead whizzed on a shaft of golden power until it was ten feet away from her, then split up like a star-burst so that each individual part of the arrowhead could seek out its target. The running corpses stumbled, collapsed, and fell.

Now Xaxxa flashed away from the ground, soaring high above the field on his shining pathway of pure power. He turned to the right, lifting himself higher than Kasyx had ever seen him before, like a jet reaching the very top of its turn at an air-display. Then he was sizzling back across the thunderous sky, his knees bent in perfect balance, the surfer of the power-slide, his face concealed behind his mirrored mask. Kasyx turned his head to watch Xaxxa as he flashed along the line of corpses, just above their heads, and then turned again to come back and hit them with everything he had.

This time, he was so fast that his fellow Night Warriors could barely see him. He streaked along the ranks of the dead, kicking and punching in a non-stop flurry of whirling arms and legs. The dead dropped to the ground like harvested corn-stalks, thirty or forty of them, one after the other; and then Xaxxa arched up and around again to knock down some more.

His last pass along the line of corpses was abruptly followed by a sonic boom, that swelled and banged and then faded. He must have slid faster than a thousand kilometres an hour.

Tebulot began to fire quick individual blasts, blowing up one corpse at a time with devastating accuracy. Samena took to using flail-headed arrows, which opened out in flight and released spinning wires with weights at each end, like bolos, which whistled through the corpses' necks and sent their heads flying like grey pumpkins.

Kasyx glanced behind him. The clockwork city was slowly and noisily dismantling itself, returning street by street and building by building to its original form; but it had been an unnerving demonstration of Yaomauitl's power. They were on Yaomauitl's territory now, fighting in the nightmare which *he* had selected, and Kasyx was beginning to feel that they were already outnumbered, already outsmarted, and doing nothing more effective than a fly can do, once it has been snared on a spider's web. Struggling, yes; fighting, yes; and still alive. But with no serious chance of ever escaping unscathed.

More and more corpses rose from the ground, white faced and maggoty, with earth in their hair – more than Tebulot could shoot, or Samena could bring down with her arrowheads, or Xaxxa could successfully slide-box. Kasyx shouted. 'Back! Let's get back! There are too many of them!'

They fired off two or three more bursts of power. Corpses flared and shrieked and fell to the grass, guttering and crackling like burned-down candles. But more corpses rose behind them, pale and screaming, a huge jostling multitude that overwhelmed the Night Warriors at last. The four of them topped the ridge and began to run down towards the clockwork city, while behind them the dead swarmed up to the top of the hill, shrieking their rage and their agony up to the sky.

The Night Warriors were only halfway down the slope when more corpses appeared on either side of them. Tebulot stumbled and skidded to a stop, and fired a heavy multiple burst of energy, first to the left, and then to the right. There were more fires among the corpses. A severed arm flew high into the air, as if it were waving to oblivion. In patches, the grass caught fire, but the corpses continued to come screaming through the flames, some of them running with their dresses and their frock-coats on fire.

Now the Night Warriors were running in earnest. The slope gradually flattened out into a wide, grey, dismal plain, a place of ashes and wild timothy, which separated the hill from the clockwork city. In the distance, about a half-mile away, a clockwork train sped along a tinplate track, the windows of its passenger-cars alight, and high behind it a clockwork crane rose up, tick-tocking as it turned.

Their feet crunched in the ashes as they jogged nearer and nearer to the bulky skyline of the clockwork city. But Kasyx glanced behind him and saw that they had very little chance of reaching it. The armies of the dead had come running down the hillside; they had already outflanked the Night Warriors on the left, and were quickly overtaking them on the right.

Abruptly, Kasyx stopped running. The other three went on for a few paces, and then stopped and turned, too.

'What's the matter?' asked Samena. 'Kasyx? Are you all right?'

Kasyx said, 'We're making fools of ourselves! Look at us, running! We're doing exactly what Yaomauitl wants us to do!'

'What else are we going to do, man?' Xaxxa demanded. That's an *army!*'

'Yes, Xaxxa, but so are *we!* As long as we fight together, instead of separately.'

'What are you trying to say?' asked Tebulot.

'You said it yourself, earlier today. We have to fight together, and as equals. So let's do it.'

The front-runners of the army of corpses were only fifty or sixty feet away now. Tebulot raised his weapon and zapped off a burst of glittering explosive power that brought seven of them down.

Kasyx said quickly, 'What we'll do is this. I'll send out

NIGHT WARRIORS

a field of power to bring them all closer together. Xaxxa –
you can fly behind them, and station yourself there. Then
Tebulot can fire charges at you, which you deflect with your
power-slide into the back of their ranks. Samena meanwhile
can pick them off from the front.'

Tebulot looked uncertain, but Kasyx said, 'I'm sorry.
Maybe I'm being authoritarian again. But it should work, if
we do it quickly.'

'I'm game,' said Xaxxa.

Samena said, 'I'd rather fight it out than run away. And
I don't fancy *that* place one little bit.' She nodded towards
the clockwork city.

'Okay, then – let's do it to them before they do it to us,'
said Kasyx.

'Oh, God,' complained Samena. 'You've been watching
Hill Street Blues.'

Kasyx frowned at her. 'What on earth is *Hill Street Blues?*'

Xaxxa took up his slide-boxing pose, and flashed off over
the heads of the rapidly advancing corpses. Tebulot took an
extra charge of power from Kasyx, and then knelt down
ready with his weapon fitted up to his shoulder. Samena
armed her finger with more flail-headed arrows.

Kasyx stood just behind them, and stretched out his
arms. He closed his eyes, and concentrated deeply, and
his armour began to come alive with spitting electrical
charges. Samena, who was standing closest to him, could
hear a deep generator hum that meant he was about to
build himself up to maximum power.

Kasyx strained harder and harder, and at last opened
his fingers, so that a vibrating sheet of pure electricity
streamed out on either side of him like some kind of

impossible cloak. It streamed wider and wider and wider, until it reached the corpses who had been trying to outflank them, both on the left and on the right. The first corpses ran right into it, shrieked and pirouetted and exploded into blazing pieces.

Behind them, the others hesitated and then retreated, shuffling and pushing and panicking, and screaming even more loudly.

Some of them tried to go back towards the hill, but Tebulot fired a quick burst of energy at Xaxxa, and Xaxxa dived and swooped in the air and caught the energy against the bottom of his power-slide, so that it ricocheted off in a shower of sparks and zipped into the corpses like red-hot daggers into ripe cheese. Bodies burned and toppled and crackled into fragments.

Kasyx now brought his arms slowly towards each other, so that the electric fence which he was radiating out of his fingers began to close in on the corpses from either side. He was using full power, and he knew that he would be unable to sustain it for very long, but this was the only way he could think of to annihilate Yaomauitl's army of corpses quickly and completely.

Soon, the screeching corpses had been herded by Kasyx's fences into a narrow corridor, only a dozen feet wide. Around them, the burning bodies of their fellow corpses lay littered on the ashes of the plain. They began to wail and cry and mill around in desperation. They were already dead; but if they failed Yaomauitl he would summarily deprive them of their immortal souls. They were doubly afraid now – not just of being dead, but of being sent by Yaomauitl to eternal nothingness. And the human fear of eternal nothingness is the greatest human fear of all. It is the one fear which every religion in the world seeks to assuage. It is the fear of being totally gone.

Tebulot fired again and again, and Xaxxa leapt and swooped and looped in the air, kicking at each energy-bolt so that it tore through the corpses like lightning. Samena stood with taut confidence in front of the corpses, bringing them down in tattered heaps with volleys of bizarre arrowheads – whirling wires and multiple barbs and arrows that exploded in one body, zipped through to the next, exploded a second time, and then zipped through to a third.

One corpse – taller and stronger and less rotted than the rest – although half of his naked jaw was leering from out of the side of his face – came staggering out from the burning crowds of Yaomauitl's army, and lurched towards Samena with his hands clawing at the air. Samena fitted a simple arrowhead to her finger, straightened her arms, and hit him *zap!* straight in the middle of his forehead.

The corpse swayed but kept on staggering forward. Samena tried to reload, but she dropped her next arrowhead into the ashes.

'Samena!' Kasyx yelled at her.

Screaming harshly, the corpse fell against Samena, wrapping its rotted arms around her. Then it lifted her up into the air, squeezing her and shaking her in an attempt to break her back. Samena cried out in agony, and pummelled at the corpse's arms, but even though she broke off large chunks of decayed flesh, the corpse still clung on to her, and squeezed her even more ferociously. Kasyx could smell the corpse from ten feet away, and he saw with disgust and horror that every time it squeezed Samena more tightly, it squeezed a liquid flood of yellow-and-grey putrescence out of its own insides.

'Tebulot!' Kasyx shouted, and Tebulot turned around and saw what had happened. He couldn't shoot, though: the danger of hitting Samena with an energy-bolt was far too great. But Xaxxa, flying high above the remnants of the army of corpses, looked to see why Tebulot had stopped feeding him with fire-power, and he understood what was happening in an instant. He circled, paused, and then came surfing in across the battlefield at high speed, feet first, leaning back at an angle of nearly forty-five degrees.

There was a moment when Kasyx thought that Xaxxa was attempting the impossible. The corpse gripped Samena even more tightly, forcing its leprous forehead down against her throat, and clutching at her back until she began to jerk in spasms of pain. In that moment, Kasyx was tempted to shout out to Xaxxa to pull clear, to pull away, not to take the risk. But then Xaxxa streaked unerringly up to Samena and the corpse, and drop-kicked the corpse's head smartly off its shoulders, sending it over a hundred feet away, rolling and jumping across the ashes and the timothy grass.

The corpse's neck fountained with yellow-and-grey liquid, and then it spun around and buckled at the knees and collapsed on to the ground, releasing its hold on Samena at last. It gave one last trembling kick and then lay still.

Samena climbed to her feet, shuddering and pale faced; but she managed to give Kasyx a fleeting smile of relief. She had been captured by the Devil, and she had understood what total evil can do. Nothing – not even a rampaging corpse – could ever equal the terror of that.

Kasyx allowed his power-fences to die down, and the

four of them patrolled around the huddled army of corpses, occasionally firing at those which were still moving. Tebulot's weapon was hot in his hands, and almost empty of power; he looked around the plain of ashes and he saw corpses lying everywhere, over three hundred of them, and he knew that the Night Warriors had won a great victory over the forces of darkness.

The wind blew the ashes over the bodies, and flapped at their funeral clothes. In a day or two, they would be buried for a second time, this time for ever. Kasyx said, 'I suppose we ought to pray for them. They were only ordinary people like us.'

Tebulot came stepping over the corpses toward Kasyx, and said, 'Now we look for the Big Cheese himself, huh? Yaomauitl?'

Kasyx looked toward the clockwork city. It had taken on the shape of a huge recumbent body, but it was constantly changing, constantly reassembling itself, which showed that the boy who was dreaming about it was restless and frightened. Highway overpasses disconnected themselves from one intersection and reconnected themselves to others. Steeples and clock-towers rose and sank like the bobbin-heads of old-fashioned sewing machines. Lighted trains whirred in and out of tunnels; clockwork ticked; whistles blew.

Samena came forward with the plumes of her hat blowing in the wind. 'Yaomauitl is there,' she said, raising her hand towards the city. 'The city is made up of all the scariest things that the boy can think of. Yaomauitl has drawn them all together, and taken them over. You saw how the city rose up, like a Transformer. The city is Yaomauitl, and Yaomauitl is the city.'

Tebulot came and stood on Kasyx's right side, and Kasyx laid his hand on the machine-carrier's shoulder to recharge him.

'What do we do?' Tebulot asked. 'Do we try to blow up the whole city, or what?'

'Wouldn't that inflict damage on the boy, I mean psychologically – if we blew up all of his most intimate fears?' Samena asked.

'I don't know,' said Kasyx. 'Besides, I think the question's academic. We don't have sufficient power to destroy the whole place.'

Xaxxa said, 'Yaomauitl's got a *heart*, right, like everybody else?'

Kasyx nodded. 'I think we can assume that he has, since his offspring had an anatomy similar to a urodela.'

'A what?'

'That's a species of amphibian creature, like a salamander lizard, or a siren, which is a kind of a lizard that doesn't have any legs.'

'Okay, then,' said Xaxxa. 'If the Devil has a heart, then we can go into the city and find it, right? And hit him right where he lives.'

Tebulot checked the charge-scale on his weapon. 'That makes some kind of sense, I guess. If we don't have the power to destroy the whole city, I don't see that we have any option.'

Samena shrugged. 'It makes sense to me. We don't have very much time left, do we?'

'Question is, can we *find* the heart?' asked Kasyx.

Samena armed her index finger with an arrowhead that was designed to bury itself deep within a building or a body and then explode, like a whaling-harpoon. 'I'll find it,' she said. 'That time the Devil's offspring held me hostage – I think I developed a nose for Yaomauitl and his kind.'

They walked away from the plain of ashes where they had defeated the army of the dead, and into the outskirts of the clockwork city. Up above their heads, the sky was even more thunderous, and lightning leaped from cloud to cloud. By the time they had reached the first buildings, it was beginning to rain, a slow soft drizzle that glistened on the printed tinplate sidewalks, and beaded the printed tinplate walls. The Night Warriors walked cautiously down a dark narrow street, their weapons raised ready. They passed under a railroad bridge, and a train hurtled over them, its lights shining on the rooftops.

Samena touched her fingertips to her forehead, and closed her eyes. 'This way,' she said, turning to the left. They followed her along an even narrower alleyway, between buildings that were crowded with cogs and springs and ticking ratchets. There was a strong aromatic smell of oil in the air, as well as a curious odour of tin. Kasyx said, 'Can you smell that? I used to have a wind-up racing car that smelled exactly like that. Jesus, I feel like I'm six years old again.'

So far, they had come across none of the inhabitants of the clockwork city, but suddenly the alleyway ended, and they stepped out on to a broad tinplate mall, dimly lit, but busy with clockwork trams and clockwork buses and clockwork cars, all life-size. The noise of springs and cogs was tremendous and there was an endless skirling of painted metal tyres on painted metal pavement. The buses and trams were crowded, but only with vacantly smiling people who had been painted on to the tinplate windows. The bus drivers had been painted in profile on the side windows of the buses, and full-face on the front windows.

'This is truly weird,' said Xaxxa, as they walked past butcher's shops in which the meat was simply printed on to the back wall behind the counter, and grocery stores with printed advertisements for Wheaties and Come Brown Rice and Rinso. The drizzle sparkled in the streetlights, forming a soft halo around each one. As he walked along the wet sidewalk, Kasyx began to understand that they were making their way through some archetypal childhood, lost and gone forever in the real world, but still humming and clicking and living out its life on the fringes of every child's dreams.

This city was the boy-dreamer's creation only in so much as each individual part of it represented one of his nightmares. It was Yaomauitl the Deadly Enemy who had brought his nightmares together and made a city out of them. Yaomauitl could take on any form that he desired, and that was what Samena had meant when she said that Yaomauitl actually *was* the city.

The Night Warriors followed Samena through street after street, over narrow bridges and mysterious walkways, through silent town squares and clamorous trolley-depots. They had been walking through the rain for almost twenty minutes before she raised her hand and said, 'Listen! Now you can hear it!'

They strained their ears, and she was right. Underneath the whirring and chirring and ringing and clashing of the city's traffic, they could detect another kind of mechanical sound: the deep-throated *kachug*, pause, *kachug*, pause, *kachug*, pause, of a massive verge-escapement clock, with a swinging pendulum. This clock was the city's heart; a clock of nightmares, the kind of clock that chimed in echoing hallways, with a pendulum that swung backwards and forwards in a dark rushing arc, from wall to wall.

The four of them crossed a narrow bridge that took them high above the city's main street. Hundreds of feet below them, they could see the headlights of clockwork cars and buses, and the glitter of streetlights. The pale face of a clock on a steeple told them that it was already nearly half-past four, and that this deep-level nightmare couldn't continue for very much longer. As dawn broke, and the boy-dreamer began to stir, his mind would gradually rise up through the lighter debris of dozing dreams, and this malevolent clockwork city would be buried in darkness for all time.

'There!' said Samena, pointing ahead of them. The bridge led them to a curved tunnel, right through the sixty-sixth floor of a tall iron-grey skyscraper, and on the far side of the skyscraper there was a balcony, with tinplate railings. They jogged through the tunnel and came out on the other side, and stepped right up to the balcony's edge.

In front of them – out of the black chasm of the city's structure – a massive iron framework rose up, and inside this framework a clockwork mechanism steadily and inexorably beat away the minutes of the night. From the centre of the mechanism a pendulum swung, a pendulum that was more than a hundred feet long, and which bore on its disc-shaped weight the death mask of a goat-bearded man, in corroded bronze.

'Yaomauitl's heart,' Samena declared.

Tebulot wiped the rain away from the visor of his white helmet. 'Do you think we have enough power to destroy it?' he asked Kasyx.

Kasyx gave him a thumbs-up sign. 'One burst at maximum strength should do it. Aim for the anchor.' The anchor was the claw-shaped piece of metal which rocked from side to side with each swing of the pendulum, releasing the toothed cog-wheel one tooth at a time. If the anchor was damaged, the cog-wheel would spin freely, and release the escape-wheel from which a hundred-tonne pallet of pig-iron was suspended, two hundred feet below them.

Tebulot shouldered his machine, while Kasyx stood behind him and placed a hand on each of his shoulders, to infuse him with as much of Ashapola's power as possible. The charge-scale on the side of Tebulot's weapon shone white, indicating full energy and more. It hummed loudly, eager to be released. Samena and Xaxxa kept watch from opposite sides of the balcony, in case anyone or anything attempted to stop them.

'Ready?' Kasyx asked Tebulot. 'Then kill him – *in the dark and holy name of the Night Warriors!*'

Tebulot fired. There was an ear-shattering *zzhhh-waaappp!* and a fifteen-foot bolt of supercharged energy streaked from the muzzle of his machine. But they had reckoned without the strength and the cunning and the devilish alertness of Yaomauitl, the Deadly Enemy; for as the energy-bolt sped towards the massive clock mechanism, there was a metallic flickering sound, and a flock of curved metal plates were catapulted through the air like clay pigeons or frisbees, right across the front of the clock structure. Tebulot's energy-bolt hit the first plate in a spectacular shower of sparks, and the plate was skeeted off sideways. But it had been enough to deflect the energy-bolt by two or three degrees, and when the bolt hit the next flying plate, in another explosion of sparks, it was deflected another two degrees, and then another, and then another; a glittering bursting succession of firework ricochets, which set up a whistling and a crackling like nothing that any of them had ever heard before.

As it sparkled against the very last plate, the energy-bolt flashed harmlessly skyward, disappearing into the windblown cloud-base. The plates themselves, smoking and scorched, tumbled down into the depths of the clockwork city, bouncing off beams and scaffolding and railroad tracks with a deafening clanging and ringing sound.

The Night Warriors were stunned by what had happened. They stood on the balcony watching the gargantuan clock-mechanism continue as before, *kachug*, pause, *kachug*, pause, and they knew that, this time, they had failed.

'That's it!' said Kasyx. 'We're almost out of power! Let's get out of this dream as quickly as we can!'

But, right then, the skyscraper on which they were standing began to descend, just as other towers began to rise. They looked down from the balcony and saw the building sliding smoothly and quickly into the ground, its lighted windows swallowed up storey by storey, while a tall thin steeple right next to them began to climb into the sky at the same relentless speed. All around them, bridges and traffic interchanges swung around and reconnected themselves, without even a pause in the flow of clockwork trains and cars. Lightning forked down between the buildings, and lit up the chaos of assembly and reassembly in stark, startling relief.

As the sixty-sixth floor of their skyscraper neared the ground, the Night Warriors stepped back into the protective shelter of the tunnel behind them; but the balcony retracted of its own accord before the building slid without any hesitation into a sleeve of close-fitting steel plate. They saw a wall of greasy metal speeding upwards in front of their eyes, just as if they were standing in an elevator. Then the building slowed and hissed and shuddered to a stop, and the balcony opened out again into a series of steps.

Down here, there was silence. They were deep inside a metallic cavern, only a little higher than their heads. They cautiously climbed down the steps and looked around, Kasyx using his helmet to illuminate the furthest depths of the cavern. They could glimpse shadowy archways, and massive pillared supports, and greasy black electrical cables that hung from the roof like boa constrictors.

Kasyx looked from one side to the other, and then said, 'There's nothing here. This is way down underneath the surface. The power and maintenance department, if you ask me.'

'Shall we call it a night?' Samena suggested anxiously.

'I think so,' said Kasyx. 'Tebulot? Xaxxa?'

Xaxxa nodded. 'Let's face it, man, he outsmarted us that time, but next time we're going to be ready. Next time we're going to blast that mother right where it hurts the most.'

Tebulot raised his hand in agreement. He had been fighting hard, and his machine was heavy, and he was looking weary. Kasyx therefore took a single step backwards, and opened out his arms so that he could draw the octagon in the air.

'We shall return to fight Yaomauitl again,' he said. Samena, Tebulot, and Xaxxa gave him, bravely, the salute of the Night Warriors.

At that moment, however, they heard a grinding, clashing sound from the darker recesses of the metallic cavern. Kasyx looked this way and that, his horizontal beam flickering from one shadow to another. Tebulot, tired as he was, lifted up his machine again; Samena unhooked an arrowhead from the jingling collection on her belt. 'What the hell is that noise?' Tebulot asked, alert and nervous.

His question was answered immediately, for out of the darkness, on all sides, ten or eleven gigantic clockwork machines appeared, advancing on them in that same whirring rush that characterizes all clockwork devices. Each machine was different, but all were nothing much more than a huge wheeled collection of churning cogs and ticking springs and swinging foliots and spinning crown-wheels. The Devil's machinery – because it had no other purpose than to mangle or maim anybody who was caught in their way.

Xaxxa instantly sped away from the rest of the Night Warriors on a power-slide that illuminated the whole cavern. He banked and turned, keeping his head low so that he didn't hit it on the cavern ceiling, and streaked in to drop-kick one of the machines on its side-plate. His first kick did nothing but unbalance the machine for a moment, but then he circled around again, ducking low, and delivered another two-footed kick, right against the very top of the machine.

The machine teetered on its wheels, and for a second Kasyx thought that it would regain its equilibrium, and keep on coming. But the momentum of its own cogs swung it to one side, and it crashed to the floor of the cavern in a thunderous explosion of flying gear-wheels and tumbling spindles.

Samena ran forward, somersaulted between two machines, and fired a double-headed arrow as she did so. Each arrowhead trailed out behind it a long thin cable of braided steel, and the cables flew into the clockwork mechanisms, instantly tangling them up. The two machines screeched and ground and strained at their springs, and eventually jammed up completely, then stopped.

Tebulot blipped off four or five small energy-bolts, wrecking one machine and sending another round and round in clattering circles, shedding nuts and bolts and pieces of framework as it went. Kasyx shouted, 'Back! Back! Let's get out of here!' and lifted his arms again to draw the octagon. But as he did so, Samena screamed at him, '*Behind you! Kasyx! Behind you!*'

Kasyx heard the machine before he saw it. His ears were suddenly filled with the whirring of flywheels, close up behind him, and then he turned and saw that one of the machines was almost on top of him. He tried to stumble clear but the cogs snatched at his ankle, and suddenly half of his leg had been tugged in between the wheels and springs. He roared out in pain, hopping on his one free leg and desperately trying to push against the mechanism's framework to drag himself away.

If he hadn't been wearing armour, his leg would have been completely mangled. As it was, the cogs had crushed the greaves below the knee, and twisted the alloy of his sabatons. The machine squealed loudly as its crown-wheels tried to pull him deeper inside, and the teeth of its cogs rattled against his poleyns, or knee-plates. He gritted his teeth, and pushed harder against the framework. He felt his muscles cracking, and the sweat streaking down the side of his face, inside his helmet. His trapped leg felt as if it were on fire, and he knew that if he relaxed even for one instant, he would be pulled right inside the clockwork and killed.

He could have used his last remaining power to disable the machine. But, if he did that, there would be no energy left to take the Night Warriors back to the real world. They would be imprisoned in the clockwork city for as long as the clockwork city lasted, and then swallowed up for all eternity when the boy-dreamer awoke.

'Kasyx!' Samena shouted, and came running up to help him.

'Get back!' he gasped. 'Don't come too close!'

Now Xaxxa and Tebulot came up, and in spite of Kasyx's protests, caught hold of him under his arms, and helped him to maintain his steady pull against the devouring machine.

'Let me go!' Kasyx demanded. 'I can ... draw the octagon ... then you can – For Christ's sake, let me go!'

Tebulot said, 'No martyrs in this cause, old-timer. Hang on tight. Samena, let's have one of those wires of yours, to jam up this machinery.'

Samena came up close, and fired off a wire-trailing arrowhead at close range. The wire lashed itself around the crown-wheels as tightly and as quickly as a fuse-spring, and the clockwork juddered and snarled and came to a stop.

'Right,' said Tebulot, 'Xaxxa – see if you can kick those cogs free.'

Supporting himself against the machine's framework,

Xaxxa kicked out at the gear-wheel again and again and again. At last, one of the spindles burst out of its socket, and three cogs clattered on to the ground. Xaxxa kicked again, and Kasyx's leg came free.

The three of them lifted the charge-keeper out of the machinery. His leg was twisted at an odd angle, and he was white with pain.

'Put him down for a moment,' said Tebulot, but Kasyx violently shook his head and said, 'No – no! Let's get back! Just gather around me, and let's get back!'

They did as they were told. They all came close to him, supporting him this time instead of simply holding his hand, and he drew the sparkling blue octagon right in the air in front of them. As he lifted it above their heads, they heard more clockwork machines grinding toward them, but Yaomauitl had missed his chance. The octagon sank all around them, and when it touched the floor they were back in the sleeping boy's bedroom.

The house was quiet now; the lights were out. The sun was just beginning to lighten the sky over the Santa Monica mountains. The boy had buried himself in his covers some time during the course of the night, and now lay hot and tousled, with his arm hanging over the edge of the bed.

Kasyx winced, and half collapsed. 'Jesus! This hurts,' he gritted, between tightly clenched teeth. Tebulot said, 'Come on, I'll get you home. You should be okay, once you're back in your own body.'

Samena clasped his hand, and said, 'Take care, Kasyx. I'll call you as soon as I can.' And Xaxxa put his arm around him, and looked straight into his eyes, and gave him a short strong nod which meant more than words could ever have expressed. We're brothers; we're friends; we've fought together; we've been scared together. It doesn't matter that I'm young and black and that you're old and white. We're Night Warriors, and when we fight the Devil we're together.

Samena and Xaxxa rose and faded through the ceiling of the house, and were gone. Tebulot supported Kasyx with his arm, and helped him to lift himself slowly into the air, and fly out over the early morning canyons of Beverly Hills.

They had a long way to go, back to Del Mar, but the wind was warm and the morning was sunny and Tebulot had sufficient strength for both of them. He carried Kasyx back past San Juan Capistrano and San Clemente and Cardiff-on-Sea, slowly and gently and as solicitously as a son.

Nobody could have seen them flying past. The sun was too bright and their images were too insubstantial. But they were as graceful as the transparent wings of dragonflies; as silent as a kind thought; and they carried with them the last hope of returning Yaomauitl the Deadly Enemy to his elm-wood prison in Mexico.

Chapter Eighteen

Jennifer woke up in the middle of the night and she was drenched in sweat. She had been dreaming that dream again, that dream in which the Devil had been lying on top of her, forcing her legs apart, and whispering in her ear, '*Now you will be my little mother.*' She had dreamed it two or three times a week, ever since that encounter with Bernard at the supermarket, and it was always the same. The weight of its body, the feel of its fur, the stench of its breath.

But tonight it was different. Tonight when she woke, clutching the tangled sheets, sweating, shuddering – tonight she could still feel something. Tonight there was a stirring in her stomach, a strange slithering sensation, and a persistent nausea that refused to be swallowed away. As she lay in the darkness with Paul sleeping heavily beside her, and only the green eyes of her digital clock for company, she tried to think what it was that she had eaten that day that could have upset her so much. The passion-fruit juice, at breakfast? The herb-and-tomato omelette she had eaten round at Sandra's, for lunch? The fillets of veal which she had cooked for Paul's dinner?

Usually, when she felt nauseous, she had only to think about what she had eaten to be able to identify what it was that was making her feel unwell. But this sickness was quite different: this sickness kept turning and rolling inside of her stomach as if she were still trying to digest something that was only half chewed. This sickness had a movement of its own.

She lay and sweated for another half-hour. The sky outside the tightly drawn curtains began to lighten. She longed to get up, to draw back the curtains and make herself a cup of hot strong lemon tea. But Paul was a hair trigger sleeper, easily disturbed, and he needed his rest after five straight days in Denver, trying to wrap up the Trianon deal. So she lay where she was, rigidly, clutching and releasing the sheets, sweating, trying to suppress the rolling and the slithering, trying not to feel so desperate.

Slowly, she moved one hand down until it rested on her naked abdomen. Her muscles were churning all right, she could feel them. Yet they couldn't be her stomach muscles, they were too low down; and this slow turning-over sensation wasn't at all like gas.

It suddenly occurred to her just what this sensation felt like. She hadn't felt it for a very long time, not since the days when she and Paul had been poorer, but happier, and they had lived in that third-floor apartment over on Santa Monica Boulevard, next to the Mexican restaurant. They had *wanted* a family in those days, but that was before Paul had started getting serious about his promotion prospects, and about office politics, and about his status in the air-conditioning industry.

She remembered the happiness. She remembered the sunshine. She remembered the day that she had come back from the doctor and told Paul that he was going to be a father.

She also remembered the day when it had all ended. The pain, the spasms of labour, the blurred faces in the hospital. She had heard it cry, just once. Too young, too underdeveloped, to survive. Paul had held her hand. Her mother had brought her walnut candies.

But now, tonight – this feeling. This intermittent pushing and rolling. This was the same, or almost the same. She didn't know how – she had taken her pill religiously – and Paul had been away so frequently and for so long that they scarcely ever had sex any more. *But it was the same!* She couldn't deny it, no matter how much she tried to pretend that it was omelette or fillet of veal or plain old flatulence.

She felt as if she were having a baby. She stared at the ceiling. This was ridiculous. Of course she wasn't having a baby. Apart from the fact that she hadn't missed a single pill, she had experienced no morning sickness, no changes of mood, no swelling of her breasts. She hadn't had a period, of course, but then she took her pills continuously, most of the time; and even when she did allow herself to menstruate – to flush herself out, as she liked to think of it – her flow was always very light.

She couldn't be having a baby. And yet – what else could it possibly be? It was inside her, and it was moving on its own. She was sure that it was shifting around of its own accord; around and around as if it couldn't settle itself for a moment.

She looked across at Paul. It was light enough now for Jennifer to be able to make out his face. His eyes were closed, his mouth was slightly open. He wasn't snoring, he never did. He always looked as if he were dead. It only took one wind-rattled door, however, or one dripping tap, or one foot creaking on a wooden floorboard, and he was instantly and irrevocably awake.

Jennifer whispered, '*Paul.*'

There was a moment's pause. She knew that he had woken up instantaneously, and that all he was doing now was deciding behind those closed eyelids whether he ought to sit up and be angry, or keep his eyes closed and pretend that he was still asleep, or listen to whatever nonsense it was that Jennifer was going to tell him.

'Paul,' Jennifer repeated.

He opened his eyes. Hazel-coloured irises, too pale to be really attractive. He stared at her without speaking. Perhaps he hadn't made up his mind yet what kind of mood he was going to be in.

'Paul, I'm sorry to wake you, honey, but I think I'm sick.'

'Sick? What do you mean? You mean nauseous?'

'Well, kind of, but not exactly.'

He propped himself up on one elbow. 'Not exactly? What exactly does that mean – not exactly?'

'It's like my stomach's turning over and over. It won't stop. I feel like I want to throw up, but I can't.'

Paul dropped his head back on to the pillow. 'Jennie,' he said, tiredly, 'I don't expect to be woken up at the crack of dawn just because you have a stomach-ache. I have a long hard day ahead of me. I need to get some rest. Now, why don't you go to the bathroom and fix yourself some Pepto-Bismol or some Alka-Seltzer and then come back to bed and settle down?'

'Paul, it isn't that kind of a sickness.'

'How many different kinds of sickness are there?'

'Paul, there are lots of different kinds of sickness. This

is more like – I don't know – this is more like a period sickness.'

'Jesus, Jennie, if it's a period sickness, then take whatever it is you take for period sickness.'

Jennifer protested, 'My period isn't even *due*, Paul. And, besides, I haven't been having periods for six months.'

'Then maybe it's time you did. Maybe that's what the pain is. Your body, telling you to stop fucking around with it and treat it like a body ought to be treated.'

'Paul –'

'For Christ's sake, Jennie, what do I have to do to get some sleep around here? If you're sick, go make yourself a cup of tea and read a book or something. There's nothing I can do about it, is there? I mean, in all seriousness, what can I do? It's your stomach. Take it out of this bed and go take care of it, all right?'

'Paul, please –'

'Jennie,' said Paul, in a warning voice, and Jennifer knew then that if she persisted, he would really lose his temper. When he said 'Jennie' in that particular way, he was drawing a chalk line in the air, and that chalk line meant this far, you understand me, and no further.

At another time, on another occasion, she might have considered that it was worthwhile arguing. But this morning she felt too sick and too miserable, and so she climbed slowly and unsteadily out of bed and slipped on her pink nylon-fur slippers, and groped for her dressing-gown on the back of the bedside chair. Paul made a production out of turning over, and readjusting the pillow, and settling himself down for the short remainder of his allotted night's sleep. Not that he *would* sleep, Jennifer thought, with a startling amount of bitterness, as she turned around and looked at him from the bedroom doorway. He would lie there and smoulder in wakeful martyrdom; but he would lie there without moving until the alarm went off, and even then he would press the snooze button, to give himself five minutes more self-pity.

She went through to the brown-tiled kitchen. Outside, it was already bright, and three California quail were out on the patio, pecking at the stale crackers which she had put out for them. She filled the coffee percolator with water, and went to the pantry, but though she felt hungry, she knew that if she tried to eat anything she would probably vomit. She sat down on one of the kitchen stools, with her head in her hands, and tried to suppress the cold roiling in her stomach, while the coffee percolator went *baloop*, blip, *billip*, blip.

The coffee was almost ready when she felt the first sharp pain. It was so unexpected, but so agonising, that she jumped off the stool and screamed out loud. The stool fell clattering on to the tiled floor behind her, and Jennifer dropped to her knees, clutching her stomach.

'Oh my God!' she cried out. 'Oh, Paul! Oh, my God! Paul! *Paul!*'

The pain was right inside her uterus, so intense that she didn't believe that she could bear it. She felt as if her womb were actually being torn apart, or stabbed, or twisted around and wrung out, like a dishrag. For a moment, she went into shock, and her heart bumped as slowly as a grand-piano falling off a precipice, bump, fall, bump, fall. Her eyes rolled up into her head and she began to shudder and grind her teeth.

Paul came into the kitchen, naked, angry. White chest and shaggy pubic hair. 'Jennie! What the *hell's-*' he shouted. But then he saw her rolled-up eyeballs and the way she was shuddering, and without saying anything else he went straight over to the wall telephone and punched a number. 'Ambulance – I want an ambulance, quick! Fourteen-forty Paseo del Serra. Yes, it's my wife.'

Then he knelt down beside Jennifer and held her in his arms and said, 'Honey?'

Slowly, the pupils of her eyes sank back down into view, although she still looked glazed.

'Honey?' Paul persisted. 'Listen, honey, I've called for an ambulance.'

'Paul,' she whispered. She scarcely moved her lips, as if she were trying to ventriloquise; as if she wanted to speak to him without her body finding out what she was doing. 'Paul ... it hurts so bad ... I can't stand it.'

He started to lift her up. 'Come on, Jennie. Come and lie down on the bed.'

'Don't move me,' she whispered.

'Jennie – you can't stay here on the kitchen floor –'

'*Don't move me! For God's sake, Paul, don't move me!*'

Paul stared at her closely. 'Jennie, honey, you just can't stay here on the floor.'

Jennifer began to judder and shake, and a long string of saliva dangled from her lower tip. 'Oh God, Paul, it hurts so bad. It's like something's biting me. It's like there's something inside me and it's biting me.'

'Honey, it's probably food-poisoning. That's a symptom of food-poisoning, that sharp pain like that. It must've been the veal. You have to be careful with veal. Was that fresh veal you bought, or frozen veal? I'll sue that market for everything they've got.'

Jennifer could scarcely hear what he was saying. The pain inside her uterus was growing steadily more severe, as nerve after nerve was stripped away. The wriggling grew more excited, too, and when Paul gently opened Jennifer's dressing-gown to look at her stomach, he could see the convulsive movements for himself, quite clearly, as if her muscles were turning and contracting in grotesquely exaggerated peristalsis. Her skin was actually rippling, and rising, as if something were pushing at it from inside.

She threw back her head, so that the veins in her neck stood out like dark blue worms, and she screamed. It was the most terrible scream that Paul had ever heard in his life, even worse than the woman he had heard screaming on the Ventura Freeway, after her arm had been severed in a car-crash. This scream was so agonised, so desperate, that Paul found himself screaming, too, shouting at the top of his voice, begging her to stop it. '*Stop it! For Christ's sake, stop it!*'

Suddenly, unexpectedly, she did stop. She stared at Paul as if she didn't know who he was, and then she slowly lowered her eyes until she was staring at her stomach. An extraordinary hissing noise came from the back of her throat, a low hoarse hissing, as if she were having difficulty in breathing.

Paul said, fearfully, 'Jennie? Jennie, what is it? For God's sake, Jennie, you've got to tell me!'

His eyes followed hers, down to the stomach. The wriggling continued, but now a darkish lump had appeared under the skin, like a very severe bruise, or a constricted hernia. Jennifer was staring at the lump in horrified fascination, and even though she was suffering pain far more terrible than anything she had ever experienced before, she remained quiet, expressing her agony by hissing, and clenching her fists, and by praying and praying inside of her head that this was all a nightmare, that it wasn't real at all, and that she would have only to say, 'Paul – wake me up,' and it would all be over.

She didn't ask him to wake her up, however, because she knew that it wasn't a nightmare, and that if she *did* ask him, it wouldn't make any difference. She was awake, and the gnawing pain inside of her body was real. Oh Lord, please save me. Oh Lord, please don't let me die. Oh Lord, whatever you ask me, I'll do it. *Please, Lord; please, Lord; please!* Paul heard the distant yipping of the ambulance siren, and squeezed Jennifer's hand. 'You hear that, honey?' he reassured her. 'Only a few minutes longer, and the medics are going to be here.'

Jennifer lifted her head, and said, hoarsely, '*Too late.*'

'Now, come on now, Jennie, that's no way to talk. Why, they'll have you in the hospital in ten minutes from now, and then you'll feel fine. Come on now, honey, I promise you.'

Jennifer repeated, even more hoarsely than before, 'Too ... *late*. Too ...'

Then she buried her hands in her hair, and clenched it so tight that Paul could hear her scalp skin tearing away from her skull. She opened her mouth wide, and this time she screamed and she screamed and she wouldn't stop. She screamed so loudly that Paul didn't hear the ambulance turning into Paseo del Serra, nor did he hear the paramedics ringing at the door.

'*Jennie! Stop it! Jennie!*' he roared at her, over and over, until their faces were only inches apart – she screaming white-faced and agonised, he screaming red-faced and furious.

Suddenly, Jennifer's scream turned to a descending moan of disgust and terror. She looked down at her stomach again, her hands still tugging at her hair, and the black bulge was bigger than ever, and moving. Paul stared at it, too, unable to imagine what it was; all kinds of strange and horrible ideas tumbling through his head in quick succession. A kind of a blowfly, maybe, that had buried a colony of eggs underneath her skin, and which were suddenly hatching out. A hard lump of undigested food that had somehow penetrated the stomach lining, and which her body was trying to repel.

But the reality of it was even more horrible than Paul's imagination. For as Jennifer screamed and the paramedics pounded at the door, the bulge on her stomach stretched out until the skin that covered it was almost transparent, and then the dark twitching object inside bit right through it, and bright red blood splattered out – all over her gown, all over her thighs – and a flat eel-like head appeared, silvery and streaked with blood, with a staring and expressionless eye. The head waggled and turned, and Paul could do nothing at all but stare at it in total fear and total disgust. He was so shocked that he had forgotten that Jennifer was still screaming, and he certainly didn't hear the glass breaking as the paramedics forced an entry with a fire axe. '*Paul!*' screamed Jennifer. '*Oh, Paul! Oh, God!*' Paul snatched wildly at the eel's head. The first time, too scared, he missed it; but the second time he went closer and the eel darted forward and caught the side of his hand in between jaws that hurt as much as a red-hot barbecue fork. Automatically, Paul whipped his hand away. The eel clung on, and he dragged the whole length of it, four feet, out of the hole in Jennifer's stomach. Jennifer fell back on to the floor. Paul heard her head crack. But all he could think about was the eel that had fastened itself on to his finger, and wouldn't let go.

He lashed the eel against the wall, but still it kept its grip. He lashed and he lashed in rising panic, but however hard he hit it, it refused to let go. He was so confused, so frightened, that when two paramedics suddenly appeared in the kitchen, all he could do was hold up the eel like a fishing trophy.

'*Snake!*' one of the paramedics shouted, and immediately unhitched a large knife from the back of his belt. 'You see to the woman – I'll deal with this.'

The paramedic came forward, lunged, and then gingerly grasped the eel by the middle of its body. The eel thrashed and struggled, but the paramedic managed to hook it over the kitchen table, and keep it pressed down against the butcher block.

'You want to look away?' the paramedic asked Paul. He had a young serious face with large brown eyes and a bushy brown moustache. Paul swallowed, closed his eyes, and said in a voice that didn't sound at all like his own, 'Just do what you have to do, okay? But quick, it hurts like all hell.' The paramedic placed the edge of the blade close to the eel's head. Meanwhile, the other paramedic, who was kneeling over Jennifer, said, in awe, 'Jesus, Tony, this woman's got a hole in her stomach you could drive a truck through.'

Tony said, 'Okay, Levi, just wait up one moment,' and sliced through the eel's body with one swift movement, as if he were skilled at filleting fish. The eel, however, was no ordinary eel. As the paramedic severed its head, its jaw-muscles went into spasm, and it bit off Paul's little finger, as well as most of the knuckle and a diagonal piece out of the side of his hand. Paul opened his eyes and lifted up his hand in disbelief. Blood sprayed out of it like a garden fountain.

'God Almighty,' said Tony.

Levi turned around, and exclaimed, 'What the hell –?'

Paul tried to clutch his wrist, in the confused hope that he might be able to stop the bleeding by pressing on his artery; but then he stumbled forward and collapsed on to the floor. Blood pumped crimson graffiti all over the tiles, all over Jennifer's shuddering legs, all over Tony's green-and-white shoes. Both paramedics immediately knelt down beside him.

'The woman's dead,' said Levi, tightly. 'Severe trauma to the abdominal area, presumably caused by snake-attack. Shock, loss of blood through catastrophic internal haemorrhage, cardiac failure, fractured skull.'

Tony opened up his medical case in silence and began to apply a tourniquet to Paul's wrist. Then he cleaned and dressed the devastated finger-joint, and gave Paul an injection of tetanus toxoid and 1.2 mega-units of benzathine penicillin. He tried to prize open the eel's jaws to release Paul's bitten-off finger, but the eel's muscles remained too firmly locked. He wrapped up the head and the finger in a sheet of kitchen towel, and then said, 'I'll get this guy to hospital. There's a chance we could save his finger. Meanwhile – you'd better call the coroner.'

Paul was beginning to recover consciousness. He opened his eyes and stared at Tony and Levi, and said, 'Jennie ... is Jennie all right?'

Tony knelt down beside him. 'Don't you worry, sir. Jennie's going to be fine. Right now, the most important thing is getting you straight off to hospital.'

Outside, the sun was shining brightly. Tony drove Paul off toward Hollywood West Hospital on La Brea, just as a police patrol car was arriving. Tony gave the cops a brief salute, and then turned on his siren, howling his way eastward with Paul lying semi-conscious in the back, and Paul's finger lying on the passenger-seat in a sheet of kitchen-paper, still trapped inside the eel's jaws.

Levi had just finished calling the medical examiner when the two police patrolmen stepped into the blood-splattered kitchen and warily looked around. Levi hung up the phone, and said, 'How're you doing?'

'Okay, I guess,' said one of the cops. 'What happened here?'

'Snake-attack,' replied Levi. 'One dead, one missing his right-hand pinkie.'

'*Snake-attack!*' said the other cop, wrinkling up his nose. 'Are you kidding, or what?'

Levi pointed out the eel's decapitated body, lying curled-up on the tiles. 'That's the snake – at least what's left of it. My partner had to take the rest to the hospital with him.'

The first cop hunkered down beside the eel's body, and prodded it with the tip of his finger. 'This ain't no snake,' he said after a while.

Levi stared at him; then looked away; then put his hand on his hip.

The cop stood up. 'I'm telling you, man,' he repeated, 'this sure as hell ain't no snake.'

'It isn't a snake?' said Levi. 'What is it, then, if it isn't a snake? A necktie, maybe? Something that fell off of the back of somebody's Davy Crockett hat?'

'That's an eel,' said the cop, emphatically. He pushed his thumbs into his belt and gave one of those puckered defiant looks that almost all cops adopt as soon as they begin to suspect that your attitude toward their omnipotence isn't quite all that it should be. Three more contradictory responses and you are likely to be arrested for having an attitude problem. Levi however did not have an attitude problem. He knew from experience how to cope with cops. He whistled softly in admiration, and said, 'An *eel*, huh? I never would have guessed an eel. Right out here, so far from the ocean?'

'Still an eel,' the cop insisted.

'Well, um ... how come you know that?' asked Levi. 'How come you're so sure?'

'Fishing,' said the cop.

His partner said, taking off his cap and waving it around as an aid to explanation, 'Josh here fishes anything. Tuna, snapper, you name it. He was Santa Monica champion three successive years.'

Levi looked towards Jennifer's body, completely draped now in a green sheet. 'It seems like it bit her. The eel, I mean.'

'Well, eels can be vicious, some of them,' the cop called Josh remarked. He kept on looking around, his neck bulging first from one side of his collar, and then the other. He had one of those bland pugnacious faces that always reminded Levi of Marion Brando when he could have been a contender.

'In your kitchen?' asked Levi.

'I beg your pardon?' Josh retorted. Polite words spoken with menace.

'Eels can be vicious in your kitchen?'

'Sure eels can be vicious in your kitchen. Eels can be vicious anyplace at all. Friend of mine flushed an eel down the John, next thing he knew it came straight back up again and bit his wife in the ass.' Josh obviously found this hilarious, because he suddenly shouted, '*Ha!*' just once, and slapped his thigh. He looked around again, and then jerked his head towards the body under the green sheet. 'Where'd it bite her?'

'Stomach,' said Levi. 'Just to the right of the navel. Bad bite, too. You could have driven a truck through it.'

'What d'you think happened?' asked the cop's partner. 'I mean – do you have any idea how the eel got in here?'

Josh said, 'What kind of a question is that, William? An eel lives in the water, right, and an eel this size is an ocean going eel, right?'

William nodded doubtfully.

'So how do you think it got in here? It didn't *walk*, did it? It didn't hitch a ride from the beach, on the back of some wetback's pick-up? It must have been brought here – either by the deceased because she wanted to cook it and eat it, or by the husband because he'd been out fishing and he was stupid enough to bring the fucking thing home.'

Levi stared down at the eel's body distastefully. 'Somebody would want to eat *that*?'

'Sure they would,' Josh told him. 'Smoked, stewed, jellied, you can eat eel any way you like. Maybe the deceased was trying out that Chinese recipe, where you throw the live eels into the boiling pot, and you have to hold the lid down until they stop struggling.'

'*Chao shanhu*,' said William. Josh turned his head and stared at him fixedly. William shrugged and looked vaguely embarrassed.

'This guy doesn't eat nothing except Chinese,' Josh explained.

Levi checked his watch. 'The medical examiner should be up here soon. How about your people?'

'Don't ask me,' said Josh, wiping his nose with the back of his hand. 'They had a serious shooting down at the Burger King on Highland.'

The three of them stood around with their arms folded, trying not to step in the patterns of blood that looped and squiggled all over Jennifer's kitchen tiles. Josh said, after a while, 'Some accident, huh? You're just about to eat your supper and your supper eats you?'

William smirked because he was supposed to, and glanced down at Jennifer's green-sheeted body. He frowned, and took a second look, and then he nudged Levi's arm, and pointed.

'Look there,' he said, 'she's *moving*.'

Josh turned around. 'Moving?' he exclaimed, with morbid amusement. 'You don't mean to tell me she's still *alive*? Boy – are you going to get it if she's still alive. Some paramedic! Leaves the badly injured victim of a serious domestic eel accident lying on the cold tiled floor of her kitchen for ten minutes solid, while he passes the time of day with two police officers. Demotion, at best. Dismissal, more likely.'

Levi could see that William was quite right. The green sheet was humping up and down, and moving from side to side, as if Jennifer were trying to raise her body up off the floor.

'*Riboyne ShelO'lem!*' Levi cried, and quickly crossed the kitchen, and picked up the sheet, dropping on to one knee as he did so.

The eels swarmed out everywhere. Levi shouted, a coarse terrified shout, and one of the eels jumped at his face and clung on to the side of his jaw. Another bit at his ankle, and a third went for his calf-muscle. There were nine or ten more, and they slithered their way blindly around the kitchen floor, their tails making patterns in the blood that had been spilled there, looking for a way to escape.

Levi screamed with pain. He staggered one step backwards, and then another, with the eel waving from his face. Josh yanked open two or three kitchen drawers, scattering cheese-graters and egg-slicers and clean tea-towels everywhere, and at last found a drawerful of knives. He snatched out a poultry-knife, and dodged his way around Levi, while William banged away at the other eels with his night stick.

'*Don't cut it!*' Levi shouted. '*Don't cut it, for God's sake! It 'll bite my face off!*'

'Hold still" Josh yelled at him, 'Hold still, will you?'

Levi tried to stay where he was, trembling with pain, while Josh slowly approached him, glancing quickly downwards now and again to make sure that there were no eels around his feet, and kicking them to one side or the other when they were too close. Levi stared at him, his eyes wide, the long silvery eel swinging from the right side of his jaw, its teeth tightly fastened in his flesh. Every time Levi spoke, the eel swung some more, causing him acute agony. But he had to speak. 'The guy ... who was here before ... my buddy ... cut the eel's head off ... and it bit his finger clean through ... The jaw muscles ... *closed* ... instead of opening ...'

'All right,' Josh said, softly. 'If that's the way they play the game – this is the way that *we're* going to play it.'

He beckoned to his partner, and indicated that he should hold Levi from behind, under his arms, to support him, and keep him comparatively still. Then, coming closer, he took hold of the eel's swinging tail, touching it with all the expertise and care of an experienced fisherman, and gradually slid his hand up it until he was holding it just behind the head. The eel's eye stared without any emotion or expression whatsoever. The eye of a creature without feelings, which lives only to sustain its own life.

Josh then lifted the poultry-knife, and slid its long thin blade in between the eel's partly-open jaws, with the sharp edge facing towards him.

'You see what I'm going to do?' he asked Levi. 'I'm going to hold on to the eel's body, and then I'm going to slice towards me, so that the knife separates the eel's jaw muscles. He won't get a chance to bite you, believe me.'

Levi nodded. The eel was hurting him too much now for him to want to speak. The eels on his ankle and calf were causing him even more agony, too. His right trouser leg was stained dark with blood.

Josh grasped the eel's body carefully, stroking it, so that its nervous system would grow accustomed to the sensation of being held, and not recognise it as a threat. 'All right now,' he said, 'I'm going to count to ten, and when I say ten I want you to brace yourself because that's when I'm going to cut this bastard's head wide open. You got me?'

Levi grunted to show that he did.

'One,' said Josh. Levi's eyes widened.

'Two,' said Josh, not noticing another eel which had slithered its way close to his shoe.

'Three.' The eel beside his shoe raised its head, its bright eyes glistening yellow in the sunlight which criss-crossed the kitchen floor.

'Four.' The eel nudged aside Josh's trouser-cuff, and began to lift its head up past his sock.

'Five. You ready there, my friend? This is where we do it.'

'Six.' The eel poured up inside his trouser-leg. 'Seven – what – *ahhhh!* Shit! Shit, get out of there! *Gaahh*, you bastard!' Josh violently kicked his leg, and dropped the knife so that he could grapple with the eel that was running up inside his trousers. He spun and jumped and pirouetted, and slammed his leg against the side of the breakfast-bench again and again. But the tough slippery eel slid right up as far as his thigh, and even when Josh realised what it was after, and clutched himself tightly in both cupped hands, the eel still forced its narrow head underneath his hands and bit him.

Josh roared like a madman, and fell backwards on to the floor, jerking and convulsing and kicking his legs. He wrestled his belt open, and dragged down his trousers. His shorts were brightly stained with blood. The eel's silvery body protruded from the side of them, coiled tightly around his thigh like one of the classical serpents of Laocdon. '*The knife!*' he roared, his face crimson. '*Give me the fucking knife!*'

William scrabbled on the floor for the poultry-knife. Levi, in desperation, tried to tug away the eel that was suspended from his jaw. Its teeth audibly snapped, and it bit away a chunk of Levi's face, right down to the bone, enough to fill up a small coffee cup with blood and flesh. Levi shouted in pain and horror and awful relief, and fell to the other side of the kitchen, leaving a foot-wide smear of blood all the way down the side of Jennifer's oak-fronted units.

William found the poultry-knife and handed it with jittery fingers to his buddy. Josh's face was strange and grim. He was biting the flesh inside his mouth to stop himself from screaming, and blood ran freely down each side of his chin. He lifted up his buttocks, bit by bit, and gradually edged down his shorts. The eel had swallowed his penis almost up to the root, and although its teeth had penetrated the skin, it had not yet closed its jaws. Its eyes stared up at Josh with predatory calm.

'I can't –' Josh said, bloodily. 'I can't get the knife between its jaws.'

His partner inspected the eel in fear and disbelief. 'What are you going to do?' he asked, in a voice as pale as milk.

Josh bit even harder at the flesh inside his mouth, and his eyes filled with tears.

'You're going to have to – take hold of its jaws – see if you can keep them open – long enough to pull it off me–'

'These are real powerful, these bastards,' William said, worriedly. 'Supposing I can't hold its jaws open for long enough?'

'Well, what the fuck *else* am I going to do?' Josh hissed at him, his lips bubbling blood. There was a scream from the other side of the kitchen. It was Levi, tearing off another eel, and another chunk of flesh. But the cops took no notice.

'Listen, listen,' said William. 'That paramedic – he's bound to have some sedative, right – some real powerful sedative. Supposing I can inject that bastard eel with enough sedative to send it to sleep – then it will drop off, right? Fall asleep and drop off – and you won't – well –'

Josh was turning grey with shock, and with the tension of sitting on the floor with the eel holding his manhood and even his life between teeth as sharp as a gin-trap. 'Yes,' he said, thickly. 'Try it. Maybe it'll work. Ask him to get it ready for you.'

William loped across to the other side of the kitchen and hurriedly spoke to Levi. The paramedic was in shock himself. He had torn off all three eels, and now he was lying next to his medical box, dressing his terrible injuries and preparing to inject himself with anti-tetanus toxoid. He could barely understand what William was saying, but at last he nodded his head, and with trembling blood-smeared hands made up a hypodermic of thiopentone sodium. 'This should ... send a whale to sleep ... okay?'

William loped back again, holding up the hypodermic. 'He said to inject it right behind the head.' Josh nodded, his whole chin running with blood now, because of the pain. William looked at him, and said, 'You're sure you want me to do this?'

'For Christ's sake, just do it,' Josh urged him, between clenched teeth.

With infinite care, William raised the hypodermic, and positioned the point of the needle right behind the eel's gleaming head. He licked his lips, and sniffed, and then he lowered the needle until the point was actually indenting the eel's skin.

The two cops stared at each other. They had been through three years of service together, over a thousand days of violence and tedium and danger and injury. This, however, was something different. This was the night when they had unwittingly come face to face with the Devil himself.

Josh nodded. William stuck the needle into the eel's body, with a faint pop of punctured skin. The eel showed no sign that it had felt the prick of the needle – nor did it move when William gradually depressed the slide, and filled its nervous system with anaesthetic.

The cops waited, nervously. The sun came out from behind a cloud and the kitchen suddenly brightened. They looked around them. The rest of the eels had disappeared now, leaving the body of the woman who had borne them lying bloody and ravaged. Levi had injected himself with an analgesic, and was lying with his head drooping between his shoulders, too shocked and dopey to do anything at all but hold on until Tony returned.

Josh looked down at the eel. 'What do you think?' he asked. 'Do you think it looks like it's sleepy?'

William peered at it closely. 'Do they have eyelids?' he asked. 'I mean, when they go to sleep, do they close their eyes?'

Five minutes passed. Josh was beginning to tremble with fatigue. 'The damn thing must be asleep now,' he said, in a hoarse voice.

'You want me to try to take it off?' William asked him.

Josh nodded, but before William could take hold of the eel he raised his hand. 'Wait,' he said. He carefully reached down to his holster, unbuttoned it, and eased out his .38 revolver.

'What's that for?' William asked, scared.

'In case,' Josh told him, and cocked it, holding it up so that the muzzle was touching his right temple.

'Josh –' William protested, but Josh snapped, 'Do it!'

William reached up until his hands were positioned on either side of the eel's jaws. His idea was to grip each jaw between finger and thumb, and to keep them stretched apart while he removed the creature from his buddy's body. He prayed on his mother's life that the anaesthetic had worked, and that the eel's reflexes were now totally deadened. There was no outward way of telling whether they were or not. The eel's body remained coiled around Josh's thigh, its eyes remained wide open.

'This is it,' he said, more to himself than to anybody else. He took hold of the eel's jaws, feeling their bone structure through the slippery skin, and slowly lifted the sharp teeth out of the skin of Josh's penis. He paused for a moment, sweating, holding his breath. The eel's eyes stared at him coldly, mockingly, like the eyes of a dead fish in a supermarket freezer, or the eyes of a man who is determined to see you dead.

The jaw muscles were far stronger than William had expected, and it was everything he could do to keep them apart.

Josh breathed, 'Take it off, William. Slowly now, slowly, but for Christ's sake take it off.'

William swallowed. He had just begun to ease the eel downwards, however, when the broken kitchen door banged open, and two detectives walked in.

'What the hell's this?' one of them demanded. 'What the hell's going on here?'

William glanced up, and as he glanced up his fingers slipped.

Josh shouted, as the eel's teeth punctured his skin yet again, and he tried in panic to wrench the creature loose. The eel's jaw muscles snapped shut, with a gristly crunch.

Josh roared like a kamikaze and pulled the trigger of his .38. With a thunderous report, his head emptied itself all over the kitchen.

He fell sideways, and, as he did so, the eel unwound itself quick and silvery, and slithered away to the other side of the room, and disappeared. William wasn't watching it anyway. He was kneeling in front of Josh, his face spattered with blood, his hands still held helplessly up, the way they had been when he had lost his grip on the eel's jaws.

The two detectives had whipped out their guns when Josh had fired, and were crouched on the far side of the kitchen in perplexity, wondering what they ought to shoot at.

'You want to tell us what's happening here?' one of them asked, reholstering his gun, and distastefully hop-scotching his way between the splashes of blood.

William shrugged. 'I tried,' he said, with his voice choked by tears. 'I tried my level best.'

Outside, two sirens cried in the sunshine. Levi the paramedic tried to raise his head to see what was happening.

Nine eels, meanwhile, had slithered out of the house, seeking places to hide. Three of them buried themselves in the dry sun-baked soil in Jennifer's garden, next to her rose-bushes. Another coiled itself up in the darkness at the back of the shed which housed the swimming-pool pump. Two more managed to find a way through to the neighbour's yard, where one of them slid into a squirrel-hole, and the other found a niche for itself in the disused outside toilet. Two poured like liquid mercury down a nearby sewer-grate, and would gestate in an archway which was regularly flooded with raw sewage. The last tried to cross Paseo del Serra, just as the local road-sweeping truck was crawling its way past, and was whipped up by the brushes and carried, still alive, to the garbage dump, where it was buried under tons of newspaper and gravel and Coke cans and dried yucca leaves and excrement.

It lay there, with its eyes wide open, its gills opening and closing, waiting to grow.

Chapter Nineteen

It had been seven weeks now and the Night Warriors had found no trace of Yaomauitl. After they had failed to destroy the Devil in the clockwork city, they had gone out night after night, criss-crossing the darkened landscape of Southern California, searching for the slightest heartbeat that would tell them that Yaomauitl was concealed close by. They had penetrated dream after dream. Dreams of carnivals, dreams of love affairs, dreams of drowning. But although they had glimpsed many demons, and many dark anxieties, although they had felt the scuttling of many guilty figures, and heard the whispering of many evil names, they had failed to find the Devil they sought.

'Maybe we've scared him off,' Tebulot suggested one night, as they silently sailed by moonlight over the Sepulveda Dam Recreation Area.

Kasyx looked grim. 'I don't want to scare him off. I want to get him back in that box in San Hipolito where he belongs.'

After the third week, they had agreed to split their nightly patrols, so that only two of them went out at once. Although their mortal bodies had remained peacefully sleeping in their beds, their minds were growing weary from nights of searching. After the fifth week, they had given up patrolling every night, and instead flew out twice a week, spreading their search as far as San Luis Obispo in the north, and Palm Springs in the east. Kasyx had felt that it was unlikely that Yaomauitl had returned to Mexico.

These days, they hardly saw Springer at all. Occasionally, she was there when they went to the house on Camino del Mar, but she was quiet and uncommunicative, and her clothing was growing increasingly lavish and decorative, as if to show them that every day the Devil remained free, the world grew a little more decadent.

The Night Warriors still met each other during the day. Henry's cottage had become something of a casual headquarters, where they came and went whenever they felt the need to talk. Lloyd stayed over a couple of nights, despite protests from his mother, and Gil was a regular visitor. Occasionally, Susan dropped by, too, when she came down to the beach to swim, and they would all sit out on Henry's verandah drinking Cokes and talking about the battle they had fought on the plain of ashes, and what they would do next time they came face-to-face with Yaomauitl.

They had nobody else with whom they could talk about their adventures as Night Warriors. They had nobody else in whom they could confide their fears. They had all been terrified that night in the clockwork city, but who were they going to tell?

'If I said anything to my analyst about it, he'd have me bouncing around in a padded cell before sundown,' Henry had remarked.

Henry was finding it increasingly difficult to resist the vodka bottle. As each night ended without any trace of Yaomauitl, his sense of failure and frustration began to irritate his nerve-endings again, and he would have done anything to anesthetise those nerve-endings in Smirnoff. He went to the liquor cabinet two or three times a day and opened it and stared at the half-bottle of vodka that stood there, and then closed it again. He felt that he had entered into a solemn agreement with the other three Night Warriors not to drink. After all, they were young, and their lives depended on him.

But, as each night went by, and the Deadly Enemy remained hidden, Henry's craving grew stronger and stronger. One drink, he thought. Just one. Just to give me that glow, just to give me that extra confidence. Just to relax this whirling overloaded brain of mine, and to give me some peace. His equilibrium had not been helped by the matter of Salvador's death. Although the police had eventually been satisfied that the presence of Henry and Gil and Lloyd at the Scripps Institute had not been contributory to Lieutenant Onega's accident – mainly due to evidence given by Andrea – the Institute themselves were considering a prosecution for unlawful trespass and damage to their property, and the police made a point of calling Henry at all times of the day, as if they were checking up on him.

And whether the police were satisfied or not with what had happened that night, Henry and Gil and Lloyd all knew that while they might have saved Andrea, they had certainly been largely responsible for what happened to Salvador. It was no good making excuses about 'casualties of war'. Henry had been around to see Salvador's widow with a bunch of flowers and a Fisher-Price wind-up Ferris-wheel for her children. The children had sat on the green sculptured nylon rug and the Ferris-wheel had played *In*

The Good Old Summertime, and afterwards Henry had sat in the passenger-seat of Gil's Mustang with tears running down his cheeks.

Daffy, Susan's friend, kept complaining that Susan was 'eons away' and that she just wasn't *fun* any more. Susan apologised just as often as Daffy complained, but there was nothing she could do to explain how she felt. Even if she could have told Daffy about that day when the Devil had kept her captive, even if Daffy had *believed it*, she wouldn't have been able to understand. Not even Henry and Gil and Lloyd could understand. Because even though Susan had been alone, she had been frightened that day beyond any fear she had ever known. That day, she had understood exactly what she was, an assembly of bones and skin and convulsing muscle, and she had understood that the difference between life and death was nothing more than a fragile spasm.

That understanding brought her closer to her grandparents. These days, she could even tolerate her grandfather's corny ribbing. But it took her further away from her own generation, to whom death remained comfortably remote.

Daffy was right. Susan was no fun any more. But she was far more caring and far more sympathetic than she had ever been before; and she knew that when they defeated Yaomauitl at last, her sense of fun would soon return. If only she could have told Daffy how hard it was to laugh during a war.

Gil's experiences had divided him from his friends, too – and from his parents. Quite apart from the matter of the borrowed gun, which had cost him two weeks' allowance and a month of working mornings in the store, he found that he was completely unable to confide in his father and mother the way he used to. Phil Miller tried to talk to him several times to find out what was wrong. 'You're not sick, are you? You're not in love?' But Gil found it impossible to give his father any kind of explanation that would have described how he felt, even remotely. He felt like Tebulot, and how could he tell his father that? He felt strong, philosophical, aggressive, moral, and dedicated. He felt a need to fulfil his destiny as a Night Warrior by finding and destroying Yaomauitl, the Deadly Enemy. How could he put any of that into words that his father could accept – his father, whom he loved dearly, but whose horizons were bounded by pepper salamis and boxes of Cap'n Crunch?

The changes that had occurred in Lloyd's life were more oblique. He had always been thoughtful, and deeply involved in everything he did, whether it was schoolwork or athletics or developing a friendship. His father was a serious man; a man of such honesty of spirit that in his own small way he was almost a saint. Lloyd had inherited that honesty, combined with the passionate enthusiasm of his mother, and so when he had started to close himself away from the rest of the family to think over his experiences as a Night Warrior, nobody had noticed anything particularly unusual.

This time, however, Lloyd had begun to feel that there was a great fulfilment awaiting him. Not just the fulfilment of winning a five-hundred metre track race; not just the fulfilment of scoring top marks in English. Not just the fulfilment of being black, and doing well in a white man's world. Lloyd had begun to smell greatness in the wind; the sharp aroma that stirred up ordinary men and made them heroes.

One evening, in the sixth week of looking for Yaomauitl, Lloyd's father came into his bedroom and stood there for a long time with his spectacles in one hand and his folded copy of the evening paper in the other, and at last said, 'Lloyd, I want you to tell me the truth.' 'Daddy?'

'Lloyd, are you sniffing anything? You tell me the truth, now.'

Lloyd had actually smiled. 'No, Daddy,' he had told his father, quietly, his face half shadowed by the light from his desk-lamp. 'No, I'm not sniffing anything.'

On the third morning of the seventh week the skies along the Southern California coast were grey and hazy, but the early weather forecast predicted that the sun would burn through the haze before ten o'clock. After the weather forecast came the local news, and Henry was sitting in the kitchen eating a bowlful of muesli when it was announced that the body of a young woman had been found in a house on Prospect Street, La Jolla, with massive abdominal injuries.

The newsreader said, 'Police were reluctant to say last night whether the slaying was the work of a ritual killer, or whether the girl's death resulted from some kind of bizarre accident.'

Henry slowly put down his spoon. Massive abdominal injuries. He wondered whether at last he had found the key to Yaomauitl's long silence. Leaving his breakfast, he went through to the living-room and leafed through his telephone directory until he found the listing for the San

Diego Coroner's Office. He punched out the number, and ran his hand repeatedly through his untidy hair while he waited for an answer.

'Mr John Belli,' he said, when he was eventually connected.

John Belli sounded tired and unhappy. 'Who is this?' he demanded, clearing his throat.

'Mr Belli, this is Henry Watkins, Professor Henry Watkins. I was one of the three people who originally discovered the body of Sylvia Stoner.'

'Yes?' John Belli asked, suspiciously.

'Well, sir, I'm sorry to bother you, but I heard this morning that another girl had been found dead. On Prospect Street, in La Jolla.'

'Yes.' Flatly this time. Cautiously.

'Can I ask you just one question about her?'

'You can ask. I can't guarantee that I'll give you an answer.'

'Well,' said Henry, 'you don't have to say yes, if what I'm going to ask you is true. But if it isn't true, then I'd be obliged if you would say no.'

There was a pause. Then John Belli said, 'Go ahead, ask.'

'The question is, does the evidence indicate that the girl found at La Jolla was killed in the same way as Sylvia Stoner?'

There was another pause. Then John Belli hung up.

Henry held the receiver in his hand for a moment, listening to the endless burring of the dial tone. Then he slowly cradled it, and stood up. So that was it. Yaomauitl had been waiting for his new offspring to be hatched. A girl at La Jolla had died; and who knew how many more women had been impregnated by a Devil who could disguise himself as anything and anyone he chose. There could be hundreds of eels, greedily eating their way out of the wombs of scores of women. And even though they were not yet grown – even though they were only embryos – they could begin to dream, and once they could begin to dream, they could join their father and master Yaomauitl as reinforcements.

Yaomauitl was preparing to annihilate the Night Warriors, and carry his invasion through the dreams of every living American. He might not be able to exert any influence during the day, when men were rational and wakeful and alert, and sceptical of Devils. But at night, as they slept, his evil influence could coax them and tempt them and turn their minds. His shadows would rise up in their nightmares, and preach intolerance and cruelty and self-indulgence; and all the achievements of religious civilisation – those achievements which had been won by hundreds of years of war and anguish and human suffering – would be toppled, and swept away. Out of a nation's nightmares, a new Dark Age would begin to flood, staining the map of the world like ink.

Henry called Gil. 'Gil? This is Henry. Did you hear the news this morning?'

'I was slicing corned beef.'

'Listen, Gil, it's happened again. They've found a girl in La Jolla, dead, with her stomach eaten open. No eels – at least the news didn't mention any – so presumably they managed to get away and bury themselves.'

Gil said, 'What does this mean? I'm not sure that I understand.'

'The way I interpret it,' said Henry, 'Yaomauitl has been waiting for the birth of some new embryo Devils, so that he can outnumber us, and wipe us out completely.'

'When? Where? Any ideas?'

'Not yet. But I think we ought to go out tonight, all of us, and see whether we can pick up his scent.'

'All right, you're on. Eleven?'

'Eleven it is.'

Henry called Susan and then Lloyd. Lloyd was out but his suspicious mother took a message. Susan sounded quite grave on the phone, and asked Henry if he thought this was the showdown.

'Showdown? You make it sound like *High Noon*,' joked Henry.

'He wants to kill us, though, doesn't he?' asked Susan, still grave.

Henry hesitated, and then he said, 'Yes, he does.' 'And if he kills us when we're Night Warriors?' Henry reached down and rubbed the leg that had been bruised during their last battle in the depths of the clockwork city. 'You know what Springer said. If he kills us as Night Warriors, then our physical bodies will never wake up.'

Susan said, 'Eleven o'clock?'

'You don't have to come if you don't want to,' Henry replied.

'You need me,' said Susan. 'How are you going to find Yaomauitl without Samena's sixth sense?'

'You still don't have to come. We'll find him somehow.'

Susan said, 'Henry – the very worst that can happen is that I get to rejoin my parents.'

Henry didn't know how to reply to that. It was both mature and mystical; a statement of adult resignation and a statement of child-like faith. He said, with a thickness in his throat, 'All right, then. Eleven o'clock. I'll look forward to seeing you.'

The day seemed to take an eternity to pass. Henry went to the liquor cabinet even more frequently than usual, and once he even went as far as unscrewing the cap of the vodka bottle. He sniffed it, and let the fumes of it rise up into his nostrils. One drink, just to focus his mind. One single solitary drink, just to prepare him for the battle that he knew the night would be bringing him.

He screwed the cap up tight again, and put the bottle back, and went outside for a short walk along the promenade, breathing in the breeze from the ocean. He had thought that he was over the worst of his desire for alcohol, especially after seven weeks without it. Surely his system must have dried out by now. But the craving seemed to be worse than ever, and he wondered if he would ever be rid of it. His mind was already spinning out ready-made excuses for him to drink. You've been teetotal for seven weeks, you deserve a drink. *One* won't hurt you, you'll be able to prove to yourself that you're not an alcoholic after all, if you just have one. If you have one, you'll be drinking like normal people do. You'll be cured. After all – how you can say that you're cured if you're still not drinking any alcohol at all? Staying completely on the wagon is like admitting that you're still sick.

He met by accident an old friend of his called John Lund, a hoary old history professor who wore fraying Panama hats and linen coats that looked as if they had previously done service as mail sacks. John was short and bespectacled and voluble, and he didn't drink, so Henry suggested that they have lunch together. They linked arms and went to a vegetarian restaurant further along the strip called Brother Bread, and Henry managed to pacify his desire for vodka with a cool bowl of home-cultured yoghurt and a plate of fresh-sliced melon. While he ate, he listened to John's latest interpretation of the War of Independence, which was something to do with the English not wanting to win it anyway.

While John spoke, a man sitting opposite, who was eating alone, opened out his copy of *the Los Angeles Times*. Henry only glanced at the main headlines at first, out of the corner of his eye, but then he peered at them narrowly, and read them with a rising sense of fright. *'Killer Eels Slay Wife, Attack Husband And Cops.' 'Officer, emasculated, shoots self.' 'Medic and husband suffer multiple bites.'*

'And after Valley Forge ...' John was saying, earnestly, as he cut up his melon into small pieces.

'John, excuse me,' said Henry, and went across to the man with the paper. 'Could I borrow your front page for just a minute?' he asked him, and the man shrugged and peeled it off for him.

John Lund watched Henry through the lenses of his smeary spectacles as Henry quickly read about the eels that had attacked a middle-aged couple, as well as paramedics and police, on Paseo del Serra in Hollywood. The wife's body, the report said, 'had been very severely mutilated ... with stomach wounds which Sergeant Garcia described as "worse than anything that Jack the Ripper ever perpetrated".' Only a detailed examination of the body would reveal exactly what had happened. 'What is it?' asked John. 'You look worried.'

Henry said, 'I am worried. Actually, I'm *more* than worried, I'm scared stiff.'

'You? Scared? What on earth does a professor of philosophy have to be scared of?'

Henry handed the front page of the newspaper back to the man at the opposite table. Then he said to John, with his hands clasped in front of him, 'Supposing you were told that you had to fight one of those Japanese sumo wrestlers?'

John guffawed. 'I'd lose,' he said. 'No question about that.'

'Supposing you were told that, if you lost, the whole of the human race would die out?'

John said, with a frown, 'What is this, one of your peculiar Oriental riddles?'

Henry shook his head. 'What would you do? How would you feel? Would you fight, or would you funk it?'

John very slowly stirred his cup of coffee, and then helped himself to another spoonful of brown sugar. 'I'd fight,' he said. 'But I'd be scared.'

'Exactly,' said Henry.

'You mean that you – ?' asked John, unable to get to grips with what Henry was telling him.

'Me,' said Henry. 'Me and the sumo wrestler and the whole human race. Only it's not a sumo wrestler.'

'May I ask what it is?' asked John, in mystification. He had heard Henry talking sober nonsense, and he had heard Henry talking drunk sense, but he had never heard Henry talking like this before.

Henry leaned forward, and grasped the coarse linen shoulder of John's coat. 'It's the Devil,' he whispered; and of course John smiled, and sat back, and shook his head, and smugly crossed his legs, and didn't believe him for a moment.

They all arrived well before eleven, serious and eager. Springer was there, too, a man this time, dressed in a strange suit of grey and black that rustled like tissue paper when he walked. He touched the hands of each of them, and looked into their eyes one after the other with his own eyes that were like slanted windows into outer space. Absolute emptiness, and distant stars, and meanings that you could only dream about.

'I knew you would be here tonight,' said Springer. 'You have interpreted Yaomauitl's manoeuvres well.'

Kasyx lifted one crimson gauntlet and slowly parted his fingers. Sparkling blue electricity jumped from one fingertip to the next. He had never before absorbed so much of Ashapola's energy, and he knew that one accidental discharge would be catastrophic. But tonight, if they were to encounter Yaomauitl yet again, they would need all the power they could possibly muster.

Springer said, 'Tonight will be your greatest adventure. Tonight you will know the true power of being Night Warriors. In the name of Ashapola, and of all the sacred Warriors of ancient times, may you be protected from evil, and may your light cleave the darkness for the liberation of the world of men.'

These words were plainly words that Springer had repeated time and time again, in years gone by. Words from the greatest days of the Night Warriors, when scores of Devils had walked the earth, and those who had fought them in dreams and nightmares could be counted in their thousands. A dark company, who had brought the virtues of peace and understanding to every corner of the world, no matter how uneasy that peace and understanding may have been.

The Night Warriors rose up into the evening air. Springer

had alerted Samena that he felt cold vibrations somewhere to the east, so they glided over the golf courses and condominiums around the Fairbanks ranch and headed up into the hills, where the night air was pungent with the aroma of eucalyptus, and lights sparkled from expensive Spanish-style homes, hidden among the lemon groves and the yucca.

'Any feelings?' Kasyx asked Samena, as they sailed silently over Rancho Santa Fe, where light from the windows of the white-painted Inn cast bright green patterns across the croquet pitches that surrounded it. Then they were back into the darkness again, searching the hills for the slightest sensation that would warn them that Yaomauitl was close.

Xaxxa said, 'Maybe we were wrong, man. Maybe he isn't ready to fight yet.'

'He's ready,' Kasyx affirmed. 'He wouldn't have allowed those embryos of his to be born so publicly, if he wasn't ready to fight. He knows we know about it, and he knows we're out here looking for him.'

'Well, any time, man, any time,' said Xaxxa.

Tebulot said nothing. He was too deeply in thought about the problems he was having with his parents, and about the dangers that the Night Warriors were going to be facing tonight. He hadn't lost his nerve. Far from it. But he wanted the fighting to start, and start soon, so that he could be given some respite from his endless wrangling anxieties. He loved his father and mother. He didn't want to be alienated from them. But until they had found and vanquished Yaomauitl, there was nothing he could say to them that would bring them closer together.

They were almost ready to turn back towards the coast

when Samena said, quietly, 'He's here. He's quite close by. I can feel him.'

The three other Night Warriors moved in closer to Samena, gliding together in ghostly formation between the hills. They followed every turn and dip she made like an acrobatic team coming in to land in total darkness, using only Samena's abstract senses to guide them to their target.

'Right a little, right,' said Samena, and they banked towards the right, until at last they were rustling through a thick grove of fan palms, and into the grounds of a large ochre-painted house that stood by itself on a bend in the highway.

'This is it, he's here,' said Samena, and without hesitation she penetrated the clay-tiled roof, and entered one of the bedrooms.

An Oriental-looking man lay asleep with his wife on a wide brass bed covered with a black satin sheet. The rug was white, the furniture was white, and there was a large stylised painting by Sotaro Yasui on the wall. The Night Warriors stood at the foot of the bed and looked at the sleepers with caution. 'Which one of them is it? The man or the woman?' asked Tebulot.

'The man,' said Samena. 'The feeling is really strong; stronger than it's ever been before.'

'Are we ready for this?' asked Kasyx.

They nodded. Kasyx lifted his hands, and drew the octagon. When he divided the night air in between it, he saw whiteness, and snow falling.

'Looks like this is going to be a cold one,' he said, but without hesitation he raised the octagon over their heads. As it slowly descended all around them, he gripped the hands of each of them in turn, giving them encouragement and extra strength. We're going to win this time,' he assured them. 'This time, we're going to send Yaomauitl back to Mexico, and on a permanent basis, too.'

The octagon reached the floor, and immediately they were engulfed in utter silence, a silence so complete that none of them moved, none of them spoke. All they did was lift their heads and listen.

They were knee-deep in the softest of snow, and more snow was falling thickly all around them, without a whisper. There was no wind blowing whatsoever, and so the air was surprisingly warm. They looked all around them, but as far as they could see in every direction there was nothing but snow.

Tebulot came wading over to Kasyx, his machine slung over his shoulder. 'I never saw snow like this before,' he remarked, his eyes darting uneasily from one side to the other.

'Maybe it's Japanese snow,' said Kasyx. 'Samena? Do you have any ideas where our Devil might be?'

Samena cupped her hands over her face and was silent for almost a minute. The snow dropped silently on to the feathers of her hat, turning them white. Xaxxa meanwhile was walking around in circles, holding out his hands and watching the snowflakes melt in his palms. 'Do you know something?' he grinned. 'I never saw snow before in my whole life, not ever. Isn't it weird?'

Samena at last pointed vaguely to the right. 'Over there, I think. It's difficult to tell. I can feel something, but the feeling doesn't seem quite right.'

'All the same, we'd better give it a try,' said Kasyx, and the four of them began to trudge in the direction that Samena had indicated, leaving wide deep tracks in the fluffy white surface.

'I wonder if this is a nightmare or a dream?' asked Tebulot, still looking around suspiciously.

'It feels like a nightmare,' said Samena. There's something not quite balanced about it, like it's peaceful, but that's only a sham. I keep picking up the idea that somebody's died, and that they're holding a funeral nearby.'

'For many Orientals, white is the colour of mourning,' said Kasyx. 'Maybe this whole dream is some kind of a funeral.'

They continued to push their way through the snow. Where the ground dipped, it had drifted, and they found themselves buried almost up to their waists. But the soil beneath the snow seemed firm and hard packed, and so they managed to make quite good progress. The snow kept on falling all around them, densely and noiselessly, out of a sky that was dark red with cold; and still there was no sign of Yaomauitl.

'Do you think we're making a mistake?' asked Tebulot, as they paused for a rest.

Samena shook her head. 'There's no mistake. He's here someplace. But he's probably trying to disorient us and tire us out.'

'He's not making too bad a job of it, either,' said Tebulot.

Xaxxa said, 'It's going to take more than snow to put me off, man.' Kasyx placed his hand over his forehead, and examined their surroundings with infra-red, to see if there were any tell-tale traces of heat – either Devilish or human. But all he could register were the glowing yellow-and-blue bodies of Tebulot, Samena, and Xaxxa, and the golden pulsing of Tebulot's highly charged machine.

'You still think we're heading in the right direction?' he asked Samena.

'As far as I can tell,' said Samena. 'It's stronger than it was, but it keeps breaking up and dividing, and sometimes it's hard to say exactly where it is.'

Kasyx said, 'All right. We'll keep on going for another couple of miles. If we haven't located anything by then, we'll leave this dream and see If we can't find Yaomauitl someplace else.'

Samena told him, 'He's here, Kasyx, I promise you.'

'Come on,' said Kasyx, and they began to march slowly through the snowdrifts once more, four small figures in a huge whirling landscape of white. As he marched, it struck Tebulot as totally amazing that this entire world could exist Inside one man's sleeping mind; and that this one man would only have to turn over in bed, and he could start dreaming about another world altogether, quite different, but just as vast. That was one thing that his experiences as a Night Warrior had taught him: that inner space was just as infinite as outer space, but far more complicated, because it obeyed none of the laws of the material world. In inner space a building could float in the sky, an animal could talk, a dead husband could come to life again. In inner space, snow could fall in the hottest month of the summer, and Devils could hide like Arctic wolves.

It was then that they heard a sudden and terrible clashing. The snow shuddered as it fell, and began to spin around in wild eddies. They heard whoops, and cries, and the shaking of dozens of small bells, and out of the snowstorm a huge sledge appeared, as large as a truck, drawn by over a hundred harnessed Polar bears. The sledge passed by them only fifty feet away, its wooden runners sliding over the snow with a chilling hiss. It was constructed entirely of yew, articulated in the middle so that it could turn quickly. The front section was three stories high, and heaped with hundreds of animal furs. The rear section was crowded with masked soldiers in breastplates and winged helmets that reminded the Night Warriors of the hordes of Genghis Khan and each soldier carried a strange wide-barrelled rifle. At the very back of the sledge there was a wooden tower, sixty or seventy feet high, whose sides were clustered with silver bells and ribbons, as well as the carcasses of dead wolves and snowshoe rabbits, and the flowing black scalps of human beings.

At the very top of the tower, in midnight-black armour that resembled a beetle's carapace, stood a being whose eyes gleamed yellow and malevolent: the lord of all darkness, Yaomauitl.

Tebulot yelled, '*Hit the deck!*' and the four Night Warriors plunged face down into the snow. The jangling sledge wheeled around them in a wide circle, and they could hear the harsh cries of the Tartar soldiers screeching through the snowstorm like strangled crows. Kasyx lifted his head, and immediately the snow all around them exploded into hundreds of powdery white plumes. He ducked down again, and glanced across at Samena, and said, 'I think we take it all back. You found them all right.'

Tebulot eased back the T-bar of his machine. 'If I can hit Yaomauitl himself, maybe we can get this over with.'

They heard the terrible sledge sliding closer. The paws of a hundred bears made the snow shake as if an earth-tremor were impending. Tebulot made a confident circle of finger and thumb and gave Kasyx a wink from behind his face-mask. 'Here goes nothing,' he said, and lifted himself up out of the snow.

Instantly, there was an ear-splitting barrage of fire from the soldiers at the rear of the sledge. Each shot made a sharp, breathy shriek, like a bicycle-pump drawing in air, only twenty times louder. As the sledge thundered past them, towering high above their hiding-place, Kasyx saw three soldiers lean over the sides of it and fire at them, and then he realised what the whistling noise was all about.

The Tartar's rifles, instead of firing a projectile, *sucked in* whatever they were aimed at, over a distance of nearly a hundred metres. When they missed, and aimed at the ground, a thin bullet of snow would be plucked up and zapped backwards into the gun's barrel. It took only a little imagination to picture what would happen if they managed to aim straight at a human being.

With the sledge almost past them, Tebulot rolled on to his back, and fired a single dazzling blast of concentrated energy at the wooden tower. The energy-bolt screamed in through one of the tower's windows, and for a moment nothing happened. Then the tower blew up, in a tumbling shower of shattered wood and scorched wolf carcasses, and a ball of orange fire rose up over the sledge, then vanished. Two rear runners collapsed, and the giant sledge ground to a halt in a spray of ice. Immediately, the Tartar soldiers began to swarm down the sides of the sledge, and drop into the snow, so that the Night Warriors would find them more difficult to hit. One of the Tartars ran around and cut loose the bears, waving a bright red flare at them to frighten them away. Samena watched this particular Tartar for a while, and then unhooked a single arrowhead from her belt. She crossed her arms, and fired the energy-arrow *zip!* along the side of the sledge. The arrowhead pierced the soldier's hand so that he dropped his flare. Immediately, two of the bears turned around, and shuffled towards him, snarling and roaring. The Tartar cried out, and began to run, but the bears could run much faster. They came up behind him like two white locomotives, and knocked him down in a spray of blood. One of them went for his head, and from two hundred feet away the Night Warriors could hear his skull crunch.

The flare, meanwhile, had dropped among the furs, and the front of the sledge began to burn. Within three or four minutes, the whole sledge was thundering with fire from end to end. Kasyx kept a lookout for Yaomauitl, but there was no sign of him. He said to Xaxxa, 'How about making a quick pass overhead? Do you think you can do that without getting hit? I want to see where Yaomauitl's hiding.'

Xaxxa said, 'You got it,' and lay flat on his back in the snow. Then he covered his face with his mirror-like mask, and double-somersaulted backwards right out of the pit in which they were sheltering, streaking up into the snowy sky on a slide of shining gold.

For a moment, Xaxxa disappeared completely, and they waited anxiously for his return. The wooden sledge crackled and popped, and there was a thick nauseating smell of burning fur. The Tartars kept their heads well down, especially since Tebulot was ready for them with his machine fully cocked and ready to fire a multiple horizontal burst.

Samena said, 'You don't think he's lost, do you?'

But before Kasyx could reply, they heard that familiar jet-plane whistle, and Xaxxa came flashing across the snow, only two or three feet above ground-level, crouched on his shining slide like the greatest surfer that ever was.

One of the Tartars lifted himself out of the snow, and aimed at Xaxxa with his wide-barrelled rifle. But Xaxxa weaved and ducked in mid-air, and kicked the Tartar straight in the jaw with a perfect two-footed drop-kick that must have had an impact velocity of three hundred miles an hour. The Tartar was flung bodily across the snow, and his rifle dropped and fired straight at one of his comrades, who had been crouched next to him. It was then that the Night Warriors saw what the weapons could do. A six-inch plug of living flesh was snapped out of the soldier's thigh, and sucked bloodily into the rifle's open barrel. The soldier screeched, and dropped to the snow, clutching his leg.

Xaxxa made another fly-past, and then circled around and rejoined the other three Night Warriors.

'Terrific kick,' Kasyx complimented him. Then, 'Any sign of Yaomauitl?'

'I don't think that creature we saw was Yaomauitl himself,' Xaxxa panted. 'I saw his armour lying in the snow, empty, and something lying next to it that looked like that Devil we burned at the Scripps Institute, only smaller and redder. Whatever it was, it was dead meat.'

'One of Yaomauitl's new offspring,' Kasyx breathed. 'While they dream, they can take on his grown-up appearance, but when you destroy them, in their dream, they revert back to what they really are. Embryos, undeveloped demons. What did Springer call them? Joeys.'

Samena said, 'How about the rest of the soldiers? Do you think we can manage to beat them?'

'I'm not so sure,' said Xaxxa. 'They've dug themselves in pretty good. It's going to take a lot of energy to shift them.'

'Energy is one thing I don't want to waste,' said Kasyx. But then Tebulot lifted his hand and said brightly, 'I've got an idea. Listen! I read it in a cowboy book once. It was something the Cheyenne Indians used to do, to distract their enemies.'

'I hope you realise the Cheyenne Indians got beaten, in the end,' said Xaxxa.

'Well, come on, it's only an *adaptation* of what the Cheyennes did,' Tebulot explained. 'What we could do is this: pick up that Tartar soldier, the one who's been wounded in the leg, and fly him down the whole length of the Tartar lines, spraying them in blood. Then we round up the rest of those bears, and drive them back here. As soon as they smell that blood – well, they're going to go crazy, aren't they?'

'When you say *we*, you mean *me*, if I understand you right?' Xaxxa asked him. 'I mean, seeing as how I'm the only one who can fly.'

Tebulot said, 'We'll be covering you.'

Xaxxa looked at Kasyx. Kasyx said, 'It's a good idea, but you don't have to do it if you don't want to.'

'No, I'll do it,' said Xaxxa. 'I just wanted to make sure that nobody here was taking me for granted.'

'Are you kidding?' smiled Samena.

Without any further delay, Xaxxa flashed off through the falling snow, and vanished once more. This time, when he came back, he was travelling so fast that they didn't see him until he reached down out of the blizzard and snatched up the wounded Tartar like a buzzard picking up an injured gopher. The other Tartars lifted their weapons, and fired a sharp shrieking salvo at him, but he managed to fly the whole length of the Tartar lines with his victim hanging bleeding from his arms, without being hit.

He dropped the hapless Tartar into a deep snow-drift, and then climbed away into the sky to round up the Polar bears.

Kasyx waited impatiently as minutes passed by. The snow was still falling thickly, covering his crimson armour like white wool. Samena sat beside him, her face calm, turning around now and again to make sure that the Tartars hadn't yet decided to attack them. Tebulot kept his weapon ready and humming but he knew that there was nothing he could do, not at the moment.

Samena said, 'I hope Xaxxa isn't lost. He doesn't have the same directional senses that I have. Not in this kind of weather, anyway.'

'He'll be all right,' said Kasyx, although he wasn't completely convinced of it. Xaxxa was a little too fast and a little too flamboyant. If he had accidentally run into another of those articulated snow-sledges, then he could have been killed without any of them knowing about it.

Ten minutes passed. Then Samena said, 'They're advancing, look.'

Kasyx raised his head, and changed his sight to telescopic. Samena was right. The Tartars were rising up from the snow, their winged helmets showing black against the blizzard, their masked faces expressionless. A shot screeched past Kasyx's head – not a bullet, but a thin column of air, sucked back into the rifle at twice the speed of sound. He dropped down, and said, 'There have to be thirty of them, at least. Do you think you two can hit them all?'

'We'll try,' said Tebulot. 'We hit ten times that number of corpses when we fought them on the plain.'

'Sure you did,' said Kasyx. 'But those corpses weren't armed with suck-guns, the way that these jokers are.' Samena said quietly, 'We have to take the risk, Kasyx. Xaxxa took the risk.'

'Well, I know,' Kasyx replied. 'It's just that you're-' 'Young?' smiled Samena. 'Yes, we are. But warriors have always been young. That's what makes their sacrifice so much greater.'

Tebulot lifted his head. The Tartar soldiers had fanned out, and were now making their way across the snow towards them in a wide pincer-movement, dark and sinister, their rifles held high. Tebulot aimed his machine, and fired three bright energy-bolts that burst into jagged 'shrapnel' – uncontrolled electrical charges that could tear their way through armour-plate. With a crackling sound, six or seven Tartars dropped to the ground. Smoke drifted through the falling snow.

Samena dropped two of them with wire-flailing arrowheads, immaculate shots that killed them with scarcely any waste of energy at all. But then the remaining Tartars began to fire at them from three sides, and they had to drop back down into the snow.

'Where the hell is Xaxxa?' Tebulot demanded, more to the snow in front of him than to anyone or anything else.

Tebulot needn't have worried. For suddenly, the shrieking of suck-guns died away; the three Night Warriors heard confused shouting, and then screams. Cautiously, they looked up out of the snow, and there was Xaxxa, floating towards them through the snow, twenty feet up in the air, his arms outspread, his mirrored face inscrutable and terrifying, even to them.

Ahead of him, roaring and rumbling, jogged sixty or seventy full grown Polar bears, the remains of the ice-sledge's harness-team. At first, they had run this way because Xaxxa had frightened them, looping from side to side in shining figures-of-eight. But now they could smell the fresh blood that he had spattered all over the Tartar soldiers, and their hunger drove their legs like superheated pistons.

Kasyx rose to his feet, and so did Samena and Tebulot. The sight was extraordinary. Each of the Polar bears must have weighed close to a ton, yet they all shambled forward at nearly twenty miles an hour, their teeth bared and their black lips curled back and their yellow eyes staring with mindless hunger. The Tartars opened fire on them. Bloody strings of flesh were snatched from the flanks of four of them, and three of them collapsed on to the snow, but the rest began to canter forward even more quickly, their breath smoking, their claws scratching on the ice-crust. The Tartars wavered, and then dropped their rifles and began to run.

With a last unstoppable rush, the bears brought down the soldiers in showers of bloody fury. The four Night Warriors watched with a mixture of horror and relief as their enemies were overtaken one by one and clawed down on to the snow, where their bodies were ripped and their helmets were scattered and their entrails were dragged blue-grey and steaming for yards across the snow. The bears circled and circled their prey, their yellowish fur streaked with red, their snouts dark and glistening, shreds of soldier meat hanging from their jaws.

A little way off, almost hidden by the thickly falling snow, the ice-sledge had been burned down now to a trough of ashes. A wind rose and began to blow away the sparks.

The Night Warriors cautiously retreated from the scene of the battle, so that they wouldn't disturb the bears. Following Samena's instincts, they trudged their way off through the snowstorm again, and within minutes, when they looked back, all trace of the sledge and the bears and the bodies of the Tartars had vanished.

For over an hour, they walked blindly through the snow. Kasyx asked Samena several times if she was sure that Yaomauitl was near, but each time she assured him that he was. 'I feel it, Kasyx, he's here. He wants to fight us to the bitter end this time. He won't run away.'

'I wouldn't even mind if he ran to meet us,' Xaxxa complained. 'He might save us a walk.'

Strangely, although it reduced visibility to little more than a few feet, the snow was neither wet nor particularly cold. It was more like thickly falling feathers – the way snow ought to be, in dreams, rather than the way it actually is. Xaxxa's and Samena's costumes were very brief, but neither of them felt affected by the blizzard. Their body temperature, in fact, was exactly the same as that of the dreamer himself, as he lay in his black satin bed.

After a little while longer, the Night Warriors found that they were descending into a wide valley, and that the snow was beginning to clear. The sky, however, remained deep red, almost maroon, and the clouds that moved through it, stately and slow, were tinged with pink. As the snow dissipated altogether, they looked up and saw that flamingos were flying around the clouds, their wings beating lazily on unseen air-currents, and that on some of the clouds there were colonies of untidy nests.

The snow beneath their feet began to clear away, too, and soon they found that they were walking through bracken, interspersed with wild flowers, and that the sun was beginning to shine. Below them, the valley spread out wide, with a silvery river looping its way through sparkling meadows, and willows sadly washing their hair from grassy banks.

It was difficult to decide where this place actually was; whether it was in the West or in the Orient, or somewhere else altogether different. They knew that the dreamer was Japanese, or half-Japanese, but this landscape was nothing like Japan. Nor was it anything like California, either. It was still and warm and regretful, a landscape of memories and lost loves, but there was also some vaguely threatening quality about it, some indefinable instability.

The Night Warriors reached the river and slowly forded it, up to their thighs. The water glittered in the sunlight, and ran thick with fish. They climbed the muddy bank on the other side, and sat down beside one of the rustling willows to rest for a minute or two, and to look around at this extraordinary world in which they had found themselves. High up above them, the flamingos still idly circled, and the clouds sailed past them with all the dignity of old-time Spanish galleons leaving Cadiz. 'Isn't this the most peaceful place you've ever been?' asked Samena.

Xaxxa was lying on his back on the grass, chewing the stem of a wild flower, his hands laced behind his head. 'If this wasn't somebody else's dream, I tell you, I'd stay here.'

Tebulot put down his machine, eased off his helmet, and ran his hand through his hair. 'I think Yaomauitl's taken a powder, if he was ever here at all. There's nothing Devilish going on in this neighbourhood, believe me.'

But Kasyx still felt uneasy. He sniffed the fresh water in the wind, and the bright fragrance of flowers, and he plucked a blade of grass and began to twist it around his finger; but still he sensed trouble. Not in the way that Samena sensed the presence of Yaomauitl and his offspring, through disturbed emotions, and subtle currents of fear; but through plain analytical logic. Yaomauitl needed to eliminate the Night Warriors before he continued his invasion of America's dreams; both as a matter of practicality and as a matter of pride. It was hard for Kasyx to believe that he wouldn't try to destroy them at the earliest possible opportunity. The longer your enemy lives, the stronger he becomes.

'Where do we go from here?' he asked Samena.

Samena shaded her eyes against the sun. 'I suppose we could try walking along to the far end of the valley.'

'You mean you don't know?'

Samena said, 'I'm not sure. I seem to have lost the scent.'

Kasyx stood up. He was worried now. Xaxxa watched him from where he was lying on the grass, twiddling the flower stem between his teeth. 'What's the matter, man? You look like something's under your skin.'

'I don't know, I don't know, this is all wrong,' said Kasyx. 'Listen – I vote we get out of this dream, now we've lost the trail. Let's go back and try again, right from the beginning. We've managed to kill off one of Yaomauitl's offspring, let's chalk that up for tonight, and leave the rest until tomorrow.'

Tebulot was down by the edge of the river, trying to scoop

up one of the fish in his hand. 'I think we ought to stay here for a while, and enjoy it. Come on Kasyx, enjoy! How often do we get into a dream like this? This is paradise.'

Kasyx said anxiously, 'Please – let's go. There's definitely something wrong here. I can feel it.'

'If you can feel it, how come Saména can't feel it?' Tebulot wanted to know.

But Kasyx didn't answer. Kasyx was staring out at the wide, reflecting surface of the river. Something had disturbed the surface of the water, and caused it to furrow as it flowed. Then something else, a small triangular point rising out of the water; and another, and another, and another. No, not points, but spears.

Utterly silently, with dreadful majesty, an entire army rose from the water; a black-armoured army mounted on black steeds that looked like horses but had the skin of reptiles. The soldiers wore huge helmets with horns on top of them, and breastplates that rose up on either side of their heads like the wings of vultures. Their eyes glowed venomously yellow, and they carried long spears which began to hum on a deep, vibrating note, like the very lowest note of an organ. The soldiers themselves started to hum too – deeply and discordantly, a triumphant hum of victory and death.

The river crept away from the horses' clawed hoofs. The grass shrivelled up, with a sound like crinkling cellophane, and turned deathly white. The willows shed their leaves and their trunks wrinkled with premature age. Behind the soldiers, the sky turned from red to threatening black, and lightning scuttled along the spines of the distant hilltops, cracking rocks and incinerating trees.

The leader of the army nudged his horse forward, and

approached the Night Warriors like a mounted nightmare. He glared down at them without speaking for a very long time, and then he addressed them in words that they could hear only inside their minds.

'*You have been warned before not to interfere in my affairs. You have caused me great grief, and for this you shall die. You will see no more mornings, Night Warriors. Look around this dream, for this is where you will meet your end, and this is where I shall bury you for ever.*'

A cold wind began to blow, tossing away the dead leaves from the trees, and drying up the last of the river, where the fish now flapped and gasped. It lifted Yaomauitl's cloak and shook it, so that it sounded like thunder. The Devil's eyes flared up, and his steed roared, and clawed at the air.

Kasyx stood forward. '*In the dark and holy name of the Night Warriors, we shall see you chained up for ever!*' he shouted.

Tebulot rolled away sideways, yanking back the T-bar of his weapon, and let fly with half-a-dozen energy-bolts. Three or four of them struck the black shields that Yaomauitl's soldiers carried, and were deflected in a spray of incandescent sparks, but two of them zapped through to their targets, and two soldiers exploded like bursting boilers, toppling from their steeds with unspent energy still crawling all over their armour.

Xaxxa shot away, out over the valley, with a shower of humming spears flying after him. He dodged and twisted, but as he circled around to fly back toward the soldiers, he suddenly looked over his shoulder and saw that the humming spears were still following him, with all the deadly tenacity of heat-seeking missiles.

Xaxxa climbed steeply, his feet sliding up the vertical strip of glowing energy as if they were on rails. The spears climbed upwards after him. He looped the loop, and still the spears pursued him, edging their way nearer and nearer.

He climbed again, as high as he dared, then paused, rolled over sideways in the air, and dived straight for the ground. Even Yaomauitl's soldiers turned in their saddles to watch him as he plummeted out of the thundery sky, a golden meteor. He disappeared behind the hills and the humming spears flashed after him.

Kasyx feinted first to one side, then to the other, and then he grabbed hold of Samena's arm and began to run. There was nothing else for it. With Xaxxa lost, they stood no chance of fighting Yaomauitl and his army of offspring in the same way they had fought the army of corpses. Tebulot gave them a brilliant horizontal spray of covering fire that knocked two more of Yaomauitl's soldiers from their steeds, and then came running after them.

A flight of humming spears came after them, but Kasyx whipped up his arm, and stopped them with a sizzling burst of energy which sent them harmlessly bounding away. Two or three more spears followed, but when Kasyx knocked those away, too, Yaomauitl uttered a harsh order that clutched coldly at Kasyx's heart as he ran up the hillside, because although it was spoken in an unknown language, he knew intuitively what it meant. He heard scythes being drawn out of metal scabbards with a steely ringing sound, and the cries of the Devil's soldiers, urging their steeds to run faster. He heard jingling harnesses and clattering armour, and clawed hoofs tearing at the ground.

Kasyx and Samena and Tebulot scrambled away as fast

as they possibly could, but the gradient of the hillside grew steeper and steeper, and they knew that they didn't have the strength to outrun Yaomauitl's reptile-horses for more than a few seconds longer.

Kasyx stopped running, and then Samena stopped, too, and finally Tebulot came to a halt, doubled over, gasping for breath. The soldiers encircled them, as black and threatening as shadows, their steeds fretting and sidestepping, their scythes gleaming in the storm-light, their eyes as frightening as the fires of hell, glimpsed through a secret grating.

Yaomauitl came forward again and dismounted. He was impossibly tall; he seemed to stretch up above them the way that a shadow stretches, as it falls across a cemetery at sunset. He exuded an extraordinary and repellent odour, like goats and musk and decaying chickens. It was more than the odour of death, it was the odour of complete physical and moral corruption.

'*You will kneel before me, minions of Ashapola, and you will kiss my feet, and then you will die. For hundreds of years, I was imprisoned by your forefathers, and you thought that you could take up their weapons and imprison me again. Well, my friends, it was not to be, and never will be, world without end, amen.*'

Yaomauitl reached down and lifted his engulfing cloak. He revealed beneath his armour the shaggy legs and cloven hoofs of Pan, the hair matted with grease and filth, and crusty with droppings.

'*Kneel!*' he commanded. '*The pure before the impure! The good before the evil! Kneel, and kiss my feet!*'

Kasyx said to Tebulot, under his breath, 'We have one chance only.'

Tebulot turned and stared at him.

'That's right,' said Kasyx. 'I can discharge all my energy at once, and we can blow the whole damned lot of them to Kingdom Come.'

'Can you really do that?' asked Samena, her eyes wide.

'*Kneel!*' roared Yaomauitl, and together the three of them knelt.

'I can do it, sure,' said Kasyx. 'The only trouble is, it'll probably wipe *us* out, too. And even if it doesn't, we won't have enough energy left to get out of this dream. Yaomauitl was right. This is where we're going to meet our end.'

'Do it,' said Tebulot, decisively.

'Samena?' asked Kasyx, softly.

'Do it,' she whispered, without hesitation.

Yaomauitl's offspring had climbed down from their steeds now, and had gathered around the Night Warriors to witness their final humiliation and execution. Their robes swished in the rising wind like the curtains of confessionals in blasphemous cathedrals. Thunder banged and grumbled in the distance, and hawks with the faces of men wheeled and turned over the naked trees.

Kasyx lifted his head, and said to Yaomauitl, 'I will not kiss your feet.'

'*Then I shall have your head cut off, and your dead lips shall kiss my rump,*' Yaomauitl replied, In the coarsest of voices.

'No, you misunderstand me,' said Kasyx. 'I recognise now that you are greater than Ashapola; that I have been mistaken all this time. I wish to do more than kiss your feet. I wish to embrace you. I wish to hold you close, and feel that you and I are one.'

Yaomauitl was suspiciously silent for a while. Then he said to Kasyx, '*Stand.*'

Kasyx got up on to his feet again, and stood in front of the Deadly Enemy face to face.

'*Should I believe you?*' Yaomauitl asked him.

'What harm could I possibly do to you?' asked Kasyx. 'You have defeated me now. I am your thrall.'

Very slowly, snow began to fall once more; the snow that had followed Yaomauitl's coldness from the Arctic regions where the Night Warriors had first penetrated the dream. Thunder and lightning and softly falling snow. It was the climate of madness.

Yaomauitl suddenly laughed. The snow seemed to have given him glittering new confidence. He could crystallise the very air, in the middle of an electric storm! He could do anything! He could ride through the dreams of men like a whirling avenger, creating anarchy and havoc wherever he went! He had defeated the Night Warriors that Ashapola had sent against him! More than that, he had defeated their spirit, too, so that they now knelt before him and acknowledged that *he* was the master of darkness, and that Ashapola was nothing more than the dust of twenty million unopened Bibles!

'*Embrace me, then!*' he roared to Kasyx, and Kasyx opened his arms wide and advanced into the huge black shadow of Yaomauitl's cloak.

For one fraction of a second, Kasyx thought that he had done it, that he was going to hug Yaomauitl as tight as he possibly could, and then release every single ounce of the energy that was stored up inside him. Yaomauitl would be exploded into atoms, beyond all possible resurrection. Even though he and his fellow Night Warriors would die in this haunted dream, unable to return to the waking world – at least they would have done their duty. But, grotesquely, one of Yaomauitl's offspring suddenly stepped forward, and stood between Kasyx and Yaomauitl.

'*You have shown no love of my father until now*,' he grated, his voice echoing inside Kasyx's head. '*Prove that you are sincere, in your change of affections. Embrace me first.*'

Kasyx tried to sidestep the embryo Devil, but the half-born creature took hold of his arm. Kasyx repelled him with a sharp burst of power. The Devil screamed out, and Kasyx pushed him aside, and lunged at Yaomauitl, triggering as he did so the mental formula that would totally discharge his energy.

Yaomauitl, however, was too quick. He whirled his cloak around, and knocked Kasyx away, sending him flying into the thick of his own offspring.

'*Kasyx!*' screamed Tebulot. But then there was a mind-splitting explosion that turned the world into dazzling white, and cracked the atoms in the air. When Tebulot could open his eyes again, Kasyx was standing with his arms straight up in the air, his hands glowing electric blue, while juddering curtains of pure energy flickered all around him, creeping and jerking across the ground, and discharging themselves with ferocious spittings and cracklings.

Samena saw Yaomauitl transfixed for just one moment, his huge cloak raised to shield his eyes. She unhooked an explosive arrowhead from her belt, and fitted it on to her finger, and took aim at him. But at the very second she fired, a lance of light, Yaomauitl's cloak suddenly collapsed to the ground, empty, and Yaomauitl was gone. Her arrowhead zipped away through the darkening sky, and vanished without exploding.

The wild bursts of energy gradually died away. Tebulot and Samena slowly approached Kasyx, who was standing on the hillside surrounded by the abandoned armour of all of his enemies, and by the dead bodies of forty or fifty embryo Devils. They were curled up and glistening and red, like baby birds who had fallen out of the nests. Blowflies began to buzz around them, even though it was snowing.

'Kasyx?' asked Tebulot, gently.

Kasyx lowered his arms, and looked down at his hands. 'I'm all right,' he said, at last. 'I've used up all of my energy, but I'm all right.'

Samena put her arms around him and held him close. 'Kasyx,' she said, and her voice was so soft that he could hardly hear it.

'I'm sorry that this was the only way,' said Kasyx, looking around at the carnage.

'Yaomauitl escaped,' said Samena. 'I tried to shoot him, but he disappeared.'

'Back to the waking world,' said Kasyx. He didn't have to add that they would never return there; that their lives would only last as long as this dream lasted; and that this dream would be the last thing that they would ever see.

'You're totally out of power?' Tebulot asked him.

'Flat,' said Kasyx, with a wry smile. 'I'm not exactly the Duracell of Night Warriors, am I?'

'I still have *some* energy left,' said Tebulot. He lifted his weapon to show that the charge-scale was still glowing.

'I have some too,' said Samena.

Kasyx slowly shook his head. 'I shouldn't think that it will be enough, even with the two of you. But here, let's try anyway.' He beckoned them to stand either side of him, and place their hands on his shoulders. He closed his eyes, and felt their small reserves of energy draining back into his system.

'Well?' asked Tebulot, anxiously.

Kasyx touched his fingers to his forehead. Then he said, 'I'm sorry. A little more, perhaps, and we could risk it. But I won't even be able to draw the octagon with this amount.'

Tebulot dropped his machine on to the ground. 'Well,' he said. 'Nice try.'

It was at that moment, however, that they heard a yell. A wild, high yell, as if somebody were whooping with glee. They turned and looked up, and there, streaking across the floor of the valley, came Xaxxa, both fists held high in the air, triumphantly. He landed beside them, and shook them all by the hand, and then admired the devastation all around them. 'Man, how did you *do* this?'

'More important,' said Kasyx, 'how did you get away from those spears?'

'World War One fighter-pilot trick,' explained Xaxxa. 'I saw it in the George Peppard movie *The Blue Max*. If somebody's chasing you, you dive straight for the ground, right – but you pull up at the last moment, and they can't.'

'But what took you so long?' asked Tebulot.

'In *The Blue Max*, they didn't misjudge it and halfway concuss themselves, that's what took me so long.'

Kasyx said, 'Xaxxa – how much energy do you have left?'

'I don't know, why?' asked Xaxxa, frowning.

'Give it to me,' Kasyx told him.

Xaxxa gave Kasyx a strange, perplexed look, but placed his hand on Kasyx's shoulder without asking any questions. Kasyx felt the energy streaming into his body, adding to the small store of energy that Tebulot and Samena had given him.

'Well?' asked Tebulot, anxiously.

The ground was beginning to rise and fall beneath their feet. They recognised the rhythm – it was the rhythm of the dreamer's breathing, as he slowly began to wake up. The world began to shudder and tilt, and they knew that if they were unable to escape from this dream, they would soon dwindle into absolute nothingness, forgotten by all humanity as if they had never existed.

'I'm not sure,' said Kasyx. 'I'm not at all sure.'

'Well, *try*,' Tebulot urged him. 'You have to try.'

'Very well,' Kasyx agreed, and held up his hands. He drew the octagon in the air – only a faint and glimmering octagon, but enough for them to see. They clasped hands, and Kasyx directed the octagon to rise up over their heads.

'I pray we make it,' Samena said. The ground trembled beneath their feet, and as the dimly flickering octagon slowly descended all around them, they all said, 'Amen.'

Chapter Twenty

John Lund was strolling slowly along the promenade, past Henry's cottage, when he saw an unfamiliar young man in a grey turtle-neck sweater and grey slacks obviously trying to force open the front door. John stood and watched the young man for a minute or two, the early morning breeze flapping his shapeless coat, and then he approached him, and lifted his Panama hat, and said, 'Excuse me, young man, I don't think that this is your house.'

The young man snapped around and stared at him. John was startled. For the young man's eyes were blazing yellow, like a panther, or a demon, and his mouth was drawn back from his teeth in the most terrifying snarl that John had ever seen.

'I, er – I – seem to have made a mistake,' he said, weakly, and replaced his hat on his head, and started to back away.

Instead of running off, or continuing to force open the front door of Henry's cottage, the young man followed John down the path to the promenade, and took hold of his arm. He was strong. His hand felt like an iron claw. He said, softly, 'You know who lives here, old fellow?'

John swallowed, his stringy Adam's-apple bobbing up and down in his soft cotton shirt-collar.' Yes, sir. I know who lives here.'

'Then come with me. I'm paying him a visit.'

'Young man, I don't think I –'

'Come along,' the young man urged. He leaned so close that John could smell his breath. It was foul, as if he had been drinking, or chewing cloves of garlic. 'Your friend won't mind if you pay him a visit, will he?'

'It's kind of early,' John protested, as the young man almost frog-marched him up the path.

'It's nearly seven-thirty. That's not early. And, besides, some people like to be woken up by their friends, don't they?'

John didn't know what to say to that. All he could do was stand helplessly by while the young man eased open the front door with the blade of a long mechanic's screw-driver, and then kicked it sharply to break the mountings that held the security chain.

'There we are, old Kasyx must have been expecting us,' the young man smiled.

'Old who?' frowned John. 'You must have the wrong place. The man who lives here is called Henry Watkins. He's a professor of philosophy at the University of California.'

The young man hissed with laughter. 'Henry Watkins! Now, that's a romantic name, don't you think? Well, he may be Henry Watkins to you, but he's Kasyx to me, and this house stinks of Kasyx!'

John said, 'You're not thinking of stealing anything, are you?'

The young man's eyes gleamed yellow. 'I don't think there's anything worth stealing, do you? A few books, a few sentimental photographs, a couple of bottles of liquor. A microwave oven. No, no, I don't think I'm going to steal anything.'

He beckoned John to follow him across the living-room to the corridor which led to the bedroom. John reluctantly did what the young man wanted, and even more reluctantly looked into the bedroom itself, where he could just glimpse Henry lying asleep.

'I don't know what you're up to,' he told the young man, hoarsely, 'but I really think you'd better leave now, before you get yourself into any real trouble.'

The young man hissed again. 'Real trouble? Surely you're joking. Only one person here is in real trouble, and that's Kasyx. He's asleep, you see, his mind is away somewhere else, dreaming; but just supposing that his mind came back and found that it no longer had a body to go to?'

'Are you a student of his?' John demanded. 'I don't understand any of this, but it sounds like nonsense to me, and dangerous nonsense at that. If I were you, young man, I'd leave – because if you don't leave, I'm going to call the police, and then you'll *have to* leave.'

Without warning, the young man produced a surgical scalpel out of his pocket, and held the blade up so that the point of it almost touched the tip of John's nose. John stared at him soulfully and the young man stared back.

'Have you ever wondered what it must be like to be one of those unfortunate people who are gravely disfigured?' the young man asked. 'One of those unfortunate people who can never go out in public without people staring at them in utter shock, because their faces are so badly distorted? No nose perhaps, or a terrible cleft in the upper lip, or a cheek that is nothing more than gristle?'

John squinted down at the point of the scalpel, and said, almost inaudibly. 'It's okay. I won't call the police, if it's all the same to you.'

'You are a man of great intelligence,' the young man

smiled. 'Now, come into the bedroom, and let us see what fun we can have with your friend Henry Watkins here. The man that *I* call Kasyx.'

'You're not going to hurt him?' John whispered, anxiously.

'Oh, no,' the young man replied. 'I'm not going to hurt him. You can't hurt somebody who isn't here, can you? And Henry Watkins isn't here, at least not yet. This is nothing but his physical body. His real personality is far away from here, further than you, my dear old friend, could even conceive possible.'

John said, in a hopeless voice, 'I pray to you, young man, don't hurt him. Please. He's a very old friend of mine, and a very good man.'

'Good, by *your* lights,' the young man agreed. 'But to my way of thinking, he is the worst of all possible pests. He is meddlesome, pompous, and sanctimonious. He deserves to die for his hypocrisy alone.'

'I pray to you, please,' John repeated, but the young man turned on him, and lifted the scalpel, and there was no need for him to warn John any further. John was a brave man, in his way, but a fatalist, too, and he knew exactly what would happen if he tried to play the hero. No nose perhaps, or a terrible cleft in the upper lip? Or even death.

The young man approached Henry's bed and leaned over Henry with a satisfied, foul-breathed grin. He touched Henry's face, and turned to John and grinned at him when there was no response. Then he tugged down the covers, and bared Henry's chest, with its wiry grey hair, and its slightly paunchy nipples, and he prodded Henry's skin with the point of his scalpel as if he couldn't decide exactly where to start his first incision.

He stood back. 'I want his heart, you see,' he told John. 'I want to cut his heart out, and hold it pumping in my hand. That will satisfy justice. A single heart for all of my children; nobody can complain about that.'

'You're crazy,' said John. 'You can't cut his heart out.'

'You don't think that I can?' the young man grinned. 'But you're going to watch me do it! You're going to witness it, in person! Come over here, come closer! I want some of the blood to pump out on you, so that everybody will know for sure that you actually stood there and watched it happen!'

The young man snatched at John's arm, but John screamed, 'Let me go! You're crazy! Let me go!'

The young man twisted John's arm around behind his back in an agonising half-nelson, and held the scalpel up against his withered throat. 'I could end it all now,' he breathed, in John's ear. 'I could cut your throat right through to your vertebrae, and then we could see who was crazy!'

'Please, I apologise, let me go,' John begged him.

The young man considered this apology for a moment, and then released him.' I'll have to think about you,' he told him. 'Having your heart cut out, that's too dramatic for you. Too heroic. Only warriors have their hearts cut out. That shows that somebody respects them enough to want to put an end to them altogether. But you – you deserve something more insulting. You deserve to have your foot cut off and thrust down your throat.'

John was backing away as the young man made these bloodthirsty threats, back towards the bed. So it was John alone who saw Henry open his eyes, and look up at the young man's back, and quietly raise his head up from the pillow.

The young man said, 'Maybe I'll cut both your feet off, and –'

He stopped in mid-sentence. His eyes had caught the sideways glance that John had made towards Henry. He froze where he was, his yellow eyes shining, and then he suddenly jumped around, so that he was facing Henry with his scalpel lifted.

But Henry was sitting up in bed now, and in his fist he was grasping the bag of nine seals that the priest had given him in San Hipolito.

'Yaomauitl,' he said, and he managed to smile. 'You know what these are?'

The young man stared at the bag and began to breathe slowly and deeply. His face lost all its colour, and his forehead broke out into beads of sweat.

'Who gave you those?' he said, in his harsh, deep voice.

'The people of San Hipolito. The people who believe that you belong there; not just now but for all time.'

'You're a fool. You cannot send me back. You have already seen my power.'

Henry climbed off the bed, and stood in front of the young man, holding the bag of seals up in front of his face. 'I've seen your power, yes. But I've also seen the power of Ashapola, and I've seen the power of simple human faith. You haven't been defeated by corpses or robots or battle-scarred veterans. You've been defeated by young people who know that they're capable of great deeds of heroism, and great acts of personal sacrifice.'

Henry loosened the drawstring on the bag of seals, brought them out, one by one, and brandished them in the young man's face.

'You think this superstitious nonsense can scare me?' the young man mocked him. 'You think these relics can make me cringe? Let me ask you this, old fellow: what do you think those relics really are? Humbug, that's what they are. Faked-up souvenirs of the son of God. And who was the son of God, old fellow? Do *you* believe in the son of God? Do you believe that he actually walked this earth, all those years ago, and that his disciples left these pitiful fragments, which survived until today?'

Henry looked at the seals, and then smiled. 'You're quite right, of course,' he admitted, 'these are ridiculous, aren't they? But, the funny thing is, I *do* believe in them. I *do* believe that the son of God walked on this earth, and I *do* believe that these relics came from his disciples. There are times, you know, when even a professional sceptic like me has to take some articles of faith for granted.'

He paused, and then he said, 'There are some things, you see, which can be proved only by the feeling in your heart.'

In front of Henry's eyes, the young man's face began to shift and change. His hair darkened, and his features altered, and in a matter of a few moments he had turned into Salvador Ortega. Henry thought to himself: the Devil certainly knows where to find a man's weakest and guiltiest thoughts.

John whispered, 'My God, he's somebody else. Look at him – he's somebody else!'

'Don't worry, John,' said Henry. 'He just looks like somebody else. He's doing it on purpose, to upset me.'

Salvador said, 'Henry? Listen to me, Henry.'

Henry replied, 'You're not Salvador. Don't even pretend that you are.'

'Henry, you're making a mistake,' Salvador persisted. 'You know what I felt about my religion, about Jesus and the Holy Virgin. But I've seen heaven for myself now, Henry. I've seen it with my own eyes, and it's nothing like the priests told me it was going to be. It's wonderful, Henry, you shouldn't feel guilty. But there's no God here, no Jesus, no angels, no Holy Mother. It's a place where you can do and think and be whatever you want. It's freedom, Henry, that's what heaven is. It's total freedom. Throw down those pieces of trash, Henry, and I'll show you. Come on now, throw them down.'

Henry shook his head. 'I'm holding on to these seals, you bastard, because these seals are going to put you away where you belong. John – I'm pleased that you're here. I want you to look on my desk. You'll find a telephone number there, on top of my notepad. It's a Baja number. Call it now, and ask to speak to the priest. When you get through, tell him you're calling for Henry Watkins, and that he should send up the elm-wood box. Tell him to send it straight away, just as quick as he possibly can.'

'Elm-wood box,' John repeated, quite mystified. 'Elm-wood box. All right, Henry.'

Now Henry stood alone with Yaomauitl. The two of them faced each other in silence for a moment or two. Henry could feel the coldness of sheer evil pouring from Yaomauitl like the vapour from liquid oxygen.

'Perhaps I can tempt you,' Yaomauitl suggested, in a throaty voice.

He twisted his hand, and produced, like a stage magician, a tall glass of chilled vodka, with an olive in it. 'Only one, Henry. Just to prove that you're cured. You deserve it, after all, now that you've defeated the great Yaomauitl.'

Henry stared at the drink for a long time. Then he looked back at the Devil. It was a curious thing, but after last night's battle his craving for alcohol seemed to have subsided; and being so blatantly tempted with his principal weakness somehow helped him to overcome it even more completely. He was a man, he was a Night Warrior. There was nothing that could deflect him from his power and his principles – especially not liquor.

Yaomauitl twisted his hand, and the glass of vodka vanished. 'Women, perhaps?' he suggested, and for one voluptuous second, Henry glimpsed bare breasts and curving thighs and provocative lips that glistened with lipstick. 'You *do* like women?' Yaomauitl smiled.

Henry said, 'You can try anything you like, Yaomauitl. But you're going back to San Hipolito, and they're going to shut you up in that elm-wood box, and that's where you're going to stay till hell freezes over, I promise.'

Yaomauitl glared at him with yellow eyes, and began to hiss. Dramatically, his head seemed slowly to explode, like a speeded-up movie of a growing cauliflower. His cheeks grew pitted and scabrous, and his forehead bulged out, and horns pushed out of his hair. His chest grew too, and his hands turned into hairy claws, with long curved nails that looked as if they could rip a man's heart and lungs out with one swipe. His legs thickened and grew shaggy with hair; and his feet narrowed into cloven hoofs. This was the true shape of Yaomauitl. This was the legendary Devil whose appearance had been described again and again by witches and warlocks and frightened priests, all the way down the centuries. Only this Devil was real, and he stank of death, and he stood in Henry's bedroom.

'*Now*,' Yaomauitl roared harshly. '*Now I am going to slay you, old fellow. Now you are going to experience hell!*'

He lashed at the air, and his claws made a sound like a thunder crack. Henry held up the seals, and shouted, 'In the name of Ashapola! In the name of God!' But the Devil gripped him in both hands, his nails piercing Henry's pyjamas and digging into his flesh, and lifted him clear off the floor.

For one second Henry was staring at eyes that blazed like blowtorches and double layers of teeth that could have bitten out his Adam's-apple in one ferocious snap. But then he screamed: '*I believe in God! I believe in the Father! I believe in the Son! I believe in the Holy Spirit! I believe in the Holy Virgin! And in the Resurrection! And in the life to come! And I repudiate you, Yaomauitl! I deny you! I have defeated you!*'

The Devil shook him and shook him until he could feel his brain thumping against the inside of his skull, and the beast's claws digging right through his flesh and scraping against his ribs.

'Oh God!' he cried out, and lifted the nine seals of the disciples and shook them in agony in Yaomauitl's face.

Yaomauitl screeched – a noise like boxcars being shunted in a railway siding, only twenty times louder. He dropped Henry on to the floor, and covered his eyes with his hands, shuddering, as if he were having a fit. Henry, bruised and bleeding, tried to crawl away across the rug. Even the floor was trembling, and a picture dropped off the wall.

Then Yaomauitl fell, but his falling was soft and silent, and when Henry at last managed to heave himself around, and to prop himself up against the side of the bed, all that he could see was a huddled figure, like a dead dog, shaggy and misshapen. Yaomauitl twitched, and then lay still.

John appeared in the doorway, his face the same colour as his linen jacket. 'I've called the priest,' he said, in a papery voice. 'He seemed to know what it was all about. He said he'll be here as quickly as possible.'

He saw the stains of blood on Henry's pyjamas, and came into the bedroom and knelt down beside him. 'You're hurt,' he said. 'I'd better call for an ambulance, too.'

'No, no,' said Henry. 'I don't think the paramedics would quite understand. Just go to the bathroom cabinet and bring me some bandages. And then go to the liquor cabinet and bring me a bottle of vodka.'

Slowly, painfully, Henry eased himself out of his pyjamas. The wounds that Yaomauitl had made in his sides were deep, but comparatively narrow. He dabbed them with his rolled-up pyjama top. Then, when John came in with the bandage and the bottle, he splashed them all with Smirnoff, to sterilise them. He winced, and clenched his teeth, as the liquor burned into his skin, but the stinging soon faded, and he was able to bind his sides with bandages.

John said, 'I suppose you can't possibly explain any of this?'

Henry nodded towards the huddled figure of Yaomauitl. 'I told you that I had to fight the Devil. You didn't believe me. But there he is. And what's more, I've won.'

'But why *you*, Henry? Why did *you* have to fight the Devil?'

'I don't know,' said Henry, philosophically. 'I suppose, one day, everybody has to.'

Epilogue

It was evening when six Mexican labourers slowly lowered the huge elm-wood box back into its tomb in the floor of the church of San Hipolito. The tiled lid was lowered over the top, and the priest sprinkled a crucifix of holy water over it. Henry and Gil and Susan and Lloyd stood a little way away, watching the ceremony with a strange mixture of pride and regret.

'O Lord, keep this Devil securely entombed until the Day of Judgement shall dawn, when he shall be required to bow down before You and acknowledge your holy supremacy. And protect all those who have incurred this Devil's wrath, and all those innocent instruments who may be used in the commission of his revenge, and may the world of men be kept free of his stain for ever and ever.'

'Amen,' said Henry.

'Amen,' said Gil and Susan and Lloyd.

They went out into the sunlit porch, and shook hands with the priest, and gave money and cigarettes to the labourers. The labourers crossed themselves over and over again, and hurried off home before the sun finally went down. One of them muttered '*Yaomauitl,*' and spat into the dirt.

The priest said, 'You have saved the lives of many, my friends. You deserve our thanks.'

Henry rubbed the back of his neck wearily. 'We deserve some sleep, I can tell you that much.'

They left San Hipolito and drove down the dusty roadway into the sunset. As they drove northwards, Gil said, 'What do we do now? Are we still Night Warriors, or what?'

Henry glanced at him. 'We're always going to be Night Warriors, you know that.'

'But all the Devils are safely locked up now.'

'That doesn't stop us from being Night Warriors.'

Gil dropped Susan and Lloyd back home, and then Gil and Henry went back to Henry's cottage for a cup of coffee.

'Are you going to start drinking again?' Gil asked Henry.

Henry came out of the kitchen wiping his hands on a tea-towel. 'I don't think so. I don't think I need it any more.'

They stayed up until two o'clock in the morning. At last, Gil said, 'I'd better get home. I have to work in the store tomorrow morning.'

Henry looked at the empty coffee cups and nodded.

'You look tired,' said Gil.

'I am,' Henry agreed. 'I just don't want to go to bed, that's all.'

Gil said nothing, but he knew what Henry was feeling.

Henry said, 'To tell you the truth, I'm afraid to dream.'

About the Author

GRAHAM MASTERTON is best known as a writer of horror and thrillers, but his career as an author spans many genres, including historical epics and sex advice books. His first horror novel, *The Manitou*, became a bestseller and was made into a film starring Tony Curtis. In 2019, Graham was given a Lifetime Achievement Award by the Horror Writers Association. He is also the author of the Katie Maguire series of crime thrillers, which have sold more than 1.5 million copies worldwide.

Visit www.grahammasterton.co.uk.